His Rebel Bride

Brothers in Arms, Book 3

Shayla Black
writing as Shelley Bradley

His Rebel Bride
Published by Shelley Bradley LLC
Copyright © 2000 Shelley Bradley LLC

Print ISBN 978-1-936596-28-7

PROLOGUE

Yorkshire, England
November 1484

Kieran Broderick exhaled in the cool, moonlit morn, blood singing as he awaited the battle cry that would come within the hour. Eagerly, his gaze swept across the rugged beauty of the Yorkshire hills surrounding Hartwich Hall.

Aye, he should have tried to sleep, and his body should be craving rest. Instead, he focused on the hum of excitement that always preceded battle. 'Twas then that men lived and died by their wits, their swords. Only one sensation exceeded the pleasure of such anticipation, and he had no wench with whom to share it now. And after last night, he might not need another for at least…twelve hours.

Grinning, he dismounted his horse and strode inside the Hall. 'Twas the home of his mentor, Guilford, earl of Rothgate—and the only real home Kieran had ever known.

As a boy, he had shared Hartwich with Guilford—a shrewd lord and something of a father, as Kieran shunned to remember his own. He had been raised with two other fine warriors, the brothers of his heart, since age eight. He still had the scar on his palm to remind him of the day they had sealed their bond with blood as boys, securing his loyalty to Aric Neville and Drake MacDougall.

At the bottom of the stairs, he heard their familiar voices

coming from a chamber near the top and smiled.

"The Campbells are below and ready for battle," said his Scottish friend, Drake MacDougall.

Aric sighed. "Will the Campbells never cease these petty squabbles with the MacDougalls? They should have understood long ago that your mother's marriage to your father was not an act of aggression."

"Aye, 'twas naught but a mistake." Drake sighed. "Let us fight them once more."

"I'll be below shortly," murmured Aric.

Kieran frowned. Aric's deep voice lacked its usual vigor. Was he ill? Troubled?

As he vaulted up the stairs, wearing a frown, he heard Drake ask, "Did you receive word, then?"

For long moments, Aric did not answer. On both sides of the wall separating them, silence stretched tight.

"Aye, as I feared, they are dead," Aric muttered, voice grave. "Suffocated September last in the Tower."

Kieran stood in the doorway. *Dead?* Though he had missed most of the conversation, he feared Aric spoke of England's young princes, Edward and Richard. The children's safety had weighed much upon Aric's mind of late. Had the boys been sacrificed to their uncle's ambition?

A *clink* of well-oiled armor sounded from within the chamber. A moment later, Drake uttered, "'Tis a grievous day, indeed. I am sorry for England's loss."

Silence held for thirty seconds more. Kieran let Aric and Drake have it together. They were ever men of reflection and deep thought—Aric especially. Kieran admired that but could not follow suit. He was a man of action.

"Kieran arrived last night after we were abed," Drake said suddenly.

"How is our Irish friend? As reckless as ever?" Aric tossed out, seeming eager for a new subject.

"At least," Kieran quipped, leaning through the doorway.

Drake and Aric whirled toward the sound of his voice. Though a golden mane framed Aric's square face and contrasted mightily with Drake's dark intensity, both men wore identical expressions— welcoming and reproving at once. Kieran restrained the urge to roll his eyes at their parental scowls.

Sauntering into the room with a jaunty grin, he teased, "Zounds, the pair of you look as happy as mutts that lost their meals. Good to see you, too."

"Aye, 'tis good," Drake replied, voice pointed. "We simply would prefer to keep seeing you in one piece."

Kieran opened his mouth to defend his actions, but through the open shutters of the window, he could see the battle beginning to form on the field below, calling to him. The horses pawed the mist-clung earth restlessly, their breaths white against the blue-black of the predawn sky. Troops lined up, over one hundred men unsheathed weapons.

The restless hunger called to him again, singing a siren's song of expectancy.

The trio of knights dashed down the stairs and left the castle to join the impending fray. Aric, known throughout England as the White Lion, looked oddly weary and reluctant for a legendary warrior. Drake, as always, would serve Guilford skillfully, with an abiding sense of duty and affection for his grandfather. And Kieran…well, he always followed the thirst for adventure until it was quenched—at least for the moment.

Kieran had his squire, Colm, assist him into his armor. Then he climbed onto his gelding and looked out upon their warring Scottish opponents. With a restless gaze, he sought out those among the Clan Campbell who looked big, fast, and skilled. Eagerness to test their mettle against his own chafed him. He tapped his fingers impatiently against his thigh.

It seemed an eternity before the battle began with a shout in the dark morn. The clash of swords declared the fighting under way.

With a nudge to his horse's flanks, Kieran urged Lancelot into the melee, his sword at the ready.

Opponents came at him one after the other, sometimes in pairs. He felt a surge of achievement as he sliced into one man. Surprise crossed the Scot's face—just before death did. Kieran let loose a battle cry as he ducked to avoid a Campbell blade on his left, only to see it enter one of the Scottish men on his right.

Feint. Thrust. Parry. Kill.

Lunge. Slice. Plunge. Defeat.

The battle was like a rhythm in his head, one he could

understand and dance to. One to which he was addicted.

The motions were automatic and rewarding, as were the results—his challengers lost.

The metallic scent of blood tinged the air, along with the smells of damp earth and dewed grass. The *thud* of metal upon bone mixed with the cries of defeat as the battle whirled all around the revelry at its zenith. Still, the sun hid slyly behind the winter-bare hills, as if to add an intriguing dimension to this game of life and death.

True, Kieran could not exactly recall what squabbles the Campbells now had with Guilford. Years past, the Scots had become the earl's foes when his daughter, Drake's mother, had wed Drake's father, an enemy MacDougall. Apparently, the union, though long over, still angered and threatened the Campbells.

He shrugged. Their reasons hardly mattered. Here was a battle to be fought. And he would not back away.

With a *whoosh* of his broadsword and a *whoop* of excitement, Kieran rode to Drake's side.

His Scottish friend smiled back wryly. "How fare you?"

"The battle is near finished and no one has killed me yet. That makes for a good morn thus far. And you?"

Drake's expression turned grim. "Ready to end this farce with the bloody Campbells."

At the sight of a charging foe, Drake tossed down his *claidmor*, then retrieved the longbow from his back. He fired an arrow, felling the man. Beside him, Kieran repeated the process when another man approached behind the first.

Kieran laughed. "Lord, 'tis an excitement, besting your enemies, pitting your skills against mighty warriors."

"Killing is never fun," Drake said harshly.

Did neither Aric nor Drake feel the excitement of testing their skills anymore? What had happened to the warriors he had always known? Kieran frowned.

"Battle is the stuff of men and life," Kieran protested.

"Aye, but not of amusement." Drake grunted. "Do you find nothing else pleasurable these days?"

With a rogue grin, Kieran replied, "How well you have forgotten me since I last saw you!"

"'Tis right you are," his Scottish friend said dryly. "You *always* enjoy a good wench."

"At least one," he shot back.

Shaking his head, Drake retrieved his sword and whirled away to discover another attacking Campbell. Kieran leaped in front of him and severed the warrior's head from his body. Then he let loose a battle cry and rode for another opponent.

Kieran whirled to the hiss of flames and discovered that someone had set fire to the cottages of Guilford's crofters. He angled his mount away from the heat—and the distant memory of flames on the wood stones of Balcorthy Castle, burning across Irish soil. Men howled, and Kieran recalled the sounds from many years past...

Shaking his head, Kieran cleared it. He never thought about the past, about his childhood. Such reminiscing served no purpose. He could not change what had happened.

Shrugging, Kieran turned to dispatch a new opponent. A moment later, fresh blood adorned his sword as he whirled to find another foe, to lose himself in the familiar dance of battle.

Within minutes, the Campbells were outnumbered and retreating.

Kieran hollered in triumph. Another day's work well done. More liquid excitement ran through his veins, slowly being replaced by a languid satisfaction.

Behind him, Aric tiredly dismounted, looking about. Kieran followed the Englishman's gaze. At the top of the next rise, he spotted Drake nearly surrounded by his fellow MacDougalls as he knelt with bloody hands next to a fallen man. Frowning, Kieran peered out at the bloodied warrior lying upon the earth.

Was that Lochlan, Drake's father?

"Traitor! Murderer!" he heard one of the Scotsmen yell at Drake as he stood protectively over Lochlan's body.

What? Do they believe Drake killed his own father?

Stunned by the exchange of accusations and protestations of innocence, Kieran charged toward the group. Aric followed beside him.

He rushed to his friend's side, his quick gaze assessing the scene and the blame upon the faces of Drake's kin.

"Drake is innocent," Aric vowed. "His love for his sire is well known by you all."

His words affected none of the Clan MacDougall. Hunger for blood was running high among the men now that the cowardly

Campbells had thwarted everyone's feast by retreating. Fury pelted Kieran as a pair of men grabbed Drake and shoved him roughly to his feet.

"Pea-witted fools, Drake would never kill Lochlan! This you know," Kieran added with fervor.

The Scotsmen still paid no heed.

Suddenly, the crowd parted to admit the old earl, Guilford. His white hair was a shock against the dark sky. "I demand you release him. Drake murdered no one, least of all his own father."

Still, a Scotsman Kieran vaguely remembered as Duff refused. "The Clan MacDougall maun judge him now."

Crows circled above, calling into the morn. Kieran watched the scene in apprehension. For if the powerful earl of Rothgate could not help Drake, he feared no one could.

He would not lose a blood brother this day!

Drake struggled, but the MacDougall soldiers contained him. Kieran drew his sword from his scabbard, ready to fight. Guilford stayed him with a firm hand until the Scotsmen disappeared.

All too quickly, Drake was taken away.

He turned to Guilford, his glance demanding an explanation.

"Let the firebrands work this foolishness out of their blood," the earl advised. "They will soon see their words as senseless and release him."

"I would rather fight!" Kieran objected.

"Of that, I have no doubt," Guilford answered wryly.

"They cannot imprison an innocent man so unjustly!"

"And so they shall not, Kieran. Leave this to me. You, too, Aric." The aging man shot his blond hulk of a friend a sharp gaze.

"Aye," Aric replied after a moment's hesitation, though he clearly liked it not.

The crowd began to disperse as morning finally burst its way over the craggy Yorkshire hills. Men pilfered through the fresh corpses on the battlefield, gathering valuable weapons, armor, and boots for later use. Aric turned away as if disgusted.

Kieran frowned. His friend did not seem…himself.

"Aric?" he questioned, unusually concerned. Beside him, Guilford looked on.

Aric did not answer. He looked instead as if life, as if his very soul, had deserted him.

A moment later, Aric gripped his broadsword in his hands. He looked at Kieran, then at Guilford, then glared at the heavy sword he held.

Then, with a mighty thrust, Aric cast his sword into the dark, yielding earth and strode from the battlefield without a backward glance.

Baffled, Kieran watched his friend disappear.

"Aric?" he called.

No reply.

He took two steps toward the victorious yet oddly defeated man. "Aric!"

Nothing still.

Guilford laid a calming hand upon his arm. "Aric requires time alone, to think, after receiving the news of the princes' deaths. Drake I will see to. You, however, I must speak with."

"Now? Drake has been accused of murdering his sire by his own kin, and Aric— What happened to my friend, the warrior? 'Tis as if some brooding monk has overtaken him."

"True, and I will deal with both soon. But this matter concerns you, and you have been in Spain for far too long." Guilford peered up at him with sharp blue eyes. "Do you recall Hugh O'Neill from your boyhood?"

Kieran recoiled. The name itself brought back memories of his youth in Ireland. Memories of the past—the shouting, the fire— flashed in his mind. He pushed them away.

"Aye." Kieran crossed his arms over his chest.

"He's written me a letter, several actually, looking for you. Your kin has worried since your mother took you away as a lad. They inquire as to your well-being and hint at land that belongs to you. I think 'twould be wise to reply."

Denial raged as Kieran shook his head. There was no purpose. His cousin Hugh was a part of his distant past—a past he had no wish to revisit.

And Ireland was not a place he sought to set foot upon ever again.

"Tell Hugh I will never return and he can gladly have what remains of Balcorthy. I have no use for it."

Guilford gave him a disapproving scowl he'd much hated as a child. "Kieran, I—"

9

"Nay," he insisted. "No more!"

At that, he made haste for his chamber within Hartwich's walls, wanting to believe he had heard the last from Guilford about Ireland.

But he knew Guilford too well to believe the earl would stay silent for long.

CHAPTER ONE

Sheen Palace, London
Mid-January 1490

After a pleasurable night in a warm bed, Kieran finally settled into his own chamber for some much-needed sleep as dawn rose over the Thames.

Stretching his naked length out upon the mattress, he turned onto his stomach and curled into the pillow with a sigh—only to be interrupted by heavy footsteps approaching his door and the sound of someone barging in.

Kieran whirled for his knife on the floor and sat up, fist clenched around the hilt.

Aric greeted him with a blond brow raised in question. "Planning to stab me?"

"Try knocking next time," Kieran grumbled, rubbing gritty, tired eyes.

"Who would have thought you would still be abed at this hour?"

Irritated, Kieran gestured to half-open shutters covering the window on the far side of his chamber. "The sun has scarce made an appearance as of yet. Why should I?"

Aric frowned. "You've a west-facing window. The sun has been up in the east for quite near two hours, as have I."

Sighing, Kieran regarded his friend of near twenty years. Aric,

11

as oldest, had always thought he knew more, had a right to guide the actions of his younger comrades.

"My goal in life is not to rise with the sun. I seek rest, and if you had enjoyed the night I had…" He grinned.

"With a wife as saucy as Gwenyth, what makes you think my night was restful?" Aric queried as if daring him to reply.

Kieran found himself scowling. "But she expects a babe within the month."

The robust laughter rumbling from Aric's chest conveyed great amusement. "Such hardly makes Gwenyth dead."

"But her delicate condition—"

"When have you ever known Gwenyth to be delicate?" he challenged.

'Twas a good point, Kieran conceded. Gwenyth had ever been full of fire, from her sharp tongue to her brave ways.

"True," he conceded. "But after losing the last—"

"Gwenyth will not lose this babe," Aric said, his voice a vow. "This one grows strong."

Sensing the issue disturbed Aric, Kieran asked, "What news have you of Guilford? Does he recover from his fever?"

"Aye. Drake and Averyl arrived a fortnight ago at Hartwich and sent word just yestereve that Guilford appears to be recovering, thank the Lord."

Knowing Aric and Drake shared his great fondness for the old earl, he nodded. "'Tis good news indeed."

"Drake also says Averyl expects another babe come summer."

Gratified, Kieran nodded. "Ah, more cause for celebration."

He cared much for fair Averyl. Her soft heart had done his friend Drake well, and the babes, this now the third, seemed to delight his Scottish friend much.

Aric's and Drake's happiness pleased him, as did all the children he could tickle and tease. Drake's eldest son, Lochlan, grew more daring each day for a wee lad of three. Their daughter, Nessa, had learned to walk this past Michaelmas. And with God's help, Aric and Gwenyth would add a son or daughter to the close-knit association Guilford held together with his gruff affection.

He couldn't be more pleased for his friends. They had overcome political strife, false accusations, near death, and much anguish, but love was now theirs. Still, Kieran had no intention of following suit, ever. Love and marriage did not seem worth such trouble and effort.

Tomorrow he would leave for Spain and his profitable journeys as a mercenary. Today he would enjoy the comforts that castles and ladies afforded him. Now that Guilford was recovering from his illness and Aric had returned to Sheen Palace, Kieran had no need to stay and see to his mentor's business any longer.

Except that another glance at Aric proved he looked like a man on a mission, a man with something on his mind.

And judging from his careful expression, Kieran did not imagine he would like what his old friend had to say.

"Out with it," he barked.

Aric did not pretend to misunderstand. "'Tis your antics, my friend."

Kieran paused, trying to sort it through. "Zounds, that could mean anything."

He soothed a hand across knuckles sore from boxing a particularly vexing swain yesterday and flexed thighs stiff from pleasuring a woman most of last night.

"You keep the ladies aflutter with your…shifting attentions—"

"Do you expect me to take but one?"

Clearly exasperated, Aric sighed. "'Twas not expected you would plough through most of them within half the month!"

Kieran shrugged. "'Twas harmless fun. And good times were had by all."

"The men complain," Aric went on as if Kieran had not spoken. "You make war freely and do not observe court rituals."

Discarding the sheet and pulling on his braies, Kieran stood. "They are fops and coxcombs. Slop jars have more brains."

With growing impatience, Aric sighed. "King Henry maintains a very sober court."

At that, Kieran rolled his eyes. "You've no need to tell me thus. How can you spend so much time here? 'Tis lucky I am the boredom has not yet killed me."

"I doubt you've had much time to be bored," countered Aric. "And King Henry has had enough of your ways."

"I'll be gone by sunrise tomorrow." He grabbed his tunic from the cold wooden floor. "I am expected back in Spain—"

"King Henry is sending you to Ireland."

Ireland? The tunic in Kieran's hand fell from limp fingers back to the floor. Nay, he had not heard that properly.

Had he?

"Did you say—"

"Aye, Ireland," Aric answered. "Henry thinks to keep you out of mischief there, as well as perform a favor for the crown."

Memories better left forgotten flashed in his mind. He frowned as he pushed them away. "I've no need to do King Henry a favor."

"'Tis not for Henry but for Guilford."

"What mean you?" Kieran asked, reaching again for his tunic, his stomach clenched with tension.

"You know King Henry seeks to rebuild his treasury and regain control over the nobles by 'borrowing' funds from them. He's borrowed a fair amount from me, but apparently fears Guilford's political influence with others, as he's borrowed much more. Guilford can scarce afford to 'lend' any more or he may lose Hartwich."

Guilford had risked his life many times over Hartwich Hall. 'Twas in his blood, as it was in Kieran's own. He could not let the old man lose his home, not after all Guilford and Hartwich had done for him, meant to him.

But Ireland?

Sighing, Kieran said, "Tell me."

"I...I negotiated a compromise."

Kieran knew he wasn't going to like it. "Well?"

"Since King Henry wanted you gone and Guilford could ill afford to give more money..."

"Aye, so you agreed to send me to Ireland?" Kieran prompted.

"King Henry is having a bit of trouble in the Pale," Aric admitted.

"The Pale?"

"Aye, that area about Dublin he has managed to keep English control over—"

"I know what the Pale is."

Did he ever. His mother had married a virtual barbarian trying to protect it for England. He had no interest in defending it himself.

"What I cannot understand," said Kieran, "is how it affects me."

Aric paused as if weighing his words. Kieran stared, hands on hips, feeling none too patient. The longer Aric remained mute, Kieran knew, the less he would like the answer.

"I grow gray waiting."

"The good word is that King Henry has made you an earl. The earl of Kildare, to be precise."

"*What?* Moments ago, did you not say he disapproved of me? So King Henry must expect something." Kieran's eyes narrowed. "Or rather, you promised some service on my behalf."

Slowly, Aric nodded. "In return for your absence and this new title, King Henry decrees that you go to Ireland. Actually, to Kildare and a certain Langmore Castle. 'Tis home to the O'Shea family."

Kieran shook his head, still not comprehending. "What have I to do with them? I know them not."

"Well, nay, not…yet. The O'Sheas make much rebellion inside the Pale and seek to incite the other leaders to insurrection. King Henry has not the funds or the army to see to the task, so he is sending you to organize what remains of the army, suppress the rebellion, and enforce peace."

"Me, enforce peace?" Kieran might have laughed at the notion if he did not loathe the thought of seeing to Ireland and this duty.

Aric nodded, as if conceding the absurdity of that. "Apparently."

"So, I'm to travel to Kildare and knock a few heads together until they behave like good little subjects once more?"

"Not…exactly," said Aric.

Kieran felt his stomach tense further. "What exactly, then?"

If anything, Aric's expression turned grimmer. "King Henry wants someone to wed and breed them to English ways, starting with the unruly O'Sheas."

"Wed? As in take one to *wife*?"

Kieran refused to believe his ears. He still did not want to believe it when Aric began to nod.

"There are four O'Shea sisters," Aric began. "Take one of your choosing."

As if he would willingly choose one!

"Once she breeds," Aric went on, "you are free to return with your babe to raise him English, then send him back to Langmore when he is a man grown. 'Tis simple."

Simple? Nay, 'twas terrible. No sane Englishman would marry a heathen Irish girl. 'Twas even forbidden by law.

At that realization, he brightened. "The Statute of Kilkenney forbids the English from wedding anyone Irish."

Aric grimaced. "Aye. 'Tis why you, my half-Irish friend, were chosen."

"But I have lived here since I was a boy."

"Still, you cannot deny your Irish blood, not to King Henry. Not to yourself."

Kieran's throat tightened. Aric spoke true, no matter how badly he wished to deny thus.

Damn his O'Neill father. Damn his love for Hartwich and Guilford.

Damn Ireland.

* * * *

A fortnight later, Kieran inched his horse along—ever closer to his doom.

Wed? He shook his head. Somehow he had never imagined the word would describe him. Aye, Aric and Drake were excellent examples of marital bliss. But such had not always been the case, and they had sacrificed much to realize those loves. Kieran could imagine not how 'twas worth such.

Besides, he expected naught but contempt to come of his union with an Irish O'Shea wench. Most like as not, each of them would be crafty hags, deeply buried in rebellion. Every time he took his wife abed, he'd probably have to search her and the bedclothes for daggers first.

Pushing aside such unaccountably deep thoughts, he looked about him, at the land he had not visited since boyhood. Ireland had left him with ill memories, but he could not deny the beauty of the country. The seemingly endless rolling hills would soon be carpeted in a misty green. Pastures swept with gentle dominance across the land until the trees met the bog in the distance.

Kieran drew in a deep breath of air. There was none of London's sour smell there, he admitted. Above him, a rook called, spreading its dark, glossy wings across a perfect blue sky. To his left, wetlands abounded, making a lattice of the land and water. Marsh thistle spread their pink spindles about, awakening to the surprisingly warm February day.

Still, he'd near give his right arm to be anywhere else,

performing any task but riding to choose a bride among four undoubtedly wretched shrews.

As he urged his mount around the bend of a dusty lane, he spotted two young women in simple garb. The one on the right had golden hair that hung down her back in waves. Her slight curves told him she was still a child, though growing.

'Twas the other woman who snared his gaze. She possessed a small waist, lush lips, and, he'd bet, delightfully long legs as well. Beneath her wimple, tendrils of curls skimmed her neck, shimmering in the afternoon sun, lighting it afire with all shades of red.

Flame-haired women had ever been a weakness for him. They tended to be shy creatures who, when properly coaxed, showed their hidden fire with passion and a flush of desire upon fair, fair skin.

Kieran felt his interest—and something more—rouse.

He had been in this wretched country for two days, been without a woman's comfort for nigh on a week—certainly a record for him. If he was to be wed to some termagant who would likely spend her days plotting his death, could he not be granted just a bit of ease first?

Slapping on his most charming smile, the one that had kept him much sated at Sheen Palace, he urged his mount closer to the redhead. Anticipation slid through him. Mayhap Ireland did have its finer points.

* * * *

Maeve O'Shea turned at the sound of a horse's hooves. She found herself staring at an unfamiliar man with the body of a warrior, the eyes of a hunter, and a smile designed to persuade a maiden to part with her clothing posthaste.

The stranger was too handsome by half, she thought as his blue-green gaze focused on her, intent, and his eyes warmed a shade. To her annoyance, she felt a flush creep up her cheeks.

With a glare, she turned away. Her reaction was unacceptable. And why, because of his pretty face? She'd not simper over that.

"Good day to you, ladies," came his voice, smooth as well-worn leather.

And very English.

Beside Maeve, her youngest sister, Brighid, gasped. With a

quiet hiss, she shushed the girl.

This man could be no other than the new earl of Kildare. Word had reached Langmore from Dublin that King Henry had executed the previous earl for treason after he supported Lambert Simnel, a Yorkish pretender to the English throne. In the wake of the plot, the Tudor king had sent this new earl to subdue the seeds of rebellion.

What did these English fear in freedom that they must always conquer and make war? She despised them, all of them, for their haughty voices and silken clothes. And their arrogance. Aye, always that. Behind her sat a prime example of grating English confidence.

Turning again to face the intruder, Maeve pasted on a smile.

"And a good day to you, fine sir." She curtsied.

Apparently pleased with her response, the Englishman dismounted and sauntered toward her, his eyes ever upon her face. Maeve swallowed against the heat of his stare while ignoring her sister's gaping expression beside her.

With a sweep of his hand, he took her own in his. Maeve scarce had time to register the strength of his fingers and the texture of his calluses against her palm before his lips touched—and lingered—on the back of her hand.

Against her will, she stared. His features were pleasant, his nose straight and even. The slash of his brown brows a masculine arc over the intriguing bluish eyes. He was clean-shaven, and he wore his hair shorn like his undoubtedly Norman ancestors. Even its color was pleasing. Black would have been too severe on him. Nay, God had blessed him with a shade not too light, not too dark, possessing a hint of auburn. And he was probably rich and smart and annoyingly charming besides.

Suddenly, she dreaded every day he spent at Langmore.

"You are a gem indeed amid such a lovely land," he murmured. "I beg the pleasure of your name, sweet lady."

'Twas doubtful with his charm he begged for much. No doubt women simply gave the man whatever he asked, all for a mere moment in his strong arms and the touch of his full mouth upon theirs. And while Maeve liked the company of her own sex, they could be such fools when a charming man sniffed about their skirts.

Ignoring the fact her hand tingled where his mouth had been, Maeve gently broke the contact and cast her gaze away as if timid.

"What would you be knowing of this fine land, sir?"

At that, his grin turned wry. Aye, he was self-possessed and strong and a warrior to the core, but he could smile. The flash of white teeth, the engaging stare, the warm interest in his lively eyes made him unlike the other Englishmen she had known. Mischief hung about him as surely as a cloak. No doubt, he had led many a maid astray.

The fact he would remain at Langmore as their lord annoyed and flustered her at once. Would he continue to focus his charm upon her, despite her betrothal to Quaid?

"I know little of the land, 'tis true," he answered, saving her from foolish thoughts. "But its beauty is clear for all to see."

Again, his gaze caressed her, roaming her cheeks, brushing her mouth, then meeting her eyes once more. Oddly, Maeve felt her heart pick up its pace again. Why, she had no idea. He was a rogue—and an English one at that—seemingly intent upon trifling with her. He cared naught for the Irish people. Like the others, he would reap the land's profits, use them to line his coffers, impregnate his kitchen maids, and jail the men.

The fact she could do naught to stop him made her want to scream in frustration. Somehow, she had to stall him, make plans for Langmore's defense. They were unprepared, for this new Kildare had not been expected until next week!

"'Tis a lovely bit of land we have," she agreed, smiling with deceptive sweetness. "What brings a fine man like you here?"

At that, his smile faltered. His eyes did not seem quite so lively. "I am the new earl of Kildare, lady."

"My lord," she cooed, pretending away—and gritting her teeth.

A furrow wrinkled his brow, and Maeve was surprised to find he did not like her show of deference.

Then the smile returned, as if it had never disappeared. "For you, lovely lass, I am Kieran. And you are…?"

She frowned. Odd, his name. It sounded more Irish than English. In fact, 'twas a Gaelic word for dark. More like than not, 'twas a comment on his soul.

And since he had likely come to subdue her family, she would wait to confess her O'Shea heritage just a bit. He would learn that soon enough.

"I am Maeve. This," she said, putting her arm around her little sister, "is Brighid."

The new earl—she refused the intimacy of thinking of him as Kieran—nodded to the young girl. Maeve noticed then that her sister stared at the Englishman with blushing approval.

"Do you steal kisses from maidens?" Brighid asked in an uncertain whisper.

Hellfire! The girl's questions about men were already too much to take. She knew this audacious knave would only fuel more, and nearly groaned at the realization.

"As often as possible," he said, grinning. "Twice if she will let me."

The earl winked at her, and Brighid flushed another shade of pink, blue eyes sparkling with wonderment.

Maeve sighed.

"Do you call this area home?" the earl of Kildare asked, shifting his attention back to herself.

She saw no point in lying…nor in telling the complete truth. "Aye, within Langmore's walls."

His smile brightened as he reached for her hand again. "As I am headed there myself, we will likely meet again, sweet Maeve."

"It seems certain." She forced a smile to hide her vexation. How dare the man use her Christian name so familiarly, speak it as if he could caress her with the sound.

When he reached Langmore, no doubt her brother, Flynn, would adjust Kildare's confidence a bit—and possibly his face, as well.

At that, Maeve cringed. She abhorred fighting. Watching grown men beat upon one another like unruly children always aggravated her. And of late, Flynn had been always ready for a nasty fight.

In this case, Maeve could see the purpose.

Prying her hand loose from Kildare's grip under the pretense of adjusting her wimple, she smiled.

Unfortunately for her, he grinned back, something wicked and lopsided and full of waywardness. Against her better sense, her stomach fluttered.

"Shall I follow you to Langmore, since I find myself lost?" he asked, voice smooth.

"We make for the village, my lord."

"I see. Can you tell me how might I find Langmore, then?" he asked, his voice ripe and unbroken with charm. "I would appreciate your kind guidance, my sweet."

His sweet, was she? Her betrothed, Quaid, would indeed be disturbed by that. So was she, for that matter.

And she was eager for Flynn to give Kildare the lumps he deserved. Neither Ireland—nor its ladies—would surrender to his dubious English charm without considerable fight.

For now, she must plan, must find a way to warn Flynn of Kildare's arrival, before the actual event.

"Langmore, 'tis easy to find from here, my lord," said Brighid at her side.

When the girl turned toward the pasture-lined lane that led straight to the keep, Maeve knew she must stop her sister.

"Aye, but you must travel on the path through yon bog," she said, pointing to the nearby wetlands and hills.

"The road does not lead to the castle?" he asked.

"It does," answered Brighid, frowning.

"But the bridge over the River Barrow is down," Maeve cut in. "Gone with a flood last spring. And the river's bank is too steep for your mount, so the bog it must be."

Brighid stared at her as if vexed. "But—"

"This way you will reach Langmore soon, so that you might meet Flynn, the leader of the O'Shea *Fein*."

Kildare frowned. Aye, he was surely disturbed by her use of the Gaelic, something the English always hated. Certainly he did not know the word's meaning. What could he know if Irish kin-groups?

As if reminded of his duty, the new earl looked toward the keep's stone towers, rising to gray splendor against the blue sky, and nodded, suddenly sober.

"You have my thanks, sweet Maeve. Brighid. 'Tis my hope we meet again soon." With a courtly bow and a smile, he mounted and urged his roan toward the bog.

Once Kildare had disappeared into the trees, Brighid asked, "Why did you lie to him about the bridge?"

"To give us time to plan. We must warn Flynn. We'll not be invaded by the English again, particularly not one who thinks overmuch of himself and has a penchant with the ladies."

* * * *

Whistling a merry tune, Kieran guided his horse toward the bog.

Aye, mayhap life at Langmore Castle would not be as disagreeable as he had once thought. The lovely peasant Maeve would be a most pleasing diversion after he had chosen a wife from among the four long-toothed O'Shea sisters.

All in all, he was glad both that he had been a tad lost and that he'd worn one of his best tunics. He was not usually one for much decoration, but in this case, he suspected the gold braiding and rich fabric had been worth the extra expense.

Sighing, he urged his mount up a hill, searching for the path. When he found none, he descended into the valley below, hooves skimming through the cold stream. Bogbean grew up from the soil beneath the water, crowned with tiny white blossoms. And the gentle trickle of water over mossy rock somehow soothed him, despite his upcoming task.

Odd, he could still find no path, despite the fact that Langmore's visitors had used this for nearly a year. He frowned. Mayhap the castle received few visitors.

Shrugging, he pressed on, making a path of his own. Of a sudden, the water began swirling higher and higher, until it nearly reached his horse's chest. Lancelot neighed in protest, whether from the cold or rising water, Kieran knew not.

But the stubborn animal made one thing very clear: he would not take another step.

Heaving an angry sigh, Kieran dismounted. A February day had turned the water to something scant warmer than freezing. It rushed about his waist, sank into his boots, and thoroughly soaked his hose and braies.

"Addle-pated beast!"

If the animal heard his curse, he cared not. Instead, he stared at the water, eyes wide, and shook his long head in agitation.

"Stubborn horse," he said again through gritted teeth as he began to lead Lancelot forward.

After a moment's hesitation, the stallion took a ginger step toward the opposite bank. Kieran damned the cold water and wondered if his feet would see the land upon yon bank before he froze to death.

They took another step forward, and the water rushed up around Kieran's chest, dousing his emerald tunic. "Ballocks!"

Though he had no real wish to meet the O'Shea wenches, he

wanted to do so looking every inch their lord. He would be hard-pressed to appear an authority whilst looking like a rat half drowned in a vat of ale.

Cursing again, Kieran bolted around the horse from side to front, certain he would persuade the beast to move on before his teeth chattered any more.

He stepped on a rock hidden beneath the water, slick with slippery moss.

Before he could catch his balance, he fell beneath the water's surface, the icy river closing over his head, sluicing down the skin of his back. His buttocks landed squarely on the offending rock with a jarring thud.

"Damnation!"

Kieran moved to rise, but Lancelot pranced nervously around him, rearing up. He saw the beast's hooves looming above his midsection and tried to roll out of the way, but the horse was faster. Closer those hooves came to his stomach—and lower.

"Nay!" he shouted, his voice echoing in his ears.

Scrambling away from the descending hooves, Kieran felt alarm tear through him. He had little time to ponder the fact that he was about to become a eunuch, courtesy of a four-legged beast.

He stared at the horse in horror.

The animal's foot landed just between his thighs, a safe enough distance away from harming the part that made him male.

Kieran sighed, relief thick in his blood. His mind slowed with it, registered that he was unharmed.

With that came anger.

He came out of the water, sputtering curses.

"You old codswallop!" he shouted, staring into the stallion's face.

In response, Lancelot lowered his head for a drink, thoroughly ignoring Kieran's dressing down.

Which only served to irritate him more.

Without fail, his first act as Lord Kildare would be to repair the bridge. He would also carve another path to Langmore's door around the bog, in case the bridge should become impassible again. If he had to make such a road with his bare hands, he would do it.

Ridiculous backward people, not fixing a vital bridge. 'Twas as if they wanted to keep visitors away, or simply cared not for their guests' discomfort.

Again, he frowned. Why would anyone want to discourage peddlers, traveling priests, or family?

Cursing, he smacked Lancelot's rear. The horse scurried out of the water and up the next hill. Kieran mounted after the next rise, much annoyed.

A few minutes later, shivering in the winter wind, he found himself nearly beside Langmore's walls. To his right stretched a well-worn path dusty from frequent use. Down the wide lane he looked, all the way to the river.

He spotted a bridge, one very much intact.

The path disappeared around the bend after that, no doubt leading to the road on which he had been traveling when he spotted sweet Maeve.

By Saint Peter's toes, that little redheaded imp had duped him! She had completely lied with those lush red lips and smiled while doing it.

Shivering with cold, tunic ruined, Kieran vowed he would repay her tenfold—at least.

CHAPTER TWO

A minute later, Kieran arrived in front of Langmore's gatehouse. He stared up at the massive gray stone structure, passing glad it stood strong and intact. The crenellated towers looked to be at least eight feet thick, though the curtain wall was not as tall as he might have liked. Still, 'twas a sturdy place. That he could be glad for.

After he got his hands about that wench Maeve's neck.

The drawbridge lay lowered, yet no sentries stood in sight. Eyes narrowed, Kieran dismounted and stamped onto the drawbridge. Did these lax Irishmen never fear invasion, siege, war? Such made no sense.

Resolved to fortify the more human aspect of castle defense at the first opportunity, he barely noticed the noise—a scrape of metal upon wood. 'Twas the sound he did not quite recognize as that of a pin being withdrawn from the drawbridge.

At least not until he began falling.

With a curse, Kieran lost his hold on Lancelot's bridle and plummeted down, down.

Finally, he landed with a *thump*, sinking into knee-deep mud. It oozed coldly into his already quaggy-wet boots. He cursed roundly.

Using a tense hand, Kieran raked damp hair from his eyes and looked about. 'Twas a dark pit, one that towered many feet above his head. He looked at the nearly black walls for any way he might crawl out.

He was not surprised to find none.

25

Foolish! His mind had been so engaged on the peasant Maeve, he had thought little of the dangers in coming to a hostile keep, knowing his own men to be but a day or two behind him. Aye, he was lord here, but the O'Sheas had not yet accepted him. He would do well to remember that.

If he got out of here alive.

"Are you the Englishman who thinks he's come to run Langmore?" demanded a hostile Irishman above him.

Peering up, Kieran was nearly blinded by the sun until the man's big body blocked the light.

He encountered the most determined dark eyes he had ever seen. The black Irish eyes spit hatred and promised a fight.

Kieran felt no shock when he saw the man lift a bow from the ground and draw an arrow through it. The grim mouth smiled with glee when he pointed the arrow at Kieran's chest.

"'Tis nothing but a bloody leech you are, thinkin' you can come to Langmore and dominate us. 'Twill be my pleasure to split your English hide in half."

Anger speared Kieran. 'Twas like an Irishman to fight unfairly without honor. His own father had done such. Apparently naught had changed.

"Would you kill me, you craven coward, without a fair challenge?" needled Kieran. "Do you fear a well-trained Englishman so much you would resort to murder?"

The man drew the bow back farther. "Why should I be fearin' any Englishman, I ask you? You're all naught but—"

A soft gasp interrupted the man's haranguing. Kieran then saw a familiar blond head peek over the top of the hole. Young Brighid gaped, her pink mouth as wide as her blue eyes.

"Flynn! Your plan worked. He is trapped!"

So this was Flynn O'Shea, already protecting what was no longer his. Kieran frowned. He should have guessed such.

The O'Shea man scowled at the young maiden. "Of course it did. 'Twill be a fine day when you learn some faith in me."

"She will learn faith, Flynn, when you think a plan through."

Though he could not see her, he recognized Maeve's sweet, lying voice as it made a dulcet path to his ears.

"And what do you mean by thinking a plan through?" Flynn directed a scowl over his shoulder.

"If you kill him, Henry Tudor will simply send another, possibly with a large army."

Flynn's scowl mutated into a thoughtful frown. Apparently the simpkin had not considered that. Whether 'twas true or not, Kieran decided to seize upon it.

"Aye. Even now King Henry awaits my word...or lack of it before he sends his real warriors."

Kieran looked from Flynn to Brighid, still hovering about the imprisoning hole. Suddenly the girl smiled. "'Twould be a shame to kill him. He is more than passing handsome."

Splendid. Though he never wanted a female barely beyond childhood to think him fine-looking, now was a particularly bad time, for Flynn O'Shea looked enraged by the comment.

"Is he kind?" asked another woman, her whispered voice one he did not recognize.

Over the top of the hole appeared another blond head, this one belonging to a young woman of perhaps sixteen years. She was lovely, with golden pale cheeks and an ample bosom. At least the women at Langmore were easy to look at. Such might make his time here more bearable.

"Kind, Fiona?" Flynn gaped at the woman as if she were shandy. "He is English. Why should you be carin' if he is kind?"

At Flynn's bark, the delicate creature looked as if she were going to tremble or cry—mayhap both. Kieran scowled.

Maeve's voice broke into his thoughts. "Perhaps we should consider why it would be better to accept a kind Englishman in our midst, rather than try to fight a mean one or any of them."

"Aye, and 'twould be such a shame to kill a man with so magnificent a face and form," added the youngest girl.

"Brighid! 'Tis the English who ruin our lives, kill our men, take over our homes," said yet another woman.

The latest addition waddled up beside Brighid, dark hair glistening in the sun, but she did not spare him a glance as she chastised the girl. He could see little of this woman's face from the deep hole, but 'twas clear she was well rounded with child.

"Mayhap he is different, Jana," Brighid defended, then offered, "He likes to kiss women, sometimes twice even. He said so."

Jana struck back. "I should kill myself before I let an Englishman kiss me, as should you."

"I want no kiss, but…if he is kind," interjected Fiona, "mayhap he would not make war."

At this point, Kieran would have gladly kissed an eel to earn passage from this cold mud pit and see the end of this odd argument, rather than watch with vexation.

Kieran opened his mouth to speak—just what, he was not certain. He never had a chance.

"Can you not see his just being here tells us he will make war, I ask you?" That from Flynn, who again pointed his bow down at Kieran's chest.

"Aye." Dark-haired Jana looked at him finally, her brown eyes narrowed with hate in a pale, tired face. "He looks a war-making man. Naught but English arrogance."

"But he winked at me!" defended Brighid. "An enemy never does that."

"You are too trusting," scolded Jana.

"You must be careful with trust," added Fiona.

"Even Fiona agrees," Jana said with some triumph.

"But we know next to naught about him. What if he is kind and not here to make war at all?" said Fiona again.

Flynn tossed another dark look over his shoulder. "'Tis all the English do is make war, I tell you. Are you listening?"

"Well…" she hedged, softly spoken. "I had hoped that you were, perhaps, wrong.

"Wrong?" Flynn thundered.

"It has been known to happen more than once," Jana snapped.

"See, he might well be kind." Fiona's voice trembled.

"Kind men give kisses," Brighid confirmed.

Kieran shook his head to clear it. Their logic completely baffled him. He wanted naught more than to make his way from this pit, which grew colder by the moment, and throttle the lot of them.

"Flynn, it might be best if you put the bow down," said Maeve calmly. "Now, if Kildare was here to make war right away, I think he would have come with his army. Since he did not, we must believe he has some peace in mind. As for whether he is kind or kisses the lasses, neither matters as long as we keep the roof over our head, our people alive, and our crops left to us. We may not like the earl's presence among us, but we have little say in the matter at this moment, unless we would like to risk the wrath of the English king."

Maeve's logic impressed Kieran. The rest of the group seemed addle-pated and mad. His clever peasant apparently had a swift, sharp mind.

"She does have the right of it," Jana conceded with a resentful curse.

"Of course Maeve is right!" declared Brighid with a toss of blond curls over her shoulder. "She is always right."

"Aye. Mayhap we should simply pray for peace. I want no more of war," said a small-voiced Fiona.

"Peace?" barked Flynn. "Let the Tudor bastard make war, I say."

"Why?" quizzed Maeve. "You cannot possibly fight him and win. We have not the men, the weapons, the—"

"There will be no peace! I'd sooner cozy up with a swine, I tell you. I care not for the wrath of the English king."

Maeve sighed. "You will care very much when he sends an army trouncing to Langmore to tear it down and kill us all."

"He would not dare," growled Flynn.

"The fact he executed Geralt and plans to see Quaid dead, along with others we know, should tell you different."

Kieran cared not who Geralt or Quaid were since Flynn actually seemed to be considering Maeve's words. She was amazingly calm in the face of her overwrought brethren.

"King Henry seems determined to hold the Pale," continued Maeve. "I see no reason not to believe him. Flynn, instead of fighting him in open war, we must choose the battles we can win. Besides, if you kill this earl, 'twill be less than a month before they send another. And that one will be less likely to show mercy."

The dark-eyed man glared at Kieran, then glanced at Maeve again. Briefly, Kieran wondered at the relationship between all of these people. Was Maeve even a peasant at all? Flynn had once been master here, and Kieran did not believe the man would ever allow someone so lowly to speak to him thus.

He frowned. Was Maeve his wife?

Shuddering at that thought, Kieran turned his gaze up again. Jana rubbed a hand across her pregnant belly. Brighid toyed with her hair. Fiona clasped her hands nervously while Flynn gritted his teeth and held his bow. Only Maeve projected an unruffled visage, as if she were correct and merely waiting for everyone to understand that.

Finally, Flynn cursed, the ripe expletive hanging in the air, before he threw down his bow and arrow.

"Pull him out, then. I will not kill him…yet."

With a dark glare, Flynn turned away.

The four women stood around for a moment. Kieran felt more mud seep into his boots and wished someone would do something to help him find a way out now.

"How do we free him?" Fiona asked hesitantly.

"I know not," admitted Brighid. "Usually we just wait for them to die and bury them in the hole."

"True," echoed Jana. "Is there a way out?"

All three of them turned to look at Maeve.

With a sigh and a strained smile, she turned away, her soft footsteps retreating.

"Good lady!" he called after her, feeling as if his last hope had left him. Jana, Fiona, and Brighid had not the mind between them to help him out.

"Maeve has a plan," Brighid assured with an impish grin. "Maeve always has a plan."

By God's oath, he hoped so. Though he could do little until she decided to reveal what that might be. Zounds, he hated idleness.

"Why do men stare at Fiona's breasts?" Brighid asked suddenly, much unexpectedly.

Kieran sent a wide-eyed glance up to the girl, then to Fiona's…assets. How, by Saint Michael's balls, was he to answer that?

He simply would not. Instead, he stared impatiently up at the afternoon sky and waited. Finally, Maeve reappeared, a castle guard trailing in her wake.

Wordlessly, she pointed to Kieran, trapped in the mud.

With no more than a nod, the guard retrieved a rope from the ground and tossed the end down to him.

He felt the smile break his face.

Now he could get out of this mud pit and begin to establish authority. He could meet the O'Shea sisters, pick one to wife, breed her, then leave this backward land and return to the mercenary life that called his name.

Such could not happen soon enough to suit him!

The rope made its way close enough that he reached out and

grabbed hold. With a good tug, he established that someone or something held the other end in place.

He lifted himself by the arms, the mud making a loud sucking noise sound as his feet emerged from the sludge. Once they were free, he planted them against the wall and began climbing his way out.

In three steps, he made his way to the top and emerged into the sunlight, surrounded by four women. The castle guard disappeared. Flynn stood away from the women, glaring in his direction.

Kieran turned to his savior. Maeve crossed her arms over her chest and met his stare with a flat expression.

Still, he felt a charge of sexual energy leap through him.

She would be an interesting, spirited woman to bed, all calm and logical on the outside, all fiery need on the inside.

After a lingering glance, he murmured, "Thank you, Maeve."

"Thank me not. I do not want your appreciation."

Though her voice held contempt, her eyes held an awareness of him as a man. He saw it plainly. And he smiled.

"Nonetheless, you have it. Now excuse me."

After executing a courtly bow, despite his muddy attire and squelching boots, Kieran made his way toward Flynn.

Now was the best time to show the Irish at Langmore—Flynn O'Shea especially—who was master here.

* * * *

Maeve watched Kildare stride toward her brother with long, purposeful steps. Flynn glared in return, stiffening as the Englishman came closer. Concerned, she frowned.

Before Flynn could speak, much less move, Kildare took the final step of his approach—and swung his fist into her brother's jaw.

She heard an audible smack, a solid connection with his flesh. Flynn staggered back, head reeling as he clutched the side of his face.

Beside her, Fiona and Jana both gasped, while she felt herself gape in incredulity.

Kildare behaved as if he knew—or cared—not about their horror. He charged her brother again, this time planting a fist in his stomach. Flynn grunted and doubled over.

31

How dare the beast! She had convinced Flynn to release him from the mud pit, and he wasted no time in harming her brother in return.

How English.

"Touch him no more!" she shouted.

The rogue spared her not a word nor glance.

Flynn recovered from the last blow and swung at Kildare's face. The rogue ducked, grinning.

"Hit me," he invited. "If you can."

"I'll be doin' it soon, I tell you," Flynn promised, then charged with raised fists at Kildare again.

As Flynn rounded his fist in attack, the Englishman caught his wrist in a solid grip. The *thwack* echoed in the air as he spun Flynn around and hoisted the arm behind her brother's back with a painful shove. Next, he grabbed Flynn's hair in the other fist and propelled him against Langmore's outer wall, face first.

With Fiona's second shocked gasp in her ears, Maeve raced after the pair.

"I'll not take this from you, I tell you," vowed Flynn. "I'm promising it will be my pleasure to kill you."

Kildare only shoved him against the wall harder, his shoulder pushing Flynn's face into the unyielding stone. As Maeve approached, she saw the miscreant still wore a smile.

Such a fight made him grin? What manner of man—or beast— was he?

"I would not deem it likely now, would you?" taunted the Englishman. "Of course, if you wish to fight more, 'twill be my great pleasure to oblige you."

The glitter in Kildare's unusual blue-green eyes confirmed his taunt in a way that made Maeve shiver. She had no doubt he would enjoy besting Flynn into oblivion.

She had wondered upon first meeting Kildare if King Henry had finally chosen a warrior to defend the territory with his own hands, instead of one who would line the pockets of others for privilege. For Kildare seemed a man who would not tolerate much idleness. He would take matters into his own hands.

Seeing such so clearly displayed did not bode well for the rebellion's future.

"Aye, now!" Flynn challenged.

With a laugh, Kildare released him. "I look forward to wiping the floor between here and the great hall with your backside."

"'Tis welcome to try, you are," sneered Flynn.

"Nay, both of you!" Maeve shouted.

The brash Kildare turned to her and actually winked. "'Twill not take long, love."

Did he truly think that concerned her? Maeve wanted to slap him. Of all the arrogant, brazen...

She sucked in hard as the Englishman made another fist and glared at her brother with great intent. Flynn was most important now. She must help him, for he had not the experience to deal with a warrior of the earl's ilk.

Grabbing Kildare by the crook of his elbow, Maeve tried to stop the next punch. He merely shrugged off her touch, then plowed his fist into her brother's face. Squarely into his nose.

Blood spurted everywhere.

Behind her, Jana gagged. Fiona gasped again, wringing her hands. Brighid was wide-eyed with shock. No help there.

Maeve sprinted after the combating men again—a moment before Kildare snapped a fist from his side to Flynn's gut faster than she could blink, then planted the other into his jaw once again.

With a snap, a crack, and a grunt, the fight ended, punctuated by the thud of Flynn falling to the earth.

As if sensing her approach, Kildare wiped the blood upon his knuckles on his hose, shrugged, and turned to her.

Again, he wore a smile. Clearly, such actions pleased him—to bully a man unprepared for such an attack.

Maeve approached the tyrant, fist clenched, and rammed it into his shoulder. "That was heathen and unnecessary, you ogre!"

With a momentary scowl, Kildare shrugged off her blow. "Of course it was necessary. Do you think, lovely Maeve, that Flynn O'Shea will question my authority so blatantly again?"

Knowing Flynn, aye. At least every day, mayhap more. But no good could come from telling Kildare thus.

Bending to her brother, she examined his face. When he woke, he would be bruised. His lip would need a stitch, mayhap two. His head would pound harder than a church bell on Sunday, but he would suffer no lasting damage.

Trying to rein in her temper, she drew in a deep breath and rose.

"Have you considered that you might rule better with kindness?"

"Like O'Shea planned to *kindly* kill me? Thank you, but such interests me not, for obvious reasons."

Again, he smiled. Maeve felt her heart pick up pace. Most like from fear at the coarse violence of his action. It had naught to do with the charm of that smile, no matter that it looked so natural, as if he'd been born with it...

She shook her head to clear the stray thought. "So, because you were but repaying his misdeed makes yours somehow more right?"

"War is not about fairness, Maeve. It is about domination, about the power to possess your claim. I have come here to do that."

Maeve could not look away from Kildare's face. Gone was the dangerous grin and easy charm. The man who stood before her with grim eyes and lightning-fast fists was all warrior. She shivered and resented her own hesitance.

Irish women bowed to no one, least of all English beasts.

"Then possess your claim, if you can," she shot out with contempt. "But do not kill my brother in the process, you oaf."

Surprise overtook his hawkish features. "Your brother? You are one of the O'Shea sisters?"

"Aye."

"And these are the other three?" He gestured to her sisters still standing beside the mud pit, fighting illness, shock, and fear.

"Aye. What of us?"

That smile crept across his mouth again, inching up the ends by degrees until his eyes danced with mischief and challenge—and Maeve's stomach began to flit, most certainly with anxiety. She refused to think of it as aught else.

"King Henry sent me here to take one of you to wife."

Maeve felt certain she could not possibly have heard him correctly. *Wife?* Henry Tudor expected one of them to wed such a fierce, conceited, glib, handsome scoundrel?

Who, unless she had too many bats in the belfry, would willingly do such a foolish thing?

Besides, she could think of other reasons not to wed him. Many of them.

"You cannot do such a thing, for the Statue of Kilkenney prohibits the English from marrying the—"

"Irish?" he interrupted, still smiling. Somehow, though, it

looked strained. "Yes, I believe that was mentioned to the king."

"And he sent you anyway?" She frowned.

Kieran nodded, the smile now fading altogether. He rubbed a hand across the back of his neck and muttered an oath of disgust when he came away with mud.

"Aye, he sent me. My good friend Aric, who has the king's ear, reminded his highness that my father was an O'Neill."

Maeve blanched. She could not have been more shocked had he told her snow would fall come July. Him, of Irish blood?

There was no trace of his heritage in his dress, his speech, or his manner. Was such possible?

"Nay," she breathed.

"Oh, aye. So you see, I can wed any of you I wish. And I will do just that, sweet Maeve. By week's end."

* * * *

Though Kieran was in no great rush to take a bride, the look of shock on Maeve's fair face, her for-once-mute mouth, nearly made the moment worthwhile.

And over the next few days, he could relish the delicious torment of reminding her that he was expected to take a wife from among her and her sisters—and give no hint as to who he might choose. True, he knew little of Maeve, but he did know such teasing would drive her to fury.

All the better.

Smiling once more, he opened his mouth to bait the wonderfully stunned Maeve, when the other three O'Shea sisters came dashing up to her side.

"What?" demanded Jana. "You're to wed one of us?"

"Aye," he confirmed, then glanced down to the woman's swollen belly with a grimace. So much for breeding this one soon. She was far ahead of him in that game.

The woman's dark eyes flashed in her pale face. Her faded lips pursed with indignation, flaring them with color. "I would end my life before breeding myself to an English dog."

"Did you not hear him say he was Irish?" Brighid asked, smiling happily, as if that solved everything.

Jana scowled at her youngest sister. "Being of Irish blood does not make him Irish of heart, you foolish girl."

With that, the pregnant woman knelt to her unconscious brother with as much grace as a woman mere days from delivering a babe could.

Kieran glanced at the remaining three. Fiona wrung her hands, and her mouth curled up in an uncertain smile. She was a truly lovely creature with golden curls and honey skin, and silent. Mayhap she might prove blessedly biddable.

Then his gaze slid toward Brighid. She possessed Fiona's golden curls, but they appeared brighter on her pink-cheeked face. He supposed her to be about twelve, give or take a year. Her face showed promise of the beauty she would be. Aye, she was young, but assuredly tamable. Thus far, she had been the most pleasant of the O'Shea sisters.

Finally, he looked to devious Maeve. There was little avoiding it. Her red hair, streaked with bits of her sisters' gold, lit up like a blaze beneath the afternoon sky.

He guessed her younger than Jana but older than Fiona, which placed her somewhere about twenty, he surmised. Long past the time to take a husband. He frowned. How could it be that such a beauty had no husband? Were all the men in Ireland more addled than he thought?

Maeve cleared her throat. Her face revealed little, except that her shock over his announcement was hidden away.

"I do not wish to disappoint you, my lord, but your choices of a bride are limited," she said, not sounding disappointed in the least. In fact, her mouth turned up in a ghost of a smug smile. "As you noticed, Jana expects a child any day."

"Where is her husband?"

"Dead," Maeve spat out in a hissed syllable. "Geralt was executed by the last earl of Kildare."

Kieran absorbed that bit of unfortunate news with a nod. No wonder the O'Sheas had given him such a dangerous welcome. Still, he had no doubt this husband of Jana's had been brewing rebellion— and had known the penalties for such.

"Aye," said the pregnant woman as she rose to her feet. "My babe will never know his father, thanks to you and your king. He's very nearly an orphan before he is even born, you English scum. Don't think I'll be marryin' the likes of you. I'd plant a blade in your back first."

Jana's face was flushed with anger, and Kieran actually acknowledged that she had once been very pretty, before grief and difficulties of pregnancy. As a wife, she would be trying, though he believed he could keep her from stabbing the life out of him. And 'twas clear she could breed. If she could prove beneficial to his post here, his wife she would be. Though he knew wedding a woman already with child would mean a longer wait until he could return to his life as a mercenary.

"And I am promised to another."

Kieran heard those words, and heard them in Maeve's voice.

A surge of denial slid through him as he whipped his gaze back to the flame-headed O'Shea.

"You are promised?"

Her gaze looked cool and smug as she nodded. "I became betrothed November last."

Kieran vowed no such wedding would take place, at least not until he had decided which O'Shea sister to take to wife. Matters of the state would come before the matters of Maeve's heart. He would choose her if it suited him, betrothal be damned.

"And when is this propitious occasion to be?" he asked, wondering at a rise of his anger.

"She and Quaid will wed when he is freed by the English in Dublin," blurted Brighid.

Frowning, Kieran remembered Maeve's earlier words. "Did you not say Quaid would be at the mercy of the hangman's noose soon?"

Maeve's wide red mouth pursed with a frown. "He did naught wrong."

Kieran raised a brow at her. Did she really believe that, or did she merely see rebellion against the English as right?

"That leaves me and Fiona, my lord," offered Brighid.

A quick glance at the two fair-headed sisters revealed Fiona trying to hide her grimace with a false smile, and Brighid's mouth turned up in a hopeful grin. He nearly smiled at the absurdity of it.

"I will wed you, my lord," Brighid offered. "For then I could learn of men and women and how babies are made…"

Babies? Brighid was little more than a child herself. 'Twould be some while before he would think her grown enough to take to his bed. But again, if wedding the imp would further his cause here, mayhap he could bring himself to do it and get a babe on her soon.

Kieran turned his gaze to the other blond girl. Her smile was too bright, inciting his curiosity.

"Fiona?"

Kieran could swear he saw her flinch when he called her name. But that fixed yet tense smile remained in place.

"My lord," she murmured, not quite looking at him.

"Come here."

He wasn't sure what possessed him to issue the command, but he knew his instincts were right when she complied, hands shaking so hard he wondered if she was ill.

"My lord," she said again when she stopped before him. This time her voice shook like her hands as it clawed its way up her throat. No doubt he terrified her.

Mayhap he should not have beaten her brother so senseless.

But it had felt too good.

Kieran regarded Fiona. "I don't bite." Then he smiled, hoping she would respond in kind. "Unless you ask me."

Fiona blanched instead. Kieran frowned and waved her away. She retreated, face relaxing with relief, hands pressed into a white-knuckled clasp.

Sighing, he gazed over the bunch once more as Jana rose to face him. Flynn moaned in the background.

With a glance down, Kieran found his hose and boots a bloody, muddy mess, his tunic torn, his dignity challenged, and his knuckles sore from punching Flynn.

And he had yet to even enter the castle.

Such ill beginnings did not bode well for any stay in Ireland.

Kieran cursed. He must get on with wedding and bedding a wife as soon as possible. Only then could he leave. Only then would he know pleasure in life again.

"Beginning tomorrow," he began, regarding the four sisters, "I will spend one day with each of you, even those widowed and promised."

Maeve objected, "But—"

"You are unwed at the moment, and that is all I require," he interrupted, then went on, "At the end of those four days, I will inform you and your brother, as well as the king, which of you I will take as my bride. Until then, I want a bath, a meal, and a soft bed."

Maeve opened her mouth again. "But—"

"And no arguing, no threatening, no frightened nor curious females." He gave each of them a hard stare. "None at all."

CHAPTER THREE

The following morn dawned gray and rainy. Though Kieran's young squire, Colm, and a few of his trusted men had arrived during the night, with the weather as it was today, they could not venture out of doors. Such idleness chafed him. Kieran wanted to be outside these thick stone walls, training the castle's army, assessing the lands, meeting its people, finding the root of rebellion. Remaining trapped with the four shrewish sisters irritated him beyond measure.

Then further unsettling news reached him upon first wakening: Flynn had left Langmore during the night and had not returned. He had no doubt the man could find the rebellion and join them, should he put his mind to such a task.

But he would bother with Flynn when the man returned. Now he had a bride to choose, despite the fact he would rather take a long trip to purgatory if it meant he might avoid taking a wife.

After breaking his fast, Kieran toured the small keep. It had been built more for defense than comfort. Its walls were thick and its luxuries—and bedchambers—were few. Still, it was a sturdy keep, and only that would matter if the Irish rebels attacked.

Knowing he could no longer put off the inevitable, Kieran returned to the great hall and reluctantly summoned Jana to his side. Since the pregnant woman had spent a good portion of the night insisting she would have the babe within hours, Kieran figured he ought not to waste any time in speaking with her, lest she actually birth the mite soon.

The dark-headed sister appeared in the great hall a few minutes after the appointed time. After clearing the room of all others, he sat

40

beside her. Her fatigued face drew a moment's pity for some unknown reason, and he hoped she found a restful night's sleep soon.

"So I'm to spend the day with you, am I?" she said, but even the contempt in her voice emerged as little more than weariness.

"Aye. I would ask you a few questions, hear about you, about Langmore. You may ask questions as you wish."

She stared into a cup of goat's milk. "You know all that is important. I grew up here in Langmore. I was wed here. 'Tis a fine castle built near a hundred years past, but she stands strong. I have no doubt 'tis why you English beasts want it."

Kieran chose not to comment on that gibe now. 'Twould only lead to an argument that would sap her of more energy.

"What do you enjoy, Jana?"

"Enjoy?" She frowned, clearly surprised by such a question. "Do my interests matter?"

Aye, they did. His parents had failed at marriage so badly because they shared naught but a son. Since Drake and his lovely wife, Averyl, both shared a love of books, Kieran thought to find a wife with whom he could share something. Such might cut down on the death and mayhem.

Mayhap…and mayhap not.

"I have been far too busy readying for this birth of late to be concerned with interests."

"What of your interests before your marriage?" he prompted.

Her faded mouth thinned into a pressed line. "I am tired and recall little before I wed. Now my only interest is in birthing a healthy babe, as Geralt would have wished."

When Kieran saw a glossy sheen of unshed tears in her eyes, he nodded. "You will make him proud."

"Not if I take an enemy as my husband. I want no part of this absurdity."

"So you've said. I want no part of marriage, either, but—"

"You did not lose the one you loved a mere two months past," she said, rising from the bench as her voice rose in volume. "You will not have to look at your innocent babe and try to explain why he has no father. You will not have to tell him that the English killed his father but his mother married one of the butcher's kind anyway!"

Tears began down Jana's face, and she crumpled back to the

bench in a sobbing heap.

Kieran flinched as she wailed beside him and rested her face in her hands. Her noisy tears echoed in the great hall, disturbing even the resting hounds. Frowning, he stared at the grieving woman. Her pain was no pretense, and he found himself shifting in his seat with discomfort.

"They k-killed him! And for doing naught m-more than what he believed was right. Freedom… 'Twas all he sought. W-why did he have to die to gain something he had been born with?"

Kieran had no answer for that. That was simply war. Some won. Others lost—and paid the ultimate price. Always he had accepted thus.

Today, watching Jana shake her own body—and her babe's—with the force of her tears, he felt…tense.

"Jana," he said softly. "Your Geralt did what he thought right, true. But he defied the law—"

"English law!" she cut in angrily, lifting her head from the table.

Misery had turned her cheeks pink, her nose red, and her eyes puffy. Grief sat stiffly in each line of her oval face, in each inch of her downturned mouth.

For once, Kieran knew not what to say.

"Why should the English make laws for Ireland? They rape our land and our women. They kill our men, then expect obedience." She laughed bitterly. "Why should we give it?"

Though Kieran knew Jana believed such, she could not see the truth: war, by its nature, decreed that those who fell would be subjugated by those who conquered. 'Twas no right or wrong in that. It simply was.

Still, he could not help an unwelcome pang of sympathy for her loss and that of her babe. He had grown to manhood without much of his own father. He knew how great that loss could be.

"Shhh, good lady. You will upset the babe." He reached out to place a soothing hand upon her own.

She yanked it away. "Touch me not, you swine! And be assured that if you are so foolish as to force me to wife, I will do all that I can to make your life hell and see you dead. *That*, you English miscreant, would have made my Geralt happy!"

Jana pushed away from the bench and lumbered away from the table. Kieran made no move to stop her.

Aye, he could force her to wed, if he wished it. 'Twas clear Jana could breed, which would ensure he could leave Ireland, but she spent more time in anger or grief than in the running of Langmore or the care of her family. She would soon have a babe to birth and raise, so 'twould be some time before he could get another on her himself and leave this miserable place. Would he not be best served to leave her be? Aye.

Kieran denied his decision not to wed her had aught to do with the enmity his parents had sharpened to lethal hatred—a fate he feared would be his own if he wed a woman who despised him. But he felt sure Aric and Drake would both have chastised him for such a denial.

Shaking his head, he tossed back the rest of his ale and rose to leave the great hall. Behind him, small, angry footsteps approached.

Kieran whirled, hand beside the dagger at his waist, ready. He saw only Maeve and felt his mind relax.

Smiling, he watched her come near. This morn, she wore her hair loose, a cascade of red-gold glory that fell to her waist. The green dress she wore contrasted with the rich, creamy underdress beneath, spilling a ripple of a sleeve down her arm. The gown fit snugly to her small waist, and though he could not see her legs, he could imagine the long and firm appendages and sighed.

A light quip sat upon his tongue, one he hoped would charm her. He bit it back when he saw the fury flushing her face and tightening her fists.

"'Tis so like an English bully to seek out the weak and hurt them," she hissed.

"Hurt? Who—"

"Who?" Maeve barked back. "Now you say that you are simple-minded as well as mean? Jana cries upon her bed great rivers of tears after less than a quarter hour's conversation with you. Leave her be! Her shattered heart can take no more."

Maeve was a warrioress protecting one of her own. He did not think her tendencies ran violent, but had no trouble believing she would sink a knife into any man's back who dared to hurt one of her kin. He admired that about her, though such could be a meddlesome penchant he must not give free rein.

"You will not take her to wife," Maeve insisted, leaning closer, jaw clenched with fury.

With her spring-scented nearness and her flushed face, Kieran's mind wandered down dark paths where an eager Maeve accepted his kiss hungrily, with open-mouthed fervor. What would she taste like?

She exploded, fists clenched. "Do you listen to me? That lewd smirk says not."

Her shout chased the thought away. Aye, he wanted her near, but not so he could hear her haranguing him.

"Aye, I hear you. You wish me not to wed Jana."

Somewhat mollified, Maeve stepped back a bit and unclenched her fists. "Aye."

"Who would you have me wed then?" he asked.

She paused in consideration, then, with a false smile, offered, "My brother's hunting bitch is in heat."

Kieran laughed. No one could deny the woman had spirit. She did not speak much, not like Aric's Gwenyth. But when she did choose to comment, 'twas clear she spoke her mind.

"As much as I must have a wife, a dog will not do, sweet Maeve."

"I am not your sweet anything." She glared at him.

"Perhaps I will change that." He gave her the grin that melted many a heart—or at least a dress away from the owner's body.

"You cannot, I assure you."

Maeve seemed so sure of herself, so certain she could resist whatever temptation he might throw her way. But she knew naught of his determination if he set his mind to something. And mayhap he would set his mind to having her, if she proved to be the wife he needed.

In response to her declaration, he merely smiled. "If you wish me to cease considering Jana as a wife, I will do so."

Maeve's golden eyes narrowed. "You would do such a thing simply because I asked it?"

"Nay. I do such a thing because I had reached much the same conclusion. Jana will remain unwed until she finds a man of her choice and my approval."

The suspicious glare on Maeve's face softened to a mere frown. "Truly?"

"Good lady, please stop looking for some trickery on my part. I will not marry Jana, and that is all."

"Thank you," she said stiffly.

He nodded, then watched her turn away.

But the devil inside him made him call out to her. "I have made no such decision about you, sweet Maeve."

* * * *

A roll of parchment arrived the following morn from Dublin. Breath held, Maeve waited for Kildare to read it. How successful had the rebellion been? Had Flynn been able to free Quaid?

She yearned to see her betrothed now, before she forgot his face, before she spent any more time pondering the mocking English smile that had kept her awake last night.

Beside the great hall's hearth, the earl straddled a bench. His wide shoulders and long legs, honed by countless hours of training and war, bunched and rippled with every move. As he read the missive, his unusual blue-green gaze made its way over the paper. She watched, swallowed, her stomach fluttering.

'Twas fear, she told herself fiercely. Only fear for her brother and her betrothed, neither big men, neither much of fighting men. Kildare could kill them both if he chose. The day of his arrival had proven that plainly. The flutter in her belly had naught to do with the hawkish, handsome face, his watchful eyes, or that strong body.

Finally, he lifted his head, rolled up the parchment once more, and cursed. Clearly the news within did not make Kildare want to celebrate. Good!

"What news have you, my lord?" she asked as if she knew naught.

He speared her with a stare that quickly turned contemplative. "Where is your brother?"

She shrugged, feigning ignorance. "Oft times, he visits a wench in a neighboring village."

"Which one?"

"I know not. Why would he share this with me?"

Kildare looked at her skeptically but said naught more. Maeve thought she might go mad with curiosity.

"Has aught happened, my lord?"

"I suspect you know this, but during the night, Malahide Castle was attacked by unknown members of the rebellion."

Maeve tried to suppress her relief and glee. Flynn had not been caught!

Instead, she gasped, trying to sound appropriately surprised. "And what happened?"

"Little, really. But they managed to damage the keep, including the dungeon."

They had reached the heart of the castle, found a way inside, and entered the dungeon. Dare she hope Flynn had been able to free—

"No one escaped, thankfully."

Maeve could not help the sinking disappointment that slid a thick path to her stomach, taking her spirits with it.

"The missive lists the names of several prisoners the rebellion seems to covet. Among them is one Quaid O'Toole. Is he your...betrothed?"

Silently, she nodded. She wanted to scream or cry in frustration, in fear. To do so before Kildare would reveal too much. Instead, she decided silence was her safest course.

"If you and your brother thought to free him and wed you off safely before I could decide who to take to wife, I will be much displeased."

Displeased? As if she wasn't sick with bitter disappointment, utterly disheartened? "My goal remains to wed the man of my choosing. If someone freed him from English clutches, I would applaud them."

Kildare's face turned hard and warring. No hint of that seductive smile lingered. "Are you disappointed Flynn failed?"

"Flynn had naught to do with last night. As I said, he is with a woman—"

"If Flynn wanted a wench to warm his bed, 'tis doubtful he would have to leave Langmore for such. From what I have seen, there are many women at Langmore worthy of a tumble."

Maeve forced herself to meet Kildare's hot gaze. "That may be, but there is not a woman here who wants a place in your bed."

She meant the words as a slur. Maeve saw instantly that Kildare took them as a challenge.

He stood then, staring, ever watchful, as if taking her measure. Maeve resisted the urge to shiver. Kildare was the enemy, no matter how well he caught her attention.

The rousing smile she knew as his returned, along with a

healthy dose of determination. "Mayhap I should prove you wrong, sweet Maeve."

"You cannot make me want you."

It was the wrong thing to say. Maeve realized that as Kildare's smile widened and he sauntered toward her. She looked around the great hall for help. No one stood about. 'Twas empty, from the freshly beaten tapestries covering the high stone wall on her left, to the huge blaze heating the room in the hearth at her right.

Kildare's smile was rich with purpose. "Tsk, sweet Maeve. How can you dislike something before you try it?"

Maeve stood firm against his slow advance and glared at him. "I already know I would find any such contact with an ogre displeasing."

He grinned yet wider. "Well, if you are certain, let us test it, shall we?"

Before she could protest or place a hand between them, Kildare seized her around the waist and dragged her close, against the hard wall of his chest. For an infinite moment, their gazes locked, his heated and determined.

Against her will, Maeve felt her awareness of his solid body rising, felt her face flushing, her belly tightening with what she could only call anticipation. Nay, she should feel this for Quaid, had always wanted to. Why should she feel this with an enemy who would soon destroy her home and make her or one of her sisters an unwilling bride?

But as Kildare stood against her, his gaze probed hers as if to peer deep inside her and see her longings so he might fulfill them, 'twas hard to remember he was the enemy.

Perspiration broke out between her breasts. She parted her lips to say something, to take in more air.

Kildare leaned in and took her mouth with a gentle sweep, surrounding her lips and plying them farther apart with an insistent caress.

The contact jolted her all the way to her tingling toes. Maeve's breath left her. She drowned in sensation. The rasp of his morning beard, the sound of his harsh breath in her ear, the feel of his iron arms about her, keeping her prisoner to his kiss—she noted all with her flushed, fluttering senses. He enticed with his lips, teasing and coaxing her surrender.

She weakened to the pleasure, then demanded more. Kildare knew how to master a mouth, how to make a woman crave more in an instant.

She opened beneath Kildare and stood on tiptoes to meet him as a craving imprisoned her. With a sound of approval, Kildare deepened the kiss again, this time sweeping his tongue about her own, taunting her, until she felt breathless, until, weak-kneed, she clutched him for support.

Kildare lifted his head, burning her with a heated smile.

Sweet Mary, what had she done?

"Cease!" she said, backing away.

Kildare reached for her. "Why, sweet Maeve? Was that not pleasant?"

"Nay."

"Nay?" He pretended confusion. "I do not recall a protest from you. Did you issue one?"

"Swine," she muttered, flushing with heat.

Kildare merely flashed her an insufferable grin.

She kicked him in the shin. "Do not kiss me again."

Her reaction was childish, she knew. But he roused her ire, blast him.

He laughed as she left the room with her head held high.

* * * *

The following morn, Kieran found himself in a familiar place, in the great hall, awaiting an O'Shea sister.

Today, 'twas Fiona's turn to spend the day with him. He did not relish the hours ahead. In fact, he found his thoughts disturbed by thoughts of her surly brother, who had returned last night well into his cups. He also could not forget her redheaded sister.

Aye, his blood heated at the thought of kissing sweet Maeve. He had not expected her to react with such abandon. Nor had he been prepared for the force of his own want.

Such only increased his curiosity more. But his curiosity was temporary and must not be given free rein. Passion meant naught in marriages born of politics. Today, he would speak with Fiona, see if she might make him a suitable wife.

"Good morn, my lord." Fiona stood before him suddenly, her

approach so silent he had scarce heard it.

As usual, she looked lovely, dressed in a soft blue that accented her eyes, pinkened her cheeks, and outlined the curves of her ripe bosom. But she still wore that feigned smile and pressed her hands so tightly together he felt sure she could hold water without a single drop falling.

"Good morn, Fiona. The rain has now stopped, so we might journey to the garden for a stroll."

Fiona flinched, skin paling. If possible, her body seemed to grow more tense.

"You do not like the out of doors?" he asked, much curious.

"I-I do," she stammered. "I… 'Tis cold this morn."

Kieran frowned. He had been out earlier this morn, questioning a defiantly silent Flynn about the rebellion after suffering a strangely sleepless night. At the end of the fruitless inquisition that made him more suspicious of what he could not prove, Kieran had sought solace out of doors. He had thought the dawning day warm for February.

With a shrug, he gestured her to the bench beside him. "As you wish, good lady. Sit here."

"Thank you."

Her voice was so quiet in the huge room the sound of it was near lost. She reminded him of a wary kitten, all wide eyes and furtive movement.

"Tell me what you enjoy."

She frowned, but even that was no more than a gentle furrow of her delicate brow. "My lord?"

Did these O'Shea women not understand the meaning of enjoyment? Did they naught but…whatever these Irish folk did? And why did they do it, if not for fun?

"I am Kieran, not my lord, please," he corrected. "What makes you smile, Fiona?"

"Mass, my—Kieran."

Mass? So Fiona would smile in the Lord's home. Would she ever smile in any bed he might want to share with her? And what was *he* to do with a woman who would not?

"Aught else? Perhaps you enjoy festivals?"

"Nay, too many people about."

"Music? I find there is little more fun than a rousing tune and a good dance."

She shrugged and looked away. "I enjoy thoughtful music, but not dance."

What woman disliked dancing? He had yet to meet one who didn't enjoy kicking up her heels until she fair lost her breath from the rhythm and the laughter. Odd, indeed.

"Have you traveled any?"

Fiona wrung her hands. "Traveled, my lord? Where to?"

"Anywhere." He threw up his hands in exasperation. "Dublin? London?"

"Nay."

Simply *nay*. Not *nay, but I should like that*. Not *nay, and I wish you to perdition*. Just one word. How was he to hold a conversation like that? Much less learn about her?

"Tell me of your parents," he said, switching to another question, which she could not answer with one word.

"They are dead."

Her whisper distracted him silly. Her brevity near drove him to madness.

"Aye, Fiona. That I know. What I asked is, what manner of people were they?"

There. Now 'twas doubtful she could answer with a mere word. He nearly dared her to try.

"Caring."

By damned, she had done it.

He sighed. "Caring? Did they sit you upon their knee? Did your father buy you ribbons for your hair? Did they dote upon you?"

"Aye."

To all the questions, she said but one word. And she could not even look at him when doing such! If the wench could not meet his gaze when talking, he could only imagine how far into the distance she would gaze if he tried to share a marriage bed with her so that he might get a babe upon her and leave this accursed country.

True, he had never wanted a woman who chattered a great deal. A woman like that was not being kissed enough, to his way of thinking. Kieran frowned. Although Aric's wife, Gwenyth, was the exception. They kissed frequently, but naught had curbed that woman's sharp tongue, which Aric needed to keep him in line.

But this lack of conversation with Fiona... Kieran knew he was here for the next year or so, long enough to take a wife and get her with child. But he could scarce imagine sitting beside Fiona each meal, lying beside her each night, with no words exchanged, no glances met for that year.

He had met dying soldiers with more to say.

True, that made her biddable. 'Twas unlikely she would argue with him about Langmore, about the rebellion…about aught.

Somehow the thought of a wife that docile seemed tiresome.

"Fiona, would you excuse me? I need to see my squire for a bit."

Relief lit the woman's face in an instant. So much for the unfailing charm Aric had accused him repeatedly of possessing.

She rose from the bench and began backing out of the room. "Of course, my lord. 'Tis certain I am you are busy."

With those two sentences, she was gone. Hellfire, the woman had not said that much to him all morn. Kieran supposed he ought to be grateful.

Instead, he felt surly.

For now, his choices in bride were but two: a budding girl-child…and an irksome wench with a kiss like fire.

CHAPTER FOUR

Another morn, another O'Shea sister.

Kieran sighed tiredly as Brighid appeared in the great hall directly after Sunday's Mass celebrating the beginning of Shrovetide. She wore a high-waisted dress of bright green, with patterned sleeves. The shining mass of her golden hair lay about her shoulders. Atop her head rested a decorative headdress of gold that was wider than the whole of her head. Kieran stared.

Brighid had dressed with all care, and he had no doubt the garments she wore were her finest and newest.

Unfortunately, such elaborate garb made her look all the more youthful, as if she were a young child who had chosen to filch her mother's clothes.

Trying to hide his grimace, Kieran reminded himself that he had chosen to speak with Brighid today for a purpose. If she would make a suitable bride, pliable and tolerable, able to be a helpmate here, he would consider wedding her. After all, of the four sisters, she was the friendliest—and the least likely to bring a blade to their bed. Kieran could not deny he disliked the idea of a child bride, but he knew he must be careful. With Jana and Fiona eliminated as potential wives, his choices were fast dwindling.

And he must do his duty by Guilford. He owed the man too much to allow him to lose Hartwich Hall to King Henry's nervous machinations. The old man had taken him in and fostered him after he had been ripped from Ireland by a distant mother, then abandoned for his unruly ways.

He focused on Brighid, clearing his mind of the past.

"A good morn to you, my lord." She curtsied prettily.

"Good morn, Brighid. Will you sit and break your fast?"

She bowed her head and sat beside him on the bench, bringing her closer into view. A flush lit her skin from the top of her low, square bodice, all the way to her pointed hairline.

He squirmed in his chair and turned his attention to the warm cider in his cup, aware of Brighid sipping likewise beside him.

Uncertain what he should ask her, he took a sip of the fermented liquid.

"What are you wantin' in a wife, my lord? A woman who will enjoy you ridin' her each night?"

Kieran choked at her question and nearly spit out his cider. Aye, such a woman sounded pleasurable, but how would this girl know of that? "What?"

Her bony little shoulders rose in a shrug. "Flynn says all men want such a bride."

Most did, and though Kieran knew many girls her age who were already wed, he had never thought the practice a wise one. His thought on the matter was, if a woman had not yet developed a bosom to please a man's eye, she had not the bosom to suckle a babe. Until she appeared a woman, she could not possibly be one.

And though he thought Flynn a coxcomb, he had not imagined the maggot would be so shandy-minded as to say such a thing to his young sister.

"But that is not all men seek in a wife," he answered.

At that, her shoulders fell in a dejected slump. "Aye, I hear Flynn say a man wants a wench who can kiss as well. But I ask you, where am I to get such practice? Every man who looks my way, Flynn scares to the devil!"

Kieran believed that. "'Tis not important now, little one. In a few years' time—"

"But how else will I learn so I might be a good wife?" She bit her lip, and before Kieran could respond, her face brightened. "Of course! You might teach me. Even though you are more English than Irish, as Jana says, you are fierce handsome." She blushed again. "And since we might soon be wed—"

"I have made no decision, Brighid. We might not be wed."

The idea of kissing the girl—much less bedding her—made him flinch. Why? He had no such compunction about her sister.

53

True, Maeve was older. But Brighid was simply sweet and unfettered, unlike maddening Maeve. He suspected Brighid would be great fun to laugh with, which he always enjoyed in a female. He would bet her inhibitions were few.

But the girl was merely a child.

"I shall be ten and three in April. If not now, when?"

Ten and three? As he had imagined, she was too young.

"Not much longer. Two or three years."

Brighid's mouth dropped open when she looked at him with an indignant glare. "Two or three years! I will near be a spinster by then, I tell you."

He laughed, and for that, the girl kicked him beneath the table.

"Do not chortle so at me! It's very unkind, you ass."

Kieran bent to rub his offended leg and bit his lip to hold in another chuckle. No doubt, the girl had spirit.

"You smile still!" she complained. "I asked you for a kiss, which you should have requested from me, and I am but mocked?"

"Sir? I-I mean, my lord?" came Colm's query from the entrance to the hall, saving Kieran from a reply.

Kieran turned to regard his young squire. Colm's gaze met his gaze, then strayed to Brighid before meeting his own once more. A familiar expression lit Colm's dark gaze—one of interest.

His squire and young Brighid?

He smiled. "Aye, Colm. Come, sit."

Eyeing him warily, Colm did as he was bid, sitting on Kieran's left. Again, the young man's gaze flitted past him and landed on Brighid. He turned to his right and found the youngest of the O'Shea sisters turning even pinker under his squire's regard.

Colm was himself but ten and five. Possibilities lay there... His squire was a kind soul, too gentle to be trained for battle. But Kieran liked the boy.

"My lord, those remaining of the last earl's army are outside, awaiting you."

"Thank you. I will see to them soon. Have you met this fair maid?" he asked his squire.

"N-nay, my lord."

The boy looked as if he were about to turn red and sweat, and Kieran smiled again. "This lovely lass is Brighid O'Shea." He turned to the girl, then finished the introduction. "Little one, Colm

Colinford. He is my squire."

Silence reigned for a full ten seconds. Colm finally broke the quiet.

"Gre-greetings, mistress."

Brighid turned from pink to red and seemed to find sudden fascination with the hands folded in her lap. "And to you, good sir."

Again, silence. Furtive glances were exchanged by both. Kieran saw in his awkward hesitance that Colm had little experience with females. He sighed when he realized he'd been neglecting such an important part of the boy's education.

And now he fancied Colm and Brighid might be good for one another.

Wearing a broad grin, he rose from the bench, leaving an empty space between them. They both looked at him in question.

Kieran gave Colm a friendly pat on the back, then teased, "Brighid is looking for a man to kiss her. Mayhap you could teach her whilst I go start with the men."

Smiling, he walked away from a pair of identical stunned expressions and left the great hall. Around the corner and down the stairs, he strode.

No sooner had he begun down the stairs when he saw Maeve.

She climbed up in the opposite direction, taper in one hand, balancing a book in the other, with wooden spectacles perched upon her small, round-tipped nose. Her lips moved a bit as she read. She appeared not to see him.

Watching her, Kieran thought she looked learned—something he had *never* fancied in a woman. It reeked of deep thought and an aversion to action. Aye, she could kiss sweetly, but he could not imagine her romping in the rain nor enjoying a good hunt. She belonged indoors, a book close to her face, mayhap with a hound at her feet.

He shuddered, for he could not imagine a life so…settled. His boyhood had been anything but, and today that suited him well.

"Good morn," he said an instant before she would have collided with him.

Maeve tore her gaze from the pages before her to his face. When she caught sight of him, she eyed him warily.

"Good morn," she replied, then frowned. "I thought you were to spend the day with Brighid."

"Aye."

Maeve waited, as if expecting more of an answer. Kieran smiled, happy to let her wait. Vexation crossed her lovely features, giving them more color, more expression.

"And so where is she now?"

"In the great hall above."

"Breaking her fast?" she asked, closing the book she held.

"Kissing my squire, I presume."

Though he but teased her, Kieran couldn't stop his grin when ire overtook Maeve's golden gaze.

"Kissing?"

More fresh color lit her luminous skin, and for some reason, Kieran wished her remembrances of their kiss, not her anger, had caused such. After all, had that kiss not kept him awake last night, tempting him? Making him wonder if Maeve would be his best choice of a wife, even though he had not spoken with her and all her sisters?

"Brighid has no need to be kissing anyone," protested Maeve, "much less some English fool of a squire. Likely he will trifle with her an-and leave her with child—"

Kieran erupted in laughter. "'Tis unlikely Colm yet knows how to trifle with himself, much less a female."

With a wink, he walked past Maeve as she attempted to sputter a retort. It pleased him to render her near speechless, and he whistled all the way outside.

* * * *

Kieran had scarce worked with the last earl's soldiers for a quarter hour before he decided they were a pitiful lot.

Standing on the grassy plain in front of Langmore, he looked over the "army" once more. 'Twas an abysmally small group. Out of the two dozen *galloglasses*, permanently employed soldiers who had stayed since the last earl left, four men looked as if they spent all their days gorging from dawn to dusk—and beyond—another three looked as if a stiff wind would blow them to their arses. Several others, with their grayed hair, showed they were much closer to the grave than the cradle. Fully a dozen had no real knowledge of wielding a broadsword, an ax, or a mace. Who in Hades had trained them? The rest were Irishmen, the *kern*, only there for the coin, and such showed in their defiant demeanors.

'Twould be a long road before he could make warriors out of this motley lot.

With a disgusted sigh, he turned away. Clearly, he would need to best the men well and often for most to listen or respect his ability.

He had not the time for this. Taking a wife and getting her with child so he might leave—that should be his focus. Except the wife hunt had not gone well. Jana was too lost in grief to make a suitable bride. Fiona seemed trapped in some nervous silence that made him want to find the nearest cup of ale. Brighid was fun…but terribly young.

Damnation! He wanted no wife. But Guilford needed him. And now he had no O'Shea sister to consider but Maeve.

He felt trapped, as if the walls at Langmore were closing about him, squeezing him off from air and light. He shuddered, wanting it to stop, wanting to be free.

Holding in a curse, he turned to one of his own captains, who had arrived in Ireland with Colm, and bade him to continue instructing the deplorable castle soldiers.

He needed to be away!

In minutes, Kieran sat atop Lancelot, aimlessly heading east as if for the sea and England, or anywhere else that might bring freedom.

The sun's zenith came. He passed the River Slaney, pausing only to sip from its cold waters as it babbled across mossy green rocks.

As he traveled on, the landscape turned mountainous. The sun began a sharp descent from the sky. Rock-strewn glens and bogs abounded, covered with dormant heather of muted purple. And green everywhere, budding shades of it, beginning to come alive with the coming spring and cover the hilly land.

And the land looked hauntingly familiar, like land he had not seen since the days after he had turned eight.

In the explosion of a colorful dusk, he dismounted before a *lough* and followed the water's edge around a gentle slope of a hill.

He encountered a waterfall, one that looked much like one that had been his favorite place to play as a boy. Chilly water cascaded over craggy granite, seemingly locked together in nature's hold.

And suddenly he felt quite certain that beyond the next rise lay the remnants of Balcorthy.

Nay. He would not see the ruins of his boyhood home. He had no need.

Settling again on Lancelot's back, he decided to make his way back to Langmore, to face the task of taking a bride and seeing her birth a babe.

Instead, he found himself urging Lancelot forward, to climb the next ridge.

Moments before the sun disappeared behind him, Kieran looked over the pasture. The ruins of Balcorthy sat in stately neglect, utterly abandoned.

Fire had turned the stone black in places. Battle and disregard had caused some of the walls to tumble down. He would even bet some of the nearby townsfolk had taken blocks from the once-imposing keep and used them to build their own homes with more security.

Whatever the cause, Balcorthy looked naught like the important, bustling castle he recalled. A sadder monument to the hate with which a husband and wife could hurt each other did not exist, he felt certain.

'Twas merely another reason to return to Langmore and complete his duty. He would assess his options, take a damned bride, and be done with the mess. The sooner he left Ireland, the happier a man would he be.

* * * *

The following night, Kieran sat in the middle of the raised dais for supper. Jana sat stiffly to his left. Maeve, doing her best to ignore him, sat to his right. 'Twould be a long evening, no doubt.

As the servants brought in the meal, Kieran glanced at Fiona, who sat at the next table, close beside his. Flynn rested beside her, looking bruised and malcontented. No doubt the man had taken part in the recent rebellion, but he had not accomplished a thing, particularly not the release of Maeve's seditious betrothed, Quaid O'Toole. But 'twas no matter, Kieran planned to punish the O'Shea man very soon.

Looking away from Flynn, Kieran glanced toward Brighid and Colm, smiling shyly at one another, as they sat a bit farther away. Perhaps Colm had taught Brighid to kiss, after all.

Everyone ate in silence. Kieran was aware of Maeve beside him, smelling faintly of this afternoon's damp rain. She kept her gaze in the trencher they shared, barely eating.

He speared a bit of garlic-spiced mutton with his knife. Their arms brushed, sleeves warmed by their bodies. Maeve tensed. So she *was* aware of him. Kieran felt his blood stir.

He tossed a bite of meat into his mouth. Maeve reached for her cider and took a small sip. When she finished, her berry lips looked glossy-wet and luscious. Enticing. Edible.

Then she mopped up the apple-spiced alcohol with her tongue. Kieran knew he stared, knew that Maeve was aware when she stared back, frozen. Her tongue stilled across her upper lip as her eyes flared wide. The feminine flutter of her pulse pounded at her throat. Kieran felt lust flood his loins.

Even when she looked away, he pictured her thus, tongue upon upper lips, golden eyes wary and wanting at once.

He had never been good at denying his wants. And he could not deny Maeve topped his list of desires at the moment. He wanted to kiss her again, to feel her heat and hear her mewl in his arms once more. He wanted to share the delights of the bedchamber with her.

Why, he knew not. Too oft, he found her now with a book in her lap and those blasted spectacles upon her face. She strolled in the garden occasionally but never raced outdoors for the fun of it. In fact, never did anything for the sheer joy of it that he could see.

How could he want such a woman?

Yet when he looked at her, flowing red-gold hair, firm jaw, gracefully sloped neck, breasts he could not forget if he lived to be one hundred, he wondered how any man could not want her.

"So, I see you've settled into Langmore as if you've owned the place all your life, you ratty Englishman. But I wouldn't be getting too comfortable now, I tell you."

Kieran jerked his gaze from Maeve to Flynn. "Do you think to threaten me?"

Flynn shrugged. "'Twould be unwise to think too little of an Irishman's mettle."

"Tell him, Flynn!" cried Jana.

Kieran ignored her. "It would be unwise to think too little of a trained warrior's skill. Have you already forgotten?"

"Forgotten? 'Tis not likely I am to forget a bastard who attacks another man when his back is turned. But that is the way you English like to fight."

"Odd, Flynn, for I recall seeing your eyes wide with fear when I first punched you."

A few feet away, Brighid gasped and Colm chuckled. Fiona looked warily between him and her brother.

Flynn turned a deep rose, which mutated into a red that soon became mottled and glowing. Kieran smiled.

"But if you think me mistaken," he continued, "I can be persuaded to go outside so we might fix the puzzling matter once and for all."

Beside him, Maeve prodded his ribs with a sharp elbow. "We are eating a peaceful meal."

"Are we, now?" he asked with a raised brow.

She was riled again, her face alive. He enjoyed seeing her thus, to see her when she could think of naught else but him.

"Just remember," Flynn growled, "that an Irishman never gives up. We will never let a little thing like blood stand in our way."

Kieran presumed Flynn meant his blood. And ordinarily, he would laugh. Flynn was no match for him alone, but if he had a group of soldiers willing to fight for his cause… Well, Kieran was not anxious to test their tenacity against that of the "army" left by the last, now late, earl. He feared more than half of them would desert to the enemy cause.

And thus he must tread carefully here.

"May the enemies of Ireland never meet a friend!" said Jana, reciting an old Irish curse.

Before he could reply to Jana or Flynn, Maeve stood beside him and glared down the table at Flynn. "Peace with bloodshed is no peace at all."

Kieran expected a retort from Flynn, at the very least about managing females. Instead, he looked…chagrined.

"Freedom cannot always be won without bloodshed, Maeve," argued her brother.

"But it is, at least, best to try."

With that thought, Maeve sat again.

To his pleasant surprise, Flynn said not another word throughout the rest of the meal. Aye, O'Shea continued to glare at him—as if he should like it if the English invader would be the next meal slow-roasted upon the spit for a freedom festival. But he kept his mouth closed.

All because of two sentences from Maeve.

Kieran knew he could not have accomplished such a feat. Of course he did not agree with her. Conducting the rebellion—and handling it—would require bloodshed, but to have said as much would only have incited Flynn to further mutiny.

With her quiet logic, Maeve could silence her rebellious brother. Indeed, she seemed to have some power over this unusual family, despite their differences in personality. Whether calming the nervous Fiona or quieting the defiant Flynn, she seemed to know exactly what to say.

Swinging his gaze left, he watched the second O'Shea sister as she now kept a watchful eye on Brighid and Colm, who stole clandestine touches of their hands beneath the table.

As if to remind him that their budding attraction was his doing, and therefore his fault, she turned her fiery gaze to him.

Somehow, despite all her learnedness, he found her intriguing. How would she look in laughter? Flushed with passion?

Kieran knew of one simple way to find out.

The kitchen maids came in and began clearing away the rest of the meal, carefully saving the trenches for the almoner to give to the poor. A troubadour emerged from the corner of the great hall, as he did most every night, to entertain the small crowd of seven. Kieran stayed the man and the lute player beside him with a hand.

Puzzled, Maeve stared at him.

Kieran merely stood and smiled. To his satisfaction, everyone in the room turned to watch him, even Colm and Brighid, who appeared until now to have eyes only for one another.

"Flynn, ladies," he addressed, "I have chosen my bride and should like to inform you all."

Fiona and Jana exchanged glances, then Brighid joined them. Maeve frowned. No doubt, she was aware he had not spent a whole day with any of her sisters, and no time devoted just to her.

"I won't have you makin' one of my sisters an Englishman's whore," warned Flynn.

"Wife," Kieran growled. "We will be wed by the priest. 'Twill be nothing improper or unsanctioned about the union."

"But you'll be takin' her to your bed, is that not so?

He smiled just thinking about it. "Definitely."

"Nay!" Jana shrieked in horror. "I won't have you touching me!"

"Nor will I, good lady, for I've no intent to wed you." Kieran frowned.

At that, Brighid stood and scampered up the steps of the dais to his side. She motioned him down, and he bent so she could whisper in his ear.

"I know you are bound to consider me and that I asked you to teach me to kiss, but Colm has done that, you see. Though you are a handsome man, I—"

He patted her shoulder, holding in a laugh. "Go sit."

With a tense sigh, the girl did as he bid, sliding closer to Colm. A shaking Fiona next caught his eye as he stood once more, but he refused to be distracted from his purpose again.

"We must plan a wedding and a feast."

"Lent is upon us," said Fiona. "We can have no such event until after Easter—"

"We can," Kieran insisted. "Tomorrow is Shrove Tuesday."

"You mean to wed tomorrow?" Fiona gasped, then clapped a hand over her mouth as if to keep further protests in. But her fearful eyes told him she had plenty of them.

"Aye, tomorrow. Then we will celebrate." He turned to gaze at the redheaded vixen by his side, whose eyes began to widen beneath his attention.

"We will celebrate my marriage to you, Maeve."

CHAPTER FIVE

Maeve stood beside Kildare on the chapel's steps and glared at her groom. Why had he chosen her to wife? He'd not spent a day with her, as he had with her sisters. She'd had no opportunity to prove why she would make him an unacceptable wife, blast him.

And why would Kildare assume she would celebrate the event that would bind her to an Englishman against her Irish cause and spell the doom of her betrothal? The thick-headed dolt. 'Twas his arrogance and cocksure nature that allowed him to believe she would rejoice this day.

Soon, she would show Kildare how wrong he was.

Listening with half an ear to Father Sean intone the ceremony that bound her to Kildare, her mind wandered. How had this come to pass? She should be wedding Quaid. Had Flynn been able to free him, she might well have married her dear friend this day. Such would be as she had always planned, as her mother and Quaid's had plotted for years.

Kieran Broderick had disrupted a lifetime of plans with a single sentence and a wicked smile.

Aye, she was unhappy with this turn of events! If he bedded a woman with the skill he used to kiss, he could well overwhelm her. With but a touch of his lips, she felt as if her senses were drowning. The thought of giving him more—nay, all—of herself... 'Twas frightening indeed.

Not that she had any interest in giving him any more than the sharp side of her tongue. She might have forgiven him for kissing her without her permission, someday mayhap. But then he announced his intent to rush her into marriage without asking her wishes, without even telling her he wanted her as a wife before making such a pronouncement. 'Twas unforgivable! Maeve had no doubt she had been the most shocked person at the table that night.

Tonight, he would expect her to yield, demand she be a willing bride in his bedchamber.

And she had a ewe that might sprout wings this very moment and fly away to London.

She risked a glance at her groom. Morning sun slanted behind them in a clear sky as they stood on the chapel's steps, bathing Kildare's sharp profile in golden light.

He looked to be in the height of health, drat him. Such meant she could not reasonably hope he would soon perish. So she must live with him, whilst finding a way to hide her role in the uprising, as well as forward the seedlings of rebellion with minimal bloodshed.

A difficult task, indeed, but the task before her.

Suddenly, silence filled the space around her. Maeve sensed all eyes upon her and her husband-to-be. Before she could grasp his intent, Kildare bent his head to her and brushed her lips with his own in a manner so gentle and brief she could scarce find fault with such—except that this wedding he forced made such a kiss necessary.

That…and even a touch so fleeting made her heart pick up its pace.

Kildare broke the contact a moment later. Maeve met his gaze. She tried her best not to appear affected or timid. But with her breathlessness and fluttering of her lashes, she feared she failed. By the saints, the man had kissed her in a manner appropriate for their setting. Why, then, was a foolish part of her remembering the time he had kissed her with passion?

As if he could read her mind, he raised a mischievous brow. The glint in his eyes promised a much more thorough kiss later.

But he smiled not. Such was very unlike Kildare.

Though it was not rational, Maeve found herself missing that irksome grin.

As she dismissed such a foolish notion, Kildare took her by the hand. She looked everywhere but at him. Still, she could not deny the solid warmth of his palm against hers. By Virgin Mary's heart, could she not get this man from her mind?

Above them sunlight beamed. Green budded everywhere. Birds sang, as if celebrating their union with song. Even flowers looked a breath from blooming, and a slight breeze stirred the air with perfume.

Such a beautiful day—marred by the fact that she had just taken the enemy as her husband.

Flynn had made his displeasure much known. She hoped he would not make trouble, or worse, seek her new husband's blood this night. 'Twas her dilemma—and one about which she was none too happy.

Tonight, she would make certain her groom knew as much.

Moments later, Kildare led her into the chapel.

Mass ensued, and Maeve found she could not concentrate on the priest's words of faith. Kildare, standing warm and broad beside her, took up too many of her thoughts.

More than an hour later, he escorted her from the chapel, his hand holding hers atop his forearm. When he cast her a stare that bespoke sin, Maeve nearly lost her calm.

"You can cease with that rapacious grin," she hissed.

Kieran sent her a teasing glance, making Maeve want to grit her teeth. "You think this rapacious? Wait until later."

Then he winked.

Maeve felt her control on her temper slipping as Kildare took her to Langmore's great hall. There, a feast awaited. A pig had been roasting for hours on a spit, along with a goose and three kinds of fish. The scents of rosemary and yeast also hung in the air, along with the ale and wine awaiting merriment of the guests.

Inside, one of the villagers toasted her new union. "May God be with you and bless you, may you see your children's children, may you be poor in misfortune, rich in blessings. May you know naught but happiness from this day forward."

A lovely toast indeed, but purely impossible!

Maeve sighed, refusing to take part in this farce. The castlefolk and her groom could make merry without her. She had done all the duty she had planned to do this day.

Behind her and Kildare, members of her family filed in, as they had traveled from a neighboring village to Langmore to witness the wedding. A look at their faces told her that no one appeared ready to make merry. She understood their sentiments. Even Kildare seemed oddly subdued.

So why had he ordered this feast?

Maeve made her way to the dais and motioned for a kitchen maid to bring her some mulled wine. She returned with the drink, along with a mighty mug of ale for her groom. Grabbing the cup from the maid, Maeve tossed the warm liquid down her throat and wished again for more.

She could not recall the last time she had been so nervous.

Then again, she had never thought to be wed to a man whose very mission was likely to see her betrothed and her brother dead, her home confiscated, and her sisters wed to his kind.

With that unsettling thought, she wound her way through the thin crowd as the serving maids began bringing forth all the food. She was aware of many gazes upon her, Kildare's burning most.

Drawing in a breath of courage, she left the great hall and retreated to her chamber. People would be achatter with her actions, aye. But she desperately needed this moment alone.

Yesterday she had been too dazed by his announcement to do much more than gape. Last night had been a sleepless tangle of uncertainty and fearful anticipation.

Now her time to consider the situation and decide how best to handle Kildare had run out.

After throwing open her shutters, she leaned against the narrow window ledge and gazed at the setting sun. Clutching the last of her mulled wine, she focused on her dilemma.

Kildare liked a challenge. She knew thus from their first kiss. She must not, under any circumstances, present herself as a woman in need of conquering. He would take up the gauntlet and use every bit of his persuasive charm to win her over. And she wanted no part of him, only of peace. For no other reason except the hope of peace for a free Ireland did she wed him.

Draining the last of her wine, Maeve let the warm liquid slide down her throat and warm her stomach. How not to present herself as a challenge? Could she conceive of such a strategy? Short of greeting him this night wearing naught but the skin she had been born with and begging him to bed her—a truly ridiculous idea—she saw no such option.

Sighing in frustration, she looked over the land she had known all her life. Mayhap she could drive him away. Perhaps with ill-prepared food and quarters, clothing ripped in the wash, rodents finding their way into his bed... Such a plan was thin, she admitted, but mayhap over time, such discomforts would annoy him enough to leave Langmore.

Even if he decided to make Dublin his home with only occasional visits here, that might be enough to keep the rebellion alive, keep her role as scribe and messenger hidden—and keep him and Flynn from sparring until one died.

"Do not leap out the window," demanded Kildare from the door. "As a husband, I promise I will not be that troubling."

Maeve gasped and whirled about at his sudden presence, then realized he thought her willing to jump to the middle bailey below and end her life to avoid him.

"You think overmuch of yourself." Maeve glared at him.

She wanted to rail at him further, tell him 'twas clear he always thought overmuch of himself, given that he had both kissed and wed her without her consent. But that would only goad him to vanquish her.

"Perhaps I but take note of your displeasure, Wife."

Maeve shuddered to hear that word on the tongue of a man so cocksure, so arrogant. Why could she not be wed to steadfast Quaid? She ground her teeth together and held in her slurs. They would only fuel Kildare to spar with her, and that, she understood now, he greatly enjoyed.

"I think naught at all. I merely wished a bit of air before the feast began in earnest." She stepped away from the window, past her modest bed, toward the chamber door. "Now that I have accomplished such, we should—"

He stopped her with a sure grip on her arm and used it to pull her body against his.

As her betraying heart picked up pace at his nearness, she felt every firm inch of his chest and belly against her own. His arms curled around her waist, holding her close—so close. His blue-green eyes sparkled with life, a promise of pleasure she feared.

She swallowed nervously. "We should return to the feast, my lord. 'Tis rude to keep our guests waiting."

"I instructed them to start without us."

Of all the overbearing assumptions! That he could simply walk up the stairs and take her. That is what all and sundry would think.

Aye, the Church and their vows gave him that right, but only a rogue would insist upon bedding his wife before they had even broken bread together.

"It is still ill-mannered, my lord."

"Kieran," he demanded. "It is my name, Maeve. I would hear you say it."

She would rather eat her own tongue first. "I do not think it wise to have our guests believe so quickly that we cannot finish a meal without arguing. Appearing below in harmony will do much to quiet dissension."

He considered her thoughtfully for a moment, before that smile she had come to know so well broke across his face. "Why think you they will assume we fight? That is not what most newly married couples do on the night they wed. Remaining here for some hours will portend better for the union and the peace than gorging on well-prepared foods with your kin."

Biting the inside of her lip, Maeve realized Kildare was right. Everyone below would assume some happy connection if she stayed here alone with him for some hours. The O'Sheas had long known she was promised to Quaid, so for her to closet herself away with her new husband willingly, everyone would likely think her pleased with the match.

So here, sharing this small chamber, laced now with his spicy earth and wood scent, would be wise for her cause. But staying alone with her new husband and his roguish grin, the one that suggested things she had never before felt, worried her. Being held against the breadth of his chest, his hands splayed upon her back, with his gaze probing hers, such would not be…comfortable, either.

"As you wish. Could I ask to you release me, please?"

Kildare frowned, as if he disliked her polite tone. "You could ask."

Maeve bit her tongue to keep a lashing retort from release. "And how would you reply?"

"Without words, sweet Maeve."

Before she understood his meaning, his arms left her waist and his lips captured hers.

Desire jolted her in the next breath, her response even quicker and stronger than before. When he angled his mouth over hers to deepen the kiss, Maeve found herself opening beneath him, giving his tongue the admittance it sought.

Maeve knew only the taste of him then, like ale and man, as well as the wild quality that sent her head spinning. Her senses reeled with his nearness, their chests pressed together, the heat and breadth of him surrounding her.

She felt her breaths coming in short gasps and he kissed a trail to her ear.

"This is how I would speak to you all night long." His teeth nipped at her lobe, his warm whisper sending shivers of heat along the back of her neck. "And well into the morn."

Then he pressed his mouth to the curve between her neck and shoulder. Breasts taut and heavy, Maeve pressed against him, unconsciously seeking ease.

No doubt, Kildare was good at seduction. Aye, 'twas likely he'd practiced it many times over. She was no match for his skill, his charm. 'Twas best to end this havoc he inflicted upon her senses now. If she let him touch her mouth more, she would be lost.

Why he had this effect upon her, she did not know. She did not love him. By the saints, she did not even like him.

But he could kiss like sin personified, enticing her with all the temptations of the flesh.

Maeve stepped back. 'Twas only then she realized Kildare's arms hung at his sides. He held her not. His kiss alone had kept her in the embrace, coupled with the sinuous slide of their heated bodies against one another.

Such had been enough to make her heart race, her stomach dance, her breasts tighten, and her woman's place… She did not want to consider its reaction to his touch. Such was dangerous, indeed.

Keeping that realization in mind, Maeve took another step back. Kildare looked at her then, his gaze knowing, predatory, dancing with mischief. He was granting her a reprieve but believed she could not long withstand his seduction.

Maeve prayed to God he was wrong.

She seized upon the one subject designed to cool his ardor. "Our marriage need not be a regular one, my lord."

"Kieran," he corrected automatically. "Regular in what manner, sweet Maeve? It seems much regular thus far."

"I would tell you first," she said, hoping her voice did not shake, "that I have every intent to help you keep peace here at Langmore and in the Pale."

He nodded, suddenly serious. "'Tis one reason I chose you. The people here listen to you. They respect you."

"Then we have a common goal," she said, vastly relieved. "But I would have you understand that we need not make this marriage a real one in every way."

Kildare took her meaning immediately and looked at her as if she had lost all the apples from her cart. "Why think you I would let this marriage go unconsummated?"

Knowing 'twas important to appear casual, she said, "Well, I know you have no feelings for me."

"Oh, I have feeling." He grinned like a large cat.

She cleared her throat. "And I love another."

The smile faded. "Quaid."

It wasn't a question. She replied with a nod.

"Aye, since we were to be wed soon, I pledged him my troth."

"You are not bound by marriage vows to him."

"We bound ourselves in spirit."

He made a sound of vague contempt and stared as if her words meant naught.

Finally, she told him all. "We bound ourselves with our bodies as well. We shared a bed."

At that confession, Kildare tensed. Anything that had ever resembled a smile disappeared, replaced with a watchful stillness that reminded her of a hunter.

"You are not innocent?"

His words were sharp. Maeve resisted the urge to tell him her lack of maidenhood would never be his concern. But he would no doubt see that as a challenge. Oh, but she yearned to fling a stinging retort in his face.

"As I have said, I am not," she answered instead, using her calmest voice.

Kildare stood quietly for very nearly a minute. And he stared, his gaze roving her face, staring into her eyes. His expression hardened from displeasure to anger.

Finally, he looked away. "It is of no consequence. We are wed, and I will expect you to perform all the duties of a wife. I cannot afford to disappoint King Henry."

Maeve resisted the urge to shut her eyes and block out the forthright expression on his face. Damn his practical hide! Why could he not be incensed or revolted at the fact his new bride had lain with another? Why did he have no qualms about bedding the enemy?

She had told him her most shocking secret. And it seemed to matter little to him, other than a moment's annoyance. Maeve knew not what to do now. She was ill prepared to share a bed with him tonight. She could not share sheets with an Englishman, let Kildare overrun her senses, muddy her mind with passion until she forsook the rebellion and Quaid.

Such was unthinkable.

Her only choice now was to stall for as long as possible until some other plan presented itself.

"Of course you do not want to disappoint your king," she said, trying not to speak through gritted teeth. "I must humbly ask you to give me some time to adjust to the idea of wedding and bedding a man other than the one promised me for some years."

"How long?" he quizzed.

Maeve floundered. A few days was too little time to ask, a month assuredly too much. "Perhaps a fortnight...or so."

Again, he remained silent for long moments. Her request seemed as uncomfortable to him as a gash in his flesh.

"A fortnight and no more," he barked finally.

Holding in her relief, she nodded. "Thank you, my lord, for your understanding."

"It is Kieran," he corrected. "As my wife, I expect you to use my name."

"Of course," she assured, vowing hell would see snow first. "Shall we join the feast? I find that I hunger now."

Maeve prayed her lie would sway him to leave her chamber and join the celebration—anything to avoid the possibility he might seduce her now and be done with their agreement to wait.

The notion seemed particularly possible as his rapacious gaze remained on her, unwavering, intense.

"I hunger as well, but we shall join the celebration instead," he murmured.

In an instant, Maeve took his meaning and blushed.

"But first, I have a few...rules."

"Oh?" Maeve feared he could mean anything, everything.

"No more lying to me about bridges and such."

Despite his scowl, she nodded, relieved. With a man as wicked as Kildare, she expected far worse.

"No ill-run keep. Seeing to this deplorable army will take much of each day. I have no time for matters of household."

He would leave her to run the keep? Even better. Much of the rebellion communicated within these walls. Mayhap Kildare would present less impediment to the rebellion than she feared. If so, it would reduce the chances for bloodshed at Langmore.

"I understand." Eyes downcast, she presented a demure façade.

Kildare's hand tightened about her arm. "And each night for the next fortnight, you will spend one hour in my chamber, alone with me."

The moment the words left his mouth, Maeve's mind raced with possibilities, most of which roused both heat and anxiety. Each night?

How could she thwart this request?

How could she resist his seduction?

"You vowed not to touch me for a fortnight," she reminded.

"Nay," he corrected, a smile playing about his full mouth. "I agreed not to bed you. You said naught of touching."

By the spirits, he was right. Oh, goodness. She took a deep breath, wondering what she would do.

Maeve pretended to misunderstand him. "We should become acquainted, I suppose. We could use the time to talk."

A wayward glint danced in his eyes that made Maeve instantly nervous. "We will divide the hour into halves. You may spend yours talking, if you wish."

And his half hour he would spend touching her. And she could not stop him.

Her body heated thinking of it.

"My lord—"

"Kieran," he corrected, his voice hinting at irritation.

She ignored him. "Touching will lead to…more."

Kildare shrugged as if that concerned him not. Maeve wanted to scream with anxiety. Certainly the man wasn't so thickheaded he did not understand.

Nay, he understood, she realized. He simply did not care.

"I want no touching," Maeve demanded.

His face hardened with resistance. "I have given much, Maeve. A wise person knows when to cease."

True, but she could not afford to be wise. She also could ill afford to become a challenge. Breathing deeply, Maeve forced herself to calm.

"Perhaps we can compromise," she suggested.

"Perhaps," he replied, then said naught for silent moments, his face full of possibilities.

Maeve wondered what outlandish ideas he was mulling over.

Finally he spoke. "We will compromise. I will not touch you with more than this hand"—he held up his right—"and my mouth."

Maeve hesitated. Logic told her he could not make love to her with his mouth and one hand. How seductive could that be? Yet his suggestion scared her in an elemental way she scarce understood.

"Take the compromise, Maeve. 'Tis the best I will offer."

Certain Kildare spoke true, she nodded. But deep down, she feared she had just struck a devil's bargain she would regret.

* * * *

She was not innocent.

Kieran pondered Maeve's admission all through the wedding feast, which was about as cheerful as a funeral, as well as the long, solitary night that followed.

As he tossed in his cold bed, he wondered why her lack of maidenhood bothered him. He had long avoided virgins, preferring instead a woman who knew what to expect in a tryst—and what not to expect, like undying devotion. He wanted a woman who would not be tense or rigid with a maiden's fears, a woman who knew sex could be both serious and fun. So why had he been disappointed to learn Maeve had shared another's bed?

Because they were wed, he supposed. While a man wanted some experience in a lover, he wanted a wife to come to him pure. But why? So he might make her truly his? Such a sentiment had never appealed to him for the permanency it implied.

With a frown, Kieran rose. What was done was done. Maeve would come to his bed experienced in another man's caresses. 'Twas up to him to put Quaid from Maeve's mind and establish himself as her husband. He should be thankful there would be no blood, likely no tears or fainting.

The thought merely gave him the urge to pummel Quaid O'Toole's face instead.

The thought of waiting even a few nights to claim his bride only frustrated him more.

Aye, he had agreed to wait a fortnight to set her at ease. He had been through enough negotiations in war to know the tactics well. She wanted a concession, wanted to believe she had power. Kieran had granted it, but had no reason to doubt Maeve would share his bed—happily—in less than a fortnight. Seduction worked on other women; he had no reason to expect Maeve would not follow in kind. She was, after all, his wife.

He had no doubt the castlefolk—and Flynn—laughed about the fact Maeve shared a room this night with her sister, instead of her husband. But that would be short-lived, and soon the people at Langmore would know Kieran no longer slept alone.

Grumbling, he threw on his clothes. All this brooding was not good for his mood or his character. He left these black ponderings to Drake, who had been especially good at them. Even Aric had his dark moments. Not him. Life had too much to offer to waste the precious moments thinking in gloom.

Instead, he would seek the outdoors, gather the army, continue the training, and be grateful for their slight improvement.

Suddenly, thunder rumbled. Kieran turned to see lightning illuminate the dawn-tinged sky. Then rain began to fall like water poured from a bucket.

Simply wonderful. Now he would be trapped inside for the morning at least. And if this rain was anything like the last, he might be caged in the keep all day.

Would nothing go right?

The storm reminded him how much he hated this infernal country, despite its beauty. Besides the fact it rained too much, Ireland held more than its share of mutiny, and now his wife would come to him with carnal knowledge of a damned rebel.

Before he could stoop to unhappy thoughts again, Kieran thrust on his boots and headed out his chamber door, toward the great hall.

Once there, he spied Jana, who sat in a chair, rubbing her belly, crying again and staring at a baby cradle.

Something inside him turned annoyingly soft as he approached her.

"Are you unwell? Has the time come?"

"It is near," she said between sobs. "And Geralt n-never had a chance t-to finish the babe's cradle."

Kieran looked at Jana's flushed, tear-ravaged face, then the cradle itself. 'Twas nearly complete, its framework of good workmanship. He thought it a nice enough cradle, not that he had seen many. But the one Drake had made for his children with Averyl seemed similar. The one Aric had made and would soon fill was elaborate enough for a royal babe.

"What is not complete?" he asked.

Jana looked at him as if he had not the sense of a swine. "It does not rock."

When she pointed to the bottom of the cradle, Kieran noticed two thick wooden slabs, one at each end. The head had been carved with rounded ends so that, when pushed gently, the cradle would rock. The other end still possessed square corners.

"I see," he murmured.

Jana only began to sob harder. "What kind of life will my babe have? His father is dead, his mother is alone, and he has not a suitable bed."

Kieran watched the woman's shoulders shake with sorrow. He knew little of breeding women, but he could not imagine such upset was good for her or the child. Nor were all these tears good for his disposition, sour as it was already.

The thunder crashed in the sky again, and Kieran realized he had naught better to do.

"He will have a bed. I will fix the cradle," he offered softly, wishing he had Aric's expertise with a knife and wood. Still, he could finish the job well enough.

Jana ceased sobbing and fixed him with a suspicious stare. "You will? Why?"

"Have you anyone else to fix it?"

"Nay. I waited, hoping…" Her tears began in earnest once more. "I hoped 'twas a mistake, that Geralt w-would come back to m-me, that he had not been t-taken from me…from our babe."

Kieran repressed the urge to comfort the woman. She would not welcome it. Nor did he want to become too involved in her sorrow.

Still, he could not abandon the woman. 'Twas clear she grieved. And still she had this babe to birth. Jana needed his help, even if she did not wish it.

"Let me finish the cradle," he offered in a low voice. "You lie down. Such tumult cannot be good for the child."

The hope and misgiving on her face told Kieran she was uncertain. "'Tis no problem of yours if the wee one has nowhere to sleep."

"But it is. As lord here, I'm to see that all at Langmore are cared for. Besides, your chamber is not far from mine. If your mite is unhappy at night, 'tis likely none of us will sleep well."

Kieran did his best to send her a teasing grin. Jana responded with a weak smile.

"Thank you."

He waved her thanks away. "Think naught of it. Rest now."

With a nod, Jana rose and left him with the cradle.

* * * *

At midday, Maeve lifted her head from her reading and went to the great hall in search of a bit of bread to ease her hunger from Ash Wednesday fasting. She prayed she would not see her new husband.

When she entered the great hall and found Kildare shirtless, she knew her prayers had been heard not at all. In fact, 'twas as if God took great pleasure in placing enticement in her path.

Maeve stared at the wide expanse of Kildare's muscled back as he bent over something he blocked with the breadth of his body. His torso tapered down to a lean waist, marked here and there with idle scars. His discarded shirt lay in a heap at his feet, and a fine sheen of sweat now covered the skin his shirt did not.

Rhythmically, he worked at something with a small knife— some wood, she suspected from the sounds. With each movement, his wide shoulders flexed. The hard flesh of his back and arms rippled.

Maeve's eyes widened. Her jaw dropped. She had never seen such a well-built man. She tried to remember something that her mother had always said. "Put silk on a goat and it's still a goat." But she could not deny he was a very attractive goat.

Crossing herself for such lascivious thoughts on a religious day,

Maeve began to back out of the room.

Suddenly, Kildare tossed the knife on the table before him, rolled the tension from his shoulders, and turned.

He caught her staring.

But his chest only drew her gaze more. The firm bulges of his shoulders and the hard swells of flesh sculpting his chest prefaced the ridges of his tight abdomen.

Then he smiled that grin, as if he knew a secret and wanted to whisper naughty words across her skin as he held her naked against him.

Dear God, this perfectly formed man was her husband? How was she to resist such masculinity, coupled with his bawdy humor, his energy, his smile?

She must remember he hailed from England. He was here to subjugate the Irish. He could see Quaid dead tomorrow, if he wished it. And he had no aversion to battle.

How could such a man capture her attention?

Quaid had always been gentle, soft-spoken, sharing her serious nature.

Aye, and he had never ensnared her interest so deeply.

"A good day to you, sweet Maeve. Did you cease speaking to me altogether, or is your muteness momentary?"

Kildare teased her, as if he could read her restless, confused thoughts.

Maeve closed her eyes in mortification. 'Twas likely he could read her mind. No doubt her thoughts were plain upon her face. She held in a grunt of frustration.

"As I've said, I am not your sweet anything," she snapped and began to walk around him, toward the kitchen.

When she spotted Jana's baby cradle perched upon the table beside Kildare, she paused. Was he so heartless as to take a bed from a babe not yet born? He had no use for the cradle.

"What do you do with that? Her babe will come any day, and she will have need of it."

He nodded, the glint in his dark hair shining by firelight. Maeve wondered if 'twas as silky to the touch as it looked, then thrust the thought away.

She was not a simpleminded girl to lose her head over an enemy possessed of more brawn than heart. She was an O'Shea, the most learned in her family. In her heart, she was betrothed to another, so had no reason to ogle the man, especially a man who would take a cradle from a babe.

Kildare frowned. "I am finishing the cradle, not taking it from her."

Glancing down at the baby bed, Maeve could see now the remaining corners were rounded for rocking, as they had not been before. In fact, he had added some curves to the spindles and finished the rough edges off. It looked beautiful.

Geralt, God rest his soul, had not much talent with wood. Kildare, however, did. 'Twas no surprise the man was good with his hands.

At that thought, she swallowed.

Maeve looked at her husband again and could not look away from his striking blue-green eyes—and the consideration within them. Something within her softened, despite her wishes.

Why, blast him, had he done something kind?

CHAPTER SIX

Kieran stared at the marks in his candle-clock, waiting eagerly for Maeve to come to his chamber. He had no notion what she might do with her half of their hour together.

He had a fine idea of what to do with his.

But since he agreed to give her at most a fortnight before consummating their marriage, he would have to content himself with less—for now.

Frowning, he tried to recall a time he had done something with a woman as comely as Maeve other than take her immediately to his bed. Naught came to mind.

With a yawn, he glanced past the open door, down the narrow hall. No sign of his bride.

Annoyance chafed him. The first of their hours alone, and already she defied him. Somehow, Kieran felt no surprise.

Making his way out the door with a mutter, he strode down the hall until he reached the chamber Maeve shared with Fiona.

The door stood ajar and he peeked in.

There Flynn stood, chest puffed forward, looking mightily pleased with himself. Maeve stood before him, holding a rolled parchment, wearing an expression of giddy surprise.

"How did this reach you?" she asked her brother.

"Don't be tellin' me you don't have faith in me now."

Maeve frowned. "I have faith in you, Flynn."

"At times," he grumbled. "All will be well this time, I swear to you, Maeve."

"How?" she asked, lifting her uncertain gaze from the page to

Flynn's face once more. "I know naught of any plan."

"Worry not. I will keep my promise."

As answers went, Flynn's told Kieran little, except that Flynn had likely promised Maeve he would see to Quaid's release, which he had already suspected. The conversation said naught of who was involved in this rebellion or how they planned to thwart the English charges against Maeve's betrothed.

He knew Maeve had received a message, most likely of a personal nature, from a man whose bed she had shared. And from the manner in which she clutched the note, Kieran guessed his wife was happy to have it.

Disappointment pierced him, and his reaction chafed. Naturally, he expected loyalty and fidelity in a wife. Knowing his own bride felt joy receiving the court of another lover left him unsettled. Any man would understand that. 'Twas no more than his attempt to protect that which was now his.

"Thank you, Flynn."

"Read the missive now. I'm off to a late supper."

Hiding in the hall's dark shadows, he watched Maeve nod and Flynn slip out of her chamber. A moment later, she unrolled the note and thrust on her spectacles. Through the curved lenses, he watched her gaze move quickly over the page.

Her expressions changed. Smiling one moment, frowning the next. Distress followed, then a gasp. Finally came the expression that irritated him most—wistfulness. Her animated face and soft mouth said she longed for the man. The thought made Kieran want to growl and rip the note from her hands.

Why?

And why was he, a grown warrior, crouching in hallways to see what his own wife was about? Aye, he did not want the wife, at least not forever. Nor did he truly want the castle. But they were his now, and by damn, he would hold them.

Striding forward, he entered the room and shot her an accusing stare. "What do you read, Wife?"

Maeve jumped, then rolled the parchment quickly. She looked at him, though her gaze did not meet his eyes. "'Tis naught, my lord."

"Kieran," he bit out.

She nodded. "I did not see you at supper."

"The men and I were training. I would ask who sent you that

note in your hands."

"This?" She held up the parchment casually. "'Tis but a letter from a distant cousin that Flynn received. He asked me to reply."

Maeve's smile was a nervous one as she turned away, as if dismissing the subject. Dismissing him.

Kieran refused to have any of that. "What does Quaid say to you?"

She whirled back to him, golden eyes wide. She opened her mouth, as if to reply, but no words came forth.

"Does he vow devotion, my sweet Maeve?"

"I know not of what you speak."

"Rubbish. Quaid sent that note. Flynn brought it to you."

Again, she paused in silence. Kieran watched the pulse flutter at her throat. She swallowed. Her hands tightened around the parchment.

"Quaid has always vowed devotion," Maeve said finally.

With an angry shake of his head, Kieran cursed. "Once, he had the right to vow such. No more."

"Just as you had no right to begin the raising of Langmore's curtain walls, but you did anyway."

Kieran had no wish to be a ruffian with her on this. Quaid had written the note. Aye, she had received it, but 'twas up to him to cease others from coming, lest her connection to the other man stayed strong.

"The walls are of no consequence. Their raising will make Langmore less vulnerable to attack, which is my right—and my duty. O'Toole, however, is of consequence to me. Write him and tell him you've married."

She paused, jaw tensing, before she said, "I had planned to do that. He has a right to know."

"The only right he has is to stop courting you."

Finally, Maeve looked at him. In fact, glared, her turbulent gaze on his face. "Why behave as if Quaid's feelings for me—or mine for him—matter to you? You have Langmore at your feet, an army ready at your call. For all your charm, I doubt you came here wanting me as a wife. And someday, probably in less than a month, you will be bedding every kitchen maid and smithy's wife who will have you. Can you not leave me be?"

She was exceedingly keen and free with her tongue. Somehow,

that only irritated Kieran more.

"You would have me allow my own wife to cavort with her lover—"

"We can hardly cavort while you and the rest of the English dogs have him under lock and key!"

Her shout echoed off the stone walls and undoubtedly through the open door into the halls. He wanted no one aware of his business. Damnation, he had no desire to deal with it himself.

But deal with it—and her—he would.

Turning, he kicked the door shut, then faced her again. She looked startled, uncertain. And through it all, he found her uncommonly lovely. Auburn lashes framed her wide golden eyes, which brimmed with intelligence and rightness.

How could she believe herself right to pine for Quaid O'Toole when the man was not her husband?

Mayhap she needed a reminder of what she missed in asking to keep their marriage unconsummated.

Kieran focused his intent gaze upon her face and walked slowly to her.

He came close. She backed up a step. Aye, he made her nervous, and with good reason, he supposed. For he was none too happy now. It must show.

Did it also show that, despite her disloyalty to him in thought, he wanted her still?

"The only person you will ever cavort with from now on, my sweet Maeve, is me."

"I am not like a"—she threw up her hands, flustered—"a horse. You cannot command my every movement, and you cannot own me in such a way."

"The law says otherwise," he tossed back.

"As I've always said, your English laws are foolish!"

"By marriage, they are your laws now. So you will tell Quaid you are well wed now and to cease his correspondence. And you, Wife, will cavort with only me."

Kieran took hold of her arm and used it to bring her against him.

Maeve's head snapped back, eyes widening. She gasped and a shiver raced through her.

His body throbbing with lust, Kieran bent to her and took her lips with his own in a rush of breaths.

Possessing, sliding, seeking, his lips glided over her moist mouth. A soft press here, a nibble there. He curved his arms around her middle, hands on the small of her back, pressing her ever closer.

His next kiss was deeper, hungrier. He felt like a man starved who intended to make her his banquet. Suddenly, he floated in hazy pleasure, aware somehow he had wanted this, wanted her this way, all along.

Clasping his fingers upon her face, he touched her, swept his caress down her throat…and lower. She responded to the demand of his kiss, staying with his insistent rhythm. Yet he kept the pressure light enough that she might yearn for more.

With a mewling sound in the back of her throat, Maeve leaned into him. The sound vibrated through his aroused body. She seemed to seek that bit he withheld, more of the pleasure that intoxicated his senses, too. He groaned at the thought of giving such to her.

The tips of her breasts stiffened against his chest, through her soft garments. And he could think of naught but touching her until she cried out with a want that equaled his.

Determined to have just that, his teasing finger swirled around the edge of her nipple once, twice. She stiffened and leaned into his touch, her every sense seemingly attuned to him.

Then he encompassed her in broad palms, taking both breasts into his hands, rippling his thumbs back and forth across their tips. She panted beneath him, her mouth pressed to his as if asking for succor.

"Aye, sweet Maeve," he whispered as he trailed kisses from the corner of her mouth to the sensitive spot behind her ear. "Show me your fire."

Maeve hesitated, then arched her neck. He kissed his way to her throat, until his lips and teeth tantalized fragrant skin, toyed with her ear, shooting another shiver down her back.

Aye, now her body wanted him, even if her mind did not.

Suddenly, she stiffened, then broke away from his embrace. Backing away, chest heaving, she gulped in large breaths of air. Her wide golden eyes seemed to accuse him of something heinous.

"Leave me," she demanded.

Kieran frowned. "We will share a bed, Maeve."

She shook her head. "Your seduction is well practiced, my lord. You can make any woman want your touch, so find another, one willing. I vow I will resist, for my mind is stronger. It will not let me forget you are the enemy."

"I am your husband," he countered.

At that truth, Maeve closed her eyes. "You have done your duty to King Henry in taking a bride. Please leave me be."

Though Kieran had not done his full duty to the king, since his bride did not breed yet, he saw no reason to anger Maeve by telling her thus. She would only resist him more if she knew the king thought her much like a brood mare. Instead, he dropped his hands from her and stepped away.

"This marriage is sudden for you. And I have agreed to give you a fortnight to reconcile yourself to our union. In exchange for this, you agreed to spend an hour alone with me each night. Keep up your part of the bargain, Maeve, and I will do the same. But never think I will leave you to your lover."

Kieran knew he was angrier than he should be. Somehow that only made him angrier still, for Maeve had that effect on him, blast her. When he was with her, emotions seemed more common, more vivid.

He hated it.

Perhaps, 'twould be best if he let her be—at least until tomorrow night.

* * * *

The following morn, Maeve was still shaking from that kiss. Body and mind warred until she felt exhausted.

She cried at the injustice of feeling such desire for Kildare and not her own betrothed. Why? Why could Quaid rouse naught in her but a loyalty to the Irish cause and an abiding friendship? Always she had known they were destined to wed. Always she had refused the advances of others because of it. Quaid cared for her. His was a kind soul. And he loved her.

How, then, could she kiss and crave a man who would cheer at Quaid's hanging and do his best to coax her into his bed for little more than the sport of it?

The sounds of horses, many of them, riding toward Langmore interrupted her thoughts. Curious, she left the comfort of her bed, despite the morning chill, to open her shutters and peek out the narrow window.

English soldiers, about two dozen of them. Damnation, what could they want here?

Her heart began to race. Had they come to arrest Flynn?

Maeve knew she must hide Quaid's last missive to her—and hide it well. Mayhap such would protect her brother. As she turned away, she collided with Fiona, who peered out the window in wide-eyed horror, countenance chalky white.

No O'Shea liked the English, true. But Fiona seemed a bit more afraid than the others. Then again, her quiet nature had never provided for outright bravery.

"Come," she said to her sister. "We will dress and sit in the solar."

"Nay," resisted Fiona.

"We must appear as if we have naught to hide," Maeve insisted. "We must appear as if we have not a care."

Fiona looked at her, stricken. Finally, she nodded, then turned away.

Maeve sighed with relief, but her sister's reaction worried her. Aye, Fiona had always been the quiet one. But she did not like this fear.

Pondering the matter as she dressed, Maeve could think of naught that made sense.

Shrugging, she waited for Fiona to finish dressing, then took her by the hand and led her to the solar. Thankfully, Jana was already there. Their gazes met, and Maeve realized her elder sister had decided a group of sewing ladies would rouse less suspicion than those going over household accounts—and a rebel missive or two.

"Where is Brighid?" she whispered.

"Breaking her fast, I think."

"Alone in the great hall with a lot of soldiers?" gasped Fiona.

Maeve frowned, seeing the problem in that. "Let us find her, shall we?"

Fiona hesitated. She looked back at a largely pregnant Jana, then to Maeve again. They both nodded. Finally, reluctantly, she followed.

* * * *

Inside the great hall, Kieran greeted the lieutenant from the English army in Dublin.

A few days past, he had realized the army at Langmore would need reinforcements to hold the castle in case of rebel attack and had requested more men, particularly until the curtain walls could be raised for their defense. Today, they had arrived, and he could breathe more easily now.

Maeve was another tale altogether.

As if the thought of her conjured up his wife, Maeve stepped into the great hall, Fiona by her side.

His wife looked about the room, past all the soldiers, sparing barely a glance for him. Finally, she found her youngest sister in the corner, giggling with Colm and drinking a mug of ale.

With purpose in her stride, Maeve made her way to Brighid.

Kieran wondered if she was aware of all the male eyes of appreciation following her.

The soldiers also gazed at Fiona with rapt eyes. But where Maeve had ignored such stares, Fiona stood rooted in place, her face ashen. She seemed to tremble, gaze fixed on a pair of men who eyed her with more interest than most.

True, she did not seem one who wanted much attention, but she looked more than merely overwhelmed. He frowned. Did she think the soldiers would harm her here? Now?

When Fiona swayed where she stood and began to crumple to the ground, Kieran raced to catch her. He narrowly saved her head from hitting the hard floor.

Maeve dashed to his side, Brighid's hand in hers. "What happened?"

"I know not. Take Brighid away. I will bring Fiona up."

With a worried glance at Fiona, then Brighid, Maeve nodded and disappeared up the stairs.

Behind him, Kieran heard several men laugh.

"Sent her right into a swoon, Freddy," joked one lanky man missing two front teeth.

"That we did," answered Freddy, a dark-haired swain with a barrel chest.

Irritation swept through him. The girl had fainted. 'Twas no matter to laugh at.

He turned to reprimand them. "Shut your mouths, both of you."

Their laughter ceased immediately.

"Aye, my lord," Freddy said.

To all the soldiers, he said, "Sit. The maids will bring you ale and a small repast. When I return, I will give you further assignments."

As all the men ambled to the benches to do Kieran's bidding, he left the great hall to take Fiona to her chamber.

Once there, he laid the girl down upon her bed. Still she moved not. She looked like a fragile bird, one whose wings had been broken. One who would rather see death than face life.

Concerned, Kieran snapped his fingers next to Fiona's ear.

A moment later, she began to open her eyes and moan.

Upon seeing him, she bolted upright and gazed around the room, blue eyes glassy and wide.

To know she was not ill should have been enough to convince him to leave Fiona to recover on her own. But the panic on her face gave him pause.

"What is it?" he asked, voice low. When she did not reply, he pressed on. "What is it you fear?"

Realizing they were alone, Fiona fixed her gaze solely on him. The terror in her eyes shook him, startled him.

"Release me, please."

Her voice shook so violently Kieran could scarce understand her.

He did as she asked but could not keep his alarmed gaze from her wounded expression.

"What is it you fear?"

"'Tis naught." She tried to smile. "Too many people in a room overwhelm me."

She lied. He knew that by the way she glanced at her shaking hands, the way her voice held forced cheer. He more than suspected it had to do with the Englishmen.

"Why do you fear the soldiers?"

At his question, her eyes widened with horror. "I-I do not. I—"

"You do," he countered softly. "I saw you. I watched your response to the one called Freddy and his friend."

At that, Fiona's eyes became huge pools of terror.

Kieran watched her, wondering what in Hades' name he should do. A part of him wanted not to become involved in Fiona's struggle, whatever it was. But somehow, he could not leave the terrified girl.

By Saint Peter's toes, Aric was wise, knew when to be gentle, how to soothe when necessary. Even Drake, who had an uncanny ability to ferret out people's thoughts and motives, would know what to do with Fiona.

He, however, had no damned idea.

Slowly, he reached for her hands and took them in his. Her palms were icy, clammy. She flinched at his touch.

Then she tried to jerk from his grasp, began shaking her head violently from side to side.

"Nay!" she screamed. "Do not touch me."

Kieran held fast. "Freddy and his friend, did they hurt you?"

She only struggled more. "Do not ask me. Please!"

The answer was clear in what she tried not to say. His ire soared. Aye, he might have seduced more than a few women in his life. But he had never wanted to incite fear, never hit one, never taken one by force.

Suddenly he feared something like that had happened to young Fiona.

"They hurt you," he stated, willing her to tell him all.

She said naught. Tears began to fall, slowly at first, then more rapidly. Color returned to her face as despair and something that tore at Kieran's gut took over. Her whole body trembled with these silent tears. Kieran's anger multiplied.

"They hit you?" he asked.

Fiona squeezed her eyes shut. More tears fell—one, two.

Then she nodded.

Kieran kept his curse to himself. "Did they rape you?"

This time, Fiona tensed and paused for a long minute. She seemed not to breathe. Her chin trembled with an effort to hold in more tears, to hold in her words.

"Tell me. You can trust me," he assured. "I will never hurt you."

"I can trust no one," she cried. "If-if my family knew…Flynn would seek rev-revenge. They would kill him—mayhap all of us—for it."

Gripping Fiona's hands, Kieran willed the girl to calm, to understand he was not her enemy. He willed the girl to tell him the truth.

"Did Freddy and his friend rape you?"

A long moment passed. Fiona's eyes slid shut. She bit her lip as if to keep the words within.

"I will tell no one," he vowed. "I but ask you to tell me the truth, lass. Did they?"

A terrible moment passed and the tears came again, now in a stream.

Finally, silently, she nodded.

"Both of them?"

More tears fell, wetting her ravaged face. Tight white fists came up to block her desolate face.

She nodded once more.

Kieran felt anger explode within him. Fiona was a fragile creature, at six and ten barely a woman. They had stripped the innocence from her and replaced it with fear. They had left her with a terrible secret to bear, lest her brother die defending her honor.

And the awful deed would not go unpunished.

"When?" he asked softly.

"Six months p-past." Her voice shook, but she continued. "Before his arrest, the last earl came to L-Langmore and brought soldiers. I was in-in the garden alone…"

He needed no more information to know Freddy and his partner had attacked the girl, who had been unaware of the dangers warring men who craved power presented.

Fiona was not unaware of such dangers now, damn them.

He had known such deeds happened after battle. 'Twas not uncommon for triumphant soldiers to conquer the female half of the vanquished, pillaging and raping. Though he had always found such distasteful and refused to participate, he had left the others to their whims.

Clearly, he'd been very wrong.

Those men did not engage in mere sport, but fright and pain and suffering—the kind he saw in Fiona's eyes.

Squeezing her hands, he tried to soothe her with his voice. "They will not hurt you again."

Fiona closed her eyes against him.

Still, he kept talking. "I vow this."

Nodding, Fiona squeezed his hands in return, then released them to sit up.

When she looked away, gaze cast down to the floor, Kieran

knew she wanted to be alone.

"Fiona?" Maeve called from the door suddenly.

His wife caught sight of her sister's wet face and raced to her side. "Oh, sweet sister, what ails you?"

Fiona did not answer but hugged Maeve instead in silent healing.

Kieran stood. Maeve looked up from her sister's embrace and shot him an accusing look, one that asked what he had done to make Fiona cry.

The irritating wench! Could she not see he had but tried to help? Nay, for she was convinced he was the enemy. And Kieran wanted to defend himself, but he could not…without giving away Fiona's secret.

With a curse, he headed out the door. Maeve he would deal with later. Now he had justice on his mind.

* * * *

Later that night, Maeve paced her husband's chamber, waiting for him to appear. 'Twould seem she had guessed wrong about him again. Instead of inciting her sister's tears in some fit of meanness, as she had assumed, Kildare alone had found a way to convince Fiona to spill the secret of her troubles.

Maeve had wondered these past months why her sister had nightmares, spent more time in church than ever, reviled the attention of all men.

Now she knew, for Fiona had told her, as well.

The thought made her want to cry. Her dear sister raped by two English ruffians.

No wonder she had suffered.

Against Fiona's wishes, Maeve had gone in search of Flynn to tell him. Aye, she, too, feared Flynn would exact revenge, but Maeve hoped she could make him see reason.

Her brother, however, was nowhere to be found. One of the army's soldiers, still loyal to the rebellion, had said he'd left only hours past to see to business.

Maeve was not surprised, for the notes she had recently scribed told her the rebellion had plans to free their men imprisoned in Dublin and wage a final battle, the latter of which she opposed—and had told Flynn so. She wanted him here for their wounded sister today.

A sound at the portal interrupted Maeve's thoughts. She looked up to see Kildare.

His tunic sat askew upon his wide shoulders. His hair lay rumpled, and blood dotted the corner of his mouth. A bruise was forming on his jaw. He wore a huge grin, the kind he'd worn after thrashing Flynn on the day of his arrival.

She frowned. But she knew well Flynn was not at Langmore this night. Who might Kildare have been sparring with now?

"Hello, sweet Maeve. Waiting for me like a good wife?"

Folding her hands before her, Maeve forced herself to concentrate on the matter at hand, not the remembrance of their last kiss.

"I-I would thank you for persuading Fiona to tell us of the tragedy that befell her."

Kildare nodded, his face suddenly sober. "How is she?"

"Calmer now, though she still blames herself and I cannot understand why."

"She had naught to do with it," he agreed, wiping away the blood trickling from his mouth.

"What happened to you? Another fight?" The thought irritated her. Did the man have naught better to do than show his prowess with his fists?

He shrugged. "Merely seeing to a little discipline in the ranks. Naught of merit."

In other words, fighting. And whether he called it discipline or a rowdy scuffle, 'twas still all done with force and fists and violence. Done like a beast until the soldiers were forced to fight back to defend themselves, most likely.

"Is fighting all you know?"

He paused as if the question confused him. "What ask you?"

His total bafflement vexed her, and she found herself clenching her fists.

"Can you not find amusement besides pounding others with your fists, you mucker?"

"Mucker, am I? That is grave. But since you've denied me the...amusement I most seek—"

"You may leave all references to sex out of this."

"I may?" he mocked. "What if I do not wish to?"

Throwing her hands up in the air, Maeve sighed. "Why did I think I could simply thank you for discovering Fiona's worries and finishing Jana's cradle?"

Kildare took a gentle grip on her arms. "Maeve, I but tease you."

She clenched her jaw, clearly angry. "Why do you fight so much? What have you to gain?"

Pausing, Kildare wiped the smile from his face. "From the time I was eight, I lived with the earl of Rothgate in training. My closest friends are warriors. Here"—he held up his palm to show her a small scar running its length—"this is where I took vows of blood to protect and care for them like brothers. I've known battle my whole life. It is what men understand, Maeve."

"Quaid was never so full of bloodlust."

Kieran gritted his teeth at the man's name on Maeve's tongue. "I am certain your half of our hour is near done. Since you chose to spend yours berating me, I choose to spend mine sleeping. So I bid you good night, sweet Maeve. Unless you wish to join me in my bed."

Maeve shivered at his seductive tone. She tried to tell herself it was revulsion, for who could want a warring man so primal and primitive?

Who would not want a man who could kiss with all the sweetness of spiced mead, who tasted like pure temptation?

Ignoring the troublesome voice in her head, Maeve left him and went below to the great hall. There she would wait for Flynn. Anything to avoid her vexatious husband.

At the corner table sat two men, both blue and swollen and bloodied. She shuddered.

Dear God, what had happened to them?

Beside them, another Englishman saw her reaction and laughed. "Looks like your face ain't pleasing to the ladies, Freddy, now that Kildare tousled you well and good."

Fiona had told Maeve that a man named Freddy and another soldier had raped her. These bruised men had brutalized her sister? Anger and a shocking need for vengeance pricked her. Then she realized Kildare had mauled these toads' faces with his fists. For Fiona?

"Close your mewling mouth, Benny," hissed Freddy.

Benny kept on laughing. "You look as ugly as my mother's feet. Between that and the rebuke Kildare made about touching the women at Langmore, 'tis likely you'll be an old man afore you bed another wench."

"You'll be as old as me, you damn fool. Shut up."

As if Freddy had not spoken, Benny kept laughing.

Maeve turned away, stunned.

Kieran had punished Fiona's rapists? He had told the men to not touch the women of Langmore? Such sounded as if he protected them from men of his own kind, warring men, Englishmen. Why?

Had he thought Fiona's plight as terrible as she? Maeve could not conceive the man of Kieran's teasing, bloodthirsty nature would consider her sister's attack aught but the spoils of war.

Had she misjudged him once more?

CHAPTER SEVEN

Kildare spent the following day, all day, with the soldiers, training for the battle Maeve prayed would not come. She wanted peace for Ireland—and that included a peaceable solution to the differences in the Pale now.

As ferocious as her husband looked practicing war, she feared he'd be doubly lethal on a battlefield.

Sighing, Maeve dismissed the thought and paced his chamber. Surely he would show up soon. Then she might find out, once and for all, what manner of a man he was. Now she could not decide between the arrogant, unfeeling rogue who had taken her to wife without a word of her consent, or the man who had completed a coming baby's cradle, helped her wounded sister, then punished the bastards for their crimes.

Maeve could hardly imagine Kieran was both these men, but that possibility looked confoundingly real.

The swish of the door alerted Maeve to a presence. She turned to find her husband striding into the room, his graceful economy of motion all the more evident by the muscled swells and sinews of his bare torso.

Maeve did her best to look away.

"If you've come to accuse me of some other misdeed, I will tell you I'm far too tired to hear it," he nearly groaned.

She frowned at the many questions racing through her head. Aye, they had Fiona's matter to discuss, but one query leaped into her mind and would not quiet until she had the answer, one which might tell her so much about him.

"If you do not like the training, why be a warrior? It's bloody business anyway."

He nodded as he poured some water into a bowl upon his trestle table. "Aye, but battle itself makes a man's blood race. There is naught like besting a worthy opponent."

Maeve frowned at him. The man was ever a puzzle. She understood him not at all. Battle made his blood race? It sounded trying to one's nerves, not an event to anticipate.

"Besides the fact I must train to prepare this army, naught beats a hard day's work to divert my energies."

"Divert your energies from what?"

He splashed water on his face, then wiped it dry with a cloth at his side. When he looked at her again, water had spiked his brown hair hanging over his forehead, as well as his lashes. His blue-green eyes danced with sudden mischief.

"From the fact that I have eleven days before I might claim you in our bed."

She swallowed against his words, for they incited a burn of anticipation that made little sense. Had she gone mad? Had Kieran driven her to insanity with his hot, spiced kisses? With wondering how his hands might feel upon her flesh?

Repressing the reckless feeling, she looked away from his bare skin and changed the subject. "My lord—"

"Kieran," he all but sighed.

She smiled. "I accused you of misdeeds yesterday, and I know now I was wrong. I came to express my gratitude for what you did for Fiona—and to her attackers."

Her husband's face showed surprise. Then he stared at her for a long, silent moment. "I did naught but listen to your sister, then roughed up a pair of fools in sore need of such."

"You disparage your role, but you alone made Fiona believe she could tell the truth. And though I'm loath to see any manner of bloodshed, I could not have been more pleased of your treatment of Freddy and his despicable friend."

"Careful, I may make a savage of you yet, sweet Maeve."

Looking again at the warmth of his bare brown chest, honed with years of labor, she feared he might be right, though not necessarily savage for the sight of blood.

"Truly, I thank you," she said instead.

His face fell to something more serious. "'Twas my duty and my honor. Your sister is now my sister. Such ill treatment will not be tolerated."

He turned away, and she watched as he splashed the rag into the water once more, then sponged his thick brown arms, his neck, his hard chest in long, sweeping strokes.

Disturbed by the vision, she avoided looking at him. "Still, I appreciate your effort. I suppose most of the household duties have fallen on my shoulders in years past. Flynn has been far too busy with—" She broke off in horror, realizing what she'd nearly admitted.

"The rebellion?" Kieran supplied, his gaze probing as he tossed on a tunic of black. "And where is your brother? I have not seen his mangy face all day."

"I know not," she lied, before she rushed to continue her subject. "Jana was off and married, and with my parents gone, who else would see to Langmore, Fiona and Brighid?"

"I observed such. 'Tis another reason I chose you."

Nodding, she conceded the point. "My family… Trust does not come easily for us. When Jana's husband was executed by the last earl, mayhap you can imagine her feeling for all men English. Now we see Fiona has equal reason to dislike your kind."

"I lived here for eight years. I remember being Irish."

Something in his hard tone gave her pause. His face and form, usually given to energy and expression, looked closed, impassive. Were his remembrances of living here unhappy? Somehow she sensed they were, but felt certain he would tell her naught about the matter if she asked.

"You do not speak thus and you do not rally to our cause," she pointed out finally.

"And what cause is that, beyond making mischief?"

"We seek freedom, autonomy to run our lives as we have for centuries, without interference."

"I have no wish to debate England's policies with you, good wife, for neither of us can change them."

"You have no influence?" she asked, confused.

He barked a laugh. "None. If I did, I would be in Spain now, warring for a great deal of cash and enjoying the warmer weather."

"You were ordered here?"

He nodded. "Against my every wish, I assure you."

"But King Henry made you an earl," she pointed out.

"I still would have said him nay had I been given that option."

Taken aback, Maeve stared at her husband. Just when she had decided she knew all she could about him—or would wish to—he surprised her. He would have turned his back on wealth and a title? For what, a little warmer weather in Spain? That seemed very unlike every Englishman she'd ever known.

"You look surprised," Kieran observed.

"I-I confess I am."

He grinned. "I might provide you any number of surprises, sweet Maeve."

That provocative note had returned. Maeve felt alternately thrilled and annoyed by it.

"Can you fix your mind at all on serious matters?"

Kieran shrugged, wearing that lopsided grin she knew so well. "Only if avoiding it cannot be helped. And what of you? Can you focus your mind at all on matters not serious? I've seen no evidence you can."

Maeve frowned, taken aback. "Of course I can—at appropriate moments."

"Hmm. Mayhap all of thrice a year: Mayday, Midsummer's Eve, and Christmastide? Have you not learned that life is too short to treat everything with such gravity?"

She scowled. "Have you not learned that your future may not hold what you wish if you do not treat more matters with importance?"

"You sound like Aric and Drake," he grumbled.

"Your friends?"

Kieran nodded. "Aric is always responsible for everybody and everything. And Drake"—he shuddered—"the man's mind is always working, ever the strategist."

This surprised Maeve. She would have thought Kieran would make friends with men prone to smiles, like himself. "And yet they are your friends?"

He nodded. "The best. Aric is the most dependable, firm-minded man I know… Well, besides Guilford. The old earl has years of wisdom on him. Drake is loyal, a good man to have at one's back. Fast and possessed of a quick temper, he's not someone I would want for an enemy. And now they have both been well wed for some years, I can tease them mercilessly about being so foolishly in love with their wives."

Maeve quieted at his words, for she heard their unconscious message: he would never tie his heart to hers in the same manner. Why that troubled her, she could not say. Her heart should belong to Quaid. She had nearly wed the man.

But somehow knowing Kildare thought himself immune to Cupid's arrow disturbed her.

"So they are well settled?" she asked, knowing the answer.

"Aye, Gwenyth and Averyl both should birth babes soon. 'Twill be Drake's third." He smiled. "I recall sitting beside Drake just the day after he and Averyl had wed and hearing him insist he did not love her. I knew then that he did."

Nodding in response, Maeve tried to ignore a sting of jealousy. She wanted love in her marriage. But did she want that with Kildare?

Nay. Such would be like asking for sunshine at midnight. Impossible and foolish both.

Before she could reply, Brighid burst through the door. "Come quickly, Maeve. Jana says she is contracting again."

"This is beginning to be a nightly ritual," Kieran quipped.

Maeve nodded wryly, smiling. "You are right." She nodded at Brighid. "Tell her I will be down in a few moments."

"I shall. And when I take to bed with a man, I won't let him plant a seed into me until my stomach swells and contracts like Jana's!"

Then, with a shake of her blond head, Brighid went out.

Maeve turned to see Kildare smiling with amusement, and she found herself laughing.

"You will have to explain the truth to her someday," he said, grin wide.

"Aye, and how I dread it. She is filled with questions."

"True."

Silence prevailed a moment later. Maeve knew not what to say, only that she felt an odd connection to Kildare and was surprisingly reluctant to see it end.

"I suppose you should see to Jana," he said.

Maeve nodded. "Aye, but I want to thank you again."

She touched his arm in a soft gesture, only to have her husband clasp a hand about her arm and pull her to him, until their faces lay a breath apart.

"Then I would ask you to thank me properly, sweet Maeve."

His allusive tone made her belly dance and her toes curl. Certainly he did not mean what she thought… "Properly?"

Rather than reply, Kildare swept his mouth over hers. Instead of a lusty kiss of hunger and demand, the kind he had thrice given her, his lips were gentle, probing, hungry without force.

The flavor of his soft kiss was so unexpected, so welcome, Maeve melted into him.

He brushed his mouth over hers once, again…then away, still holding her arms. Her flesh tingled where he touched. She leaned into him, seeking more, though some part of her mind knew she should not.

Kildare lifted his mouth from hers. Before she could stop herself, she made a mewling protest at the back of her throat, then hooked her hand about his neck and brought his mouth to hers for another kiss.

With a possessive growl, he obliged her, melting her will, her thought, her very skin. Maeve drowned in sensation, in wonder as he nibbled on her lower lip before sweeping his tongue through her mouth and tasting her as if she were made of honey. Feeling unsteady, she returned his kiss in kind, tasting a hint of ale and something spicy on his tongue, and sidled closer, reveling in the feel of his solid warmth.

"Maeve!" Brighid called from the bottom of the stairs. "Where are you?"

With that intrusion, Kildare ended the kiss. And though Maeve had been loath to let him, she knew that, for many reasons, doing so was best.

"Good night, sweet Maeve."

Biting her lip, she willed the pleasure to recede, her heartbeat to calm. She realized she still grasped his hard shoulder in one hand and released him.

"Good night," she said quickly, then hurried out the door.

* * * *

'Twas shortly after the next dawn that an English soldier arrived from Dublin bearing bad news.

"You're certain?" Kieran asked the man.

"Aye, my lord. Last night, they attacked Malahide Castle again, trying to free the jailed rebels."

Including Quaid O'Toole, he'd bet. Damnation, why did the rebels want the man released so badly? Or was that simply Maeve's wish?

"Did they succeed?" Kieran asked.

"Nay. The keep is still secure, but the attacking rebels escaped, my lord."

Gritting his teeth, he dismissed the soldier and went in search of Flynn. His small chamber was empty. Kieran touched the sheets. Cold, not a hint of warmth to suggest he'd passed the night here. Kieran cursed. He'd been so involved with the army and Maeve, he'd not noted Flynn's departure. In fact, after their agreeable conversation and her kiss last night, he'd been able to think of naught else.

Taking the narrow hall in a few long strides, his boots echoing off the corridor's walls, Kieran flung open the door to Maeve and Fiona's chamber.

Fiona lay sleeping in a quiet ball upon the bed. Maeve sat on the edge, dressed in naught but her shift.

Despite the urgency of the situation, he could scarce overlook Maeve's creamy skin visible at the garment's low neckline and the thick red braid teasing the top of her buttocks.

His wife's gaze whipped around at his entrance.

"Why are you here?" she asked. "Fiona sleeps finally."

He glanced at the younger girl. Her tortured soul had not allowed for safe sleep recently, according to Maeve. He did not wish to disturb her now.

"Come to my chamber."

Maeve frowned, then sighed. "As you wish. Let me dress—"

"Now," he insisted, striding across the small room to take her by the hand.

The look on her face screamed protest, but Kieran knew that Maeve would try not to wake Fiona. He also knew she would not linger in the hall in her undergarments where anyone might see her.

And so his wife came to his chamber, more undressed than dressed, while he had to question, rather than seduce her.

He frowned and frustration lent an edge to his voice. "Where is your brother?"

Maeve looked at him as though he had sprouted a second head. "You dragged me from my bed without proper clothing to ask me that? I really could not say."

With that, she turned and made for the door.

Damn the woman's hide. Could she not be more compliant or docile?

He grabbed her by the arm once more and spun her to face him. They stood so close Kieran could smell her light blossom scent, could see the rise and crest of her rounded breasts beneath her thin smock. Memories of last night coursed through his mind. She had spoken of her family, asked him of his life, his friends, seemed so…open to being with him. Then, during their blistering kiss, she had thrown her arms about his neck and demanded another kiss.

Cursing, Kieran grabbed her chin and thrust his gaze to her face once more. "Look at *me* when I speak to you."

Anger flashed in her golden eyes, tightened her mouth.

Kieran felt himself flush. Usually, he could play games of seduction like a master, letting a woman know he wanted her while remaining in control of his desire. With Maeve, he could not hide his eagerness; he felt his control slipping, to be replaced by a madness he feared only she could cure. Was it lack of sex? Of sleep? Was it Ireland? He frowned, knowing he must leash his urges or risk delaying his wife's surrender further.

He looked directly at Maeve, his gaze delving so deeply into her snapping eyes she tensed.

"I will ask again, where is your brother?"

She raised her chin. "I know not."

"Did he go to Dublin?"

"I know not."

"Is he with the rebels?" Kieran asked.

She hesitated. "I know not. I know nothing!"

"Why would your brother not tell you of a plan to free your former betrothed from imprisonment?"

"Because he does not tell me his plans."

Kieran felt sure she lied. Even if Maeve knew not exactly where her brother was, she knew his intent. Still, she had said naught to him. She had said even less of the matter last night.

Hell, Maeve had even sought him out without a word of the truth. Aye, she had come to his chamber, thanked him for his help, and passed some quiet moments. She had lingered in his kiss when she could have left to see to Jana's labor, which had again produced no babe. Indeed, Maeve dragged his mouth back to hers, distracting him from all else but her.

Perhaps, that had been the point.

Kieran's mind exploded with possibilities. Aye, Maeve had come to his room last night, keeping him occupied while turning the conversation away from her brother and his absence. Had that been her goal—even melting into his kiss, taking more—to divert him whilst the rebels did their work?

Why else would she seek him out with such amiable intent?

Such made sense. Maeve had resented his presence even before his arrival at Langmore. Only a fool would believe she had suddenly sought his company, unless for a device of her own—or the rebellion's.

Kieran regarded her through narrowed eyes. Why should he feel betrayed by the bride he'd never wanted?

That he could not answer now. He was too damned mad.

"I imagine you want to know what has become of your lover?"

Maeve cast her eyes downward. Perhaps she could sense his anger. Part of him wanted to believe she regretted sharing herself with another man, but he knew better.

That only added to his growing fury.

"He is my friend as well," Maeve murmured. "I have known Quaid all my life, my lord."

"Kieran! How many times must I tell you my name before you use it, woman?"

"That has no bearing now."

"Aye," he barked. "Now we must discuss the fact you came to me last night and accepted, even seemed to enjoy, my kiss. And why? I thought it because you might come to accept me, even want me. But nay, you did it to deceive me. Sharing your sweet mouth and distracting me from the matter of Flynn's whereabouts. 'Twas all a ruse, was it not?"

Maeve gasped. "Think you I-I let you kiss me to *distract* you?"

"By damnation, I do. I think the rebellion sent you to keep me occupied so I would not ask after your brother. And you did it admirably. But know this, sweet Maeve," he ground out, finger pointed at her shoulder, "it will not work again. I understand you now—"

"You understand a pig's hindquarters, perhaps, but you know naught of me."

Kieran grabbed her arm and held tight. "Lie all you wish, but I see the depths you will sink to in order to help the rebellion. I stood and watched you ply me with kind words, then tempt me with your mouth. What else might you have done had I not been satisfied with kisses?"

"You truly are a swine! Yestereve, I wondered what manner of man you were: the bully who beat on my brother's face for pleasure or the gallant who helped my sisters. But I see you are much more one than the other! And *if* I were of a mind to lend my actions to the rebellion and remove you from their path, 'tis more likely I would poison you than kiss you, you horse's ass!"

CHAPTER EIGHT

Two rainy afternoons later, the sun finally appeared in a still gray sky. Kildare took the last earl's soldiers and those newly arrived from Dublin out for a long session in the bailey. Freddy and his friend were conspicuously absent.

Maeve tried not to watch the men as she stared out from the battlements, waiting for Flynn's return and praying it was a safe one. 'Twas difficult to pull her gaze away, for none wore a tunic.

And none looked more virile than Kildare.

"Watch your shoulder, man!" her husband shouted to another of the men. "Be at the ready, lest an opponent beats you."

"'Tis a heavy beast," complained the young soldier.

"It is, and for a reason. Your weapon must be strong enough to kill, not merely wound, if need be. It must be heavy enough to endure the pounding of your enemy's blade. So you must be strong, as well. To be the best, you must control the sword always and at will."

Her gaze roved over Kildare's bare chest. Even from a distance, she could not miss the hardened, ridged muscles from neck to hips. Most of the other men lacked such strength. Even her own brother was not so well-honed from his fighting. Nor was Quaid. Both had rather talk of rebellion than train for it.

At the thought of the rebellion, Maeve began pacing again. Where was Flynn? Had he freed Quaid or been caught?

Sighing, Maeve stepped away from the battlements.

She bumped into Brighid.

"Lord and mighty, is he not full of power and perfection?" The girl spoke in awed tones, glancing down into the bailey.

Maeve knew not if her sister spoke of Kildare or Colm, but another glance at the field below confirmed that only her husband could be termed perfection. His squire… He was but a boy.

Either way, 'twas up to her to turn her sister's thoughts in a more pious direction. After all, Lent had begun.

"They are all men, made by God in exactly the same fashion, Brighid."

"It doesn't appear so." She giggled.

Maeve took Brighid's arm and spun her away from the scene. "Their differences mean little. They are all men, all driven to make war. Those men down there would see Ireland's hopes for freedom dashed and your brother imprisoned."

Brighid frowned. "But Kieran is your husband."

Holding in a curse, Maeve released her sister's arm. 'Twas clear the girl did not understand her husband was her enemy. In truth, Maeve wasn't sure she really understood herself.

Last night he had all but accused her of whoring for the cause, and it nettled her. Aye, his opinion of her should not matter in the least, so why did it?

Letting loose a frustrated sigh, she refused to linger on the distracting sight of him. Brighid continued to gape.

What else might you have done had I not been satisfied with kisses? His accusation rang again in her head. Though he might never believe she would not have shared his bed simply to further the rebellion's cause, Maeve knew the truth. He insulted her in saying such!

But what if Flynn had told her of the plan and had asked her to distract Kildare from his absence? Maeve paused. There was little she would not have done to help Quaid and her beloved Ireland. Oh, she could have distracted Kildare without using her body as bait. She was clever enough to think of another ruse. But would she have spoken with Kildare at length if asked? Lied to him? Invented a crisis to distract him?

Aye. She would have done all that and more to bring her betrothed and her brother home safely and move Ireland one step closer to freedom without loss of blood.

Maeve's anger deflated. Biting her lip, she tried to sort the matter through. What she *might* have done mattered little. Kildare was still an Englishman who had turned his back on his Irish blood. He was the enemy who would likely cheer at Quaid's execution, if such came to pass.

But he was also the same man who had finished Jana's cradle and aided Fiona in dealing with her tragedy. He'd had no need to do either, and Maeve wondered why he had.

Around and around, these thoughts spun in her head. Just who was Kildare? And what was she to do about him?

Lightning crackled across the sky, followed by the ominous peal of thunder. A glance upward confirmed rain would soon fall—again.

"Maeve, are you well?" asked Brighid suddenly.

Erasing the frown she felt upon her face, she sent her young sister a reassuring smile. "A trifle tired, sweetkins. Naught more."

A curse below lit the air, one so foul it could only belong to Kildare. Raindrops fell slowly, one on her cheek, another on the back of her hand. Maeve began to lead her sister inside the castle.

"I think Jana is tired, too," the girl said suddenly. "She says she has been laboring some hours."

"What?" Maeve gaped at her sister, openmouthed.

The girl backed away. "Did she not tell you this morn?"

This morn? Nay. Maeve had gone to the chapel and sought a moment alone to sort out her tangled mess of a marriage. All she could remember was that a wife's duty was to submit to the will, wishes, and whims of her husband.

She had never been good at submitting.

"How does she fare?" Maeve asked, focusing once more on Jana and her coming babe.

Brighid shrugged. "She says her labor began last night and has lasted into the morn. She asked me to find you."

"And you spent time staring at the soldiers instead?" Maeve chastised.

The girl's shoulders slumped and she cast her gaze downward. "'Tis sorry I am. I became...distracted."

As much as she wanted to lecture the girl on responsibility, Maeve delayed the topic until later. Not only did she understand the girl's dilemma, having stared at Kildare more than once herself, she also remembered Brighid was not yet a woman grown. For now, she must think of Jana.

Racing to her elder sister's chamber, Maeve thrust open the door and rushed inside.

There she found Jana lying upon her bed, hands clasping her distended belly, panting wildly. Dear Lord, would she have this babe within the hour? Maeve felt a wave of dizzy fear assail her.

Drawing in a calming breath, she looked at her elder sister again. "Ready to have your babe, are you?" She tried to smile.

Jana nodded, weakly. Maeve's rising panic returned.

Nay, no panic. She had been present for a few births at the castle. She could do this. Nature told a laboring mother when to push. She had but to make sure she received the babe and that he breathed, right?

Maeve hoped that was so but had no real notion. Her mother had always seen to the births in the castle, along with the help of one of the maids, Ismenia.

With nary hesitation, Maeve turned to Brighid and whispered, "Find Ismenia—swiftly, if you please. Send her here."

Brighid nodded, then ran back down the hall and down the steps. Satisfied with the girl's effort, Maeve turned back to Jana, who clenched her fists so hard her knuckles nearly turned white.

Rushing to her sister's side, Maeve knelt. "How long have you been thus?"

Jana did not speak at first but scrunched her face against the pain and groaned. More panting followed. From her vague recollection, Jana's time must be very near.

Suddenly, the pain seemed to leave Jana. "I cannot say." She looked out the narrow window, her limp, dark hair pasted to her temples with sweat. "Since midday, perhaps."

Alarm beat inside Maeve again, stronger now. Midday had been nearly four hours ago. She had labored this hard for so long? By herself?

Taking Jana's hand in her own, Maeve squeezed. "I am here. All will be well. How can I make you comfortable?"

Jana sent a weak smile. "Get this babe out of me."

Maeve smiled in return. "I will do my best. I've sent Brighid for Ismenia. She will know what to do."

Before Jana could reply, a wave of pain seized her again. She clutched Maeve's hand until it seemed near breaking. Biting her lip against discomfort, Maeve was not prepared when Jana issued an ear-splitting scream.

Sweat poured off her sister's face now. Her cheeks looked to be losing color. Maeve did not remember this much struggle as normal *before* the baby's appearance.

Dear God, that must be it! The babe must be coming now!

"What in the hell was that scream?" barked Kildare from the door.

Maeve glanced at her sister and felt another wave of concern when Jana did not even lift her head.

"Get out! Jana's babe comes."

Kildare glanced at Jana, frowned and hesitated, then left.

Sighing, Maeve turned her attention to her sister again. "Jana, I must see if the babe's head is visible. If so, you need to be concentrating on birthing him now."

With a weak nod, Jana agreed.

Maeve took Jana's overskirt and shift in hand and lifted them to her waist. Instantly, she saw the baby emerging from Jana's red, swollen body.

Instead of a tiny head, she saw buttocks.

Eyes widening, she clapped a hand over her mouth to hold in a squeal of panic.

Women died in breech births. Frequently. She had not had much practice in assisting births. Would she know what to do? Pray God would tell her, help her see Jana's babe into the world with a living mother to feed him.

"What is it? You see him?" her sister asked, her voice barely a whisper.

"Aye." Maeve hoped her voice did not shake as her hands did. "He comes."

"Her time comes?" asked Ismenia, who bustled into the room in a manner that belied her aging years.

Maeve nodded, then whispered, "He is breech."

Ismenia's lined face became grave. "We can do naught but pray."

The woman crossed herself, and Maeve fought off anger. "We must help her."

Maeve wanted to tell the crone she would not leave her sister to die, but knew she could not say thus where Jana might hear. No one here could afford panic flung wide.

The old maid shrugged. "'Tis all I can promise to fetch water and a few herbs. The rest will be God's will."

With that, Ismenia departed the room. Maeve stared after the empty portal, bereft and panicked at once. Would no one help her? Would no one lend assistance to keep Jana alive?

Maeve turned to call for Brighid again. She found the girl crumpled at the door in a dead faint.

Another wail, sharp and wounded, sounded from the bed. Maeve turned to see the baby's buttocks pressed against Jana, who made little effort to push her babe into the world. Blood began to seep out, staining Jana's dress and sheets.

Trembling, Maeve knelt to her sister again. "Push. He wants to come."

"No more," Jana whispered weakly with a shake of her head. "Let me sleep."

"Nay. You will birth this child first!"

Jana began to cry, silent tears squeezing from her tired eyes. Maeve mentally flogged herself.

"Please, Jana. Do not give up," she cajoled.

Squeezing her sister's hand one last time, Maeve left Jana to rush to the portal.

"Ismenia?" she yelled. "Come quickly!"

Kildare appeared in his chamber door moments later instead. "She's gone to fetch herbs from her cottage."

"Her cottage? Nay! There is not time."

Panic gripped her now fiercely. Jana began panting and groaning behind her; the sounds were growing faint.

"I need Ismenia now! Jana's babe is breech."

Kildare came closer, a concerned frown furrowing his wide brow as he stared at Jana. "Can you turn it?"

"My sister is not a horse, you ass!"

He grabbed her hands. "Aye. Stay calm, Maeve."

Jana groaned again, then whimpered. Maeve broke away from her husband and rushed to her sister's side.

Her eyes were closed. Her blue-veined lids provided the only color against her pasty skin. Even her lips looked white in a face paler than death. Maeve felt fear eating at her.

"She's going to die," Maeve whispered, voice shaking. "Dear God…"

Kildare grabbed her shoulders. "She will not die. Let us try once more."

"What do you know of birthing babes?" she snapped.

"Only slightly less than you, apparently. Get in position to catch the babe. He will come out."

With that directive, Kildare made his way to Jana's side and gripped her limp hand in a firm fist. "Listen to me," he ordered, voice stern. "You must not give up. This babe needs you."

"Nay," Jana whimpered.

"Aye. Fight! Would Geralt have wanted his child to die before knowing life?"

Maeve hoped Kildare's blustering gained Jana's resolve. She prayed anything would, for it won naught but her ire. Did he not think Jana realized Geralt's last wish for his babe was life?

Jana opened her eyes to slits. "Nay," she admitted, then groaned. "Nay," as another contraction seized her.

"Push, dear heart," Maeve coaxed.

"Push, damn you!" Kildare shouted.

"I cannot," Jana cried.

"By hell's fire, you can. Now!" he insisted.

Jana cried out, her shoulders jerking off the bed. And she pushed.

"She is falling. Get behind her!" Maeve shouted.

Without hesitation, her husband did, sweat dotting his brow with the effort to keep Jana upright for the long minute. Though he wore a bemused expression, Kildare did not move, even when Jana screamed, the sound so shrill it bounced off the chamber's walls and vibrated the very air.

Maeve glanced down and saw the baby's buttocks had emerged, as had his hips and lower back.

"He's coming!" she cried, hope and joy mingling in her heart.

Kildare laid Jana back on the bed as the contraction subsided. Maeve was shocked when he grabbed her sister's hand and crooned, "I knew you had fight in you. You're a brave woman. Geralt would be proud."

"Is he born?" Jana asked weakly.

"Almost," Maeve assured. "One more push, mayhap two."

To her relief, Jana slowly nodded.

Time stood suspended for long moments until the next wave hit her. She gripped Kildare's hand. He grimaced against Jana's hold and nodded to Maeve, who grabbed hold of the infant's protruding behind and tugged gently.

Jana reared off the bed once more. Instantly, Kildare got behind her, holding her frail shoulders in his massive hands. Maeve tensed. Her sister let loose a cry that curdled her blood. Long and pain-filled, the scream tore at Maeve's composure. Blood oozed everywhere, and Maeve again feared 'twas too much for Jana to overcome.

"Push!" Kildare shouted. "Push!"

Teeth grinding, Jana made another attempt. Another long cry filled the air.

Suddenly, a slippery bundle of flesh dropped into Maeve's waiting hands with a wail.

Maeve looked down at the babe she held, caked with blood and full of displeasure.

"'Tis a boy!" she shouted. "A boy!"

Jana nodded and gave a tired smile.

A moment later, Ismenia, having returned, stepped forward, cleaned out the babe's mouth with her finger, cut the cord, then swaddled him in a cloth she'd brought with the water.

"Congratulations, good lady," the old woman offered, handing the babe to his exhausted mother.

Jana took him and smiled at his red, blood-smeared face. He loosed another hearty wail. Kildare laughed.

By the door, Brighid roused and rose, mouth agape and eyes joyous, to meet her nephew.

Maeve looked at her husband, his face full of awe, his eyes sparkling. For some unknown reason, she felt tears prickle her eyes.

"We did it," she gasped. "I can scarce believe it."

He came to her side, his eyes warm and full of life. "You did it. I but yelled at her."

Ismenia appeared at her side with a fresh bowl of water. "'Tis a miracle, I think."

Maeve washed her hands and looked down to find the new babe suckling noisily at Jana's breast. It seemed a miracle indeed.

They were alive, thanks in part to Kieran's help. All would be well now with Jana.

"You did more than yell," she assured Kildare. "You helped." At his dubious expression, she rushed on. "Truly. I was most fearful until you came."

Kieran shrugged, as if he could not conceive how she believed such but would not argue again.

The babe soon tired, as did Jana. Ismenia took him from his mother's arms, then washed the infant.

Kieran curled his arm around Maeve's waist and led her away. "Come. They need us no more."

Without a word, Maeve followed Kieran to his chamber.

Once there, quiet fell between them, but she sensed no tension, only…gladness.

As he poured wine, she ambled to the window and looked out. In the hours during the babe's birth, night had fallen completely over the land, tossing milky stars into a blue-black sky. The moon hung high, casting a silvery glow over the hill-dotted landscape she knew so well. 'Twas so quiet she heard frogs croak. In the distance, she heard the River Barrow trickle. Not even a breeze disturbed the cool air. She sighed with the peace of it.

Tonight seemed as if God had declared a holiday from strife. He had brought forth a new child into the O'Shea fold upon an eve so blessed, harmony sang in her veins. 'Twas as if calm enveloped Ireland and the walls of Langmore. Though she knew it was all temporary, a fleeting illusion, it still made her smile.

Kieran put a cup into her hand, and she sent him a tired smile. "You did very well by your sister."

She shrugged. "I am glad they are alive and the boy looks healthy."

"He does. He looks like a boy she can be proud of."

Maeve nodded, and Kieran's hand came up to soothe her back, first in a gentle caress, then a firm stroke, easing tension from her tired muscles. He sent his fingers over her shoulders, about her tight neck, as he sipped wine.

A lazy contentment stole through her, a combination of the day's life-changing events and Kieran's easing caress.

Had she ever imagined his touch would rouse aught but apprehension or passion? Nay, but now that she had felt his comfort, she was loath to let it go. She should—she knew that. But right now, she could not deny herself such small solace.

She closed her eyes, feeling his hands upon her and languor wash through her.

"You amaze me," he said softly.

"Me?" she queried, opening her eyes a fraction.

Then she saw his gaze focused on her face, her mouth. Her lips tingled in anticipation of his kiss.

Instead, he spoke. "You are brave and smart and kind. You care for your family."

Against her will, she flushed upon hearing his praise. "I do only what I believe to be right."

"You keep Langmore and your family together."

She frowned. "You would do no less."

Disagreement flickered across his face, but he said naught, simply continued his questing fingers over her back, fluid now where stiffness had so recently reigned.

As he gazed upon her, a new tension slid through her, one she welcomed in a way she did not understand. She opened her eyes to regard him with honesty and all the uncertainty and need within her.

As if he read the emotions in her eyes, he swallowed. He wore no teasing grin tonight as he eased his thumb along her nape. The pleasure of it seemed to steal straight to her heart, and she melted closer to him.

"Sweet Maeve," he breathed, brushing the hair away from her face as he leaned closer, closer.

He pressed his mouth to hers. Tonight, there was no hurry in his kiss, only a soft hunger, a joy for life she, too, felt. 'Twas a yearning she could not resist answering.

With a brush of his lips, he claimed her mouth again, his tongue dusting her lower lip with a light stroke.

Maeve felt it all the way to her belly—and lower. She opened her lips to meet him, needing to taste him. Tonight she would think about naught, tomorrow and yesterday be damned.

Thought disappeared as he accepted her invitation with a groan. His tongue made a sweep through her mouth that was somehow lazy and thorough at once. Turning to him fully, she clung to him, drawing him in. She pressed closer, her breasts against his wide chest, as they shared each breath. He touched her cheek with gentle fingers.

Quivering beneath his soft touch, his attention, she wondered briefly how such a warrior could treat her with such tenderness.

Then he claimed her mouth again, hunger mounting.

Her own rose a notch as she felt his hard shoulders tense

beneath her hands, began to hear her heartbeat in her ears, urging her to dive into the deep, endless kiss.

He angled his head over hers more, now seizing what she offered. Again, she swayed against him restlessly, seeking the ease of the ache he was building, building.

Heat curled in her limbs, swirled in her blood, set her adrift in a hazy sea of sensation where only his mouth and her ache for him existed.

The hunger seemed to seize him, too, as he wound his hand behind her neck and made her mouth his captive.

Then he truly kissed her, insistently, hungrily, rapaciously.

Maeve had never imagined a mating of the mouths so deep she drowned in its hot urgings. His scent slid across her senses, heightened to his every breath, his every groan. His lips played with her need, surging it skyward until she boiled.

Maeve scrambled to thrust her fingers under his tunic. Kieran sighed his approval as one of his hands made its way from the small of her back to the underside of her breast.

Tensing, Maeve felt his thumb playing just beneath her nipple. His mouth continued to plunder and give, always demanding and bestowing complete assurance.

Her nipple tingled, tightened under his ministrations. She felt herself moisten and swell, hunger howling like a fierce wind, drugging her veins like the heaviest wine.

This need consumed her, stirred her. Surely such desire for her enemy was a sin.

The thought chilled Maeve. What of Quaid? What of Ireland?

Horror, then guilt, crushed her ardor, and she jerked from his embrace. She hated that she panted and ached, that her mind felt somewhat sluggish and uncertain.

Pressing her temples, Maeve closed her eyes and willed rational thought to return, but she could still scent Kildare in the thick air between them, still feel the throb of her need pulsing with every heartbeat.

"Maeve?"

She opened her eyes to regard him. His tunic sat askew on his shoulders. His hair lay rumpled from her fingers. Those unusual blue-green eyes looked dilated and heavy-lidded. From pressing against him, she knew the state of his arousal. And she wanted him.

Biting her lip to keep in her cry, she shook her head. 'Twas unfair she should be married to the one man who challenged her, who could make her blood dance to his rhythm—and that Fate had chosen him as her enemy.

"You promised me a fortnight's wait, my lord."

Disappointment hardened his features. "To adjust you to the idea of our marriage, *my lady*. A few moments ago, you seemed quite reconciled to our…union."

Maeve looked away and tried to muster up some anger for him for such a sneer. But he only spoke the truth.

"It is Lent, the time for sacrifice."

He regarded her with a cynical stare. "And you decided to give up sex until Easter?"

"Nay, I-I merely feel uncertain."

"Your thoughts are uncertain," he corrected. "You felt more than fine."

'Twas no use trying to argue with him in this mood. She had broken their unspoken truce. Part of her mourned that, for she hated the anger between them. Part of her knew there was no other way. She was not ready to give herself over to him, to be intimate with him in every way he desired. He wanted more than a husband sought from a wife. With him, there would be no fleeting kisses, no quick entry, no short possession.

Nay, he wanted a lover to envelop, to overwhelm.

The realization frightened her.

"I've asked you to wait another eight days. I shall hold you to each one."

So I might hold my sanity a little longer, she thought, fleeing his room for the sanctuary of her own.

But she knew 'twas temporary. He was a warrior, a predator. He would hunt her down, stalk her senses, and capture her eventually.

'Twas simply a matter of when.

* * * *

Flynn finally returned on that blustery Tuesday morn. Deeply relieved at his homecoming, Maeve laid aside her book and her spectacles and greeted him in the great hall with a hug.

Her brother was in little mood for family affection, and he

cursed and stepped around her, seeking a mug of ale.

"What happened?" she queried, frowning in concern.

He downed the mug's contents in a few swallows. "Quaid is still in prison, if that is what you ask."

She flinched at his anger. "I have heard thus. Did you see him?"

"Nay, but his father did. We were close, I tell you, to besting those English devils. The guards were deep in their cups. We managed to get a blade to Quaid. But by Saint Christopher, the man used it but once before it was taken from him and he was captured again. Wish that he had killed a whole lot of those English dogs."

Flynn's voice rang with contempt and bitterness. Maeve scowled. When had she last seen him smile? She could hardly recall. Now he talked mostly of war and killing the English.

Flynn also had yet to inquire about Jana or any of the others. 'Twas unlike him. Was he so involved with the rebellion that he cared for little else?

"Jana birthed a boy whilst you were away," she said, offering a smile and a refill of his ale.

"Both are well?" he asked, raking a hand through his long, dark hair. He looked as if he wanted to pace.

She nodded. "'Twas a difficult birth. Jana bled much and we worried she might die."

"Aye, well...she lives now," he said as if distracted. "There should not be a reason, I tell you, that we cannot free Quaid and the others."

Maeve scowled at her brother. Rebellion obsessed him. And it worried her.

"I will keep trying, Maeve. If it takes my last breath, I'll see you wed to him and freed from that swaggering cock, Kieran."

Fixing him with a frown, Maeve began, "You—"

"You cannot free your sister from me. She is my wife."

Maeve and Flynn both whirled to the sound of Kieran's voice. He looked imposing and large, and none too pleased. He gazed at Flynn with contempt and ire, then shifted his attention to her. To her shock, his gaze upon her seemed much angrier.

Maeve glared back. If he thought to be angry with her for refusing to share his bed, then he could stew and fume into next week, for all she cared.

"You will never wed Quaid."

Kildare's anger hardened as he spoke those words, and she saw then he smoldered over her wish to escape their union. He viewed it as a duplicity, she felt certain. Maeve swallowed against a sense of guilt and apprehension she scarce understood.

"My lord—"

"Not now," he barked, then turned his attention back to Flynn. "'Tis time for you and I to talk."

"I have naught to say to you, you English prick."

Kieran grabbed her brother by the arm in a harsh grip. His wicked grin showed traces of unyielding steel. "I have plenty to say to you, swine-sucker. And you will listen now."

Her husband began leading her brother away. Maeve ran after them, panic rising. Flynn's pride would not withstand another beating like Kildare had given him that first day, not to mention what such would do to his face. And what if Kildare should see her brother imprisoned for his suspected part in the rebellion?

"My lord—"

"Stay out of this, Maeve. I simply wish to question him."

"Do not hurt him," she implored.

"I can see after myself," Flynn insisted as if insulted that a mere woman thought to protect him.

Knowing she could do naught, Maeve watched them go, heart sinking.

CHAPTER NINE

Kieran returned to his chamber later that night, frustrated. He'd gotten precious little information from the foolish Flynn earlier. And blast Maeve, but he had been unable to punish Flynn for his rebellion with fists, as her protests had rung in his head.

And then there was the woman herself. By Saint Peter's toes, he could not recall the last time he'd had this much difficulty in seducing a woman. He frowned. In fact, he had *never* had this much difficulty. That Maeve should lead him on such a chase did not surprise him; a more stubborn creature he had never encountered. Still, why did all his charm fail him now, with his own wife?

The object of his own thoughts knocked upon the door to his chamber and hovered just inside, looking very well in a dress of shimmering gold. 'Twas no surprise he could think of little else but her lips beneath his. The blasted woman had that effect on him.

"My lord?" she called.

He sighed. Would she ever call him by his own name? He knew her refusal to say it was another form of defiance. But damnation, he could scarce handle more resistance this night.

"Aye, my wife. You have come for our hour together?" he asked, noting the book tucked beneath her arm and her spectacles in her hand.

"Nay, I came to speak to you of my brother."

"I sent him to his rooms. And you may rest easy, for I did not hit him, though he sorely tempted me."

The relief on her delicate face only irritated him more. He watched with fascination as she flung a stray lock of fire-hued hair behind her shoulder. Hellfire, how he wanted her.

She, on the other hand, hated nearly everything about him.

"Thank you, my lord."

"Kieran," he corrected futilely.

As he expected, she behaved as if he had not spoken.

"Flynn is not himself of late, and I would caution you to know that, while he can be rash, his intent is pure."

"Pure rubbish for the English position, Maeve." Kieran shook his head, weary. "I do not wish to discuss your brother. We are to spend an hour together—"

"But—"

"We *will* spend this hour together, Maeve. We have been waylaid by birth and rebellion, but no more. I'll not have you stiff and unyielding in my bed seven days hence."

A flush colored her features, and Kieran felt his energy rise again, as did his interest. Maeve was a lovely creature, full of intelligence and quiet spirit. Last night, when he told her she amazed him, he'd meant those words. Her deeds somehow only made him want to possess her more. Why, though, he could not say. Usually he cared more for a woman's pretty white bosom than her mind.

Yet as with everything else, Maeve was different.

"But—"

"I do this to ease your path between us. Accept that and read yon book to me," he said, settling into a nearby chair.

Maeve took the small book from beneath her arm and gripped it. "Th-this one? I-I do not think you would like it."

Her reticence intrigued him, and he pressed on. "Why? I enjoy words as well as the next man."

"'Tis poetry."

"And you assume I do not like poetry?" He frowned.

"You are a man of battle, not one of study."

"I can read, Maeve."

She flushed guiltily. "I meant that I cannot see you enjoying these verses."

At that, he smiled with mischief. "Mayhap you can convert me, sweet Maeve."

Looking skeptical indeed, Maeve stepped into the chamber and sat upon the stool beside the hearth, roaring with warmth. Donning her spectacles, she opened the book and looked at him with uncertainty.

Again, he merely smiled. "Please, read."

Her shoulders conveying tension, she began.

"After the day, before the night,
Or before day, after the night has gone,
For modest girls a reassuring shade,
Just the right sort of light, with curtains drawn,
Wherein to lay inviting ambuscade."

Kieran leaned back in his chair and pulled the next words from his memory.

"And there Corinna entered, with her gown
Loosened a little, and on either side,
Of her white neck the dark hair hanging down.
Semiramis could not have been, as bride,
Any more lovely, nor could Lais move
The hearts of men more easily to love."

"You know this poem?" Her face betrayed her utter shock.

"I do know a thing or two besides lances and broadswords. The earl of Rothgate, my mentor, ensured the educations of all his charges were properly completed, Ovid included."

Maeve's cheeks flushed a beguiling pink. "So you know what comes next?"

Kieran's grin broadened.

"Sheer though it was, I pulled the dress away;
Pro forma, she resisted, more or less.
It offered little cover, I must say,
And why put up a fight to save a dress?"

He rose from his chair and made his way to Maeve's side. He trailed a purposely tender thumb along her nape, then brushed the back of his hand along her cheek. Tensing, she watched him, gold eyes widening as he knelt before her.

As she took a shaky breath, Kieran kept her gaze captive and he continued.

"So soon she stood naked, and I saw,
Not only saw, but felt, perfection there,
Hands moving over beauty without flaw,
The breasts, the thighs, the triangle of hair.
"No need for catalogue, to itemize
All those delights."

As he whispered, he traced a gentle finger upon her ankle, caressing her shin, then her knee.

To his delight, she shivered and reached for his shoulders, placing her hands upon them as if she could no longer balance without him. Grin wide, he lifted her ankle to his mouth and laved a kiss upon her stockinged skin. Her fingers curled into his arms, clutching.

He leaned closer, feeling her tremble again as he whispered against her mouth.

> *"Nor could I truly say*
> *That I confined my pleasure to my eyes.*
> *Naked, I took her, naked, until we lay*
> *Worn out, done in.*
> *Grant me, O gods, the boon*
> *Of many such another sultry noon!"*

When he finished speaking, Kieran's hand rested just above her knee. Maeve looked entranced and uncertain at once.

"You know every word of it." Maeve's whisper sounded breathless—and accusing—as if that somehow betrayed her idea of him.

"I am more than brawn and battle, Wife."

"Nay." She frowned at his words.

She tensed, then gasped as he brushed his hand from just above her knee to the inside of her thigh.

"Why? Does the fact I know a few verses of Ovid make hating me harder? Or wanting me easier?" he challenged.

Maeve jerked away from his touch and closed her eyes, as if that might block out the truth. "Neither!"

"Are you certain?"

Closing the book with a frustrated sigh, she pulled off her spectacles and rose, darting for the door. Kieran took hold of her arm with a firm grip and stayed her.

When she struggled against his hold, he brought her closer with a subtle tug, then pressed his mouth to the inside of her wrist.

Her heartbeat surged beneath his lips.

With a feminine growl of fury, she wrenched her arm from his grasp. "Touch me no more!"

Kieran paused, pondering her reaction. She responded to him as a woman does to a man she desires. He had no reason to believe she would not eventually succumb to their marriage bed and the pleasures it would bring. But if she resisted him for the reasons he suspected, he feared 'twould take much time to overcome her strong mind and her convictions.

"I know this marriage has meant much change in your plans, sweet Maeve. But if you forget for a moment that King Henry sent me, you might find we can talk with much to say."

"I do not wish it."

"Since we are wed, 'tis best if you try. This marriage will only be a failure, dismal beyond comprehension, if we do not."

Though she stood half a head shorter than him, Maeve somehow managed to look down her nose at him. "I imagine you will think yourself well versed with the ladies. What I think you fail to understand, my lord, is my disinterest in you as anything other than the man who can keep peace here."

"If 'tis peace you seek, why do you aid the rebellion? And do not deny your involvement."

She arched a reddish brow at him, her expression haughty. "I merely want freedom without bloodshed. I want no war. And you've no need to worry, for I will do my duty to you as God intends, but I do not think you draw me into your kisses now that I know what you're about. I do not wish to be breathless or enthralled."

"But I will not rest until you are, sweet Maeve."

With a regal lift of her head, she shrugged. "If you enjoy a life of disquiet, that is your choice."

Cloaked in silence, she left, a vision of aloof female.

But Kieran knew a woman too well, sensed the excitement she fought, tried even to hide from herself.

And with half of her fortnight's reprieve gone, he thought now might be an excellent time to show her the strength of his charm until he found her, sighing and happy, in his bed.

* * * *

The following afternoon, the sun glowed with golden intensity across the Irish hills. Maeve watched Langmore's army. A few were still in sore need of training, and they grumbled at Kieran's directives and stared at passing maids. She repressed a grin, glad to see her cocksure husband had made little progress with the most unruly of the group. But the rest were much improved.

He worked patiently with the soldiers each day. Some of the fat ones were beginning to slim under his rigorous training. Some of the old were building strength again. Those with no training were learning, a few eager, as if sensing they learned from a master. Indeed, he seemed to be winning the respect of most of the soldiers, for they looked upon him at times as if he were a god.

Maeve only prayed she did not look at him with that same expression.

If the man would make war, 'twas double certain he could seduce a woman. Last night, his words and a few simple touches alone near made her skin dew with moisture, her heart beat, her belly tingle with wants she never felt in Quaid's arms.

Why him? Of all men, why?

Before she could ponder the question again, as she had during her last sleepless night, she watched Kieran round the men up and dismiss them for the day.

Surprise furrowed her brow. 'Twas barely after midday and nary a cloud hung in the sky to portend rain. So why did he cease their work?

As if he could sense her curiosity, Kieran raised his gaze to the battlements where she watched him and smiled. "Come down, sweet Maeve."

He wanted something, and as weak as her resistance to his charm had been last night, more contact she needed not. Her resolve could hardly be called immune to his grin, his touch.

"I am enjoying the view from here, my lord."

"I've a mind to show you something," he called up, his voice strong, sure.

And she did not have a mind to see anything he had to display. What could he wish to show her now?

Maeve shook her head. Down that path lay troublesome thoughts. Did he plot to interrogate her? Seduce her?

"Later, perhaps. I must see to supper."

"Let it wait, Wife. Come down to me now."

Maeve hesitated, aware suddenly that Langmore's army, as well as the passing servants, watched, waited to see who was master here. For so long, Maeve had held power, made decisions, acted as the lord, since Flynn was so frequently gone or occupied. And she resented Kildare assuming the mantle of her responsibility so quickly and easily.

Still, she knew his request had naught to do with the castle's duties. That knowledge was in his eyes.

She hesitated. Going to him would show all she'd been vanquished by her husband. The thought of everyone believing her subjugated chafed her pride.

"Come, Maeve, or I shall come after you. Mayhap then we will not appear for supper at all."

Shocked by his intimation, Maeve stared. Heat flooded her cheeks moments later.

Dear Lord, the man was bold, so brazen he put the Devil to shame. And she had little doubt he would carry through with his threat and scale the battlements to get to her.

"I must check with the cook. Then I will see you."

Before he could protest, she fled the battlements. Racing to the kitchen, she peeked her head into the hot room. An open fire cooked several loaves of yeasty bread. A cupboard of spices stood locked against the far wall. In her hand, the aging cook held a fat goose, plucked fresh.

The woman was so efficient Maeve scarce had to check in more than twice a week.

"How can I be helpin' you, m'lady?"

Maeve shook her head. "You are as organized as always, I see. Finish with your goose."

Knowing such an errand had been foolish at best, Maeve chastised herself. If Kieran wanted to talk, she could carry on a conversation with the rogue. She need not avoid him. Certainly she feared him not.

Only her body's reaction to his touch.

Pushing the rebellious thought aside, she made her way to the middle bailey. There, Kieran stood much as she had left him.

Upon spying her emerge into the sun, he flashed her that knowing grin, the one that never failed to make her head spin with the possibilities of his charm.

She must absolve herself of these foolish notions! Aye, his smile might hold more lure than Flynn's or even Quaid's. But it meant naught except he had practiced before a mirror catching a lady's eye.

"What wish you to show me?"

Maeve silently applauded her crisp question. Kieran could not find any invitation there.

He held out his hand to her—and his smile grew more mischievous. To herself, she denied any surge in her heartbeat.

Refusing to meet his blue-green gaze, she walked to his side and fixed on his nose. It was long and straight, though slightly bent at the bridge and just above his mouth, which maintained that wicked grin still.

She sighed. Perhaps her heartbeat was a trifle faster, aye, but no more than that.

Finally, mercifully, he turned away and bent to retrieve a bow at his feet. To her shock, he placed it in her hand.

Instantly, she dropped it. "I will not touch this instrument of death."

With patience, he retrieved the bow and placed it back in her hand, this time wrapping his hand around her own. His fingers felt firm and warm and rough against her own.

"It is an instrument of protection, as well as a means to feed the castlefolk. It is also an amusement to be mastered."

Kieran had lost possession of his mind, she felt certain. For him to believe the very instrument that could pierce armor and skewer a soldier at thirty paces was also one of recreation was the height of madness.

"Nay, do not frown at me thus, sweet Maeve. I will show you."

The protests were still forming in her mind as he took her hand in his callused one and led her to his horse. He lifted her up on the animal's back with no more effort than the wind lifts a leaf, then mounted behind her. After tucking the bow away in a pouch attached to his saddle, he kicked the stallion's flanks.

That simply, Maeve found herself out of doors, away from Langmore. Wind fingered its way through her hair, pulling loose strands about her face and nape. The sun beat its golden rays upon the fragrant earth, waking to the coming spring.

But she was more aware of Kieran's arm about her waist, tight, pulling her against the solid warmth of his chest. She could feel him breathe, feel his heart beat. When had she noticed anything so familiar about Quaid? About anyone?

Moments later, he stopped them in the midst of a small glade of trees beginning to bud after the winter. As soon as he halted his mount, he jumped to the soft earth and reached up for her.

Maeve looked at his waiting hands, into his expectant eyes. Her heart tripped dangerously. Why did this man hold appeal for her? He called to her in ways she did not understand, challenging her notions of war, of politics and marriage…of what passed between a man and a woman.

Why did he affect her in ways Quaid did not?

Sensing her hesitation, Kieran reached up for her and plucked her to the ground, directly before him. They stood so close she felt his heat, sensed his leashed desire. It sent a dangerous, foolish swirl of longing curling through her.

Remembering Quaid and the political duty she had to Ireland's future, one that did not include falling in thrall to the enemy, she stepped away.

"Why have you brought me here, my lord?"

The expected irritation crossed his face. Aye, she knew he hated her to address him thus. That was why she did it. 'Twas a small enough revenge for having altered her life without her consent.

With exaggerated patience, he pulled the bow from the bag attached to his saddle. Then he handed it to her and closed her fingers around the detestable weapon.

Fury scaled her as much as his touch upon her hand. She knew not whether to curse him or melt.

"In your hand I place a longbow. 'Tis made of two pieces of yew, so it is fairly light. This is a boy's bow, so it is smaller. You will be able to shoot it."

"I wish no such lesson, my lord. I must ask that you remove your hand—"

"In archery," he began as if she had not spoken, "you strive for four areas of practice. First, of course, is precision. In hunting, in defense, even in sport, it is important to hit one's target."

"I do not want to learn this."

"Will you use it against me by joining the rebels when they march?" The rogue had the nerve to grin.

"I've told you, I want no bloodshed. I only want freedom for Ireland."

He nodded, as if her words had solved all. "Number two, you want speed in each shot. You can hardly defend yourself or hit a moving target if it is faster than your arrow."

126

She feigned a yawn. "Must I hear more?"

He answered with a laugh. "Three, you want comfort and ease with the bow's handling. For this, you must have nimble hands."

Was it her imagination, or did his last sentence hold particular suggestion? Maeve risked a peek at his lean profile, only to find that ever-present grin of his.

Determined to ignore his intimations, she watched his hands close around the bow again.

Still, the thought of his nimble fingers lingered to discomfort, to distraction.

"Last," he said, "you must have power. 'Twill do you no good at all to merely scratch your target. You want to penetrate, deeply."

Certain he had intended every kind of suggestion with those words, she snapped her gaze up to his face.

His eyes, a striking blue-green, darkened, sharpened, at her regard.

"I understand you," she accused.

He merely smiled. "Good. Then I'll not have to instruct you much more on what I seek."

Then, as if he had not used a husky shiver of a voice to suggest acts that pass between a man and woman, he took her by the shoulders and turned to face the glade of trees.

Again, he handed her the bow. "Now, position your body directly before the target and spread your feet apart a trifle." When she resisted, he wedged one of his booted feet between her slippers and prodded them apart. "Distribute your weight equally on both legs and line up your shoulders with the target."

He placed her thus, hands roving from shoulders to her hands, then finally dropping to her hips. Even through her dress and her smock, she felt the heat of his fingers penetrating her skin, sinking deep into his touch.

"Good," he crooned. "Now hold the bow so you form a vee with your thumb and forefinger, like thus." He quickly placed her hands in the appropriate position. "Remember, you should be able to move freely after an arrow is released."

She sighed. "How would I know that before I shoot the arrow?"

"Once you practice, you will know. Now you must nock the arrow. Hold the bow in your left hand, like thus." Again, he put her in the correct stance. "That is good. Bring the bowstring against the inside of your left arm."

Frowning with concentration, she did as he bid, doubtful she could do this. Something that appeared so simple suddenly felt complicated.

Though with Kildare, nothing that seemed thus should surprise her.

"Aye, Maeve. Lay the arrow shaft across the rest, with the feather sticking up. Excellent," he praised as she followed his instruction. "Now draw the arrow toward the bowstring. Stop only when you feel the string sits firmly in the arrow nock."

Again, she followed his instructions. The motion felt awkward, but he nodded with approval, his gaze suddenly alive and serious at once. She watched him, oddly eager for his next words.

"Excellent. You must draw the bow next, using your first three fingers." He seized the ones in question and curled them around the taut string. "Aye, but hold the arrow nock with your fore and middle fingers."

Maeve tried to grip the little bit of wood between her fingers but could maintain no grip on it. She sighed in frustration as she tried twice more, to no avail.

Kildare reached into the tangle of bow and arms to position her fingers on the top and bottom of the nock. With a gentle squeeze of her hand, she clamped around the wood. Suddenly, the fit of the pose felt much better.

"That's right." He regarded her with approval. "Now draw the string back until the index finger on your right hand feels fixed in place. And remember this place, for you will use it each time you draw a bow. Different anchor points result in poor shooting.

"Are you aimed properly?" Kildare began repositioning her directly in front of the closest tree in the glade before he even finished speaking. "Now look at the target with both eyes. Imagine lining up your arrow with the tree so they align perfectly. When you feel ready, take a breath and release the bowstring."

Intent on the target, Maeve looked from the tip of her arrow to the thick tree trunk. Then she took the aim's measure again.

"Do not worry about accuracy now. Understanding aim takes some time, sweet Maeve. For now, 'tis enough to try."

Absently, she nodded, then drew in a breath. An instant later, she released the string. Kildare stood behind her, his large hands engulfing her waist, making her feel tiny and for once not invincible.

Maeve was unsure if she liked the feeling or not.

The arrow went through the air with a small whistle, then moments later, hit the tree. The tip barely embedded itself in the bark two inches above the ground. But she had done it!

"Very good!" he praised, leaning around her.

His genuine smile, his dancing eyes, combined with the familiar heat of his touch, made her feel flushed, fluttery—not at all like her usual logical self.

"Try again," he suggested and reached for another arrow.

With a surprising excitement, she plucked the arrow from his grasp. She repeated the process, missing the tree this time.

An even more surprising disappointment stole through her, and she questioned its existence. It wasn't as if she cared whether she ever mastered archery. Of course, she did not like being unable to complete a task, any task.

She glanced behind her, to Kieran's face. Relief relaxed her when she saw no disappointment there. Then she frowned. Certainly she did not care about her performance in this brutal sport because she sought to avoid his disappointment. Did she?

"Not everyone makes every shot," he assured.

"Not even you?" she challenged.

He shrugged. "I have had twenty years of practice."

"Hit that tree," she said impulsively. "I want to see how you do it."

Grinning, he took the bow from her hand and reached for another arrow. In a whirl and an instant, he had the arrow in place, his body in stance, and his shot aimed. He released the bowstring faster than a blink. The arrow whistled in its flight, the shrill cry as it sliced through the air surprisingly loud. With a solid *thwack*, the wooden tip embedded itself in the tree. Even from this distance, Maeve could see the entire tip had penetrated the bark. Deep, just has he had said.

Would he make love the same way?

The thought came from nowhere, but she could not shake it. Maeve looked up at him, caught between awe and fear and curiosity and her own unshakable desire. Why did Kieran confuse her so?

His gaze held her own. For long heartbeats, he said naught. Neither moved. Maeve felt sure he would kiss her again, and her body tightened with anticipation.

"Try again," he said softly, handing the bow back to her.

Their fingers brushed as she took the instrument from him, and she shivered. Next, he handed her another arrow, gave her another touch.

Trying to settle on the instructions he had given her, Maeve placed the arrow in the bow and lined up her aim. She was aware of little more than Kieran standing behind her, all heat and muscle, his soft breath near her neck.

She closed her eyes, demanding concentration of herself. Then she let loose the arrow. A moment later, it found its way into the tree mere inches from Kieran's.

Behind her, he laughed. "You are quite good at this, Wife. Perhaps I should be worried?"

He teased her, and she felt herself smiling, staring, wondering about him...

Suddenly, his smile faded, his eyes warmed.

Then he took her mouth.

Maeve did not resist. Instead, she felt herself open beneath him, as if she were another person, a weaker one whose desires meant more than anything. Want and warmth pounded strongly in her veins as he slanted his lips over hers again and pursued, explored, demanded, and possessed her mouth. But he gave, too, the most exquisite pleasure. She felt it building in her breasts, and her belly, coiling lower... God help her.

In the next moment, she felt his hand at her waist moving up, curling toward her heart. His fingers brushed at her fluttering belly, traced a slow, soft line between her breasts.

A strangled moan escaped her as she arched closer. Her breast ached to feel the heat of his touch surrounding her, enclosing her completely.

Suddenly, he fulfilled her wish by sliding his large palm over the taut mound. The fabric between them abraded her flesh; then his thumb followed, skimming, brushing, arousing.

And still he devoured her with his mouth. Maeve felt herself drowning in a warm, honeyed pool of desire, the gong of her heartbeat resounding in her ears, making her body throb.

Why could Kieran do this to her, make her wanton, so nearly willing to forget all she held dear just for the experience of his pleasure?

She was not that kind of woman. Duty—to family, to God, to Ireland, to Quaid—must come first.

Taking a deep breath, she ended the kiss and stepped away. She expected him to come after her, to demand they continue the intimacy.

He did not—and perversely, that disappointed her.

Kildare licked his lips, as if taking more of the taste of her. His hot stare drilled her, filled her with a shaking need, and she couldn't decide whether it frightened or thrilled her.

"In six days, sweet Maeve, there will be no stopping. Then I will take you—all of you—without your protests."

Between her illogical desire and his words, she felt without power, and she refused to let him steal her will or her voice.

"When we made that agreement, I said a fortnight, give or take a few days, my lord," she snapped.

"Less I will agree to; more I will not. I plan to hold you to that fortnight."

"And do you have that calculated to the second? Should I expect to wake up that morn and find you pinning me to my bed, regardless of my wishes?"

She tried to scorch him with contempt, but his face betrayed no reaction to her tone.

"You cannot make me want you!" she cried, frustrated.

"I do not have to," he asserted, crossing his arms over his chest. "Your body wants me. 'Tis your mind I fight now."

Maeve stared at him, wide-eyed. How had he known that?

Her question must have shown on her face, for he came closer and whispered, "A man senses things about a woman he desires: her breathing, her heartbeat. Did you know a woman's arousal has a scent?"

"And like any beast, you perceive it?"

"Yes," he said without apology. "I know the scent of your arousal, Maeve. I won't rest until I satisfy it."

With that, he turned away and stashed his bow in the pouch beside his saddle. Silently, he held out his hand to her. Knowing 'twas best if they left now, she placed her hand in his. Such proximity in the sunshine, the trees enclosing them in false privacy, gave the illusion of intimacy they needed not.

Quickly, Kieran helped her on the horse's back, sat her astride, then mounted behind her. His body engulfed her back in taut heat as they rode for Langmore. Neither could she mistake his erection against her buttocks.

Suddenly, her head felt light, her muscles weak. What was she to do? Kieran was right. He had won her body over. Even now she ached. Late at night, she thought too often of entwining her body with his. She had only her mind to resist him now, and she feared that, with his smile and unexpected acts of tenderness, he was fast overcoming that as well.

Finally, they reached Langmore. She swung her leg over the horse's head and slid off the horse's back without Kieran's assistance and sought to make her way inside.

Before she could escape, he leaped from the saddle and grabbed her arm. "You cannot run from me much longer. I will not hurt you, and soon your mind will know that."

"You know naught," she ground out.

Kieran looked ready to kiss her again, just to make his point, and Maeve steeled herself for another onslaught of warmth and tingling fire.

"My lord?" called Colm, his squire, instead.

With irritation on his lean features, Kieran turned to the boy. "What is it?"

"'Tis someone here to see you."

Kieran looked beyond Colm's shoulder, to the figure of a vaguely familiar auburn-haired man.

Maeve shuddered when she recognized the visitor as Desmond O'Neill, for she had never liked the wily man, despite his devotion to the rebellion.

She turned to Kieran, to warn him of the man's crafty nature. The shocked look on his face stopped her, for he looked as if he'd turned to stone.

Frowning, Maeve watched as O'Neill walked toward Kieran, then held up his hand in greeting.

His next words stunned Maeve.

"Hello, Son."

CHAPTER TEN

Kieran stopped. He stared, frozen. His head swam in icy shock. But the longer he stared, the more he knew his first suspicion was true.

The man was the father he had not seen in many years. Twenty-one, to be exact.

Desmond O'Neill's waist had thickened, and his auburn beard had grayed, but Kieran could not mistake the truth.

How had the man known where to find him? Where had he been since that terrible day at Balcorthy?

Kieran opened his mouth, and for long moments, no words came. His mind whirled, and he felt certain his furrowed brow showed his confusion.

"I thought you were dead," he said finally.

With a sharp edge to his laughter, Desmond came closer. The skin around his eyes gathered in deep creases, giving testament to his age and hard living.

"Is that what your mother told you, now?"

Numbly, he nodded. She had lied to him, clearly. Jocelyn Broderick, his mother, was dead, gone to find her heavenly reward some five years past, so he could not ask her why.

Still, the man had sought him out this day, and though Kieran did not know what had kept his father away, some part of him felt gladdened at this reunion with his sire.

Desmond scowled. "She always was a heartless whore. Can't

say I'm surprised she would tell you thus."

His slur took Kieran aback. Jocelyn had been many things: withdrawn, bitter, more interested in the Church than her son. But she had never lain with a man other than her husband. Irritation replaced a bit of his gladness.

Beside Kieran, Maeve tensed. She watched in silence, her face full of wide-eyed shock.

Damnation, he had not wanted to tell her—to tell anyone here— about the worst of his past. Every time memories of it crept up, he'd found 'twas easy enough to forget them with swordplay, ale, or female flesh—whichever he found handy. But a woman like Maeve, she would never forget.

"Maeve O'Shea," Desmond said, nodding toward her. "How fare Langmore and your brother, lass?"

She nodded cautiously. "Well, sir. Thank you."

"Maeve is no longer an O'Shea," he told his father. "She is my *wife*."

"An O'Neill, lass!" Desmond grinned. "Well 'tis glad I am to have the likes of you as my kin."

Maeve sent Kieran a seeking glance, then turned to O'Neill.

'Twas odd enough a dream—a father mysteriously alive, a wife who knew naught of his past. Yet, from the wind upon his face and the feel of Maeve beside him, Kieran knew it was not.

As reality replaced shock, one blinding question followed: If Desmond O'Neill had not died that fateful day at Balcorthy, where had he been for the past twenty-one years? Why had he never contacted Kieran, especially after his mother left him in the care of strangers?

"Maeve is a Broderick, like me," Kieran said.

Desmond frowned. "And did that bitch strip you of your rightful name, too?"

Irritation became anger at his father's slur. "She is dead, and maligning her does naught to change what is done."

"Dead? 'Tis the best news I've heard in years."

Kieran felt his jaw tense; his fists clenched. A simmering fury replaced the anger he'd felt moments ago.

He and his mother had not loved well, for she had never wanted a son of Irish blood. Kieran had tried to adopt her English ways, to no avail. His mother may have abandoned him, but she had at least seen to his care, written an occasional, if distant, letter. What had Desmond O'Neill ever done as a father but engage in the siring?

He gazed at his father, suspicion rearing its head, ugly as a gargoyle. "Why have you come?"

Surprise crossed Desmond's face. He leaned forward to clap Kieran on the shoulder. "To visit. You've grown to a fine son, one in whom a man can take pride. To see you as the earl of Kildare and back in Ireland, and with so Irish a wife, well…it does my old heart good."

Though the man smiled, Kieran saw the watchful gaze Desmond swept over him and Maeve.

His father came closer then and clapped him on the shoulder. "Aye, a fine son. An earl with so much power!"

Kieran heard his father prattle, seemingly happy. But his battle instincts, honed since age eight, warned him to be wary.

"Why have you come?" he repeated.

Desmond looked affronted, then flashed a false grin. 'Twas no doubt in Kieran's mind the expression was naught but a ruse.

"Have you no kind words for your old father, now? Come, invite me in for an ale. Let us talk of Ireland."

Sensing he would receive no further information until the man was inside Langmore's walls, Kieran gestured Desmond in the direction of the keep. He followed. Beside him, Maeve dug her fingers into the crook of his arm as he escorted her inside. Her every muscle felt beyond tense.

"Be careful," she whispered.

He gave her a slight nod in acknowledgment.

So, his perceptive wife did not trust O'Neill, either. Her expression said she was not pleased the man was his father.

He began to think she was not alone in that.

Once inside the keep, he turned toward the stairs. "Go. Await me in my"—he glanced at his father—"our chamber."

She looked from Desmond, then back to him. Her expression reflected concern, a willingness to protect.

Did sweet, slender Maeve think to protect him, a warrior?

He found the thought vaguely pleasing, if impossible.

Finally, she gave him a reluctant nod, then departed upstairs. Kieran watched her go, hips swaying—not like a temptress; she was too practical for that—but something elementally female and graceful. He wondered, not for the first time, how much longer it would take him to break through her resistance so he might touch her—all of her—as he craved.

"She'll make you a good wife, Son," said Desmond, intruding into his thoughts.

Kieran merely nodded as they sat at the head table in the great hall. A kitchen wench brought them ale a moment later, at his bidding. Everyone bustling about he then sent away.

Finally, he and his father were alone.

And Kieran felt anything but comfortable.

"I have visited Langmore once or twice. 'Tis a beautiful keep," Desmond offered. "Strong and defensible, a good haven in times of war."

Kieran merely nodded. "How did you learn I had come?"

"Your cousin Hugh. He has maintained a correspondence with the earl of Rothgate for some five years, Son."

Guilford. Kieran absorbed the information and stifled a curse. He would speak to the meddling old man as soon as may be. "And you've just now decided to see me. Why is that?"

"To see the man you've become," Desmond said, as if the answer should be obvious.

Kieran still distrusted his words. 'Twas a strong instinct.

"Yorkshire is but a week away. You might have seen me sooner had you merely wished to satisfy your curiosity."

"An Irishman riding on English soil? Nay, 'twould be like plunging a blade in my own heart, lad. Foolish."

Perhaps an Irishman might have such a worry, but only if he had reason to fear the English wished him harm—or if he had done aught wrong.

"But now that you are back in Ireland, we have much to discuss, father to son."

Thus far, Kieran could think of naught he wished to discuss with the wily older man. "Such as…?"

"The past."

Nay. Kieran shook his head. "It is over and done. Discussing it changes naught."

Desmond nodded. "Well, then, what of the future?"

"What of it?"

"'Tis a time of great changes for you. And for Ireland."

136

"I can see to my own matters," Kieran said, leaning forward in his chair, dreading what he felt certain would come next.

"Can you see to Ireland's as well?" Desmond asked.

Reluctantly, he nodded. Though he wanted not the duties King Henry had given him, they were his to fulfill, if for no other reason than his honor and Guilford.

"Well, we both want what is best for her now, don't we? Aye," Desmond said. "And what could be worse for a country than having foreigners with the spirit of serpents rule it?"

Kieran nearly flinched at his father's words.

Desmond merely leaned forward in his chair and whispered, "Son, I know you've come at that bastard Tudor's request, but you cannot forget your blood now. You cannot turn your back on the country that birthed you."

So, O'Neill was here to persuade him about the virtues of Ireland and the rebellion. At the cost of committing treason?

"I thought Jocelyn birthed me," he returned dryly.

"I meant the soil, lad. 'Tis not dense you are. We are a land rich in traditions that have naught to do with the English. We deserve our freedom!"

"And you want me to help you get it?"

Desmond nodded excitedly. "'Tis been the cause closest to my heart since before I wed your mother. For some years, we were winning the war. Now this Tudor bastard sends more men in here to live in our castles, breed our women, subjugate our spirit. But you"—his father pointed at him—"you are of Irish blood. You know the joy of this land. Help us, son."

Commit treason to help a man who had given more of his heart to a cause than to his own wife and son? Turn his back on Guilford to aid the rebellion he hated for ravaging his life not once but twice?

The River Thames would smell like the sweetest summer rose before that would happen.

"Get out," Kieran ordered.

Desmond's eyes widened as his frown deepened. "But Son—"

"Do not call me that."

"Kieran, I am your father."

"And a fine example you have been for the past twenty-one years."

"I wanted to seek you out sooner but knew not where to find

you, lad. I was wrong." Desmond's voice seemed to plead. Kieran knew better than to believe it. O'Neill had only visited when it suited him, when his son could aid him. The wretch.

"Aye, wrong you were. Now I want you gone."

"You are an earl now, with an ear to the king. Kieran, you can ease the rebellion's way with Henry Tudor. Ireland needs—"

"I don't give a damn about Ireland. I care even less for the rebellion. Now get the hell out of my castle."

* * * *

Maeve paced. Though her husband had not been alone with Desmond O'Neill long, she feared for him. Aye, O'Neill had long been devoted to the rebellion, but he *wanted* bloodshed in the name of freedom, even seemed to crave the sight of it red and running on the soil. And he'd begun to influence Flynn of late… And then there was the rumor that whispered word about the manner in which Desmond had driven away his English wife many years past. She knew not if 'twas true, but if it was, Maeve could see some frightening implications.

She shivered. Kieran should not be alone with the man, for he did not understand O'Neill's nature. But she did. Aye, she had warned him, but had it been enough?

The sound of the latch on the door brought Maeve whirling about. Kieran marched through the door, his face a glower. Tension dominated his body. His mouth, usually smiling, pursed instead in a scowl.

Kieran took three long strides to the hearth, then turned, stalking back to the door. Twice again he crossed the floor, his frown becoming fiercer with each step.

What had happened with O'Neill?

She'd never seen him so agitated. In fact, she had only known his imperturbable charm. And though she knew what had likely incensed him, his sudden change still disturbed her.

"What happened?" she asked.

He stopped in midstride to glare at her. "What about this damned country makes all you people fanatics to free it?"

His question shocked Maeve into silence. From whence had such a question come?

"Truly," he went on, "do you people see this place as God's Promised Land or some such nonsense?"

Kieran began pacing again before she could answer, and Maeve sensed he did not really wish a reply anyway.

"It rains too much," he ranted. "'Tis foggy nearly always. And you Irish find guileful ways of dealing with honest men."

Of what did he complain? Maeve was uncertain but had no doubt the blast of heat she felt from him was anger, more than she had ever imagined Kieran capable of.

"If you will but sit—"

"Like your brother"—he paused at the hearth to spin toward the door again—"that day I first arrived, he trapped me in that mud hole, rather than fight me like a man."

Aye, Kieran was indeed very angry. And his fury grew with each word. Had his father's visit unleashed this uncommon display? Kieran's mood before the man's arrival had been a good one. Maeve searched her memory for anything else that might have upset him, but concluded it could only be Desmond.

Then why did he not talk about it?

"Your talk with your father, it did not go well?"

He speared her with a glare and bunched a fist, paced faster, and bit out a curse.

"And you," he accused, stalking closer. "You lied to me about the bridge over the River Barrow. Did you hope I would drown in that damned bog? As it was, my horse nearly emasculated me. Would you have laughed if he had?"

Kieran's anger was now approaching fury. His accusation stung her, but she held her temper, reminding herself that something had happened to cause him strife and she would not know what it was until he was composed. Now, she could only do her best to calm and comfort him.

"I in no way wished you harm when I lied about the bridge. I merely wanted to delay you so that I might advise all at Langmore you were arrived. Flynn set that trap for you before I knew what he was about. And I did my best to see you quickly freed. I am sorry."

"Saint Maeve you are," he sneered. "Willing to sacrifice your sensibilities and distract the enemy with your words and your kiss whilst the rebels attack the safeguards of *my* people."

Maeve bit back a word of defense and approached Kieran, who

looked darker than a storm cloud at midnight. Never had she seen him without his voluble charm. His wicked grin looked years away from his current scowl. But Kieran was more than angry. Mere anger he would find some way to ignore or laugh away. The fact he displayed as much depth with his fury and pain as he did with his laughter stunned her. His pacing and cursing told Maeve his father's visit affected him deeply.

And though he was the enemy, he was also the man who had helped her sisters…and the man she had wed.

Concern filled her with both warmth and worry as she took two small steps to his side and reached up to place a gentle hand upon his shoulder. "Desmond is neither known for his deftness with words or people. He is a fair soldier, but—"

Kieran shrugged away from her touch, then grabbed her shoulders in the grip of his rough, large hands. "This has naught to do with him. I spoke of you, Wife. You, who have been disloyal and aloof."

He would not talk of Desmond. Her concern deepened.

Then his heat seeped into her. And his scent surrounded her, for he smelled of the forest—of clean air and wood and rich soil. His touch through the sleeves of her dress heightened her awareness of his looming size, his hot strength.

Maeve tensed against the sensations. Such awareness of her husband as a man, vital, virile, alarmed her. She should not think of Kieran in that way. While easing his anguish, she could not forget she had pledged herself to Quaid.

Maeve tried to step away from his touch. Kieran held firm.

"Since we spoke vows, I have not been disloyal," she said in a husky tone that made her cringe. "I have in no way engaged the attentions of another man—"

"Except to receive Quaid O'Toole's letters. Except to harbor him in your heart." Kieran grabbed her and held her tighter. "To say naught of your helping hands to the rebellion. No more! Starting now, you will accept the fact that I am your husband. You will be my wife and behave as any good wife should."

Maeve took little exception to his words, as she felt certain he lashed out at her in his hurt. A good wife would calm her husband, be an attentive ear for his words of concern, she told herself. The fact that she ached for his pain meant naught.

But his blue-green eyes held her in wary thrall. The burn of fury, tumult, and lust that appeared stunned her senses.

Determined to do what she could to calm him, she said, "I care for your home and servants as a good wife should. I do not fail to answer when you have need of me."

Kieran pulled her against the impossibly solid length of his body. He was not the tallest or biggest man she had ever seen, but he might well be the strongest and most dangerous.

Then his mouth turned into a hard snarl she would never have imagined possible. Though his fury was convincing, Kieran was hurting. A powerful need to reach out to him, to ease his pain, seized her.

"I've had need of you since we wed over a week ago."

Desire and anger roughened his voice. Maeve felt it inside her, deep where she felt his hurt and her need to comfort him—as well as her need to touch him. She shook her head, knowing she must set on quieting the turmoil of his mood. Her thoughts of him as a man, as a husband, she would examine in private, when his nearness did not distract her.

But for now, he needed this rough embrace to take his mind from Desmond and his wretched anger. So when Maeve saw Kieran lean toward her, she met him with care.

His mouth, open and hungry, seized hers. No tender brush of the lips, no delicate caress. The kiss was laden with hunger and determination. He took her, his salty-sweet tongue sweeping across her own in a gesture of both mastery and possession, his stubbled chin rough on her skin. The kiss demanded surrender. Maeve swallowed against a moan that threatened, but could not resist sliding her tongue against his.

Long moments passed filled with naught but the feel of Kieran's mouth. The everlasting kiss numbed her mind with the nectar of pleasure again and again. Maeve reeled with the sensations—his heat, his indisputable male musk, the exhilarating, frightening ache he created. She grasped him tighter.

He splayed his hands across her shoulders, pressing her even closer. She felt the fast thud of his heart against her. She felt the change in him slowly, anger melting to desire.

Then his hands parted, one at the small of her back holding her incredibly close. Maeve felt the stone-hard length of his erection.

The other hand swept the turn-back brimmed cap from her head and pillaged her plaits until they lay in reddish shambles about her shoulders.

For a brief moment, Kieran lifted his head from her ravaged mouth and stared. Gone was his anger, which gladdened her heart. But in its place burned desire so fierce she felt staggered. An answering want burned in her belly and lower, so strong. A languid weakness invaded her arms and legs, leaving her both vulnerable and afraid.

Vaguely, Maeve knew she should push him away, but she did not. Could not. What Kieran made her feel was unlike anything she had known, something that involved the whole of her body and tugged at her heart. She yearned to explore her feelings. Frightened and thrilled at once, she waited for his next touch.

Kieran groaned his approval and held her tighter, the hand at her back reaching around to cover her breast. His thumb teased the peak gone rigid with want. She arched against his hand, eager to fill his palm with her flesh, urgent in a way she did not understand. Her heart tripped at the thought of sharing herself with him, and 'twas no longer about simply easing his pain. Nay, she felt so much more.

But the tight bodice restricted him from touching her flesh. She felt his frustration. 'Twas the very one she tried to escape.

"I want to touch your skin, your bare breasts, sweet Maeve," he murmured over her mouth.

His words hit her senses like a blast of heat, honeyed, inescapable. Impatience and need gnawing at her, she nodded.

Before she could draw another breath, she felt Kieran's mouth teasing the sensitive skin of her neck. She shivered with something icy hot that grazed its way down her back, engorging her senses with pleasure. The same something filled her with a yearning to be closer to him, reach him in the same sense.

Then he pulled her bodice away from her breasts and let the dress pool at her feet. His hands were there to caress the taut mounds and their stiff peaks. She cried out as his thumbs brushed over her nipples again.

The sensation nearly obliterated her ability to stand.

One of his hands glided down her back, then slipped beneath the hem of her shift, to cup her bare buttocks and bring her closer. He made her feel alive, made her rage with need. Around him, colors seemed brighter, touch and sight keener.

Kieran drew her deeper into the hungry tempest by whispering, "I can hardly wait to taste you."

And with a sudden tug and whirl, her chemise disappeared. She stood before him, completely bare, only the length of her hair covering her breasts and belly.

As he brushed the strands away, his gaze locked on hers, gleaming with approval that gladdened her. It pleased her to please him; the delight in his gaze encouraged her to stand before him.

With a primal growl, Kieran banded his arms tightly about her and lifted her against him. When he lowered her again, 'twas to his bed.

Heart pounding and breath shallow, she waited as he spread her beneath him—her hair across his pillow, her lips with his own, her knees with a nudge of his fingers.

Joy erupted within her at his insistent kiss. She fisted her hands in his hair, arching against him as if that might somehow appease her ache to be nearer. But nay. She needed more, his nearness fueling a craving to be closer still.

Kieran gave, devouring her from lips to neck—then lower.

Suddenly he took her breast in his mouth. His tongue alternately laved and flicked across the sensitive tip until a dark madness consumed her, until she felt compelled to moan.

"Aye, love," he encouraged in a breath across her skin.

Then his teeth nipped her breast. The pleasurable friction nearly brought her off the bed. Desire thundered in her, in a way she had never imagined before. His touch brought out the urge to hold him close, give pleasure back to him.

Maeve twined desperate fingers in his doublet and ripped it from his shoulders. It caught on his elbows, and she nearly cried out with frustration. Kieran came to her rescue with soothing whispers as he slid the garment from his body.

His shirt quickly followed over his head, with only a moment's deprivation of his kiss. But even that moment was too much for her senses. Desperate to feel more of him, to experience all this connection made her feel, she dragged his mouth back to her own— and his bare chest against hers.

The heat of the embrace intoxicated her. She rushed to stroke his back, teetering on the edge of sanity.

Kieran began fumbling with his hose, and within moments, he stood as bare as she, proud, every inch solid and aroused before her gaze. Wide shoulders bulged with tense muscle. A broad chest beckoned her mouth. His flat belly and tapering hips enthralled her.

The man was near perfect. His scattering of scars only made the landscape of his skin more varied and appealing.

Before she could comment or touch him, Kieran was upon her, flesh to flesh, the full glory of their nakedness stunning in its sensation. She felt further drawn to him as he lay atop her and brought her breasts to his mouth. As he fed himself with her flesh and her response, Maeve wondered how she would survive this ferocious desire. Would she ever be the same again?

The weighty thought vanished with a sweep of Kieran's tongue over her breast and his hand upon her thigh.

Hungry to taste him in return, Maeve set her lips upon his musky neck, the hard breadth of his chest. Beneath her mouth, she felt the racing of his heart, demanding, violent. Happiness rushed through her.

Running her hands down the firm texture of his back, Maeve found his buttocks and urged him closer to her center, where she burned with an urgent, frantic need to join with him.

In response, he thrust his granite shaft against her once again. Splinters of ecstasy made her fling her head back with abandon. She gripped his buttocks in her hands, her teeth nipping at his shoulder, blindly encouraging him.

Instead, he lifted away from her, shifted down. He fixed his gaze on her intimate center. Part of her knew she should be embarrassed that he would look at her thus. But the lust that ripped across his face and tightened his hands about her thighs did naught but bring gladness.

Then he set his hands to her flesh, a stroke upon her hip, a dip into the valley of her belly, until his palm rested directly over her moist apex, as if to claim possession.

Maeve felt the touch deep within her. She surged against his hand and cried out. Kieran ground his palm into her, until she thought she might explode into a thousand pieces from the pleasure.

She had been mistaken. When his fingers dipped into her moistness and sought her sensitive bud with a damp touch, then she knew she would explode.

He added further torment when his mouth captured her breast again and tugged on its tip. The ache there met the ache between her legs to create a screaming demand in her belly. She felt a mass of tingles and aches, and she moaned at the torment.

Still, he kept on, until the pressure and pleasure built to unbearable heights, until the need within her became the most violent storm, until the scent of arousal hung in the air between them and their harsh breathing echoed off the walls.

Nay, she would not lie prone and still whilst he drove her to oblivion. She would give pleasure back to him.

She reached forth and took his manhood in her grasp.

He stiffened. His breathing staggered. A groan spilled from his mouth, tortured and labored. Satisfied with her efforts, she stroked his flesh again, taking note of his ample size, his velvet-hard skin.

Kieran redoubled his efforts to her body, rubbing her hard center with a pair of fingers, leaving her reeling and shivering. Her thighs tensed and her body shook. A sob caught in her throat. Kieran's tongue laving her breast in long strokes released the sound.

She began to quiver and writhe beneath him. The pleasure turned urgent, jagged. Maeve felt on the brink of something new, something that clawed its way into her until she knew naught but satisfying it.

Then that need exploded. The sharp edge of desire tore through her, filling her with fluid pleasure, the likes of which she had not known possible.

"Kieran!" she cried.

He answered with another tug of his mouth on her breast.

Another dart of pleasure arrowed through her.

Endless moments later, her body pulsed with satisfaction and languor, yet hummed with something new, as if Kieran had brought her to life. She did not pause to examine her joy that he had been the one to give her these sensations.

"You said my name," he whispered in a raspy voice as he lay fully atop her and spread her knees wide with his own.

"Aye," she whispered, lifting her hips to him in offering.

"Say it again."

"Kieran." She stared up into the depths of his eyes, gleaming a wicked blue-green with approval. "Kieran."

"Maeve," he groaned.

His eyes slid shut and the tip of his manhood found her portal. He surged against her once, and she felt her tight sheath take a portion of his length. But he was thick and long, and Maeve wondered if her body could accommodate him. Disappointment and a sense of panic scathed her. The thought of not fully joining with him was almost an ache.

Again, he moved within her, tempting her body to take more of him. The solid feel of him, of his heat, nearly made her stagger with new want.

Above her, he let out a deep breath. "A little more, love. Relax for me."

She met his searing gaze. "I-I do not know if I can—"

"You can," he vowed, then took her hips in his grip and tilted her a bit more toward him.

Then he took her mouth in a slow coupling that turned her blood to mulled wine, a kiss that assured her all would be well.

He sank into her further, and she welcomed him.

Inch by inch he slid into her. When she thought she could take no more, she did. Maeve felt filled, bursting with the pulsing evidence of Kieran's need. And still his mouth indulged in a slow tasting of hers, sensitizing her to the feel of him everywhere as he slid farther into her body.

With one last stroke, he pressed his full length inside her and groaned. She met him with an arch of her back.

Shadows whispered across Kieran's golden flesh as dusk settled in the chamber. He pressed into her once more, this time with more urgency. The sound of his ragged breath in her ear and the tense feel of his body bespoke his control.

Maeve wanted him to lose that control for her.

She pressed her mouth to his and let her hands roam freely upon the broad plane of his back, down his hips, where she urged him on. Rocking her hips beneath him earned her a groaned warning that filled her with delight.

"Maeve, do not make me finish this too soon."

"I wish to ease and pleasure you," she breathed.

He plunged into her again and moaned her name. "You are not ready yet."

Before she could argue, he began a fluid rhythm, his body increasing the pressure, the pleasure. She burned with the fever again, this time stronger than before.

As he filled her in long, quick strokes, Maeve moved beneath him, sensing another peak was near, this one savage in its strength. She felt as if she were drowning, mercy to the strength of rapture. And through it all, her sense of some invisible bond to him grew.

Suddenly, Kieran rolled to his back, taking her with him, never leaving her. She straddled him, her breasts taut and visible between them. And still he pressed into her, stroking her, driving her.

He found the center of her pleasure again, and dragged both his fingers across her aroused tip. The sensation astounded her. Blood roared in her ears, hammering her senses with pleasure. She felt helpless and unprepared as he thrust into her again, transforming the brink of satisfaction into a pool of it, thick and addicting and joy filled.

She felt herself pulse around him, gripping his shaft again. A moment later, he stiffened, surged hard into her, and cried out, fingers digging into her hips.

Maeve watched as, teeth clenched, Kieran spilled himself deep inside her. Then he stilled and opened his eyes, his lids heavy, his eyes blue-green pools of satisfaction.

Her heart seemed to explode with tenderness.

Still, Kieran held her. And Maeve felt as if she belonged here, with him inside her. She did not question it when he pulled her into an embrace, a melding of slick skin and beating hearts.

She had wanted this in her union with Quaid, but never felt thus. This sense of belonging she had sought her whole life she now found in the arms of her English husband.

"Sweet Maeve," he breathed, still panting. "Did I hurt you?"

Concern. In the wake of his pleasure, he held concern for her. Somehow she had expected the conqueror to swagger with triumph. That he did not surprised her and touched her more.

Battling a prickling of tears at her sudden happiness, her sudden sense of being complete, she nodded. "You hurt me not at all. I felt only more pleasure than I knew possible."

He sighed with seeming relief. "I meant not to be rough, but you—your body—'twas clenched so tight, as if it knew not what to do."

Maeve flushed. "Quaid... We shared a bed but once."

Surprise flashed briefly across his face at her whisper. Then he pulled her closer in his arms. "I vow that will not be the last time I share yours."

Part of Maeve knew she should protest, should point out that naught had changed, that he was still the enemy. But he did not feel like the enemy now, with his warm skin damp against her own. He felt like a husband, a lover, a man she could no more stay away from than she could stop her heart from beating. He seemed thoroughly vital to her in so many ways.

She swallowed. "I am agreeable."

At that, he smiled. "Are you, now? I am not surprised."

His confidence was both galling and appealing. Maeve did not remember ever feeling so much confusion. She glared at him.

His smile slipped. "Do not frown at me. I assure you that, as amenable as you may be to sharing a bed again, I'm twice as eager to get there."

Maeve felt a shadow of a smile creep across her mouth. "'Tis I who am not surprised."

And he laughed, a right, hearty chuckle that echoed off the stone walls and shook the bed. Maeve found herself laughing with him, a lingering glow of warmth settling over her.

Kieran held her tight as the laughter subsided. Silence took over until he whispered, "I'm sorry I yelled at you earlier."

Maeve sobered. "Your father angered you."

He hesitated, then reluctantly nodded.

"Why did he come?"

His expression turned blank, flat. "He wanted my help with the rebellion."

She stiffened in shock. She'd always known Desmond to be bold, but that request went to brazen and beyond.

"You said him nay?" She touched his shoulder in comfort.

"And told him to leave Langmore."

Kieran's voice and his earlier actions told her O'Neill had hurt him. Maeve held him closer, stroking his back.

"The worst part, Maeve," he whispered against her neck, tense beneath her. "The man came here, after all these years, not to be a father but to be a rebel. He never once asked how my life has been since I last saw him."

Kieran would not cry, but somehow Maeve wanted to do it for him. She squeezed him tight, offering her silent support. A million questions about the past raced to mind, but she said naught. 'Twas not the time.

He kissed her temple, softly caressing her back until he drifted to sleep. And he looked so peaceful in repose. Maeve found herself wishing that kind of peace for him always.

But she feared 'twas not destined to be.

* * * *

Kieran woke before the sun to the feel of Maeve slumbering beside him, her hand splayed over his belly. Though his mind felt heavy with sleep, his body was awake and eager.

He smiled, hardly surprised. Maeve had been every bit as womanly and passionate as he had suspected. In fact, she had responded beyond his expectations, pulsing around him in gloried abandon.

His erection tightened, thickened, demanding her attention.

Rolling to his side, he lifted the hair covering her cheek and shoulder, placing it behind her back. He brushed her mouth with his finger. Maeve frowned and moaned before rolling away. Kieran smiled. The woman slept with as much vigor as she made love.

Had she made love with Quaid O'Toole with such abandon?

Kieran scowled, disliking that question. Maeve was here now, in his bed. Here she would stay. And he would do his best to see she forgot another man had touched her, even if only once.

He reached for Maeve again, determination and possession heating his blood.

Someone knocked on the door. He cursed.

"What?" he ground out, sitting up in bed.

The door opened, and Colm peeked in. "My lord? Sorry to catch you...abed." He glanced at Maeve's bare shoulders above the sheet, then quickly away. "A messenger just arrived. You've been summoned to Dublin, to Malahide Castle."

Kieran cursed again, soundly this time. Maeve stirred beside him but did not fully wake.

"Why?" he asked.

Colm shrugged. "He would not say, my lord."

Kieran had thought for some while the other Englishmen in the Pale would wish a meeting, but why now? "When must I go?"

"This very morn."

"And they gave no reason for such urgency, boy?"

Colm shook his head.

Kieran had little doubt such secrecy boded ill.

CHAPTER ELEVEN

Kieran arrived in Dublin two days later, exhausted, irritable, and damned tired of the rain.

Malahide Castle sat in gray splendor along the banks of a peaceful loch. The structure was solid, worthy, and accessible from but one road. Kieran had no trouble imagining why the other Palesmen thought it best for imprisoning the rebels. Thus far, Malahide's dungeons had held them.

Groaning with cold, he swung off his mount. Guards greeted him immediately in the dusk and took him to the great hall. There, fifteen lords sat with tankards in hand.

"Why should we not tax the heathens?" spouted one thick-waisted Englishman.

"Their land is more profitable, man," said another, this one younger and heartier of voice. "If we take the land and let them keep what pittance of funds they have, we'll have them by the throats."

"Why not both?" suggested a third, raising his tankard with a lopsided grin.

The group laughed.

Kieran scowled at their greed. None of these men appeared to need the funds, the lands, or the food either would provide. Did they not see taking the people's lands and funds would leave women and children to starve? Break up families? Force men to take up arms who had not previously, just to survive?

"Tax policies are directly solicited to King Henry though my correspondence, gentlemen."

At Kieran's words, all heads turned in his direction. Wariness,

151

curiosity, and distrust inhabited different faces around him.

Suddenly he felt sure this would be a long trip.

"M-my lord, you've arrived," stuttered the nearest fop.

"You summoned me with such urgency, what else could I do?" he returned dryly. "I have business back at Langmore. What needs have you so I may address them and be gone?"

At the far end of the table, a frail old man rose and gestured him to an empty seat upon a bench. "We feared the worst when you did not appear as scheduled."

Kieran made his way to the bench and sat with a frown. "As scheduled? Of what do you speak, sir?"

"This parliament, of course. As governor of the Pale, you must preside over this session and vote. We have many issues before us."

Kieran had known these duties would haunt him whilst he remained in Ireland. But the timing could not be more ill suited. Maeve and the joys of her body awaited him.

"I knew naught of any plans to open parliament."

The older man frowned with puzzlement. "We sent a missive over a month past."

And he had never received it. He frowned, pondering its fate. Nearly everyone at Langmore would want him to miss this session. Flynn, Maeve, and Jana all had reasons in particular, though Flynn seemed the most likely person to engage in something so devious.

Damnation! That O'Shea man near begged to have his arse kicked from here to London with all his mighty talk of rebellion. And Kieran longed to do the dirty work himself.

Except 'twould infuriate Maeve.

Then again, his own Maeve did receive most of the correspondence at Langmore. Was shuffling information her role in the rebellion?

Muttering a curse, he sat. "Let me meet everyone and then you may tell me what business we have before us."

The older man nodded and resumed his seat. "I am Lord Burkland."

Kieran nodded in acknowledgment. Burkland then pointed out each of the others.

The thick-middled man was Bishop Elmond, and Kieran distrusted him and his pinched expression right away. Men ambitious in the Church had ever been shifty. This one appeared no exception.

The younger, hearty-voiced man proved to be Lord Butler, a swaggering prick if he'd met one. Suddenly, Kieran thought he might give his right arm to be away from these pompous men and back at Langmore.

"Well, now that we are done with introductions, my lord, we shall go on with business at hand. Most notably, we meet to discuss the rebels."

"As we should!" shouted the bishop.

"Aye, they have all but destroyed parts of Malahide trying to break their own free," said another Englishman whose name escaped Kieran's memory.

He resisted the urge to run a tired hand across his eyes. 'Twas no doubt in his mind—and probably King Henry's—that action must be taken against the rebels before they succeeded in destroying some major English holdings, and rightly so. Among other threats, King Henry would not tolerate another Yorkist pretender to his throne hiding on Irish soil. Lambert Simnel and the duchess of Burgundy's forces had attempted such an overthrow a year past. Aiding the cause had been the treasonous downfall of the last earl of Kildare.

The issue could wait no longer.

But Kieran found himself oddly reluctant to participate in this decision, and he wondered why.

Burkland turned to a pair of guards in the great hall. "Get the rest of your force and bring up the rebels."

The duo left to follow the old man's orders right away. Tensing, Kieran waited for the rebels to arrive whilst the others around him spoke of taxes, land disputes, and the king himself. Kieran could think of little more than Quaid O'Toole—and Maeve's reaction if her once-betrothed's fate was not a kind one.

Within minutes, ten motley, unwashed rebels filed in with bound hands and ankles. Their faces were grim but proud. Kieran tried to remember their crimes against the crown, everything from petty mayhem to the murder of Englishmen. In their hearts, they harbored the seeds of rebellion, which had grown, feeding others just like them. They must be dealt with.

Why, then, was he so damned reluctant?

"Shall we, Lord Kildare?" Burkland asked.

At that, a rebel's blond head snapped up. The short, stocky man fixed him with a gaze that burned hate. "You're the bastard! You've stolen my Maeve from me."

Around him, a few of the men gasped. Others stared.

Kieran gritted his teeth and met his opponent's gaze squarely. "Quaid O'Toole, I presume?"

"You knew before you wed her that she belongs to me."

"The Church and the law have decreed differently now."

Quaid's blue gaze brimmed ire. "Don't you be layin' a slimy English hand on her."

"Bind that man's mouth!" ordered Burkland, then turned to Kieran, who would rather have exchanged fists with the man. Stony silence would have to do instead.

Burkland smiled, and a guard placed a cloth firmly over Quaid's mouth. "Let us begin."

Burkland recited the murder allegations against the first of the rebels. The parliament allowed the man to speak in his defense for less than five minutes.

Burkland interrupted the rebel's words with an impatient wave. "What say you, gentlemen?"

All present voted for death. Kieran followed suit.

One by one, the small parliament worked its way through the rebels, always with the same outcome.

O'Toole, gagged until now, had his mouth freed and was allowed to speak. "I did naught wrong, I tell you."

"Do you deny killing two English soldiers?" Burkland asked.

"I but kept them from stealing my sheep and raping my sister!"

"And you required taking a blade into the belly of one and the throat of another to do that?"

"They had blades as well, blades they would have used, had I given them a chance."

Burkland cast O'Toole a disbelieving glance. "Do you have any evidence these sheep were yours?"

"Nay, but they were."

"I see," Burkland said as if he had proven his point. "And your sister… Do you have any evidence she did not welcome these fine Englishmen in her bed?"

"She screamed so loud my ears rang!"

"Perhaps she screamed in pleasure," suggested Lord Butler.

"No honorable Irishwoman takes pleasure in an Englishman's

bed," O'Toole spat, glaring directly at Kieran.

Knowing 'twould infuriate O'Toole, he gave the man a shrug and a smile.

The rebel surged forward in fury. A pair of guards stopped him, one dealing him a blow to the stomach.

"Enough!" Burkland decreed, then turned to the rest. "Your decision, gentlemen?"

"Death!" the others declared in unison.

Kieran felt his throat plunge to his stomach. Aye, he held no love for O'Toole—but Maeve did. And he doubted she would understand his part in her once-betrothed's death. He knew not why, but the rending of the fragile bonds of his peace with Maeve distressed him. And O'Toole's defense, if true, weren't crimes that warranted death.

Awaiting his answer, the Palesmen turned to hear his verdict.

Impulsively, he opened his mouth to say he would take Quaid back to Langmore and deal with him privately, starting with a meeting of his fists and O'Toole's nose. But he could not. Such foolishness was not smart or logical, for it would put the rebel directly into Flynn's—and Maeve's—paths again. Both were too dangerous. Neither could he allow.

Resisting the urge to fly from the bench and pace, Kieran gritted his teeth. He was no damned coward. War had always meant making such decisions of fate, most of which were difficult. When he took an ax in one hand and a sword in another and faced a man with intent, he took a life. Without blinking, he moved on to the next opponent. Warriors did these things in times of war. 'Twas their duty. Ordinarily, he thought not about ending a rebel's life.

But Maeve's anger would be great indeed if O'Toole died this day.

And Kieran knew he could do naught to stop it.

"Death," he muttered finally, damning Ireland under his breath.

* * * *

Three days later, Kieran crept into Langmore's keep long after midnight. In the morn, he would have to tell Maeve the truth about O'Toole. He dreaded every minute of it, knowing she would hate him for his part in the rebel's execution.

Tonight, he wanted naught but to see Maeve and sleep without seeing O'Toole's face of resigned bravery in his mind.

Treading to his chamber, he was surprised to find Maeve curled up in his bed, sleepy and warm, her hair twisted into a single braid that curled about her neck and lay between the tempting mounds of her breasts.

She wore naught but a shift, and the burning taper in his hand revealed the shadows of her dusky nipples to his hungry gaze.

Blood rushed to his shaft, making him thick, tight, and hard in mere instants. Not so unusual, he thought with a grimace. What he disliked was the tangle of thoughts in his head, careening around until his belly churned and he knew no peace.

The urge to be near her drove him to sit on the edge of the bed, beside her. He touched her shoulder, grazed his finger across her cheek.

Longing, thick and demanding, settled in his gut. He hated the thought she would not speak to him once he told her the truth. She would withdraw the sunshine of her smile. Too well he knew even his best explanation would not soothe her.

He would miss her—even more than he had in Dublin. For whilst there, they had been but separated by miles. Here, beliefs and loyalties would separate them. She would not change hers, and he could not afford to change his even if he wished to. And the torment would be greater, for he could see her each day but not hold her sleep-soft body in his arms, not win her smile—not for some while, if ever again.

Maeve moaned in slumber, and Kieran looked down, realizing he had been squeezing her hand too hard.

He also saw her golden eyes open, glowing by the dim candlelight.

"You've returned. When?" Sleep slurred her muted words.

A puzzling wave of tenderness swept through him. Had she worried? The thought held appeal. "Only now."

She groaned tiredly. "'Tis late. You must be weary."

Moments ago, he had been. Now he could think of little but Maeve and the twisted tangle of his thoughts.

"Not so weary now that you are near."

Kieran could not resist clasping her chin softly and running his thumb across her lips. Maeve lifted a heavy-lidded gaze to him, eyes darkened with the golden fire of awareness.

The want in his gut tightened, sparking his entire body with desire. Aye, he'd thought of holding her these three days past. And now she lay before him, in his bed, soft woman.

But a soft woman who would soon hate him.

His conscience warred with his urge to be near her. His battered mind needed the soothing balm of her touch.

His conscience lost.

Bending to her, Kieran arched his hand around the back of her neck and brought her mouth gently to his. He brushed his lips over hers once, then again. She smelled of…Maeve. He recognized her scent, some unique blend of woman, spring, and Ireland itself. Never had he smelled its like. 'Twas addicting, he thought, deepening the kiss, leaning in.

Maeve did not resist him, but curled her arms around his shoulders and welcomed him with a willing mouth that parted when he ran his tongue along the seam of her lips. Triumph and a belly-deep need implored him to taste her honeyed essence—unique like her scent.

He felt himself drowning, his thoughts swimming in all that was Maeve. Half lying upon her, he leaned his weight on one elbow and lifted his other hand to her breast. Thrill charged through him when he found the mound taut, its tip erect. He teased her nipple with his thumb, alternately brushing and pinching.

She arched beneath him and whispered, "I-I missed you."

He looked at her, those golden eyes full of uncertainty and longing, and murmured, "I thought of little but you."

The admission did not come easy, but he owed her that honesty. Mayhap, 'twould soften the truth he must tell later. He pushed the thought aside, knowing he needed to taste her one last time—before she pushed him away for weeks, mayhap even months, or God forbid, forever.

The possibility chilled him. He kept it at bay by caressing her cheek with his fingers.

Pleasure lit Maeve's fiery eyes. A smile touched her mouth before he kissed her again, this time deeper. She hesitated not an instant, but opened beneath him, unfurling like a petal to the morning sun. Kieran reveled in her response, running a hand across her breast again, tempting her with his touch until she moaned.

To his shock, she lifted the shift from her body, over her head, baring her nakedness to his hungry gaze. Though he had not known such was possible, he hardened further at her honest display of her wants. Though she was hardly the first woman to remove her clothes for his pleasure, he found Maeve's gesture more pleasing because it was her and it was real.

"You're lovelier than I remembered, sweet Maeve."

The candlelight lit up the glow of the red-gold wisps about her face, along with her smile. Kieran knew an uncompromising urge to touch her, to make her his again.

Seizing her mouth, he set his fingers to unbraiding her hair. He would not be satisfied until its fire lay about his white sheets as he loved her.

While his fingers worked at her tresses, his tongue swept through her mouth. Maeve arched and moaned, then surprised Kieran by sliding his tunic over his head. They broke the kiss for a mere instant, long enough to see the garment strewn on the floor, before their mouths came together once more.

Kieran could not recall anything that felt more perfect.

Then she set her hands to his chest, her fingers to his nipples. The shock of her soft fingers upon him, squeezing, caressing—'twas more arousing than he could bear.

"Maeve, my sweet, what do you do to me?"

Her mouth kissed a path to his ear, and she whispered, "I'm making you feel all the heavenly things you stir inside me."

That whisper—her very words—sent shivers through his body. He captured her mouth again, hard, urgent, driving her to meet his desire. She did, and incredibly, he wanted more.

Kicking off his boots, he knelt on the mattress and set his hands to work at his hose and braies. To his surprise, Maeve joined the effort, her hands gliding down his back, over his buttocks and thighs. With a tug on the garments, the rest of his clothing lay haphazardly across the wooden floor.

Now he lay naked beside Maeve and her delicious ardor.

She lifted her mouth to his, and Kieran did not hesitate in receiving her kiss, demanding more of her. He let his hands roam over the soft texture of her skin as he inched down her body, pausing at the slope of her shoulders, the firm weight of her breasts, the gentle curve of her belly…the soft folds of her womanhood.

Her slick flesh surrounded his fingers, wet, nearly ready. Her cry rang in his ears, calling to him. Her musk, along with the drive of desire in his belly, urged him on. His need to touch her would not be denied.

Nor would his urge to taste her.

With his thumb and finger, he parted her folds, revealing her pink nubbin, hard now from his ministrations.

"Kieran?" she called in question.

He never answered. Instead, he brushed her with his tongue. Her indrawn gasp spurred him to do it once more. He cradled the spread of her thighs in his hands. Good, she was taut and expectant.

Again, he laved attention on her sensitive flesh until she quivered. Then again. Back and forth, he lapped. Maeve grabbed the sheet in her fists and arched into him. His blood surged.

She moaned, then breathed in deep, loud gasps. "Kieran."

He answered by taking the little bud into his mouth and sucking, his tongue teasing the tip.

Maeve exploded, the flesh beneath his mouth pulsing with pleasure. She cried out loudly, bucking her hips. Her thighs trembled, quivered, then relaxed as pleasure saturated her. Gladness that he had pleased her aroused him more.

Kieran returned to her side with a smile. Maeve turned to him with a dazed expression that had him checking an urge to mount her immediately.

"You look awfully proud of yourself," she said, voice husky, enthralling.

"You don't look as if you think to complain."

She laughed. "Brute."

Her slur came without force, but she reached for him, hands to his shoulders, propelling him to his back. As she kneeled over him, she looked down at him with a determined gleam in her eye. Kieran swallowed.

Her hand wandered down his chest, over his belly, until she claimed his shaft, so hard, its head now nearly blue.

When she squeezed him, her touch blasted Kieran to the edge of his control. Her thumb brushed the engorged head, and he wondered if he'd remember his own name once she finished with him.

And then she bent to him, experimentally touching her tongue to his tip. Kieran felt sure his brain melted altogether at that moment.

He opened his eyes to find Maeve wearing a pleased smile.

The she took him more completely into her mouth, her warmth surrounding his sensitive flesh, her tongue laving him.

His melted brain mattered not, because he had just died and found paradise.

He groaned in ecstasy, the bands of desire pulled tight in his belly. Maeve repeated the process once more, then again. His need rode dangerously close to the edge. And he wanted her, to be inside her, as he'd never wanted anything else.

Grasping her by the shoulders, he clasped her to him, then rolled her to the mattress, pinning her beneath him. "If you seek to kill me, you do a fine job."

With that ragged murmur, he captured her mouth and entered her in one smooth stroke.

Maeve was open to him, ready, welcoming. Bliss resonated in Kieran as he thrust deeply, claiming her inch by inch.

"'Tis you who kills me," she muttered.

Kissing his way down the slope of her jaw, his teeth nipped at her earlobe as he breathed against her neck. "Let us find a pleasurable passing together."

"Aye," she cried as he plunged into her welcoming wetness again, grinding deep, deeper until he swore he felt her womb.

Wildness erupted within him. He wanted to reach her this way, every way, hear her cry his name over and over until she lost her voice, her very breath, her memory of Quaid's touch.

Again, he drove into her, then again, until the edge of the precipice rushed to meet him. He gritted his teeth against it, determined to take her with him.

Suddenly, she tensed and cried out. He felt her flesh close around him, squeezing in firm pulses, coaxing the fulfillment from his body.

Blackness floated in his vision as he thrust into her one last time. Rapture burst in him, filling his blood with a slow burn of satisfaction. Languor followed, so thick and perfect Kieran wondered if he would ever move again.

Beneath him, he smelled Maeve's clean skin, felt the hard pound of her heart. And he rejoiced in a joining so perfect he swore he'd never known its equal.

She smiled softly and pressed a kiss to his mouth. Her golden eyes glowed, and Maeve looked at him with ardor. Something both happy and tender, something foreign, unfurled in his chest.

"I see you did miss me whilst you were in Dublin."

Dublin. Her words chilled him with reality. Joy vanished from his body, replaced by foreboding.

He had experienced his stolen moments in her arms. And no matter how badly he wished to cling to them, to do so would be gravely unfair. Now he must tell her the truth.

He sat up and willed himself to meet her gaze, then took her hands in his. "I did. But something happened, I…I must explain to you."

She frowned, a mixture of curiosity and concern.

He bent forward to steal one last kiss, savoring the sweet honey of her mouth, of her soft response. And he knew she would only hate him all the more for it. Still, he could not leave her be any more than he could stop breathing.

When their lips parted, he was assailed by a feeling of loss. But he could not keep O'Toole's death to himself, for she would soon hear and be all the more angry.

"The parliament met," he began. "They had been planning to meet for some time, but I did not receive their notice."

Maeve flushed a guilty red.

"You took their missive?" he asked.

"Nay."

"But you know of its fate?"

She nodded. Kieran surmised then Flynn had stolen it, but Maeve would not point an accusing finger at her brother. At this moment, he could scarce blame her for protecting her kin. He would likely do the same in her position.

"The parliament decided on many issues," he began.

How could he get the words out? How could he tell her gently?

Her face turned from watchful to fearful. "Including the fate of the rebels?"

Kieran hesitated, wishing he could keep this moment at bay forever. But he knew 'twas not possible. "Aye."

"Quaid?" A sharp note of anxiety lifted her tone. He hated such concern for another man, even a dead one, so clear in her voice, so obvious on her lovely face.

But he'd known all along that, while she had wedded and

bedded him, 'twas Quaid O'Toole she had always loved.

Clamping down on a surge of anger, he stared into her wide eyes. "Executed."

"Nay!"

Her eyes widened and her face crumpled moments before she buried her face in her hands and curled her knees into her chest.

Kieran slid a soothing hand over her head, down her back. He could not say he was sorry. This was war, after all. Instead, he whispered, "I know this grieves you."

Maeve lifted a tear-streaked face wild with accusation. "You!" She scrambled away, covering herself with the sheet, fury rolling across her face. "You ordered his death."

"I have not that power, Maeve. I but voted like everyone else," he urged.

"Voted for death," she accused.

"We are at war. 'Tis common to see prisoners executed. The others before me had all voted the same. My dissent would have changed naught."

She made a rude snort of disbelief. "And you watched in glee."

"Nay, I—"

"Of course you did. You like battle, blood. It excites you. Did you cheer when he took his last breath?"

"Nay." Kieran reached for her shoulder.

Maeve jerked away. "Do not touch me!"

A moment later, horror dawned across her face, then she glared at him with such fury Kieran thought flames might lick his face.

"You took me in this bed, knowing he was dead, knowing how I would feel." Her face was rife with betrayal.

He flinched and confessed, "I but wanted to touch you."

"You wanted to dance upon Quaid's grave, to revel in your brutal triumph. Well, never again, my lord."

"Maeve—"

"Take your ease with the kitchen wenches or the Dublin whores. But do not think to take me again."

He reached for her. "My sweet—"

She batted his hand away. "From now on, I am naught but your enemy. You have betrayed me, lied to me, ruined my life, and killed the man I wished to wed."

"I did not kill him! Maeve, even if I had voted to free him, 'twould have held no weight. They wished him dead."

"You underestimate your devil's tongue." Anger hardened her voice. "Had you tried, you might have seen him freed."

Kieran frowned at the hard mask of rage that overtook her lovely face. "At what cost? To allow his efforts to further the rebellion? So that he might take you from me and make me a cuckold?"

Maeve stood, yanking the sheet about her. "So that you might see a good, worthy man live. But what would you know of such men?" she sneered. "You are naught but a heartless, violent seducer of women. Never speak to me again."

Wrapped in a sheet like the veriest of goddesses, Maeve stamped to the door and slammed it behind her. Kieran felt its echo bang in some dark, scared, ill-used corner of his body—the corner he feared lay close to his heart.

* * * *

A week passed in veritable silence. The air within Langmore's walls seemed thick yet more fragile than glass. Kieran spent day after day, hour upon hour, training Langmore's army. They were beginning to become a disciplined fighting crew, able to handle the rebellion's small forces. And Maeve worried, for 'twas as if Kieran—Lord Kildare—felt the final battle approached. Mayhap it did.

She only knew that her guilt weighted more heavily upon her than her breaking heart. How could she have lain so wantonly with Quaid's executioner? And why did some treasonous part of her miss him even now?

Pacing the solar, she looked up as Jana entered, her sleeping son in her arms. Her elder sister glowed, her heart finally healing.

Maeve wished she could say the same for herself.

"You have acted like the tempest cloud for days now," Jana said softly. "As likely to rain as to thunder at a moment's notice. Fiona, Brighid, and I worry for you."

So, Jana had been elected to speak on her sisters' behalf.

Sighing, Maeve tried to rein in her feelings and sit calmly. Still, she felt anything but calm.

"I understand grief," Jana offered. "I know you loved Quaid."

163

Aye, she had loved him. He had been a gentle friend, as interested in books as she. He had ever understood her moods, never trying to sway her from them. They had been of like minds about Langmore and Ireland. Their match had been sound.

Now he was gone forever.

"Rebellion is costly," Jana said. "We must believe Quaid's and Geralt's sacrifices will come to good."

Maeve nodded weakly. Jana spoke true. But such did not erase the depth of her anguish—or her guilt. She had welcomed Quaid's English tormenter to bed her twice. She had fallen for Kildare's guile and allowed him to sweep her up in his charm until she betrayed the man who had vowed to love her always. Worse, she had not loved Quaid in the same manner.

That secret made her feel most guilty of all.

"You are not ready to talk of it?" Jana queried.

Maeve shifted her gaze to her sister's dark eyes, soft with understanding. She shook her head.

Jana rose from her seat. "Young Geralt sleeps. I shall lay him down and rest myself then. If you change your mind—"

"Thank you." Maeve rose, too, and curled an arm about Jana's shoulder, giving her a grateful hug. "I know."

With a sad smile, Jana left Maeve alone to pace once more.

The deep mire of her feelings threatened to drown her, and Maeve knew not what to do, how to sort through her grief, her guilt, her body's shameful yearnings for her terrible husband.

"Maeve?"

Kildare's voice made her twirl about to face him. Inside the solar he stood. Maeve quivered, both from fury and something more dangerous.

Each day, he tried to speak to her, coax her into forgetting his sins, forgiving him. She refused.

Ripping her gaze from his earnest face, she grabbed her needlework from the trestle table beside her and swept toward the door.

He stopped her by grasping her arm and pulling her to his side. "Someday, you will have to speak to me."

Briefly, she glanced up at him, as if he were naught more than an odious rodent.

"Listen to me."

She sent him a long-suffering sigh and looked just beyond his shoulder, avoiding his countenance.

His grip tightened. "Damnation, Maeve! I could not have stopped Quaid's execution, even if I had wished it. I can bear your grief. I cannot bear your blame."

She merely shrugged, glancing at the far wall. Inside, she seethed. Did he not understand she hated him as much for his part in Quaid's death as she did for his lovemaking that morn when he knew the truth? Or did the lewdster see her body as his right, even after such a betrayal? Aye, he was English. No doubt, he did.

"By the saints, speak to me!" he roared.

Maeve fixed him with a dispassionate glance, though she wanted to rail at him in the worst way. Still, she would not give him the satisfaction of the exchange he sought.

Kildare muttered a curse, then released her arm. "Where is your brother?"

Flynn had disappeared six days past. Maeve knew not to where and worried for his safety. When she had told him in tearful words of Quaid's execution, his fury had known no bounds.

Again, she shrugged, saying naught.

"Woman, you try your best to kill me," Kildare ground out.

Then he surprised her by covering her mouth with his own.

Maeve kept her lips stiff and clenched against his invasion. The crush of his mouth upon hers ground her lips against her teeth. She could feel him willing her to open to him. And she resisted.

Still, his familiar scent brought an answering pang in her chest.

Tearing her mouth from him with a cry, she speared him with a venom-filled glare. "Once, you seduced me from my convictions and my loyalty to Ireland. I know now what manner of miscreant you are. Such will not happen again."

CHAPTER TWELVE

Kieran remained tenacious. Maeve refused his pursuit. Another tense week passed.

Listening to Father Sean's soothing Latin, Maeve tried to block out the presence of her sisters and the castlefolk around her this Sunday Mass. She could forget them for moments. She could even disregard her missing brother for a bit.

'Twas Kieran, who had taken to attending daily Mass beside her, she could not ignore.

He stood close. Too close. Their arms brushed. Her skin broke out in chill bumps. He shifted his weight. His thigh nudged hers. Maeve wanted to scream.

Certainly he had found a recent interest in the church simply to annoy her. She had always attended daily, as required, along with her sisters. Her parents had been adamant about that. Occasionally, she found solace in prayer when troubled. The stained glass familiarity of the chapel she had ever found soothing.

With Kildare's nearness abrading her nerves, she wanted no more than to abandon faith and flee.

Except that would put her in Langmore's walls whilst everyone else attended Mass, leaving her quite alone with the heathen Kildare. 'Twas too risky. So in Mass she stood.

The brute beside her prodded her with an elbow. She glared at him, then looked about to realize everyone was filing from the chapel. Red-faced, she followed suit, not sparing him a glance. She also prayed he did not know her thoughts.

As they went out, a blond hulk of a man, seven or eight inches

166

over six feet, stood at the door looking over her head at Kildare with a wide smile.

Curious, Maeve pulled her stare from the man to see Kildare's answering grin. "Aric! I expected you not. When—" He frowned. "How did you get past Langmore's gates?"

The giant called Aric laughed and held up a missive with a royal crest. "King Henry's name and seal opens many doors."

Kildare nodded, then stepped toward his friend. They embraced heartily. Maeve watched on in curiosity. Never had she seen Kildare's smile so genuine or his affections so clear.

'Twas obvious he thought this fellow warrior a brother. Her sisters and the castlefolk looked on with curiosity.

"How fares Gwenyth?" asked her husband.

If anything, Aric's grin widened. "Very well. Days after you left Sheen Palace, she birthed a beautiful girl. We've called her Blythe. Gwenyth already plans to wed her to Drake and Averyl's oldest son, little Lochan."

Kildare laughed, a rich, happy sound, then clapped his friend on the back. "I am happy for you, my friend. And Drake, how do he and Averyl fare?"

"Quite well. Drake is bringing order to Dunollie and the Clan MacDougall again. Every day, he grows happier, thank God. And Averyl is a fine wife and mother, as you know, and this third pregnancy progresses similarly to the first two."

Smiling, Kildare slapped Aric on the back. "Excellent. And Guilford? Has he fully recovered?"

Aric scoffed. "The old goat will likely outlive us all."

"King Henry has not 'borrowed' further funds from him?"

Grimacing, Aric replied, "Nay, thanks to your help, our fine king is much assured of Guilford's loyalty."

Kildare nodded, clearly relieved, until Aric's expression turned chastising.

"But you failed to write us of your fate, friend," he pointed out. "Have you taken a wife? Gwenyth and Averyl will have my hides if I do not ease their curiosity."

Kildare's smile turned uneasy as he cast a glance Maeve's way. His arm curled around her waist, and Maeve stiffened. Aric's gaze could not possibly miss the gesture—and her reaction.

"This is Maeve, the second O'Shea sister. We've been wed not yet a month."

Maeve sensed Kildare wanted Aric to think them happy in their nuptials. By her husband's accounts, his friends were fortunate to have found extraordinary love in their unions.

Aric did not look a daft sort of man. He would see quickly, no doubt, that Kildare had not found the same good tidings.

"Maeve," Kildare said, facing her with a tight smile, "this is Aric Neville, earl of Belford."

"My lord." She nodded and stepped away from her husband.

Aric took her hand and lifted it politely. His cool gray eyes assessed her. "I take great pleasure in meeting Kieran's bride."

She swallowed nervously "'Tis pleased I am to meet you."

An awkward silence fell. Most of the watchful castlefolk shuffled away. Maeve briefly introduced Fiona, Brighid, and Jana to the large Englishman.

Jana gave him a cool nod and departed. Fiona, wide-eyed, mumbled a few polite phrases and followed her sister. Brighid stared with obvious interest. Maeve sent the young girl scampering off with a warning glance.

Another moment of silence fell over the trio. Maeve felt Aric's regard, his taking of her measure. She opened her mouth to excuse herself when Aric spoke instead.

"Kieran, would you cast your trained eye upon my horse? He seemed to limp a bit the last few miles."

Shrugging, Kildare said, "If you wish it, but I can send Colm. He is quite good at these things."

"Aye, but my horse has been longer with me than my own good wife. I trust *you*."

Maeve frowned at Aric's scheme. He wanted Kildare away. What was the Englishman's game? Did he bear the king's news?

Puzzled as well, Kildare assented with a nod. "Take you to the great hall and rest your bones. I will join you shortly."

"I will press your wife for a tour of Langmore's walls," said Aric, offering his arm to Maeve.

Knowing she had little choice, Maeve placed her hand upon the hard length of Aric's arm and led him inside.

After a brief tour of the outer buildings, including the dye house, the ale maker's shop, and the apothecary, Maeve led Kildare's friend to the great hall and saw him seated.

"You see, Langmore is quite typical," she said.

"But 'tis lovely, good lady. Your care for it is clear."

He was sincere in his praise, and Maeve sensed he did not speak lightly. "I thank you, but my sisters and I all tend to the insides, while Kieran is responsible for the rest."

Casually, he nodded. "How fares your army here?"

She tensed. Saints above, he wasted no time in pressing his point. "You would be better served to ask Kieran."

"I would wager he has taught them well since his arrival. He is ever ready for a good fight."

Maeve gritted her teeth. This man knew of Kildare's violent tendencies and did not abhor them? Nay, no warrior of England would, she reminded herself. Both these men were animals, exercising more brawn than brains.

"Aye. He knows very much about warfare, my lord." Maeve could not contain the sarcasm in her voice. "And little else."

"Ah, so he has lost his touch with the ladies?"

Lost his touch? Nay. To her misfortune, Maeve found her own body betraying her, craving Kildare's caressing hand, his lazy smile at the oddest times—deep in the night, early in the morn. Still, she could feel his mouth claiming her most intimately... She flushed with heat.

Aric chuckled. "So he has not lost his touch altogether?"

Maeve glared at the Englishman. He was as bawdy and lacking in manners as his heathen friend!

"I will only say that he excels in matters of battle. Of more personal matters, I will speak not at all."

She rose to leave, but Aric stayed her with a light touch. "I have offended, good lady, with no intent. Pray forgive me. Drake, Guilford, and I have long been concerned for Kieran. 'Tis only that we wish him happy and settled."

Maeve accepted his apology with a stiff nod. "You would do better to speak to him about his love of war than to speak to me about matters of the flesh."

All traces of Aric's grin disappeared. "'Tis right you are. Again, I am sorry. We have worried after Kieran's need for battle for years. Guilford reminds me often that for much of his life, Kieran has known naught else. 'Tis true, but I worry all the same."

Frowning at Aric's words, Maeve tried to decipher them. Battle was all Kildare had ever known? He had his friends and his mentor all these years, had he not? What could Aric mean?

* * * *

The days blended together in relative peace, with the exception of Maeve's silence—and her absence from his bed. The entire castle likely knew of it. Kieran cursed, for he could do naught to change it without tying the woman to his bed. The idea held appeal, but not without her willingness.

England was more likely to give up the pope.

Saint Patrick's Day dawned in mist and muted green. Maeve and her sisters had planned some manner of feast today. Kieran wondered if Flynn and the rebels would appear after their long absence and make war. He vowed to be extra alert, in case such an event took place.

In honor of the holiday, Kieran had given Langmore's budding army a day's respite from training. Now, wandering idle about the bailey, he pondered why he had done such a thing. Aric was still abed; he had naught to occupy himself.

Except thoughts of Maeve warm and smiling and naked…

'Twas useless to think such things. Maeve would not allow his intimacy again soon. She made that quite clear.

Cursing, he wandered about the gathering crowd preparing for the festival. Musicians and dancers, jesters and peddlers—all prepared for the occasion. Kieran wished they might all go elsewhere.

"Lord Kildare?"

Kieran turned to the voice to find an aging peddler beside his cart. The lined face and graying beard betrayed his hard life.

"Aye," he said finally.

"Mayhap I could interest ye in some spices so yer foods might better please yer palate. Or these gemstones." The old man pointed to an array of polished, jewel-bright rocks. "Many were taken directly from the Holy Grail, I tell ye. They are a treasure indeed."

"I thank you, but no."

The old man reached down and pulled a woman up by her shoulders. "Are you sure naught here interests ye?"

Kieran paused, staring at the woman the peddler so blatantly offered. She was about ten and eight, and likely the man's daughter. And she was beautiful, with dark tresses flowing loose and wild to her hips. An incredibly red mouth and eyes that bespoke pleasure with a sinful gleam. An incredibly lush bosom did much to add to her charms as well.

"I am Isolde. 'Twould be my pleasure to assist you, my lord," she said in a husky voice as she swayed her way around her father's cart and moved to stand before him.

In the next instant, the peddler disappeared.

Such an arrangement was not uncommon. In his youth, he had availed himself of a pretty peddler's daughter or two. Why did the idea not please him now?

Isolde touched his arm and sidled closer. "My lord?"

Kieran stared at Isolde. She had incredible breasts—high, round, firm—most of which showed above the square neck of her fitted red dress. She had smooth skin, dancing dark eyes, and a pouty red mouth he knew must appeal to nearly every man.

Why, then, did he not feel even a bit tempted?

He frowned at Isolde, at himself. Such made no sense. Here stood a goddess of sin, willing to bare herself for only a trifling amount of coin. She would lay her hand, her mouth, upon him—likely every inch of him, should he ask it—and give him the release he'd been without since the morn Maeve had ceased speaking to him.

And still, he could muster no interest.

What in Hades' name was happening to him, that he could find no ardor for a woman as tempting as Isolde? He knew not, but Maeve was certainly responsible.

"Lovely Isolde, I thank you, but not today."

He saw little more than the flash of surprise on her face before he turned away.

There Kieran found Aric standing, watching with a damned hawkish gaze. Could he not have a moment's peace?

"What?" he demanded of his friend, glaring.

Aric shrugged. "I merely came to look at the festival preparations."

Kieran gestured to the burgeoning melee about him, then snapped, "Enjoy."

Leaving behind a watchful Aric, Kieran entered Langmore.

Today, he would find Maeve. Now. Finally, they would put an end to this foolish silence. 'Twas affecting his ability to think, by the saints!

He journeyed first to the chamber she shared with Fiona. He thundered inside, where he found them both. Fiona stood fully dressed, brushing her hair. Maeve stood in only a shift, her hair flowing about her in a loose, fiery cloud.

Maeve looked up in surprise at his entrance. Then her face hardened to an icy chill. "My lord?"

Ballocks! That bloody polite tone was likely to make his ears freeze if she did not cease using it.

"It is Kieran," he bit out. Then he cast his angry stare at Fiona.

Without a word, Maeve's fragile, pale sister withdrew.

Kieran kicked the door shut behind her. "Enough of this silence, woman. We are wed. I do not press you to my bed, so the least you can do is provide conversation."

She set her jaw angrily. "Shall we discuss the fact you are a barbarian with no regard for my wishes, or the fact you deceive me with no regard of my feelings?"

He grabbed her shoulders, holding tight when she would have twisted from his grasp. "Damnation, Maeve! I told you, I could not have stopped Quaid's execution even if I had wished it. I may be governor of the Pale, but the power is not mine alone. Burkland, Butler, and the others also had a say in the matter. What good think you my one vote against all theirs?"

Maeve glared at him through eyes of golden fire. She wrenched from his hold, then advanced. "I did not say you could have saved him. I say that you should have tried. But you"—she sized him up with contempt—"what have you ever sought but battle? Even your own friends say 'tis too steeped in your blood. You would rather see war than peace."

Fury exploded, both at Maeve's dimness in this matter and Aric providing her with ammunition. "Men fight. It is the way of the world. I do not create the battles. I am merely there when they occur."

"If you refused to fight—"

"If I refused to fight, someone else would. And I would be without a livelihood, without that which makes me a knight."

She sniffed. "If you refused to fight, mayhap others would as well and we would have less war."

"What fantasy do you spin? If I refused to fight, I would be the subjugated, conquered by default. Nay, if you want aught in life, you must wrest it for yourself. If that means battle, 'tis common enough. You must know this."

"I know only that you have no heart and no honor."

The insult blasted him, and Kieran felt his anger multiply. "I have both, woman. If you would but listen to me, you would understand I have been ordered here to secure this land as best I can for King Henry."

"Why should I listen to a man of Irish blood who bows and scrapes before an English king but deceives his own wife?"

Kieran grabbed her arms again, jerking her close. Her breasts met his chest in a firm press. Her breathing became heavy. Her nipples slowly hardened against him. A raw surge of triumph burst through him as he lowered his mouth to hers.

Maeve turned her face away. "I would not touch a man who could hide a vital truth from me so he might bed me."

"I did not intend to deceive you!" he insisted. Why did she refuse to understand that, to understand a word he said?

"I simply wanted to touch you.... When you woke and spoke to me, soft and sleepy and so beautiful, I could not resist."

Her face flashed with surprise, then suspicion.

"I vow it," he said, near pleading. "Please understand."

Suddenly, she shook her head and pulled from his embrace. "Go make war with your friends and your army. 'Tis what you savages like best. Do not bother me again."

* * * *

After the festival, Kieran sat that night—or rather, early that next morn—in Langmore's great hall drinking ale. It had been his fervent hope that the brew might turn his sharp ache for Maeve into something dull and manageable.

Four hours and many tankards had brought no luck.

Dawn began filling the hall with soft gray light. Still, Kieran stared into his brew, wondering where he had gone so wrong. Never had a woman resisted him this much, for this long. Why did he have to find himself wed to such a stubborn woman? How had he wed a woman who completely failed to understand the very nature of men, of war, of him?

What the hell was he to do? Following King Henry's orders meant making his wife despise him. Pleasing Maeve could likely mean treason and death.

"Be you up early, or late?" asked Aric, who stood near suddenly.

Where had he come from?

Kieran frowned and squinted until the two images of his friend became one. "I am up late. And you, up early?"

Aric shrugged. "Aye."

Beside him, Aric sat and folded his large hands upon the table. "If you are troubled, friend, my ears listen well."

Kieran cast Aric an annoyed glance. Everyone at Langmore knew he and Maeve did not speak—or do anything else—together. Why should his observant friend be different?

And why would this blasted problem not leave him in peace?

"I have naught to say, except that I've imbibed a bit too much." He tried to give his best lopsided grin.

Aric merely shot him a skeptical scowl. "I doubt it has escaped your attention that your own wife speaks not to you."

Irritation chafed him. Could Aric not leave the matter alone?

"She is ill-tempered and I can do naught to change it."

"And you, of course, have done naught to provoke her."

Kieran glared at his friend. "Not any more than you had provoked Gwenyth after you first wed."

"I was wrong then to believe she wanted only my money and my position, instead of me. I righted my wrong with an apology. What of you?"

"I can do naught to change what is," he bellowed. "And I will thank you to remove your nose from my affairs!"

Aric hesitated, then rose with a sigh. "As you wish."

As his friend walked away, Kieran muttered a curse and rubbed a tired hand across his stubble-laden jaw. His own wife spoke not to him, and now he had offended a man who was like a brother. When had he become so clumsy with his words?

Would naught go right?

CHAPTER THIRTEEN

March meandered into April's stunning skies. Aric remained on the king's business—to check on Kieran's progress with the Pale and at Langmore. Kieran knew not whether he appreciated the familiar company or resented Aric's duty.

Flynn had not returned to Langmore, and Kieran knew well the sly fiend plotted more rebellion. Various reports from other Palesmen paired Maeve's brother with his own father, no doubt stirring up ire in the hearts of Irishmen. But he knew not where they were or what they plotted so he might stop them.

He fared even less well with Maeve. For nigh on a month, she had refused to speak to him more than a word or two, despite his constant efforts. Always, she snubbed him, ignored him. He would have preferred her voice raised to the heavens at this point. Anything but this killing silence.

Damn, but he could not remember a time of more frustration in his life!

Forcing himself to concentrate on the business at hand, Kieran crossed swords with one of his kernsmen, Shane, as they practiced. Barely grown from a pale boy, Shane held his sword in a tight fist, arm trembling. He gritted his teeth.

"Use your strength," he encouraged the boy. "Remember this could be a fight for your life."

"Aye, my lord, but 'tis frightful heavy."

Kieran nodded and engaged the young man's sword again.

A drop of water splashed on his arm, another on his face. Within moments, the rain poured down, as it had nearly every day for the past week. With a vicious curse that reflected his need for sleep and a soft woman—not necessarily in that order—Kieran all but threw his sword at Colm and stalked inside. Aric fell in at his side.

"Blasted rain," he muttered.

"It falls often," agreed Aric.

His accepting tone chafed Kieran. Did naught disturb the man anymore?

"Shall we have an ale by the fire?" his friend suggested.

Kieran wanted to be alone for reasons he knew not. Solitude had never appealed. Why it did now, he could not say.

"In a bit. Start without me."

Casting him a speculative gaze that was both frequent and maddening, Aric made for the great hall. Gnashing his teeth, Kieran made his way to his chamber.

Inside, he found Maeve, not seeing to wifely duties of any sort. Nay. Such would be too common, too helpful.

Instead, he found her rifling through his missives.

One after another, she unrolled the parchments, scanned them, then pushed them aside.

"Need you something in my personal papers?" he queried.

Maeve gasped and started. Placing a trembling hand to her chest, she turned to face him, golden gaze wide.

"'Tis not what you think."

Anger rose. For a month, the wench first refused to speak. When she did, 'twas to spy and lie. What next?

"Is it not? So you did not intend to glean information by reading missives addressed to me alone?"

"I merely seek information about Flynn, you bloodthirsty ruffian. 'Tis weeks he's been gone now. I worry."

"Did you think to ask me if I had heard aught about him? Nay," he answered before she could. "You simply searched my missives. Heavens fall upon us that you might actually speak to me."

Maeve clenched her small fists and shot him a direct glare. No fear there. No maidenly uncertainty or pretenses.

"I should rather speak to a rat than one of the devil's own," she yelled and tossed two rolled parchments aside.

She was angry at him? She, who had defiled his privacy and denied him her womanly comforts, was brazen enough to show him her ire? Ballocks, many a man beat his wife for such disobedience.

Kieran did not believe in doing thus to women. His father had done that too many times to his mother to count.

Pushing the memories away, he reached for Maeve and grasped her shoulders. He was tired of the rain, of Ireland, and the foolish rebellion. Tired of being unable to leave Langmore. Most of all, he was tired of Maeve's vexing manner.

But at last she spoke to him, a voice within reminded him. Loudly. Openly. 'Twas something to rejoice.

"Rodents scurry away to avoid ill-tempered wenches like you," he baited. "I have no doubt that if I am one of the devil's own, you deserve me."

"Ill-tempered? I am one of the most logical—"

"Spying is logical?" He struggled not to grin.

"Tenderhearted—"

"Calling me a demon and refusing to speak to me makes you tender of heart, does it?" he tossed back.

Her mouth pinched. "Reasonable women—"

"Those are two words that have no business in the same sentence."

At his retort, she gasped. Fury flooded her cheeks with color. Kieran grasped her shoulders tighter, bracing for the coming storm he sensed. And it gladdened him, for now she had no ice in her eyes. Nay, she was all fire, all red and gold, all anger and emotion.

He could scarce contain his relief.

"Take your hands off me!" she demanded.

When he ignored her, Maeve twisted and writhed. Kieran held tight.

Gritting her teeth in frustration, she shouted, "What would you know of reasonable actions? You leave this bed still warm from our consummation and go kill my betrothed."

"You cannot be betrothed if you are wed," he reminded.

"Pretend not that my feelings for Quaid mattered to you. 'Twas the kill you sought, and he, a chained enemy, was easy."

Kieran's fingers dug into her arms. Damn, but the woman knew how to anger a man. Still, he resisted his rising ire. 'Twas more important they spoke, not argued.

"I kill in battle. I do not kill for sport. I enjoy the challenge of fending off others, fighting a good and fair fight. I do not take pleasure in sending men to their deaths."

Maeve stared in disbelief. "And next will you try to convince me you've joined the rebellion?"

Kieran glared back. "Tell me again *why* you believe yourself a reasonable woman."

"A thickheaded barbarian like you can scarce understand."

Blood racing, heart pounding, Maeve stared at the husband she despised. She chastised herself for her outburst, her anger. What did his actions matter now? Quaid was dead.

Aye, but she wanted him angered, wanted him to know her sense of betrayal.

Defiantly, she jerked one of her arms from his grasp and reached for the next missive upon the table. Quickly, she unrolled it, though with difficulty given his hold. The swine. She would unroll it with her teeth, if need be, just to show him she was no simpering creature he could smile into submission.

It held naught of import, she determined a moment before Kieran tore it from her grasp and tossed it back on the table.

She gasped. "I am not surprised you should be so rude."

His stare alone laughed at her, to say naught of his deep, resonant chuckle. "Hmm. Others might find it more rude to read another's mail without invitation."

"Such simpkins have never lived with *you*. A more violent, wretched man I have never had the misfortune to meet."

Maeve felt her face flush with heat, heard her own harsh breathing as she glared at him. Her outburst stunned her. When had she become so passionate about her loathing? Why?

"Like me that much, do you?"

She stood stiffly, working feverishly to rein in her fury, a need to rail at him she did not comprehend. "I care not at all, if you must know."

Something hard and unpleasant crossed Kieran's features at her words. Maeve found herself fiercely glad that her barb had pierced him.

Then suddenly, his face relaxed into a smile again. Dread assailed her.

"You know, Wife, that I could do naught to save your precious Quaid. You want to blame me. 'Tis easier that way. But part of you knows my vote meant little to his fate."

He lied. *He lied!* Maeve buried her face in her hands. Certainly

Kieran could have done *something* to save her childhood friend.

What? a pesky voice asked within her. If others had voted against him, his word would have swayed them little. Even if he was governor of the Pale, the other swines in the parliament would expect him to see to the king's business with an iron will, allow no tolerance. The king himself would demand it.

Still, he might have tried to save Quaid, she argued with herself.

To what end? asked that insidious voice again.

Maeve stared harshly at Kieran. Perhaps he spoke true, that he could have done naught to save Quaid. But she would be damned to eternal hell before she absolved him with her words.

"And 'twas wrong of me…" he said, voice low, somehow soft, "'twas wrong of me to take you to my bed before I had told you the truth. I deserve your anger for that, true."

Kieran apologizing?

"At least you realize such," she snapped.

Where was her elation? Kieran had admitted his fault, certainly a first. Why, then, did she not feel triumph?

"I had no intent to deceive you," he vowed.

Then he reached up to grab both her arms again. Suddenly, Maeve felt surrounded by his heat, a sudden purpose in his eyes. She watched him warily.

"To hurt you was not my goal. Remember the way I touched you with gentle hands," he murmured, voice compelling.

Images of the soft glide of his hands over her belly, enveloping her breasts, assailed her. Remembrances of his intent gaze, as if she were the only woman in the world, came rushing back.

"You still hurt me," she accused.

"Mayhap," he conceded. "But not of a purpose. And not enough to deserve a month of silence."

An instant defense rose up in her. Did he not understand how deeply she ached for him that morn? Nay, what could he know of a woman's feelings—not that her feelings were for him.

"I think," he said, drawing her closer, "that what disturbed you most was your own eagerness in our marriage bed."

Mouth dropping, Maeve stared. That pig-bellied brute! Eager to share his— He should wish for such an event! She had not been eager for his hands upon her, for the pleasure he gave, for the sweep of his tongue in her mouth…and elsewhere.

Heat coiled in her belly. Confusion followed. Then came refusal. She would not believe such a mad allegation.

"Eagerness? That is arrogant, my lord. Think you I would ever be eager for a moment in your bed? Huh!"

That wicked grin came again, transforming harsh lines of his face into something more dangerous, irresistible.

"Aye. Did I not find you asleep in my bed that morn?"

"So I might learn of your business in Dublin the moment you returned," she shot back smugly. "Not because I am a swooning idiot at the thought of your kiss."

"So 'twas some other redheaded Irishwoman who lay in my bed that morn, curled her arms about me, and told me she missed me?"

Blast him for remembering! She would like to forget herself.

"You do not understand!" she insisted. "You—you twist my every word until it no longer resembles my thought. And I will not allow you to use your wily ways to dissuade me from the fact you are a knave!"

Kieran gripped her tighter. "You know I could not save Quaid. You cannot admit thus yet, but you also know I did not bed you to hurt or deceive you that morn. What you despise is that you respond to me. You respond to my touch."

Maeve shook her head, willing the words away. But the truth was there, certain, strong, immovable. She recalled cursing her own brazenness in his arms.

'Twould be easier to hate him if he taunted her. But he stated his belief in honest tones. Damn him!

How could this man rouse her ire, her passions, her very emotion, more than any other of her acquaintance? 'Twas as if her brain ceased rational thought when he took her mouth with his. Why? He had the soul of an Englishman, the heart of a warrior, the manners of a rascal, and the mind of a miscreant.

Why, then, did she seem unable to stay away from him? Why did he, of all men, stir her so?

Casting her gaze to Kieran's familiar face, she looked at him with fury, confusion. Denial and truth raged. But one question would not be silenced: why could she not maintain her distance, her coolness, when he came near? She yearned to exchange words with him—even unkind ones—just to hear him.

Foolish!

"Have you naught to say?" he prodded.

"Speak no more to me! I will not hear your babble—"

"We have no need to speak at all the rest of this night." Kieran drew her closer, his eyes now predatory.

Maeve felt her heart pound. He looked at her mouth, and it began to tingle. Her belly tightened. Her breasts followed. All over, she felt heat coiling, insidious desire washing through her. Good Mary help her.

"Do not touch me."

Her words, intended to be a command, were instead a breathy plea. She closed her eyes, blocking the unavoidable lure of his blue-green eyes. An urge to cry hit her. She did not cry, not around others. *Never* in front of a man who would use her tears to weaken her further.

"I want to touch you in every way I can."

Kieran's voice pierced her storm of feeling. Her body responded to the dark tone, to the challenge of his words. His musk washed through her senses, even as the whisper of cloth told her he moved closer.

His breath fanned her cheek. Maeve's knees buckled; anticipation slid thick and hot through the whole of her body. Why did he affect her thus?"

Warm, male lips touched her cool cheek, then traveled down in a slow brush, dangerously close to her lips. Her heart picked up its pace, until it beat with the speed of a dozen galloping horses.

Pulling her even closer, Kieran's mouth hovered above her own, so near their lips almost touched. The fact they did not, thrust a hot wave of frustration through her. Some thoughtless part of her craved the chance to fuse their lips together. Now. Her mind resisted the urge.

Impossibly, he came even closer, his scent, his heady warmth overwhelming her. And still he did not kiss her. Trembling fingers dug into his forearms. She would not close that inch between them and kiss him. She would not go to him like a whore.

It mattered not. For when he claimed her mouth in the next heartbeat, desire surged, battered her resistance. She clung to him, opening to him, wrapping her arms around him, utterly lost.

At her surrender, Kieran wrapped his arms about her, binding her to him. He stood close, so close every inch of his hard warrior's body imprinted itself in her mind, her soul. And still, 'twas not close enough. Need and demand rose up together, urging her to embrace him, mate her tongue with his.

Kieran encouraged her with another blistering kiss—a press of lips, an aroused groan. The need to take on more pleasure, and give more, overrode the feeble protests of her mind. How could a man with a kiss this thrilling possibly be evil?

Then he was pulling at his shirt, lifting it over his head to reveal the sculpted ridges of his abdomen, his chest. In the waning daylight, he was magnificent. Breathlessness clutched at her throat.

"Lie down for me, sweet Maeve."

Lie down? Slowly, she registered the command. A protest formed in her mind. He drowned it out with pleasure when he caressed the tops of her breasts with the back of his hand. His knuckles brushed down, until he toyed with the taut crests of her breasts through her dress.

She gasped, writhing, afloat in a haze of need. Inside, she began to ache, deep in her core.

Nay. 'Twas madness.

Kieran bent, his hands freeing her breasts from the confines of her dress. Then his lips and teeth worked the distended tip with a ginger bite, a suckle, until Maeve felt aflame.

"Lie down," he whispered again.

Quivering, Maeve sat on the bed beside him and lay back, her gaze never leaving his face. She needed this—him—the connection she felt when they shared a bed. This was what she sought, what she could not refuse, the feeling of belonging, of utter rightness. The thought had no logic, but she could not deny her feeling.

Kieran followed her to the mattress and lifted her skirts about her hips. Maeve could see naught but his face and shoulders. His eyes smoldered, hungered.

Then his palm cupped her center, fingers dipping into her moist heat. Already she swelled for him. Heat pierced her.

"Do you want this touch?" He brushed a fingertip back and forth over her sensitive center.

"Aye," she groaned, arching up to him.

Why, in his arms, was she so wanton? So needful?

"Show me," he whispered.

Show him? Why did he simply not fill her, possess her?

"Show me," he repeated.

Frustrated, she reached for his face and brought it down for a kiss. She brushed her tongue along the seam of his lips, and he opened to her, sweeping inside as if he belonged there.

In the next instant, he lay at her side, grasped her about the waist, and brought her above to straddle him. His length, sheathed in hose, pulsed beneath her. She ached.

With a sensual grin, he lifted her hips with his hands, then reached down to make quick work of his hose and braies.

When his hands returned to her hips to pull her down, he entered her, filling her, stretching her tight. Maeve threw her head back at the exquisite sensation. In this position, he went deeper than before, deeper than she thought possible.

"If you want this, show me." His whisper was a groan.

His fingers tightened about her hips and lifted her until he nearly withdrew. Her body had its own will and thrust herself down onto him once more. At the friction, she moaned.

Again, she raised herself and lowered to him. Then again.

"Aye, sweet Maeve. You kill me with pleasure."

She killed herself as well.

Soon, Maeve found herself greedy for more. She quickened the pace. Her breath grew ragged. Her mind ceased. Beneath her, Kieran grew tense, his groans more frequent. She felt the heady rush of his rapture, of her own, melding, thickening in the air, until pressure and sharp need blended to splinter into a million pieces.

As her sheath tightened around his body, convulsing, Kieran's shoulders turned harder than stone beneath her hands. He cried out her name in ecstasy.

Satisfaction melted her in hot, slow sweeps. She collapsed against him, too tired to move, to breathe, to think. That could all come later.

Then there would be time to wonder why she had given in to this need—and how she could purge herself of it.

* * * *

Two uneasy weeks slid by. Though Kieran had assumed at first their latest—foolish—romp in his bed had cured the ails of their marriage, she had quickly relieved him of that notion. They had

scarce spoken since. Maeve still could not discern if the anger she
harbored was more for Kieran and his conniving, charming ways or
for her own weak will where he was concerned.

Then the rumor of the rebellion army forming for fight took
Kieran away from Langmore. Lord Belford, his tall English friend,
went with him. Flynn wrote to her to assure her of his well-being.
Maeve felt as if she might breathe in peace.

At least until Flynn sent one of his men, Ulick McConnell, to
tell her of his terrifying plans and beg her assistance.

At least until she began feeling unwell.

Shifting her position on the bench in the solar, Maeve focused
on her needlework but was so tired 'twas as if she had not slept in
days. Quite the opposite was true. For a week now, she had slept
deep and long, even napping despite her fear of the rebellion's
bloody plot.

Squinting against the needle piercing the canvas, her arm felt
leaden. Giving up, she set her mending aside.

Across the room, Jana watched her. "Still unwell?"

Maeve nodded, crossing her arms over her chest. But the
familiar action crushed tender breasts, and she flinched against the
discomfort.

Jana set her needle to the silk in her lap and threaded it through.
"Has your stomach been ill these past weeks?"

"Once, but it soon passed."

Nodding, her sister watched her with curiosity. "You have lain
with your husband. When was your last flow?"

Over two months past. Maeve knew thus in her mind. Still, she
denied the obvious answer to her ailment.

"Perhaps I have a fever, some ill-humor."

"Know you of an ill-humor that robs a woman of her flow and
causes her to need sleep, other than bearing a babe?"

Maeve closed her eyes against Jana's words. Deep down, she
knew them to be true, had suspected as much herself. Still, she could
not accept thus.

A babe? Now? So soon? Pregnancy was a matter of much
gravity. It took her further from the life she had once planned, thrust
her deeper into Kieran's path. Their marriage seemed inexorable,
more binding.

Sweet Mary, help her. Was she ready to forever be joined to a warrior, an Englishman? To the infuriating Kieran?

Nature had apparently left her little choice.

What would she tell her husband? Ought she say a word? Perhaps Jana was wrong. Even if she spoke true, Maeve was not ready to tell Kieran. Their marriage was so fragile. He, Ireland's enemy, had some hold on her she could not comprehend. A child would only complicate her feelings, her life.

Suddenly, Jana stood at her side. "You look pale, sister. Perhaps you should lie down again."

Maeve nodded. Before she could quit the room, a clatter on the stairs drew her notice. Sword sheathed at his side, Kieran approached the door, looking weary from his travels.

He barked down the stairs for a bath, then turned to Jana. "Good tidings, Jana. How fares little Geralt?"

She nodded coolly. "He is all health, my lord."

"Excellent. Will you leave us, please?" He cast his sharp gaze to Maeve.

Sitting on the edge of a chair, Kieran removed his boots with a groan and let them fall to the floor. His weapon followed, then his tunic. He moved slowly, tiredly. Maeve found herself staring at her bare-chested husband, wondering why the sight of him should affect her heartbeat even now.

"There will be a rebellion soon," he said suddenly, gaze holding hers tightly. "I smell it. I feel it. They are out there, hiding, desperate, willing to do anything for their cause." He scowled. "My father is in the center. The whispers I hear tell me his plan is pure madness."

Maeve returned Kieran's stare, her heart now beating with fear. Ulick's messages from Flynn had mentioned Desmond O'Neill. They had told her of his dangerous ploy.

She hated it almost as much as the role he'd asked her to play.

"I fear people, many of them, will die if your brother and my father succeed. Maeve, I know our marriage has not been an easy one. I know you disagree with my support of King Henry. But you and I are united in our wish to save innocent lives. Help me," he implored. "Tell me what you know."

Maeve looked away. If she helped him, she would betray her brother, perhaps condemn him to Quaid's fate. And for all of Flynn's faults, he had protected the O'Shea sisters since their parents' deaths.

He was blood. She loved him.

But if she refused Kieran's request, dozens, perhaps hundreds, of innocent people could well die. Fathers, brothers, sons, some mere children, would follow Flynn's vision for an Ireland born in bloody rebellion, having no notion of the awful price they would pay in deaths for an uncertain future. Did none of them see that only freedom, borne of peaceful negotiations with the English, would be lasting?

"Maeve." He reached for her hands and took them in his. "I know what I ask of you is great. I know you have little reason to believe I want this war to end in peace. But I do."

She desperately wanted peace, so Jana might raise little Geralt without fear, so Fiona's memories of her horror might fade, so she could birth her own child in a land not oppressed.

But how could she entrust Ireland's future to the hands of a man whose very soul resounded with English loyalties? He *believed* the Irish should be under English rule.

Sweet Mary, her mind understood what her traitorous body did not: she could not place her brother's fate in the hands of a warrior who had done naught to save her betrothed from execution. Aye, mayhap Kieran had not the power to save Quaid, but had Quaid not been a rival, he might have tried at least. 'Twas no secret her husband and her brother felt much dislike for each other. Would there be no harmony at Langmore until one of them left...or died? Maeve shivered at the thought.

"Maeve?" He squeezed her hands.

"You give me much importance in the eyes of the rebellion, where no such faith exists, my lord," she began.

Betraying her brother, possibly condemning him to execution, was unthinkable. She could only hope to give Kieran hint enough to stop the worst of the rebel plan without sacrificing her brother's location.

"I know you have information, Maeve," Kieran stated. "You have conveyed missives from rebel to rebel over the past year."

How had he learned that? Panic seized her. Maeve breathed in and looked away, lest he see the truth in her eyes.

"Think you the rebels would trust a woman with such an important task?"

"They would trust an Irishwoman whom the English would not

suspect. They trust you, Maeve."

She shrugged, not meeting his gaze. "I hear but whispers, like you, my lord."

"What whispers have you heard?" he asked sharply.

Maeve tried to think of details that would not expose her brother. She thought of several, then thrust them aside as too dangerous before saying, "Malahide is but one English fortification the rebels would like back in their possession."

Kieran's gaze drilled into her. "Do you say their ambitions are to reclaim the whole Pale at once?"

"Such would not surprise me if the idea was met with favor."

"With but two hundred men, how can they think to do this?"

Maeve disentangled her hands, relieved when Kieran let her pace the chamber to retrieve some blank parchment. "I believe they have found weapons in household necessities."

With that, she tossed the parchment onto the fire. It flared, with the sudden kindling, burning orange and hot, flickering and gyrating with power and hunger.

Kieran watched with dawning horror, his face ashen.

Satisfied he understood what he must, Maeve quietly left.

CHAPTER FOURTEEN

"So what will you do now?" Aric asked late that night.

Kieran looked across the empty great hall with a shrug and clutched his tankard of ale. He had spent the evening writing missives to other Palesmen, warning them of a massive attack, one he knew would happen within days. He plotted a scheme to defend Langmore using its army. With the divided loyalties of the soldiers, he could only wonder on which side they would fight and pray 'twas his.

Those tasks completed, he'd sat with Aric for the past hour, telling him all he knew of the rebellion—all Maeve had hinted at. Exhaustion ate at him. Still, he felt the need for Aric's counsel without rebel ears nearby.

"Do?" Kieran raked a hand through his shaggy hair. "I must wait. I know not where to find Flynn or my father. Maeve would not tell me as much." He paused. "She trusts me not."

"You represent her enemy, a threat to her family. In time, she will accept you."

Kieran laughed bitterly. "You are full of hope. More than I." He shook his head. "Maeve will not come. She may be a quiet creature, more inclined to books than battle, but she will fight accepting me until her last breath."

"That disturbs you."

'Twas not a question. As always, Aric's gray gaze seemed to see his every thought.

Both relieved and resentful, Kieran nodded.

Aric's gaze questioned. "Why do you suppose your feelings are thus?"

Kieran pictured Maeve, mouth pinched in anger, head thrown back in rapture, wearing one of her teasing smiles, her hair a fiery wreath about her face. Something in her quiet manner drew him in, always had. Yet beneath her surface beat the heart of a passionate, brave woman, a woman of intellect, capable of great caring for those around her. When he was with her, she confused him. Yet through her eyes, he saw life as he'd never seen it—with a hope of peace, of promise for something beyond the next battle. He saw a life of joy.

"Because..." He sighed, paused, then realized his terrible dilemma. "Because I love the wench."

Setting aside his tankard, Kieran buried his head in his hands. Did he truly love Maeve? Aye, he did. When? Why her?

Beside him, Aric laughed. "Welcome to the fate Drake and I share. 'Tis pitiful to love a woman so that she twists your mind, but there is no escape, I'm sorry to say."

The fact his friend was clearly not distressed made Kieran rise with a frown.

"'Tis easy for you to say. Your wife returns your regard."

"And so will Maeve, and soon, I believe."

A heady thought that filled Kieran with a bright wish, but an impossible one.

"Nay. Because of Quaid, Flynn, and the rebellion—Ireland itself—she will never trust me, never cleave to me."

Aric smiled. "You have ways of coaxing her to you."

"Even if I coax her now and again, her silence and resentment will run deeper each time I do. I begin to wonder if the pleasure is worth the price."

"Oh ho! That is serious," Aric said. "You do love her, to desire her conversation and goodwill more than her body."

Kieran shot him a killing glance. "Thank you for pointing out what a perfect idiot I am."

"Nay, I think your choice a wise one," he countered.

"It means naught," Kieran declared. "For she will never take me into her heart."

"She will." Aric waved his fear away.

Kieran stood, his bench scraping across the floor in the echoing silence. "You do not understand. You cannot, for you never wondered if Gwenyth loved another."

"If you recall, she pined for Sir Penley Fairfax when first we wed," Aric reminded.

"That prick? Gwenyth did not *love* him. She sought a position as his wife, as a lady. Once Gwenyth surrendered to you, 'twas with her whole heart. And Averyl loved Drake almost from the start of their marriage."

"Maeve cannot wed a dead man," Aric pointed out.

"I do not believe he is dead in her heart," Kieran argued. "And she blames me for his execution. She blames me for persuading her to be unfaithful to him and his memory."

Aric paused, thoughtful. "Of course. 'Tis easier than facing the fact she cares for you."

"How I wish that were true." He sighed, sitting once more. "But your thinking is only wishful."

"If you say," Aric murmured, his tone clearly indicating he did not agree. "So, what will you do if she conceives? Will you leave Ireland and return for the babe, or stay?"

A good question, that. Kieran cast his gaze to the ceiling, but no answer came. Life away from Ireland had long been his goal. Now, the idea of parting from Maeve distressed him. To his shock, even this green, if wet, isle had a certain appeal. But living by Maeve's side for years to come, his feelings unrequited while she pined for a dead man and plotted with the rebellion—'twould be pure misery. They would come to hate each other, as his parents had. Still, what if Aric was right?

"I know not what I will do if she conceives." He sighed, then reached for his tankard, taking long swallows until the contents were gone. "I truly know not."

* * * *

"The rebels come!" sounded a predawn shout, followed by a pounding on his door. "The rebels come now."

Kieran sat up, instantly awake, heart pounding.

"Gather the men and rouse Lord Belford. I will be down shortly," he shouted back even as he jumped from his solitary bed and pulled on his tunic and hose.

Colm knocked and stepped inside the chamber. "Lord Belford is awake, my lord."

"Is everything else at the ready?"

"Aye. They finished digging yesterday morn."

"Good." Kieran sent the boy a grim smile. "How many men march our way?"

"Fifty or so, my lord."

More than he had thought. "Send another pair of kernsmen to scout their progress. Then you must return to see to Langmore's women and little Geralt. Gather them."

Swallowing hard with a wide-eyed nod, Colm scurried off.

Muttering a curse, Kieran made his way to the bailey. Never did he recall a time when he dreaded the fight to come.

In the hall, Colm stood with Brighid against his side, her long, pale hair hanging around her. She looked more frightened child than budding woman. Jana cradled her son, seemingly made of stone. Fiona clutched Maeve's hand in the portal of their chamber. His wife looked weak and pale.

He frowned at their apprehension. Did these women await soldiers fighting for their cause with fear?

Again, he looked at Maeve, wishing he could read in her face caring, knowledge of the coming battle—aught to guide him, give him hope. She merely looked strained and white. Still, he ached for her.

He was not so foolish to believe that she would ever love him. But he wanted her touch, her smile. Like a fever consuming him, he could not purge her from his system.

And for the past three days, she had scarce spoken to him, claiming illness. She stayed abed. Brighid whispered that she did naught but sleep and vomit. He'd gone to comfort her. Jana had turned him away—at Maeve's request.

Kieran sighed, his gaze lingering on his wife. "Are you well, Maeve?"

She looked away. "Go fight your battle."

The bitterness in her voice wracked him with frustration. What would he do with a wife who loathed him, while his heart belonged to her? He supposed this love of his explained his disinterest in the pretty peddler's daughter. And he cursed. How had he come to this pitiful state?

He could do naught about it now, Kieran realized as he made his way down the circular steps to the bailey, where his army waited. To his shock, he saw all twenty-three Irish soldiers, plus a dozen new ones.

He turned to his guard. "Who are these men?"

Shane offered, "Beg pardon, milord, but they're Irishmen who aren't liking the rebels' plans. The soldiers say you are a fair man, so they came to take their chances."

Before he could reply, Aric strode up to his side, and a pair of guards ran up the lane, breathing hard.

"My lord, the rebels are bringin' at least fifty men. They march on foot, and half carry blazing torches."

Kieran began to sweat. 'Twas as he'd feared; the rebels would burn them out, uncaring of who died. No doubt they felt that if they had no fortification, the English encroachers should have none, either.

Such actions had a way of balancing the power in a war, but often at great cost of life. Women and children died in the twisted, burning flames. Did Flynn not see that? Not care that these plans meant the destruction of his home and his family?

Clearly, he cared not.

And Kieran wanted to spare Langmore and its people from the same fate Balcorthy had suffered all those years ago.

Whirling to the outnumbered army, he barked, "Be at the ready. You know our plan. Where are my archers?"

Four of the kern stepped forward, bows and arrows in hand, faces filled with determination. Aye, these four he trusted.

"Good. You will march first on foot to the top of Langmore's battlements. While I ready the rest of the troops, you do your best to wound the rebel force as they come up the road. They must not reach Langmore's walls."

As the four men scrambled away, Kieran faced the rest. "Keep your weapons and your courage at the ready. Watch one another's backs. We all have family here to protect."

"Aye, my lord," shouted the guard. The rest echoed.

"Does everyone remember the plan?"

All the faces, even the unfamiliar ones, registered understanding. Kieran disliked that complete strangers, with untested loyalties, knew his ploy, but all he could hope for now was that he'd earned his men's trust and they did not plot to see him served up to the rebels for execution.

"When I give the command," he said, "be quick. Our advantage will not last long."

The men indicated their understanding by word or gesture, then made their way outside the gates of the castle.

Kieran followed, glancing at Aric. His pulse pounded. "Will this work, my friend?"

"I can think of no better plan."

"Nor I," murmured Kieran.

He did not take comfort in that fact. Either way, many would die this night. And he ached for Maeve, knowing how much she hated bloodshed. He found himself wishing he might stop it for her.

That was as impossible as seizing the moon.

Making his way to the side of the dirt lane leading up to Langmore, he jumped to the trench and crouched low, pulling the grass covering he and the soldiers had fashioned over the past days. He could only hope that with the rebellion's small army, they had not the men to spare for spies. The sun had yet to prove more than a hazy gray light for the coming rebels. If he could surprise them, that would aid this deception.

Still, he feared they would see through this ruse and Langmore would lie in rubble within hours, only to be abandoned and forgotten like Balcorthy.

Shaking the maudlin thought away, he waited, listening. Finally, he heard footsteps, many sets of them, coming across the bridge, then heading up the road. The light of their torches reached him in the next moments. Kieran swallowed a lump of fear, recalling the heat, the screams, the stench of charred flesh.

The rebels marched closer, between the trenches on either side of the lane. Suddenly, the *whoosh* of arrows filled the air, mingling with the sounds of booted feet. Grunts and screams came moments later, followed by the sounds of men falling, men dying.

The remaining rebels did not stay to help the fallen. Instead, they charged toward the castle, away from the archers' range, until they flattened themselves against the half-finished curtain wall for cover, below the battlements.

Kieran's pulse raced. Sweat trickled from his temple.

"Now!" he shouted.

As one, the men tossed their grass coverings into the air and charged the rebels. Running over the fallen bodies, Kieran followed, looking into the shocked faces of his enemies.

The fight ensued. Sword in hand, he parried and thrust, his blade finding men's vulnerable flesh repeatedly. At his side, Aric staved off two rebels with little difficulty. The Irishmen were ferocious, but Aric was by far more skilled.

The scent of blood tinged the dawn as the sky exploded with orange and pink. Sweat dripped into Kieran's eyes.

The rebels who held torches made their way around the side of Langmore. A bolt of panic surged through him.

"Aric, the others!" he shouted.

"Go. I will keep these," he said of the few uninjured rebels still in front of Langmore's gate.

Nodding, he tapped three of his men on the shoulder and motioned one to follow him. The other two he sent around Langmore's other side. The rest of his men stayed with Aric to aid the defense of Langmore's gate.

Seconds later, he came upon a trio of miscreants, one with a torch. Two found the wooden scaffolds used to erect the castle wall. The third drew the torch near. The light from the fire touched his fevered grin.

Flynn!

How could the man destroy his own home? All his sisters had ever known? What if they died in this blaze?

Enraged at Flynn's stupidity, Kieran charged him, sword poised. By his side, Langmore's soldiers followed and dispatched one of the other rebels to his maker. Kieran dealt quickly with a blade to the gut of the second rebel.

Now he stood with Flynn, and he itched to plant his blade deep into the miscreant's belly.

But Maeve would forever hate him.

Instead, he watched as Flynn threw his torch on the scaffolding's dry wood and reached for a dagger at his thigh.

"Put out that fire!" he shouted at his soldier, then rushed toward Flynn.

O'Shea tried to dodge him, but Kieran was faster, his sense of purpose so urgent. He caught Flynn about the shoulders and tackled him to the ground. Not surprisingly, Flynn struggled and cursed.

Kieran punched him in the stomach.

Flynn grunted, then glared at him through eyes of hate. "Don't be tellin' me you think you can change our victory."

At his sneer, Kieran pinned him roughly to the ground. "I have stopped you."

With a shrug, he said, "Such matters not, you English maggot. The rest of the English fortifications will be so damaged we will have no trouble taking Langmore later. Don't you be forgettin' that."

"I would not be so confident," Kieran returned. "Every Englishman in the Pale knew of your plans. All are prepared to meet your forces."

A stunned expression transformed Flynn's face. The rebel leader began to struggle, kicking, growling. Kieran punched him in the jaw.

Flynn went slack beneath him.

"The fire is out, my lord."

Kieran looked up to see the man had trampled out the budding flames with his shirt and boots. "Good work."

Coming to his feet, Kieran looked about for other rebels. Finding none, he bent down to lift Flynn and hoisted the man to his shoulder with a grunt.

"Go to the others and help them if need be," Kieran ordered the soldier.

With a crisp "aye," the lanky Irishman disappeared around the front of Langmore's gate. With a tired sigh, Kieran followed.

At the keep's door, Aric and the others had subdued the rebels, but fight still burned in their eyes.

The fight turned to shock at the sight of their leader slung over his shoulder.

"Nay!" shouted one rebel.

"Aye," he yelled back. "You are defeated, and I take you all prisoner."

With the help of Aric and his soldiers, they led the defeated group of rebels into Langmore and down to the depths of the dungeon. There, they put the men into groups. The wounded were kept together, and Kieran ordered two of his men to find the healer, Ismenia, and bring the old woman there.

Flynn he put by himself at the far end of the dim hall, dropping him on a worn wooden bunk with a thud. The man groaned.

Kieran backed out of the small cell, closing the heavy wooden door behind him. He signaled the guard to secure the lock with the key.

Satisfied that Flynn could not escape and the rebellion had ended that night, Kieran made his way upstairs. A need to see Maeve, assure himself of her well-being, tore into his gut. His mind said the rebels had not breached Langmore's walls. Still, he worried.

Inside Kieran's chamber, Colm stood over the O'Shea sisters. Brighid had fallen asleep at his side. Jana held a mewling babe, seeking to comfort him with a soothing voice. Fiona sat next to her eldest sister, wringing her hands. Maeve stood away from the others, stiffly, by the fire.

'Twas to her he went first.

"It is over," he said. "You are safe."

Maeve turned his way, cold gaze studying him. Her pale, distraught features concerned Kieran. Unable to resist, he reached out for her, placing a gentle hand upon her shoulder.

Stiffening, she moved away from his touch. "How many are dead this morn?"

He held in a sigh. What would she say when he told her Flynn was his prisoner and that the Palesmen would likely want his execution in Dublin soon?

She would surely hate him forever.

"I know not yet. Perhaps thirty."

Maeve drew in a sharp breath. "I suppose you are disappointed the number is not greater. 'Tis a sad day when you do not shed enough innocent blood."

Innocent? She was a fool, and her blind devotion to Flynn and the rebels was naught short of dangerous.

Casting a glance to Colm and the others who watched eagerly, he barked. "Out."

Without a word, all complied. Colm shut the door behind him.

He rent the silence with a growl. "Killing is not some merriment for me. I do not revel in spilling blood. But I defend what is mine. This morn, that meant Langmore. And those *innocent* men had come to set your very home on fire with you, your sisters, and a helpless infant inside."

Maeve paled at his words. "Even Langmore?"

"Every English fortification. Did you expect me to stand by and watch them set Langmore ablaze, to watch you scramble to leave the fire alive?"

"Nay," she conceded, voice small.

"You even provided me enough hints to aid in ceasing this rebellion, so you must have believed their plan evil."

"But I did not expect you to kill them, only stop them!"

"Sometimes"—he sighed—"that is the same thing."

She bit her lip so hard Kieran feared 'twould bleed.

"Maeve…" He reached for her. She stood stiff as he wrapped an arm about her shoulder, but did not pull away.

"The dead— Do I know any among them?" Her voice broke.

"I know not. I've sent Ismenia to the wounded in the dungeon." He paused, not knowing how to tell her of Flynn's capture. "Your brother is in the dungeon as well."

"Flynn!" She jerked from his hold. "He is wounded? I must go to him—"

Kieran wrapped an iron hand about her arm. "He is well and will have no more than a few bruises."

She relaxed a bit in relief.

He closed his eyes, hating what must come next. "Maeve, he is in serious trouble. I cannot lie."

"Nay! I will speak to him, ask him to cease. Only spare him."

Her golden eyes pleaded, and she clutched his hands. Reveling in her touch, Kieran squeezed them. "That may be beyond my power, Maeve. The Palesmen are to send all the captured rebels to Malahide Castle…where parliament will deal with them."

Maeve wrenched her hands from his. "You mean send them to their deaths."

He saw no point in lying. "In all likelihood, aye."

"And you would like naught more, I am certain, than to be King Henry's battle hero, the conqueror of the rebellion. What pleasure that should bring, at the expense of your own wife's brother."

Kieran grunted bitterly. "You think I wish to partake of glory resulting from this wretched rebellion? I hated coming upon Flynn with a torch in his hand as he lit the scaffolding about Langmore's wall. I wanted to kill him for his treachery, for putting you in danger. To spare your feelings, I did not. I see I'm the fool for thinking 'twould matter."

Glaring, Maeve remained mute, chin raised stubbornly.

He cursed. "Do you fail to understand that Flynn made a choice to engage in this rebellion? He *chose* to participate in a plan designed to kill people and destroy homes. Think you that warrants no punishment?"

"But none of that happened," she argued. "So must he die for it?"

"Flynn will not rest until he sees English blood run. I cannot spare him so he can kill others."

Turning away, Kieran made his way to the door and slammed it behind him with all his fury. He prayed the anger would last long, for once it waned, misery would take its place. Marriage between the English and Irish would not work. His own parents had proven that well.

Kieran felt painfully certain he and Maeve were well on their way to proving that again.

* * * *

"You plan *what*?" Aric demanded of Kieran the following day as they rode about Langmore's walls to survey any damage the rebels inflicted.

"Damnation!" Kieran cursed, tightening his hands about the reins. "What choice have I? If I give Flynn over with the rest of the rebels, parliament will execute him within the week. Already, I have received missives from most of them. The few rebels who lived through the battle are to be sent to Malahide within the week. If I do this duty, I will lose my wife forever."

Aric wanted to point out that refusing to do it might be seen as treason, but refrained. Having nearly lost his own wife over issues of duties soon after marriage, he understood Kieran's dilemma.

Still, he believed his half-Irish friend made the wrong choice. Flynn was dangerous and angry; he would not cease this rebellion until he took his last breath.

"What will you do with Flynn if you keep him at Langmore?"

Kieran shrugged. He looked haggard, his usual smile most recently replaced by a frown. Aric prayed it would not last. Surely Maeve would see the impossible position in which she had put her own husband, choosing sides where he could not without risking a king's wrath.

Then again, his own Gwenyth, despite his boundless love for her, had proven a time or two that where women and feeling were concerned, logic did not always rule.

"I know not what to do," Kieran said finally. "From the information I have gathered thus far, I surmise the rebellion has been all but destroyed. Over three-quarters of their men are either dead or captured. Their weapons are only crude at best. They have no strongholds and no monies to sustain them. Given that, perhaps I can detain Flynn in Langmore's dungeon until England has achieved more stability in the Pale."

"That may be years yet," Aric pointed out.

"Aye, but he will not be dead."

Nodding, Aric asked, "And what will you say if the other Palesmen—or King Henry—discover what you've done?"

Kieran's jaw clenched as he stared straight ahead, over the landscape awash in greens, pinks, blues—a feast of color for the eye. Aric doubted his friend even noticed.

"I..." Kieran sighed. "I suppose I will prepare to have my neck stretched by the hangman's noose."

"You would take that risk to spare Maeve's hurt?"

Kieran laughed bitterly. "I know such actions are foolish beyond words. This plan... It goes against all logic. Of that, I am aware. But I cannot be the one to cause her pain."

Aric understood that sentiment well.

"Then do what you must. We forged these blood bonds as boys to become like brothers," Aric said, holding up his palm, displaying the thin scar upon it. "I will help all I can when I return to London, which I must do next week."

"What do you say?" Kieran faced him, frowning.

"I will tell King Henry the rebellion is all but over and all its leaders have met their justice."

"You cannot!" Kieran insisted as he stopped his mount. "Such a falsehood would be dangerous for you, perhaps deadly."

Aric smiled. "Ah, but that is the risk I choose to take so I may help you, my blood brother."

Kieran paused. Aric wondered for long minutes if he would respond at all. Finally, he nodded. "I am blessed with such friends as you and Drake."

"Never forget that," teased Aric.

CHAPTER FIFTEEN

A week passed in which Maeve stayed in her chamber. Each morn, extreme stomach unrest ailed her. Each evening, weariness plagued her.

The afternoons… She refused to take the chance of encountering Kieran and weakening from her anger at the mere sight of him. It was cowardly, she knew. Still, the afternoons gave her ample opportunity to ponder this dilemma with Flynn and his imprisonment.

Pacing to her window, Maeve sighed into the rain. Why had her brother strayed to such extreme measures of rebellion? They had been making slow but steady progress toward their freedom with the minor theft of documents and supplies destined for English strongholds.

Then Flynn and the others had become impatient, their plans reckless. She wanted to rail at her brother. His foolishness and arrogance had led to his capture.

Kieran had shown no compunction about throwing Flynn into the dungeon. He had not even hesitated.

Could he have done aught else? asked a voice inside her. She had no answer to such a question.

As spring blushed its way across the wet land, Maeve looked out, scarcely noticing such dewy beauty.

What would she have done in Kieran's position? She wanted to believe she would have spared Flynn, even if only to keep her hands free of blood. But as Kieran had pointed out, war was upon them. Selective acts of mercy could free a man who might later plant a blade in his back.

Maeve shook her head at the argument. Flynn would not attack Kieran without provocation.

Would he?

Recalling Kieran's first day at Langmore, he had been trapped within the mud pit and Flynn loomed above him with taut bow and arrow... Perhaps Flynn would kill her husband.

Aye, now he would do so without a second thought.

Still, Flynn was her brother. Did that mean naught to Kieran?

Or did the fact that Flynn had tried to set Langmore afire overshadow, in Kieran's eyes, the blood that tied her to her brother?

Maeve shook her head in confusion. The circle of her thoughts had been thus all day. Still, she could not unravel the tangle of her feelings and her logic, each telling her something different.

Taking a deep breath, Maeve looked into the drenched bailey below—just in time to see ten of the castle guards lead twenty rebels, filthy and bound, out the front gate, into the rain. With haggard steps, they ambled down the muddy lane. They were too far away to identify, but she feared Flynn marched among them.

Would that wretch she called husband not even allow her to say good-bye to her brother one final time?

Anger allowing her to summon her energy, Maeve tore out of her chamber and wound her way down the stairs. Through the great hall, out the damp day, past the gardens and the dye house, until she reached the garrison. Mayhap the guard there could tell her Flynn's fate.

At the dungeon door, the guards stopped her.

"No need for ye to be in there now, milady," said Patrick, an elder castle guard who had once served her father.

Tears stung her eyes, then rolled down her cheeks. She mourned all of Ireland's doomed soldiers, but her brother most particularly. She and Flynn had not been terribly close of late, but he was family. Her parents had once had much hope for his future—and she feared the worst had befallen him now.

"They've all been taken to Dublin, then?"

The old man hesitated, then said, "All but Master Flynn."

Surprise, hope, and joy all skittered through her. "He's still here? How? Why?"

"He remained on milord's orders."

Kieran had allowed Flynn to stay? Relief bubbled within her. She trusted Patrick; he would not tell a falsehood. Her brother stayed and lived!

Why had Kieran done that? Why had he risked the ire of his fellow Palesmen and his king to keep Flynn hidden here?

Maeve knew of but one reason: he honored her request.

Something inside her lifted, lightened. She smiled as if her heart had grown wings. Her vexatious husband had taken an unexpected, kindhearted turn. Saint Mary above!

"I cannot be allowin' ye down there, lass," said the graying Patrick.

Nodding, Maeve smiled. "I understand. And thank you."

Whirling, she raced back through the slow, steady rain, toward the main keep, hoping to find Kieran somewhere within.

Dashing to the great hall, she spotted Aric by himself, composing a missive.

As she entered, he looked up and smiled.

"Greetings, my lord," she called with impatience.

"Greetings, my lady." He stood, nodding. "You are wet."

Maeve looked up a long way before she found his face again. "Aye. Have you seen my husband about, my lord?"

"Well, my lady—" He stopped with a mock frown. "We both have names. Ought we use them, perhaps, instead of this foolish formality?"

She had never been one for such ceremony herself. Besides, she liked Aric. Aye, he was English through and through, and a man of great consequence to King Henry. Still, she found she liked him, his dry humor, his honesty. And she felt a great urge to make haste to Kieran's side.

"Indeed…Aric," she said.

He smiled. "Thank you, Maeve. Now I ask what you seek, since you ran in here from the rain with all possible speed?"

"I seek my husband. Know you where he is?"

"Try his chamber. I believe he sees to his correspondence, as do I."

"Of course. Forgive my intrusion."

"I but write to my lovely wife. You will have to meet Gwenyth someday soon." He smiled, then offered, "For now, I believe Kieran would very much like to see you as well."

With that cryptic comment, Aric sat again, attention on the parchment before him. With a last, curious glance, she turned away and made for the stairs.

Within moments, she stood at Kieran's door. Her hand shook as she lifted it to knock. Would he truly wish to speak to her? She had offered him naught but insults for weeks. And still, he acceded to her wishes to keep Flynn here, at great peril to himself. Only a warrior who cared for her feelings would take such a risk.

She tried to tell herself his loyalties were English, that he had come here to wed her to conquer her family and her people.

She had known the first time he held her, when he comforted Fiona, and when he had assisted her birthing Jana's son, that his loyalties were English.

Still, he had proven himself capable of compassion, no matter if 'twas someone Irish who ached.

Aye, but Kieran watched Quaid die.

Maeve's hand faltered as she held it up to the door. She drew in a deep breath.

Kieran had said more than once he could have done naught to stop Quaid's execution. Knowing what she knew of Bishop Elmond, Lord Butler, and the others, she could believe they wanted Quaid and all the rebels dispatched to hell, posthaste. One voice against many would likely have meant little.

Besides, Kieran had apologized for bedding her before telling her the truth, endured a month of her silence, then protected Flynn, whom he liked not, all at great peril to himself. If he were truly bloodthirsty, he would have sacrificed Flynn to the Palesmen—or killed her brother himself.

Her husband was more than an English warrior bent on battle. He was warm and concerned, at times tender, at times fiery, and always beloved.

Beloved? Did she love him?

The truth hit her like an anvil.

She could find no other reason why she had been unable to set him from her heart, why it soared when she thought of his smile. No other reason came to mind as to why she ached when they were parted for long days and weeks, and why her whole being lit up with joy when he came near.

Such could only mean that she loved him.

Trembling in earnest now, Maeve finally set her hand to knocking on his door. A moment of silence ensued, and she drew in a ragged, nervous breath.

"Enter," he called a moment later.

Swallowing, Maeve did as he bid as she pushed the door open. Inside, firelight glowed in golden radiance about the chamber, lighting the familiar stone walls, the curtains about his bed—the bare flesh of his strong back, as he wrote with a bold hand across the parchment before him.

"Kieran?"

At the sound of his name spoken so freely from her mouth, his head snapped up. He rose to greet her, clearly surprised.

"Maeve. How fare you? Your sisters say you've been ill."

The babe. She must yet tell him of that. And she vowed she would, as soon as she had thanked him for sparing Flynn.

"As you can see, I stand before you very much alive."

"Are you well? Clearly, you have been out in the rain."

He sat again, looking tense. "Maeve—"

"Let me speak," she interrupted. "I know what you've done for Flynn."

Surprise crossed his features, lit his blue-green gaze. Again he stood, this time turning in profile as he faced the fire. "I—"

"I merely wanted to thank you," she insisted. Approaching him with a raised hand, she set it upon the taut flesh of his arm. "You heeded my wishes at great risk to yourself."

He hesitated. "I did not want to cause you more pain."

Though she wanted Flynn safe and the rest of her family whole, something compelled her to ask, "What if the other Palesmen or the king learn Flynn lives? Will they not accuse you of softening? Of treason, even?"

Kieran gave her a casual shrug. But Maeve knew better, for he stiffened further, his arm bulging beneath her fingers.

Maeve stared openmouthed at her husband. He would risk his life to spare her feelings?

A wave of concern, of joy and love, warmed her body, beginning with her heart. "Oh, Kieran."

Standing on the tips of her toes, Maeve wrapped her arms around him and drew him down to her embrace. Slowly, he wound his arms about her, damp dress and all. Then he buried his face in the crook of her neck and held her tight.

They remained thus for long moments, heart to heart, caught in the rich texture of a moment where feelings reigned in silence—but they seeped into her all the same.

Kieran stood straight then, backing out of her embrace. She clung to his arms, stared up into his eyes, charged with need. 'Twas a need she shared with everything inside her.

Leaning forward again, she placed a soft kiss upon his lips.

He hesitated. Time stood still as she waited for his reaction. And she feared. Did he care for her but refuse to accept an Irishwoman into his heart? Did he even wish to love as she did? Could he?

Kieran drew in a jagged breath. His arms tightened around her waist. His hands splayed across her back.

Then he opened his mouth above hers.

Relieved, joyous, aching, Maeve met him halfway, parting her lips and seeking him with her tongue.

Tenderness held sway in the timeless world of their kiss. He sampled her mouth with patience and reverence. Maeve felt his wanting in every slide of his hand across her damp back, in every breath exhaled upon her cheek.

After a lingering kiss, Kieran nibbled his way down her jaw, to her neck. "Maeve," he whispered. "I have missed you."

Another wave of feeling swept over her heart, nearly swaying her mindless with its power. Never had she loved with so certain a heart. She would have wed Quaid because her parents and Flynn had wished it. He would have been the kind of man to make her content.

Kieran sent her into the stars. For all their differences and their quibbling, he made her understand the joy of connecting with a mate, of feeling whole in his arms.

Eager to feel him, Maeve slid her hands from his shoulders to his back, urging him closer. He was heat and steel, but so careful with her, his touch soft across her breast.

Leaning into him, she glided her hand across the breadth of his wide back, entranced by the hardness of male flesh covered in velvet skin. Again, she indulged in the sweep of her hand across his back. In turn, Kieran sent her a stare so fixed, 'twas as if he wanted naught more than to look at her all night, please her all night.

A moment later, his mouth caressed her neck, then whispered kisses past her collarbones, down to the tops of her breasts. There, he tasted her skin in an unhurried sampling.

Within the confines of her dress, her breasts tightened, crying for his touch. The brush of his lips slipped lower, over her wet dress. She felt his breath upon her nipples, the care with which he held her. Maeve reeled from the sensations, the joining of her body and heart in something so right.

"Sweet Maeve," he whispered just before his mouth delved into the valley between her breasts.

And she could wait no more to feel him everywhere, to fully accept the fact they were husband and wife for always.

Slipping her hands to her side, she began working on the hooks of her damp gown. Gladness lit Kieran's features before he set his fingers to helping her. Moments later, she stood clad in her chemise, the rich green of her gown on the floor in a forgotten heap.

Kieran's palm was like a warm breeze upon her skin as he lifted the shift from her hips, abdomen, and breasts inch by inch. He dragged it over her head and tossed the garment away.

Lashes fluttering, Maeve closed her eyes and gave herself over to his touch. Kieran did not disappoint, skimming his rough palms down her shoulders before cupping her breasts.

Thick desire wound through her, until she knew only this moment, this man, his touch, and the soft golden candlelight about them.

Kieran continued with his slow loving as he bent to her and eased his mouth over her breast, tongue stroking lightly. Her pulse skipped. She went nearly limp in his arms as he cradled her breast, thumb caressing the tingling side, and laved kisses upon her.

Maeve wrapped her arms about his neck and held him there as he fanned the fire of her want into something burning and strong. Still, he would not be rushed as he turned the same mind-reeling attention to her other breast for an endless minute. Heat coiled deep in her belly.

In the next instant, he surprised her by bending to lift her against him and carry her to the bed. Gaze capturing into hers, Kieran settled her back against the mattress, then stood back to remove his hose. Golden shadows played over his brown hair, his muscled body, and Maeve found herself impatient and entranced.

He joined her on the bed moments later, beside her, his hands indulging in a silky exploration of the curves at her waist, her hips.

She sighed at his touch, feeling dazed at his attention, the pleasure.

Maeve returned the favor, sliding a trembling hand down the length of his chest, caressing the top of his thigh. And still his gaze held hers, her own a willing partner privy to the fluid desire and infinite tenderness there.

When he rolled her to her back and covered her with his warm length, Maeve welcomed him by clasping him tightly. His mouth found her in a smooth, unhurried stroke. When his knees gently nudged her thighs apart and he eased his hard length inside her to treat her to that same slow pace, Maeve felt certain she had been transported to heaven.

On the next long stroke, he sank deeper, then deeper again. Need shimmered in her blood. Her beat caught at his gentle rhythm. Her body, her heart, rose up to meet him each time he entered her.

Pleasure resonated in her hips, warming her, as Kieran fit his hands beneath her hips. His breath on her neck was pure fire. With each thrust, he seemed to pour himself into her. Pleasure swirled and grew until she found herself dangling dangerously close to the edge of passion.

Above her, Kieran moaned, his body growing taut. His strokes lengthened, quickened.

"Maeve," he gasped as he crashed into her once more.

He transformed her pleasure into a bright, glittering release that scattered a satisfied glow throughout her body. Tensing, he cried out above her, delving into her once more, and again. Then, with a deep exhalation, he lay upon her, utterly relaxed.

Maeve held him, his heart racing against hers. Peace and joy overtook her mind. The past mattered not. The future lay before them with perfect promise.

"Kieran?"

He groaned. "A moment please, you vixen. I think you robbed me of my mind."

Despite the serenity deep in her blood, she laughed. "I'm a thief now?"

"Consider, my lady, that I'm certain I've never been so thoroughly boneless and expended in my life."

Smiling, Maeve decided she liked the sound of that. Hugging him closer, she hoped he would welcome what she must say next.

"I stole naught what I did not intend to give back to you in some way."

He sent her a low rumble of laughter. "Oh, you gave back, my sweet wife."

Maeve felt herself flushing. "That is not what I meant." She batted a playful hand at his shoulder, then took his hand in hers. "I meant this."

As she placed his palm on her abdomen, his eyes widened in question, then in shock.

"A babe?" he whispered.

"Most like before Christmastide," she confirmed, nodding. "'Tis why I've been sick."

"Maeve…"

Uncertainty shadowed her heart. "Does that please you?"

He drew in a deep breath. "'Tis so unexpected, I scarce know what to say."

She regarded him with a frown. "Your pleasure would be best, as he will come whether you want him or not."

"True," Kieran conceded, still looking somewhat stunned. "I…I will protect him, as I protect you."

So badly, Maeve wanted to tell Kieran of her love, explain she kept it secret because of anger she now would not allow to spoil their future. But 'twas clear the news of the babe had been enough for the day. Soon, when he was reconciled to being a father, she would reveal all—and hope he felt the same.

* * * *

Lying beside Maeve that eve as she slept, Kieran tossed in their bed, feeling as if Maeve had, with her touch, robbed him of rational thought, stripped him to the bone of feeling.

Then she had stunned him senseless with her announcement.

A babe? 'Twas the ticket to the freedom he had long sought, his means to leave Ireland now that the rebellion was so severely crippled 'twould be some time before it would rise again—if ever.

He cast his gaze down to Maeve. The richness of the red-gold spread across the white pillow, her fair skin still flushed from the tender, shattering love they had shared.

Kieran tried to resist the urge to brush his fingers along her cheek but could not. She smelled of rain, of pure female, and of him.

She looked a like a sleeping goddess, relaxed but still fiery.

Aye, he loved her. But what did that solve?

So much divided them he could scarce list all of their differences. And the magic she made him feel was frightening for him, a man of battle, of logic.

Leaving the bed, he began to pace. Movement helped him to think better. Still, given their clashes, he could only wonder if he and Maeve were destined to share his mother and father's fate—eternal hate. Kieran rebelled against that thought. He had not his father's battering bitterness. Maeve had not his mother's narrow, pious mind. Still, so many parallels existed...

And what of his life as a mercenary? During his first days in Ireland, how he had yearned to return to Spain, earn his coin, a bed, a willing señorita, and drink into the night if it suited his whim.

Fondly, he recalled those days. They could be his now.

Did he want them again—or something else entirely?

Cursing, Kieran dressed in quiet and strode down to the great hall. Many of the castlefolk lingered there, supper just past, listening to Brighid play the light notes of a harp.

At his entrance, Kieran glared over the crowd. Chattering ceased. The dancing stopped. Brighid's harp fell silent. Aric rose.

Kieran's gaze found its way to his friend. Wearing a concerned frown, Aric crossed the room to his side.

"What ails you?" he asked, voice low.

"Everything," he choked, seeing the castlefolk stare.

With a glance over his shoulder, Aric nodded. "Let us go outside, hmm?"

Nodding, Kieran turned numbly, not certain why he had sought his friend, except for the man's logical mind.

Aric led him out into the falling night, where milky stars brushed the sky. Night sounds invaded his head—frogs, crickets, the rush of the River Barrow nearby. Damp ground beneath his feet seemed to suck him down.

"What has happened?" Aric asked, leaning up against the stone walls of the keep.

"Maeve," he whispered. Still, his mind could scarce form the words. "She is breeding."

Surprise crossed Aric's face just before a smile curled up his mouth. "Wondrous news! Gwenyth and I waited years for God to bless us with Blythe. Consider yourself—"

"I know not what to do!" Kieran ground out.

Confusion fell across Aric's face. "You love her?"

"Aye." The realization still did not please him.

"She will give you a child."

He nodded. "By Christmastide."

Understanding dawned on Aric's strong, tawny face. "And you still consider leaving?"

Kieran exhaled into the chilly fog. "She will come to hate me. Already she hates the English cause I represent. And Maeve will forever stand for Ireland."

"You can find an understanding with her," Aric encouraged. "She is not an unreasonable woman."

"Aye, as long as I bend to her wishes. I have done all I can, and still it will not be enough. I cannot keep her brother safe forever. Sooner or later, the Palesmen will discover his whereabouts, and I will be forced to send him to Dublin, I fear, else King Henry will see me dead, as well as punish you and Guilford for my choices. I cannot risk that. Nor can I release Flynn to wreak more havoc with the rebels."

"Kieran—"

"How much will Maeve hate me when Flynn is executed? And what if more battles ensue? I must fight them—'tis my job. Maeve will not understand or approve. And I will lose her."

The thought made Kieran's gut clench, his heart squeeze.

"You know that for certain?"

Kieran nodded. "She speaks to me now, even acts the wife with me. Perhaps 'twill last a month or two, mayhap longer if my luck holds. But this end is inevitable, I fear."

"And you do not want to leave her side?"

He shook his head and exhaled heavily. "'Twould be like ripping out my heart."

With a rueful smile, Aric clapped Kieran on the back. "Though I love my wife to foolish measures, I think you have fallen the hardest of us three."

The corners of Kieran's mouth lifted in a sad gesture. "I think you are right. But I must ask myself what would be least painful to Maeve."

"To clasp her to you for a few stolen months and grow more

attached until reality intrudes, or simply leave?" Aric said.

His English friend had a way of finding the crux of a matter that Kieran had always admired. Today, he saw his only real choice so clearly—and it brought him much pain.

"Have you considered that in those few stolen months," Aric began, "your love might grow strong enough to withstand the tides of politics, family strife, and your differences in temper?"

Kieran frowned, enveloped in sadness he had never before felt. "'Tis a fantasy, my friend, one that will ne'er happen. Maeve cannot help what she believes any more than I can help what I believe. Though I love her, she does not love me. 'Tis better that I leave before she comes to hate me."

"How much have your parents to do with this belief?"

Again, Aric seemed to discern the inner workings of his mind and drew upon them. "Some."

"Perhaps too much," Aric counseled. "You are not the same people. Nor would you make the same choices that resulted in their enmity. Think on that."

* * * *

"Good morn, Maeve," called Aric across the great hall. "Would you sit with me?"

At Aric's solemn greeting, she abandoned her morning stroll and sank to the bench beside him. "Are you well?"

"Aye, merely concerned for my friend." He hesitated. "Your marriage is not my place, and I well know that. But my friend's heart is in peril, and as I leave on the morrow, I cannot remain silent."

"In peril? Kieran's heart?" Maeve would have laughed if the assertion wasn't so confusing.

Aric nodded. "He is not a man given to many ties. Long I have thought—we have all thought—such bonds would serve him well. 'Tis been over twenty years since he has known a true family. Guilford, Drake, and I loved him as well as could be. But he needs your softness in his life to remind him of what is good, to dissuade him from war."

Slowly, Maeve nodded, though she understood not. What did Aric try to say?

"You are confused." He sighed. "Let me be plain. Why did you choose to tell him of the babe on the heels of the rebellion's collapse? Do you want him gone so badly?"

Staring at Kieran's friend, she tried to understand his question, but 'twas as if he spoke a different language.

"Want him gone? Nay. I but told him of the babe because I—his decision to keep Flynn at Langmore pleased me and I thought he had a right to know of the coming child."

"What of his bargain with King Henry? Did you not consider that?"

Maeve looked at Aric blankly. A bargain with the king?

"Or Kieran did not tell you." Aric spoke the phrase like fact, throwing up his hands in the air. "That fool."

Foreboding shot down Maeve's spine. "Since I know not of what you speak, I must assume he did not tell me."

At that, Aric stood. "I suggest you ask him—and listen with an open ear. Your future may depend upon it."

CHAPTER SIXTEEN

Maeve raced back up to Kieran's chamber. A deal with the king he had? Most like, it involved her, and she would not rest until she knew what he plotted.

Up the stairs she trounced, the sickness in her belly she had awakened to all but gone in the face of her anxiety. She ignored the glowing wall sconces, except to allow them to light her way. Every thought focused on her wayward husband.

At the chamber, Maeve pushed open the door. Kieran pulled on long boots, which served to emphasize his long, muscled legs. The image burned itself in her brain, in her belly. Idiot she was! She could not think of such now. At this moment, she must have answers, not succumb to his charm.

At her entry, he looked up, a cautious greeting on his face. "Good morn, Ma—"

"Aric let spill you have some bargain with King Henry. Out with it!"

Kieran paused, his body going still. He sighed, but Maeve heard the muttered curse under his breath.

"Aye, damnation will be yours if you do not tell me all."

He reached for her. "Maeve…"

She eased from his grasp. "What have you to say?"

Drawing in a deep breath, Kieran frowned with reluctance. "Before I left London, King Henry made me the earl of Kildare and bade me to take a wife amongst you and your sisters."

"You tell me naught I do not know," she said impatiently.

Kieran held up a hand to stay her. "I did not wish to come to

Ireland or take a wife. I was due back in Spain, and longed to be there. Aric knew this. 'Twas his deal with the king…though I agreed."

"And this bargain, it was…?"

He hesitated again. "Sweet Maeve, 'twill sound damning to you, and I meant you no ill will."

Her impatience grew. "Do not stall me with your glib tongue. Tell me now."

He paused, then admitted, "We agreed that if I quelled the rebellion and I got my wife to breeding, I was free to leave Ireland, and need only return once the child was birthed."

Fury washed over Maeve.

From the first, he had planned to fill her belly with child and leave her. Had that, and stupid lust, been his motives for bedding her as often as she allowed it? Had he no feeling for her? For their marriage?

His touch, indeed some of his actions, seemed to say he cared. This bargain said he cared only about freedom, about leaving.

Either way, she hated the confusion, the uncertainty that allowing herself to care for him had wrought. One day happy, the next betrayed. 'Twas more than she could stomach.

"Maeve, I know what you think," he rushed to say, reaching for her. "I planned to leave before I truly knew you. I coaxed you into my bed because I wanted you, not to satisfy this bargain."

She backed away from his hold. Perhaps 'twas true. Perhaps he merely said what he thought she wished to hear. Confusion spun about her until her head near burst. Always, he found ways to make her believe in him. And always, she discerned the manner in which he'd made her a fool. No more!

She glared at him. "And what of the babe? What was to happen when you returned at his birth? You were to take him from me, to England. Is that not so?"

Kieran raked a hand through his hair, sighing. "Aye, to raise him English, then return him to govern."

Finally, he spoke true, but much too late to save her from making the terrible mistake of conceiving a child with him. Betrayal seeped into her skin, into the corners of her heart. Pain hit next, blinding, devastating, soul rending.

She had loved him. To the end, he had hidden his cause for

coming, pretended to care for her, deceived her sisters into believing him a fair-minded man. Only Flynn had refused to believe the yarns he had spun about his duties in the Pale. Mayhap he had even been responsible for Quaid's execution. Had every day with Kieran been a lie?

At this moment, it felt thus. And she had never hurt—or hated—more.

"You are contemptible!" she cried. "Every word and deed from you is naught but a falsehood designed to gain what you wish. Never mind the hurts to others, so long as you obtain what you want."

"Maeve, that is unfair! I never wanted to be here. I told you thus!"

"Then why did you not leave me untouched, let me wed Quaid, and leave me in peace?" she yelled.

"My duty forbade it and…and…" He swallowed. "And something inside me refused to let another man wed you."

"How tender that sounds!" She gave him a bitter laugh. "Have I any reason to believe the word of a man who would impregnate his wife to steal her child? A man who would create the child to satisfy his king?"

"I agreed to the bargain to help my mentor, Guilford. Henry had threatened to take his money and power if I did not comply. I owe Guilford my very life. What was I to do? Let an old man rot in poverty?"

His words gave her pause. Kieran's motives sounded pure enough, but was that not always the case? And if he only wanted to save an old man, why had he not enlisted her help, instead of deceiving her?

"You could easily have told me of your bargain, perhaps allowed me a say in this tangle. After all, I am the one bearing the child!"

He held his hands out to her, face supplicating. "For some weeks now, I have not known whether I wanted to abide by the bargain. Why do you think I held back my joy when you told me of this child? I know not what to do!"

Excuses, all of them. Maeve was heartily tired of them.

"Then I will help you, *my lord*. Leave." She pointed to the door. "Travel far from Langmore and *never*, for any reason, come back. There is naught more I loathe than you!"

Desolation claimed Kieran's face, and she nearly reached out to him to offer comfort. She stopped herself short. Was the anguish on his face another method of drawing her in?

"Maeve...I see now I should have told you. But Saint Peter's toes, you scarce spoke to me for weeks. Should I have trapped you in a corner and forced you to listen?"

"If need be."

"You would only have resisted me more, and I had every intent to claim you as my wife, bargain or no."

"Regardless of whether I wished it. Exactly my point. You know not how to care for another. You know not how to love." She glared at him, hoping her fierce expression hid the fact she felt shattered and betrayed—and as if she would never be the same again.

Resignation overtook his face, until he looked weary and defeated, and Maeve's heart ached all the more.

"I was a fool to think we could live as man and wife in any sort of harmony," he said, his voice somber. "Politics predestined us to hate. 'Tis unlikely that will change." He turned away. "I will be gone within the hour."

* * * *

Kieran rode west as night fell. Every part of his body ached, from his seat, which had sat a saddle for endless hours now, to his head, which whirled at the day's events.

As he had thought, feared, Maeve was lost to him. Upon his leave-taking, Aric had tried to convince him to remain at Langmore. Aric had said he was certain Maeve would understand in time that Kieran belonged with her.

Rarely was Aric wrong, but now was such a time. Weariness, sadness, defeat, all tumbled in his blood until he could scarce think—misery had known no better soul mate. How had Maeve wrapped herself so thoroughly around his heart so quickly, when others had tried and failed?

Kieran shook his head. Knowing 'twould do him little good to dwell on this failure, he put his morose thoughts away, in the back of his mind, and buried them deeply. Now he would decide where to travel, what battle to join. Aye, he would.

For some reason, the decision brought no excitement.

Dusk settled across the mountains. Kieran gazed into the vivid pinks and oranges settling at the horizon. He pictured Andalusian Spain, her dark-haired women, her golden beaches, the wild Sierra Morena Mountains.

His mind replaced it all with images of fire-haired Maeve on a windswept hillside of heather, golden eyes beckoning.

Cursing, he forced himself to focus on the view before him. The Wicklow Mountains, his boyhood home, loomed close.

A moment's glance told him he was little more than a mile from Balcorthy. Compelled there in a way he understood not, Kieran turned his mount north, headed up the mountain, past the stream, to look at the charred ruins of his home.

The once stately keep now looked black and twisted, crumbled with the passing of time, bowed under the pelting of rain, snow, wind, neglect. Yet, closing his eyes, he could picture Balcorthy as it had once been: alive, full of intrigue, rife with violence.

The inevitable day, the last one, came rushing back. His mother's quiet contempt for his father's barbarian ways—the battle, the lack of courtly dress, the rough manner in which he did nearly all things. And his father had railed, always trying to prove himself more manly, more powerful. To this day, Kieran knew not whether Desmond had sought to impress his wife in his own way or repel her more.

Urging his mount forward, Kieran entered the remains of the castle. As he looked about, he felt cold. The roof in most places had fallen after the fire without the wood beams to support it. The black walls screamed misery, and Kieran wondered again why he was here. Memories he'd held at bay for over twenty years assailed him, vivid and terrible. Inescapable here at Balcorthy.

He wanted to leave, to continue forgetting. Yet something about the fading old place drew him to dismount, cross the fragrant grass growing where the wooden floor once lay, touch the dying walls.

As if they could show him the past again, he saw his father yelling at his silently defiant mother as she clutched her Bible in one hand, Rosary in the other. Desmond called Jocelyn a whore, accusing her of bedding down with any and all of his kin. Kieran recalled his puzzlement, as he'd oft seen his father sharing a pallet with other women of the castle. Never had his mother done aught but cling to her spirituality and ignore her husband.

Then the battle had come. Jocelyn said her family had finally come to free her from oppression. Desmond swore she would never leave. Then he hit her. Again and again and again—and not for the first time.

Kieran shook his head, refusing to remember what happened next. 'Twould do no good. He could not alter the past.

He feared that, if he followed his heart's impulse and returned to Langmore, it would become much like Balcorthy someday, its spirit dying, walls filled with hate, until 'twas abandoned. He also feared its people would suffer the same fate, and he could not do that to Maeve.

If he returned, Maeve's hate for him would surely only grow. As he loved her, Kieran knew he could not endure that.

In return, he would have the cold consolation of knowing he had done the best he could to see her happiness—and miss her always.

* * * *

A week later, quiet reigned at Langmore, except for the occasional cries made by little Geralt.

Each night, Maeve muffled the sound of her tears in her pillow and hoped Fiona, with whom she still shared a chamber, could not hear in the silence.

Another dawn burst over the spring-laden land. Maeve woke but did not open her tired eyes. Those, along with her aching heart and roiling stomach, were all intimate reminders of Kieran, of the husband she could never forget.

'Twould be easy if she could bring herself to hate him as she had told him she did. But her heart would not be merciful in this, and it pined for him, yearned to see his wicked smile, feel his tender touch again. It remembered the happy moments, the occasional teasing, the help he gave her sisters, the care with which he'd made love to her.

Only her mind recalled his ugly bargain, considered all the ways in which he had probably deceived her with any number of glib lies. With Kieran's charm, 'twas likely he knew well how to seduce women, tell them what they craved hearing, whilst keeping his heart to himself, untouched. She'd known upon first meeting Kieran that was his game. Maeve knew he had ensnared her in his smile until she forgot the truth. And she was more the fool for it.

"Are you coming to break your fast, Maeve?" asked Jana suddenly from the door.

She looked across the room, to Fiona's bed, and found it empty. It must be late indeed.

She sighed. "Nay, food holds no appeal."

"You must keep your strength for this babe," she admonished. "You'll want him strong for you and for Ireland."

Maeve nodded. Deep in her heart, she knew Jana spoke true, but her spirit felt so battered by Kieran's departure and her unrequited love, she could scarce think about much beyond surviving this day.

Jana frowned, then crossed the room to Maeve's side suddenly. "You miss him?"

Biting her lip, Maeve did her best not to cry. Kieran deserved no more of her tears. Aye, he was capable of an occasional kindness if it suited him. But he could not return her love, could never put her wishes at equal with his, could not be honest if it meant revealing his motives or explaining himself. A man like that was not worthy of her sorrow.

So why could she not contain it?

"Maeve, I know not what happened between you, but I—"

"Then say naught. I will deal with this."

"I think he cared for you very much. The manner in which he looked at you… 'Twas more than lust, Sister. He saved Flynn and even now keeps our brother's presence secret in Langmore's dungeon. He has allowed us all to visit him. The last earl would not have done so much."

Her own sister defended the enemy? Must she endure rebellion within her own family?

"I was not wed to the last earl!" Maeve cried. "I cared not if the last earl lied to me. Kieran stood in silence and watched Quaid die. He made a bargain with the king to destroy the rebellion and conceive a babe so he might have his freedom, and did not tell me thus! Why should I want a man like that?"

Jana sat on the edge of the bed beside her sister. "Did he leave before you dismissed him from Langmore?"

Maeve hesitated. "Nay, but—"

"I think, Sister, that you turned him away before he could leave you. I think, once you heard of his bargain, you feared the man you loved would leave you forever, and you cast him out first. Did you think 'twould hurt less that way?"

Maeve paused, still now. Had she done what Jana accused?

A fresh wave of despair rushed up to claim her. Anger followed. "Why did he leave?" she cried. "Not because I ordered him to, I know. He ne'er listened to me of his own will."

"Maybe 'twas your will he followed. I think he cared for you, Maeve, and did not want your contempt and distrust. He left, rather than upset you more."

"Why do you defend him?" Maeve demanded. "He is English and he came here to subjugate us, enslave us to the English ways."

"If that were true, he would have seen most of us dead or reduced to servants, imprisoned, or starved us. Instead, he wed you, cared for Langmore, cared for you, helped with little Geralt's birth, and saved Flynn's life. His bargain with the king was made long before he met you."

True, all of it. But something inside Maeve still fought back. "But he never told me of his odious deal!"

"If he had, what would have changed?" Jana prompted, touching a soft hand to Maeve's shoulder. "Would you have been able to resist him forever? Nay. You would have loved him, only fearing sooner that he would leave you."

Maeve closed her weary eyes. 'Twas ugly, but she feared Jana had the right of it. Her elder sister had no reason to defend a man so aligned to the English cause. Could it be Jana saw what she herself did not?

"I know not what to do," she whispered, feeling fresh tears sting her eyes.

Jana drew her into a sisterly embrace. "It will come to you, Maeve. Just listen to your heart."

CHAPTER SEVENTEEN

April blurred into May, which quickly passed to the first of June. Kieran gripped his mug of ale and tried not to remember that forty-eight days had passed since he'd last held Maeve, had last wanted to smile. 'Twas hard to forget with so many reminders haunting the keep of Harwich Hall.

"Averyl, love," Drake cajoled his breeding wife, whilst holding their two-year-old daughter, Nessa. "You cannot mean to spend the day riding about to visit the villagers and Gwenyth. You are fragile now—"

Gwenyth snorted at that as she came down the stairs and entered the room. "She has twice been through a breeding, you mutton-head. I will watch over her. She will not break."

The women shared indulgent grins. Maeve would fit in well here, Kieran thought. Or she would if she didn't hate him.

But she did, and he knew naught would change that.

The thought came with pain. He pushed it away and watched his friends with dispassionate eyes.

Drake threw a mock glower at Gwenyth. "And why should I trust you? You ever lead my wife astray, you English hoyden."

The Scotsman's teasing tone had Gwenyth laughing.

"I like that quality in my wife," Aric called as he stepped down the stairs behind Gwenyth, holding the bundle of their infant daughter.

"Besides," Averyl murmured, grinning at her husband, "'Tis you who leads me astray, and I will soon have a babe to prove it."

Standing in a small circle, the foursome laughed. Drake kissed his daughter, who squirmed for release. As he let her down to join her three-year-old brother in the nearby garden, he wore a contented grin, the likes of which, a few short years ago, Kieran had not believed his Scottish friend would ever display again.

Drake caressed his wife's shoulder in a tender gesture, then flashed her a grin. "And I thank God you let me lead you astray often."

More laughter ensued. Kieran took another swig of his ale and cursed beneath his breath when he found the tankard dry.

Their happiness should gladden him. His best friends, the brothers of his heart, had found such joy in life and in marriage. 'Twas plain to see.

But jealousy festered like a canker in his heart. He wanted their contentment, the bliss so evident on their warrior faces. And, God help him, he wanted it with Maeve. Such wishes were foolish and impossible, but he could not stop them.

"What say you, Kieran?" Drake called. "Is it not Gwenyth's wayward manner that has led Averyl astray?"

He tried to smile. "Blame Gwenyth not for your sins."

"Ah ha!" she said in triumph. "Kieran sees the truth."

Drake groaned. "But you give my sweet wife such rebellious ideas."

Averyl faced her husband with a saucy smile. "How do you know the ideas are hers?"

Aric clapped Drake on the back. "She has you beat there, my friend. Poor Averyl has been wed to you now for nigh on four years. Certainly, you must blame your influence on her."

"Me?" Drake pointed to himself in mock insult. "I am all that is innocent and pure of thought."

Laughing, Averyl faced her husband. "Now we all know your ability to lie. Take you off to the chapel. Such a falsehood cries out for confession!"

"You are supposed to take my side, love," Drake whispered.

"When you are so outrageously false? Never."

At Averyl's giggle, Drake wrapped his arms around her and brushed a kiss on her lips. To their left, Aric cast Gwenyth a tender gaze.

Kieran turned away, knowing he could take no more.

Their happiness burned in his gut, dangled before his eyes like a prize just out of reach.

Springing up from his bench, uncaring that its scraping sound disrupted the joy in the room, he rose and left, fists clenched at his sides.

"Poor Kieran…" he heard Averyl say.

He strode faster to block out their pitying conversation, destined to follow.

To his surprise, Kieran looked up and found himself in the chapel. Ordinarily, the House of God had little appeal for him. Battle and war left little time for commune with a higher being and reflection on the soul.

Today, it sounded perfect.

He knelt on one knee and crossed himself before rising to his feet again. What should he do next? Kneel again? Stand here and pray? He sighed. And what would he pray for besides a miracle? Surely naught less would bring Maeve back to him.

To his right, Kieran heard a sigh, then saw Guilford struggling to his feet. Rushing to his mentor, he clasped a hand around the old man's arm and helped him upright.

Guilford shot him an irritated glance. "'Tis slow I am, not infirm."

"I am sorry," Kieran said, releasing the old man.

"What brings you here?"

Kieran shrugged. "Quiet, I suppose."

Guilford stared in disbelief. "Never have I known you to seek quiet, lad. Your wife trouble weighs upon you."

The old man's perception ruffled him. He had not been so obvious, had he? Aye, he supposed he had. Still, he did not want to be reminded of thus, and he did not want to discuss it.

"It will pass."

"I think not." Guilford frowned. "Aric and Drake at least had the sense to bring their brides here whilst sorting through the difficulties of their lives. You left your Maeve in Ireland. How am I to meet her then?"

Sleeplessness and melancholy ruled his life until he hardly knew himself, and Guilford worried over meeting Maeve?

"I will give you directions to Langmore," he snapped, then hesitated. "And do not be deceived should anyone tell you that you must trek through the bog because the bridge is down."

Guilford chuckled. "Maeve's doing?"

With a sad, self-deprecating smile, he nodded.

"Ah, boy, 'tis clear you love her. You've scarce smiled since arriving. You have not looked at any of the wenches you used to fancy, and you even snarled at one you used to find more than passing pleasing, as I recall."

Ballocks, Kieran had been aware of that himself. "I need no reminders of my recent history, old man."

Kieran tried not to look glum, but he felt thus, and was all but certain it showed on his face. Why else would Guilford smile so smugly?

"Leave me in peace," he said. "Aric and Drake do well with your guidance. They are men of reflection."

"And you have been a man of action these past days, aye. Staring into your ale, refusing opportunities to return to Spain or join the battle in France, glowering at all and sundry. Aye, it must be difficult to think much with so grueling a schedule."

Kieran glared at the old man's sarcasm. Then he realized Guilford was right, as always. Naught pleased him anymore but the thought of returning to Maeve. Naught hurt him more than knowing she would never take him back.

Kieran sighed. Bleak days stretched out before him, and he had no notion of what to do, how to rebuild his life without Maeve. Why should it be that the very freedom he sought before he wed her was now the freedom that would likely kill him?

"Did you tell her you love her?" Guilford asked simply.

"Nay." He had been too certain she would never return the sentiment. He'd been too afraid that baring his heart would only make their inevitable parting more painful when politics and their beliefs clashed again.

"Mayhap 'tis time you did," Guilford offered. "With a woman, ofttimes a true apology and a few tender words will melt the anger from her heart."

"Think you I've never known a woman, old man?"

Guilford's blue eyes turned serious. "I think you've known plenty of women, but never stayed long enough to know their hearts."

The words took Kieran aback with their simple truth. Aye, he had ever known how to coax a woman into bed. What had he known of keeping her ardor after? Naught, for he had never wanted such.

"Of you three, I feared you, Kieran, would find making an attachment most difficult. Your parents did not love."

Kieran fought a grimace. He had been thinking about Desmond and Jocelyn's dismal marriage too much of late. Certainly, he had no wish to discuss it, either.

"Kieran, do you hear me?"

"I cannot help but hear you." He sighed. "Aye, my parents did not love."

"But if Maeve disagreed with you in silence, would you have beat her for it, as your father did to your mother? If she turned to the Bible to ignore you, would you do your best to force your attentions upon her?"

The very idea repelled him. "Nay!"

"And would Maeve destroy everything in her path for the simple purpose of hurting you?"

Kieran frowned at the foolish image. "Maeve seeks peace."

"Hmm. There you have it."

"I have naught! Just because we would not seek the other's pain does not mean we will love. Too much divides us."

Guilford's blue eyes pinned him in place with a healthy skepticism. "Come now. Impetuous you might be at times, but you are not a rash man. And Aric tells me Maeve has good sense. Politics can only divide the fools who allow thus. If you love her, I cannot imagine why you would keep yourself from her. And if she is already breeding, 'tis clear Maeve does not avoid you or think you a vulgar barbarian, for I know you would not force your seed upon her, as your father did to your mother."

'Twas more complicated than that. Was it not? Certainly, he had done more than merely assume at the first hint of conflict that he and Maeve were destined to share his parents' fate. Had he not?

Thoughts buzzed in his head, louder than a thousand bees swarming a hive. "What say you, old man?"

"Compromise, son. Good talk. Consider that Drake and Averyl have not allowed the fact they came from warring clans to affect their happiness."

"They are perfect for each other."

Guilford smiled as he clapped Kieran on the shoulder. "Perhaps Maeve is perfect for you, eh?"

* * * *

June brought relief from Maeve's morning-sick stomach. But she could spare no time to celebrate such relief once the rider from Dublin came.

Ulick McConnell, one of the remaining rebels spying now in Lord Butler's keep, rode for Langmore as if hell pounded at his back. Maeve rushed out to greet him, along with Jana.

The young man dismounted, gasping for air. Brown locks fell across his forehead as he regarded her with apprehension.

"What is it, Ulick? What news do you bring?" Maeve demanded.

"'Tis—'tis Lord Butler. I know not where from," he gasped, "but Lord Butler hears rumors."

Concern assailed Maeve. "Rumors?"

Ulick nodded. "He knows your lord husband has gone."

The spy, only a few years older than she, shot her a look of speculation. Maeve did not shy away. "Aye, he has. What of it?"

"Now that Kildare is not here to say him nay, Lord Butler has decided he will demand a look in Langmore's dungeons."

Maeve gasped. "He knows Flynn is prisoner there?"

"He suspects." Ulick drew in more air. "Some of the other rebels, trying to save their own necks, told Lord Butler of Flynn's capture."

"We must do something, now," Jana said quickly. "Somehow we must break him free."

Jana had said this before, that they should not leave their only brother and the chief of their *Fein* a prisoner in his own home. Until now, Maeve had disagreed. First, Kieran had, before leaving, placed Patrick and two of his most loyal guards in charge of keeping Flynn inside the dungeon. The rest of his army still held the castle. She'd not known how to break her brother free without harming the soldiers. And she refused to see them injured. Her other reason for hesitation was Flynn's violence. These past few months, he had seemed to crave bloodshed. That she would not abide.

But with one of the powerful Palesmen coming, she had little choice but to see her brother free or watch his blood spill.

The decision relieved her. But it had naught to do with Kieran.

She did not see Flynn free to protect her foolish husband from his fellow English brutes if they discovered he had kept Flynn's capture secret, for she scarce thought of Kieran at all.

Only every few moments…

"We must hurry, good lady. We have but a few hours before Lord Butler comes with his guards."

Jana grabbed Ulick's hand. "Come with me. I know of a way we can distract the guards."

Apparently, Jana had discerned the same challenge. Still, Maeve warned her, "I want no one hurt."

Her older sister smiled, something she did often since little Geralt's birth. "No one will be hurt, unless Ulick here cannot run."

He puffed out his chest, looking much affronted. "I can run better than any English knave."

Jana nodded and smiled slyly. "Then let us go. Maeve, once you hear the scream, watch for Patrick and the others to abandon their posts. You'll have but a few minutes, so be quick."

The scream? Maeve wasn't sure she liked the sound of that. "What of the keys? The door inside the dungeon—"

Grimacing, Jana paused, clearly in thought. "Old Patrick has ever been fond of you since you were a wee babe. Would he not be letting you visit your brother this fine day?"

Maeve nodded. Why had she not thought of that?

Because Kieran plagued her mind, day and night, with no respite. Why could she not forget the man?

"Wait a few moments before you…scream, Jana."

She nodded and began to lead Ulick away. "We shall go discuss the plan."

Had Jana interest in Ulick? Her smile seemed to indicate thus. And she found Ulick's gaze fixed on Jana as well. Apparently the man was not immune to her sister's charm.

"Ulick?" The question slipped from her mouth.

The young rebel flushed. "Tell Flynn my horse will wait him just off the road after crossing the River Barrow."

Then Jana tugged on his hand and they disappeared into the dawn.

Knowing she had little choice, Maeve strode to the dungeon with purpose. She hated to deceive the old man, one she had known a great part of her life, but her brother's life—and possibly

Kieran's—depended on this.

Nay, she must put Kieran from her thoughts now. He had abandoned her after learning of the babe that would free him from responsibility. He had left, making it clear that while he might have some feelings for her, he did not care enough to stay. So she had demanded he leave. Maeve had not really expected him to listen, which made her wonder if he had somehow maneuvered her into those rash words.

Shaking the confusion from her thoughts, she smiled at old Patrick and pushed thoughts of her infuriating, tempting husband away.

"Good morn, Patrick."

"Milady, good morn to ye."

Now came the difficult part. "Might I see my brother for a moment? I shall be quick."

Maeve prayed the old man would not refuse her. His reluctant expression made her insides clench.

"I have questions for him about Langmore's books. With my husband gone, I have no guidance."

Playing so helpless a female irritated her, but Patrick nodded.

"'Tis not easy, I'll be guessing, for a woman to understand sums and such." He paused. "Aye, ye can spend a few minutes with yer brother."

She gave him the most radiant smile she could muster, given her clammy hands and beating heart. The old man responded to it and let her in.

After a short walk down a dark, musty hallway, they arrived at Flynn's door. As usual, the overpowering odors of human waste, sweat, fear, and vomit nauseated her. Maeve reined in her reaction with what she hoped appeared a friendly expression. Patrick nodded at her as he let her in Flynn's cell and walked away, locking the door behind him.

Maeve turned to her brother, who sat on the straw-covered floor with fury burning in his eyes. Taken aback by his fierce expression, she approached with care.

"Flynn?"

In an instant, he stood and crossed the room, bearing down upon her with a scowl. "That English maggot you call a husband is long gone, and yet you scarce come to see me? Get me gone from here!

Time is of the essence."

Confused by his words, she frowned. Flynn grabbed her arm, grip impatient, before she could ask him his meaning.

"Well, what do you wait for? An invitation from Christ?"

Flynn's voice grew alarmingly loud. Maeve shushed him with a quick hiss.

"We have a plan," she whispered. "In a minute, Jana will scream to divert the guards. I will call for Patrick and tell him I must go join the search for her. When he comes to free you, grab him and lock him in your cell. Ulick McConnell left his mount on the side of the road, just after you cross the river. Ride far away."

"Aye, I will do that, now that you've finally decided to do as you should and release me."

Flynn had never had a nasty temper, and Maeve tried not to take his tone to heart. Instead, she grabbed his hand in sisterly affection. "I will free you, but I must have your promise that you will seek a rebellion free of blood. Flynn, I cannot have innocent lives on my hands, nor should you want them on yours. We must try negotiations, find peaceful ways to seek resolution."

Her brother's expression turned narrow-eyed with anger. He looked ready to explode, to refuse her request in the most ruthless of terms. Maeve opened her mouth to implore him, reason with him.

Jana screamed.

Loud, filled with panic and terror, the sound rang from just outside the curtain walls all the way down the dungeon. At little Geralt's birth, she had known Jana capable of great noise, but not on command.

As they hoped, most of the castle guards went running for the sound, including the old Irish guard.

"Patrick!" she cried, doing her best to sound panicked. "I would have you release me now!"

The old man turned to her, face rife with impatience. "Milady, ye cannot help. Stay here where ye are safe and let us search for the lass."

Maeve shook her head adamantly. "That is one of my sisters, I know. I must help. Do not say me nay!"

The old man hesitated, then muttered a curse as he thrust the key into the lock of Flynn's cell and swung it open. Maeve raced out.

Before the guard could shut the door, Flynn grabbed the older man by the throat, thrust a savage kick into his genitals, then tossed him to the ground. As Patrick lay writhing on the ground, Flynn bent to mumble something low and menacing, thieved his dagger from his belt, and darted out, locking the guard inside.

Maeve greeted him with openmouthed horror in the corridor. "I asked you to cease the violence."

"He did not bleed," Flynn sneered as he gripped her arm and propelled her down the darkened hall. "He is an Irishman now loyal to England. What use have we for such a man? For any man loyal to England? None. Any good Irishman would take delight in watching English blood run to death."

"All English blood?" she choked as he led her out of the garrison, to the curtain wall.

"Every drop of it," he growled. "Especially that of your lice-ridden husband."

As Flynn tried to lift her over the curtain wall, Maeve resisted. Did he mean to take her with him?

"Go on," he prompted with impatience. "We have not much time!"

She shook her head, hoping Flynn did not see how her hands shook as well. "Nay, I must stay here. Lord Butler will be here within hours and expect me to greet him."

Flynn smiled then. "He was coming for me, to take me to Dublin?"

Maeve hesitated, then nodded.

"Perfect! Now you must come." He tried to push her over the wall again.

Still, Maeve clung to the stones and tried to push herself to the ground. "He will know you are gone, that I am gone, and that something is afoot! Surely you want to surprise them."

At that, Flynn laughed. "No need. By then, 'twill be much too late."

Before Maeve could inquire after his meaning, he pushed her over the curtain wall. To prevent falling head first and to protect the babe, Maeve clung to the wall and swung her legs over. Her knees scraped the stone and she bit back a cry. A moment later, Flynn followed over the stone wall, then dropped to the firm ground with a hop.

Her brother grabbed her arm and ran through the encroaching

forest until they came to the bridge over the River Barrow. With a curse, he pushed her onto the dirt road.

"Hurry. If we're seen, they will give chase."

At the top of the bridge, she stopped. "Flynn, you need me not. Leave me here and go on."

He sighed with exasperation and urged her across the bridge. "I do need you. Ireland needs you."

"Me? Flynn, I've done all for the rebellion I can."

Taking hold of her wrist, Flynn searched about for Ulick's hidden horse. When he finally spotted the animal tethered to a tree, he dragged her to it.

Maeve stood her ground again. "Where do you think to take me? What is your plan?"

Flynn glared at her, brown eyes blazing. "Ireland's finest hour is upon us, lass, and here you stand flapping your lips." He shook his head, then lifted her onto the mount. "Aye, I have a plan."

"Tell me," she urged, fearing the worst.

Why would her brother insist she come along? What could she contribute to the cause that Flynn would feel necessary?

"You will come with me, and I will make certain your husband knows the rebellion has taken you. He will turn Langmore over to us so that we can move forward with our plan to oust this Tudor prick from our land."

'Twas as if he spoke the language of the Norse or some other she did not understand. "How would telling Kieran that you had taken me coax him to relinquish Langmore?"

Flynn cast her an impatient glance, then mounted Ulick's horse behind her. "'Tis simple, Sister. We tell him he must withdraw his soldiers and surrender Langmore or see you dead."

A chill invaded her. She was too shocked to even gasp. "Dead? But—but you would not actually see me dead."

He patted her shoulder. "Maeve, 'tis a small price to pay for Ireland's freedom. And I'll be doing my best to make it painless, I promise."

Icy fear invaded Maeve. Her own brother would see her dead for his cause. Had he gone mad?

Run!

'Twas her only thought as she made to slide off Ulick's horse. Before she could, Flynn grabbed her arm, kicked the mount's sides, and they flew like a shot down the dirt road.

* * * *

"If still you miss her," Drake said, sliding onto the bench Kieran occupied in Hartwich's great hall, "do something besides stare into your ale."

Kieran turned tired, bleary eyes to his friend. Drake's dark eyes were too earnest, too honest. He turned away.

"Guilford sent you," he accused.

"Nay. I grow weary of watching you brood. 'Tis unlike you."

"Love does that to a man."

Drake raised a brow. "Only if he allows such."

"Before you took Averyl into your heart, you did little except brood day and night," Kieran pointed out.

"I never said I had not my thick-skulled moments." Drake sighed. "You love the woman. Sit here not and drink. Fight for her. Coax her. Tell her what is in your heart."

How often had Kieran wished he could do just that? He had taken fewer breaths in his lifetime, he felt sure. Still, he knew Drake's suggestion was impossible.

"She hates me," he admitted. "She ordered me gone."

Drake laughed, then quelled the sound at Kieran's glare. "Maeve hates you not. She is merely angry."

Kieran snorted. "Spoken like someone who has never met my wife."

"Is she not a woman with a woman's heart?" Drake folded his hands upon the table. "Aye, and she cares. Did she not, 'twould not have mattered to her if you stayed at Langmore. You would have been little more than irritating, hardly worthy of such emotion. Because she cares, and because you hurt her and her pride, she renounced you, demanded you leave, and regretted it moments after you were gone, I would wager."

Why did Drake make everything sound so simple? So right?

Should he seek out Maeve, try to win her affection? Misery propelled him to think so. He knew not what else to do.

"Kieran," called Aric as he crossed the room to his friends. "This came for you."

Aric held out a rolled parchment in his large hands. Kieran

looked at him in question. Who could want him? Who knew where to find him? His belly rumbled with apprehension.

"'Tis from Langmore," Aric said softly.

Kieran took the missive, frowning with trepidation. Rolled within that was another small piece of parchment. Quickly, he scanned the first. The first was from old Patrick at Langmore explaining that his lady wife had disappeared and Flynn O'Shea had escaped. Cold fear tore through his gut. Hands shaking, he forced himself to open the other missive.

Fury and fright roared in his gut as he read the second note. Flynn had written one sentence designed to incite a terror such as Kieran had never known:

Return to Ireland and relinquish Langmore to the rebellion or Maeve dies.

Shaky and cold, Kieran dropped the notes on the table before him with a curse. Drake grabbed them and read quickly, Aric peering over his shoulder. They cursed within moments of each other.

"Dear God, why her?" Kieran whispered, wishing this horror to the realm of nightmare. But naught would change its truth.

"We will rescue her," Aric said.

"Aye, all of us," Drake offered.

Shocked and dizzy, Kieran shook his head. "The battle is mine."

"Any battle of yours is a battle of ours," Aric said fiercely. "Had you a need to fight at Bosworth Field? Nay, you said you went for Guilford, but I know you entered the bloody battle for me as well."

Drake nodded. "My fight with my half brother was my own as well. But you and Aric came to help me, to see Averyl safe. Now let us see your wife safe and help you."

"Never forget we are brothers." Aric held up his palm, revealing the thin scar where they had sealed their pact in blood nearly twenty years past.

"We are brothers," Drake repeated, holding up his palm.

Gratitude, relief, fury, terror—all filled Kieran at once. Through it all, he saw that Maeve would have a much better chance of surviving if they all attended to her rescue.

Kieran held up his palm, too, and briefly swiped it across that of the other men. "Thank you, my brothers. Let us ride."

CHAPTER EIGHTEEN

After five hard days of travel, Aric, Drake, and Kieran arrived at Langmore, his squire, Colm, in tow. The June sun cast its full glory on the tall stone structure. Clouds hung in the periphery, dotting the piercing blue sky. Towering trees swayed to the rhythm of the breeze, leaves whispering of age-old tales of love and danger.

Dismounting at the gates, Kieran thought he had never seen a sight so welcome—or so painful—as Langmore. The gentle flow of the River Barrow, the lush hills of green, and the yellow blossoms of the meadow vetchling—all had seeped their way into his blood. He had missed this place.

And he had missed Maeve, fiercely.

"It is a good keep," Drake commented as he led his mount to the gate. "Sturdy and well placed."

Beside him, Aric smiled, holding his horse's reins. "Aye, and that it sits amid such beautiful land does not hurt, eh?"

Kieran looked about him again and satisfaction—belonging even—wound through him like honey. "It is beautiful."

"So you finally admit it," Aric shot back. "And you chose to leave all this to brood into your ale at Hartwich?"

"It was a foolish choice," Kieran conceded, handing his reins to Colm, who trailed behind them.

"Indeed," Drake concurred.

In silence, they strode through the gate and the garrison, his soldiers greeting him as he passed. The trio wound their way through the lower bailey, the outer buildings, until the middle bailey and the keep came into view.

"Every bit is impressive," said Drake. "'Tis clean and efficient. Has it always been thus?"

He nodded. "Maeve is a fine chatelaine."

At the mention of her name, Kieran tried to push back the rise of fear threatening to seize his heart and shred his guts. He forced it down.

"We will save her," Aric assured him in the stilted silence.

Nodding, he looked about the familiar walls as they made their way to the great hall. Still, Kieran found himself watching for his redheaded minx, foolishly hoping she might appear at any moment.

But he knew such would not happen. He only prayed now he could save her from the rebels' fervor.

"Kieran, thank God you've arrived!" cried Jana, bustling in with little Geralt in her arms. "Thank you for coming as well, Lord Belford." She nodded at Drake. "Good sir."

Aric nodded. "I am here to help in whatever way I can."

"As am I," said his Scottish friend.

Fiona and Brighid followed, and the youngest sister grabbed Kieran's hands earnestly.

"You will save her?" Brighid questioned.

He squeezed her hands, moved by the concern in all her sisters' eyes. "I will."

"We will," murmured Colm as he entered the room, staring at Brighid with the look of a hungry man, not a wishful boy.

The girl flashed his squire an answering gaze, flushed a becoming pink, and looked away.

In the silence, Kieran introduced Drake to the remaining O'Shea sisters, then moved to the question most on his mind. "What happened? How did Flynn get free? Where did he take Maeve?"

"We received word that Lord Butler traveled to Langmore to search our dungeons for Flynn," Jana supplied.

Damnation! "He knew I had imprisoned Flynn there?"

She shook her head. "Nay, but he suspected. So Maeve and I concocted a plan to free Flynn. We could not simply let our brother die, and Maeve did not wish to see those greedy Palesmen accuse you of treason. 'Twas the only way."

As much as Kieran hated to admit thus, Jana was right.

"Maeve told me she planned to speak to Flynn about his violence in this rebellion," the eldest O'Shea sister added.

"And…?"

"We know not," Fiona answered quietly. "Jana created a diversion with one of the rebels. All the guards ran to save her from the soldier's mock assault."

When the young woman cast her gaze downward, Kieran felt certain Fiona remembered her own attack and the two men who had destroyed the innocence of this sweet girl. Without thought, he squeezed her hand and nearly smiled when she did not flinch.

"So you discovered Maeve gone after that?" he prompted.

Brighid nodded. "We knew not what to do. Jana screamed, Fiona cried, I looked and looked and looked all about the keep but could find naught. Finally, old Patrick found signs of footsteps and a scuffle near the curtain wall. We knew Flynn would race for a horse the rebel messenger left for him in the woods. When we searched for the horse and found it gone, we felt certain Flynn had taken Maeve and we knew not why."

"Then Desmond O'Neill came," said Jana.

Kieran closed his eyes and held in a curse.

"Your father?" asked Drake.

Slowly, he nodded. "What did he want?"

"At first, we were uncertain," said Brighid, her face the picture of fury beneath her blond curls. "He said only to tell you when you returned to Langmore that you would know where to find him."

Saint Peter's balls! Kieran had no time or inclination to deal with his father now, especially since the location Desmond referred to could only be Balcorthy.

"He said Maeve and Flynn are with him," added Fiona. "Then he gave us Flynn's note, which we sent to you."

Even worse. He'd always known that Flynn and Desmond together were more combustible than a raging blaze. That Maeve was in their power frightened him more than anything in his life ever had.

"What plan have you?" Jana demanded. "Do you know of their lair?"

He nodded. "The ruins of my boyhood home, Balcorthy. 'Tis in the Wicklow Mountains. We will leave come morn."

Jana nodded. "'Tis glad I am you have returned to save Maeve. She…she needs you."

Kieran swallowed against the lump of emotion that threatened to choke him. Never had he felt thus, as if his heart had overruled his logic. But today, it did. "I need her, too."

Jana smiled brightly at that, as if she approved of him, of their union. Gladness would have overtaken him then had he not been so stunned and worried.

"Promise you will do your best to save her, and I will have a maid show you and your friends to your chambers."

Standing, Kieran regarded Maeve's eldest sister. Her dark eyes were wise with loss and love and all that life brought. And brotherly affection—for him, even more evident when she leaned forward to place a kiss on his cheek.

"Promise?" she whispered.

"Aye. That is a promise I freely make."

I only hope 'tis a promise I can make real, he thought silently, hoping his worst fears—fears of his wife's murder—would not come to pass.

* * * *

Huddled in the castle's ruins, chilled by the falling mist, Maeve stared out into the open night, then glanced back at Flynn and Desmond O'Neill. Her brother had imbibed so much ale this night it seemed likely he would soon find oblivion. And Desmond was no longer a young man. He had fallen asleep an hour past. A dozen rebel guards wandered around the perimeter of the ruins, true.

Still, Maeve had to believe she would escape.

Flynn's chilling words rushed back to her as he'd calmly informed her of the "painless" sacrifice he intended she make for the rebellion, should Kieran not come to her rescue and agree to surrender Langmore.

And after the manner in which she had thrown the man out of his own home, she doubted very much that he would come.

Nay, she was on her own—and now seemed the time to escape.

With slow movements, Maeve pushed aside the thin blanket her brother had provided, and inched toward a large hole in the ruin's walls, her backside dampening with dirt and rain as she crept. Her heart hammered so fast in her chest the sound pounded in her ears like a frantic drumbeat.

As she reached the thigh-high gap in the wall, she eased over the side and stood to run.

"Maeve!" she heard Flynn scream from behind.

A look over her shoulder proved her worst nightmare a reality as her brother, Desmond, and all the rebels began to give chase.

Maeve forced herself onward, through trees, down a hill, splashing through the cold waters of a shallow loch, praying desperately to reach the other side and find freedom.

Behind her, she heard more splashing. A terrified glance backward proved Flynn and his henchmen were gaining.

Determined not to be their victim, Maeve put all her energy into sprinting away. Mist ran into her eyes, and her heart and lungs felt ready to explode. Her thighs trembled with effort. In her mad dash, her tresses fell free of their confines and streamed behind her like a red beacon in the dark. Knowing such made her much too easy to find in the dark, she grabbed at it, clawing at her head to reel it in.

Before she could, Flynn grabbed her hair from behind and gave it a vicious yank, tumbling Maeve to her backside.

"I begin to think you do not support our cause, Sister," he ground out, wrapping his palm in her hair and giving another cruel tug.

Maeve gasped. Her eyes watered both in pain and fear. "I-I want a free Ireland. I vow." Her voice trembled, and she cursed her fear, for Flynn would only feed on it. "But I have long said I want no bloodshed, least of all my own."

He grunted impatiently. "Your head is filled with ideals that lie nowhere near reality. War means blood, Maeve."

Sighing, Flynn released her hair, grasped her arm, and jerked her to her feet. He sneered into her face. "You are a coward, and I am ashamed. Do you think Geralt or Quaid were afraid to give their lives for the noble cause of freedom? Nay, they gave freely, and here you sit sniveling."

"There are other ways to achieve freedom," she argued.

"Not if we want it now. Too long we have watched them pillage our land, rob us of coin whilst calling it one tax or another. They rape our women and steal our property. No more, I tell you now! The English in Ireland must die, every man, woman, and child!

"Each I would stretch on a rack myself until they near broke apart, then gut them as they watched, as they felt the very blood leave their body toward death."

Maeve shuddered at the horror of his words, his wishes. That he would wish such a terrible end upon anyone startled her. That he would even inflict such a death upon a woman—or worse, a child—terrified her.

The realization that the child growing inside her was part English filled her with a fear unlike she any had ever known. For if Flynn learned she had conceived, he would kill her that moment and be pleased with his work, no doubt.

"Flynn," she tried to reason with him, despite her shaking voice. "Kieran will not come for me. He cares not about me."

And Maeve feared she had no one but herself to blame for that sad fact. Long ago, she should have followed her heart, found some way to build a family, despite their divided loyalties.

"He is smitten with you. And why not? You are a beautiful lass and an O'Shea. Nay, he will come, and soon."

"Please," she implored. "Let us find another way to free Ireland. I will help you, only spare the lives of innocent people."

"Including you?" With a grunt of disgust, he pushed her away, into Desmond's arms. "She is your daughter by marriage. Take her."

Kieran's father put his arms about her and began to lead her back to the ruins. With Flynn and the soldiers following in the night, Maeve knew running again was impossible.

"Maeve, do not be frightened. If that stubborn son of mine does not come within a day or two…well, Flynn is good with a blade. 'Twill not hurt very much."

Maeve held in a scream of fear. Flynn, Desmond, the rest of the rebellion—had they all lost their senses? No rebellion was worth so much pain and death. 'Twas true the English presence here had been unwelcome and uncomfortable. Losing one's freedom chafed.

But this pain and death… The rebels had wrought those with their fervency and impatience. No rebellion could possibly be worth so much blood, so many lives. Aye, she wanted freedom, but not at the expense of innocents and people she held dear.

Maeve knew she could do naught to stop it, for she and her blood tie to her brother held no sway over him. Her short life loomed in the middle of her thoughts, exploding all her hopes that would never come true, her dreams destined to remain unfilled. She anguished that she would go to her grave, taking with her a babe who had never had the opportunity to experience life.

But Flynn was right in one thing: she was a coward. She had never told Kieran how deeply he moved her, how much she loved him.

That she regretted more than anything as she faced the coming dawn and the death that lay close at hand—and a warning of the desperate, deadly plan she had heard Flynn and Desmond discussing that would die with her.

* * * *

Kneeling behind the wild growth of brambles, Kieran watched as dusk fell dank and gray on the black walls of Balcorthy's shell. Today, the pathetic shell of the keep was alive with activity. Flynn started a fire in what had once been the garrison. The drawbridge had decayed with age, now rotting on the ground, lying open in dangerous invitation. Close by stood Kieran's father as he spoke with several of the rebels. Soldiers in poor tunics, lacking hose or shoes, patrolled the walls about Balcorthy.

And Maeve sat in a corner beside Flynn's fire looking bedraggled, confused, and furious.

Kieran felt violence pumping through him at the thought of anyone, especially her own brother, hurting his wife.

Aric approached from behind and squatted down beside him. "What make you of this?"

"There are fifteen at most. Flynn surrounds himself with rebel soldiers. There"—he pointed to the burned-out garrison—"he keeps Maeve behind him. She will be hard to reach."

Clapping a hand on his shoulder, Aric reassured, "We will do it, my friend."

Aye, Kieran would gladly give every bit of his heart, muscle, and soul to save her. As long as he drew a breath, no one would harm her, not even her own brother. Still, naught would change even if he managed to free Maeve. His wife would go on hating him. And if her brother should find death this day… Her hate would then be irrevocable and boundless.

And well Kieran knew Flynn was not likely to abandon his cause—and the captive who could further it—before death claimed him. But with Flynn gone to Hell, at least Maeve would be alive, even if 'twas to hate him.

He spit out a long curse.

"Kieran, stay calm." Aric frowned, clearly confused by his behavior. And why not, Kieran asked himself. He was no less confused by his own actions. Truly, he was lovesick.

"Drake is helping Colm secure our mounts," Aric went on. "Langmore's army will stay with them. We have but to signal and they will come running."

What Aric said was true, Kieran knew. But still he feared. "Flynn is so close to Maeve. He could kill her thrice before I could reach her undetected. That mountain at their backs makes surprising them from there impossible."

"We need no surprise," Aric soothed. "Flynn wants to hear what you have to say. He will listen before he raises a hand to Maeve. Negotiate with him. Mayhap he will then let his guard down. We will fight our way out when the time is right."

"I cannot simply give him Langmore," Kieran argued. "The consequences to you and Guildford... Besides, I am not convinced relinquishing Langmore will convince him to release Maeve. He will think of some other rebellious need, I'm sure."

"I know." Aric laid a calming hand on his arm. "Flynn has only to believe you for a few minutes, long enough to see Maeve freed."

Shaking with urgency, with apprehension, Kieran nodded. "Let us go."

The sun fell another inch as Kieran and Aric topped the hill and stepped into the gray shadows. Flynn spotted them right away and gathered five of his soldiers to his side. As the small group approached, Kieran glanced at Maeve long enough to see her stand and return his long stare, surprise in her wide eyes.

No shrieking, no trembling. Always shrewd and calm—that was Maeve. And that was only one of the many things he loved about her.

"Take their swords," Flynn ordered his soldiers.

Kieran placed a hand over his. A quick glance beside him proved Aric did the same.

"Nay," Kieran said. "You offered me my wife in exchange for Langmore. I'll not give you my weapon so you can slaughter me like a pig before a festival."

Flynn hesitated.

Desmond approached, wearing his best smile. Kieran did not

trust or believe his father for a moment.

"Your point is well taken, Son," Desmond said, then turned to Flynn. "Such would not be the first negotiation done in arms, right?"

Scowling, Flynn nodded tersely, then directed his attention back to Kieran. "By coming, I assume you are willing to surrender Langmore."

"Perhaps. I must first see my wife well and unharmed."

Stepping back, Flynn gestured to his sister, still standing in Balcorthy's ruins. "There you see her."

"Nay, I would speak with her first, be certain no hurt has befallen her."

Flynn sighed with impatience. "You cannot imagine I am eager to see my own sister harmed. While I would enjoy the opportunity to vex you, I would not have some common soldier raping her for the petty purpose of spiting you."

"Yet you are willing to kill her?" The O'Shea man's logic completely baffled Kieran.

"For the higher purpose of freedom! Exalted ventures often have high costs. I dislike such, but I accept it. Besides, I can make her passing painless, and that gives me comfort."

Maeve's brother clearly possessed a twisted mind. Stifling an urge to point Flynn's ill logic out to him, he shrugged instead. "Let Maeve approach and stand beside you. She need come no closer than that for my satisfaction."

Flynn gritted his teeth. Desmond prodded his ribs with an elbow.

"Bring yourself here, Maeve," Kieran's nemesis called over his shoulder.

Cautiously, Maeve made her way toward the small gathering, her gaze darting between Kieran and her brother. When she reached Flynn's side, he gripped her arm, halting her progress.

Up close, Kieran saw she looked both weary and wary. Her red-gold curls tumbled in tangles over her shoulders. Her gown was both torn and stained. Dirt smudged one lightly freckled cheek. But she was alive.

"Tell Kieran you have not suffered," he instructed.

Maeve looked away from her brother and fixed her gaze upon him. "I have been fed, given a place to rest, and not been...disturbed."

She did not say she was afraid, but Kieran read that fact in her golden eyes. He wanted badly to hold her, tell her he would see her free this very hour. He could do neither without jeopardizing his plan.

Kieran nodded instead. "As you say."

"Does this satisfy you?"

"Enough to talk," Kieran answered with caution.

"Good." He prodded Maeve back to her corner of the burned-out castle, then turned back to Kieran. "You will ride back to Langmore, remove yourself and your belongings, along with your army from the area by dusk tomorrow. By nightfall, I will arrive with Maeve. If all is to my satisfaction, I will bring her back here the following day and release her unto your keeping."

Immediately, Kieran disliked the plan. Flynn had built in many ways to cheat him out of releasing Maeve. By his side, he saw Aric give a slight shake of his head. Though Kieran never ignored his battle instincts, it gave him ease to have them confirmed.

"Nay. Too fraught with…problems. I anticipated you would wish Langmore's army gone, so I dismissed them already."

"I have no proof of this," Flynn snapped.

"I disagree."

He sent out a sharp whistle. It hung in the darkening silence until the soldiers topped the rise, aclatter with swords and heavy footfall, Drake leading them.

O'Shea gaped, then turned to Desmond with a nervous stare. The older man gave him a brief nod, but Flynn was not soothed.

"Who is he?" Flynn demanded, pointing at Drake.

"A friend."

Flynn snarled. "I am not liking your army here."

Kieran raised a cool brow. "You would prefer to see them back at Langmore?"

"Nay," Flynn muttered. "So if you dislike my plan, what will you be agreeing to?"

Shrugging in feigned apathy, Kieran stepped closer. "You could give me my wife now and ride for Langmore whilst my army is with me."

Flynn squinted in the dark to see the soldiers. "I am thinking you brought not every man who bears arms for you."

"'Twas all the men who wished to come. The rest rode for their homes," he lied.

"Again, I have no proof."

Kieran smiled. "Nay, you do not."

Scowling, Flynn growled. "I do not like your demeanor."

"A mutual sentiment, you must allow. Do you agree to my plan or no?"

"I do not!" he shouted. "Give way to my plans or pray to your Maker now, for you meet Him this eve."

"I have never been much for prayer," said Kieran with deceptive coolness.

As Flynn busied himself with a glare, Kieran quickly drew his blade. Realizing he had been slow, Flynn backed away, toward the firelight, and unsheathed his sword. Kieran pursued, unrepentant in his stalking.

Any man who threatened to kill his own sister for any cause deserved death.

Flynn watched him with widening eyes. "Men!" he shouted, panic in his voice. "Fight!"

Within moments, battle erupted. Aric engaged a solder near Flynn. Drake and Langmore's army charged the group, eventually engaging Desmond and the other Irishmen in warfare.

The constant clash of blade obliterated the night sounds. Dusk cloaked them further, as if hiding the evils of war from sunlight.

Beyond Flynn, Maeve looked on in horror as an Irish soldier fell to the ground, dead by Drake's claymore to his belly. Another fell to Aric's sword moments later.

She shuddered when one of Langmore's soldiers took a blade across his hand, severing all of his fingers. The man's weapon fell to the ground, and the Irish soldier ran the injured man through moments later.

Before him, Flynn lunged again, and Kieran forced his attention away from his wife. Concentration pursed O'Shea's mouth. Flynn grunted as he thrust his blade for Kieran, who sidestepped the blow just before it could do him harm. Though he was conscious of his father close, he prayed the battle would not force him to take up arms against his own sire.

Then, in a move he'd been trained to perform nigh on twenty years, he moved back into stance and swiped his blade at Flynn, scratching his tip upon the man's neck.

Blood began a slow leak down the Irishman's neck.

Kieran glanced up at Maeve, to find shock on her pale face. He held in a curse. Aye, she would not want him to slay her brother, but what else could he do? Let the fiend kill her? Allow the fiend to kill him?

"Kieran!" Aric shouted.

He turned his gaze to Flynn once more.

And found the man's blade headed straight for his chest.

CHAPTER NINETEEN

Flynn roared with triumph as he charged closer. Shocked he had been so stupid, so careless, Kieran raised his sword to defend himself, but he feared 'twas too late. Death drew near, sizzled in his blood, pounded in his heart.

Slicing his sword in an arc toward Flynn, Kieran hunched back, away from Flynn's blade, all the while bracing himself to feel the blade violate his flesh, to feel his life's blood pour from his body.

Fire seared across his chest moments later, nearly from shoulder to shoulder. He hissed against the pain, eyes slammed shut to block out the agony.

A clink of blades alerted Kieran the fight was not over. He opened his eyes to find Drake had intervened and was even now slicing his way through with tireless parries toward Flynn.

Grunting, he rose to his feet and advanced. He raised his arm, despite the fire and pain. *Maeve.* He must save Maeve.

Struggling to fend off the bigger, stronger Drake, Flynn's dark eyes widened with horror when Kieran approached, blade in hand, fury in his heart. The rebel glanced about for help but quickly saw his soldiers were either occupied—or dead.

"You'll not win!" Flynn vowed. "Ireland will not surrender to a traitor like you!"

Kieran opened his mouth to remind Flynn he was rapidly losing the battle. The man turned and ran.

Straight for his sister.

Wide-eyed, Maeve watched Flynn approach.

"Run!" Kieran shouted.

Apparently sensing danger, she already had. Flynn pursued; Kieran followed with Drake by his side, blade at the ready.

Green hills and blue sky whirled by, unheeded. His gaze, his entire being, focused on his wife, now running for her life. With every ounce of his energy, Kieran gave chase, but Flynn was too close to Maeve for her to escape.

A moment later, the wild rebel grabbed her by the hair and, with it, yanked her against his chest.

Flynn arced the deadly blade in his hand up to her throat and began to press in. Maeve's scream tore at Kieran's guts.

Only a heartbeat away now, he growled and tossed aside his sword, drew out a dagger from his belt, and leaped upon Flynn. Then, without hesitation, Kieran plunged the wickedly sharp blade into Flynn's neck and yanked on it with all his might.

Blood streamed out of O'Shea's throat in a red metallic ooze, his artery severed. Flynn sank to the ground.

The sickly sweet tinge of blood scented the air, running freely down Flynn's tunic, then into the earth.

Kieran grabbed Flynn's wrist and felt for his pulse. It was weak and fast. And with a wound such as his, 'twould be no more than a matter of minutes before he died.

Maeve screamed and knelt to her brother, shock dominating her pale, pale face. Saint Peter above! He had just wounded his wife's brother, most likely mortally.

He looked away, toward Aric. "We must stop the blood."

Aric shook his head. "'Tis too late."

"We must try! I have seen worse. Maeve—"

Kneeling, Drake felt Flynn's pulse, then shook his head.

Silence fell. Kieran felt as if his heart had stopped, as if time had stopped. He stared, motionless, stunned at his unmoving nemesis.

"He is gone," Drake murmured, taking Kieran by the arm.

He shrugged off Drake's touch and knelt to Flynn. Blood seeped from the man's open wound slowly now that his heart no longer pumped.

Swallowing against the maelstrom of feeling—confusion, anger, shock—he merely stared. Dear God, how much would Maeve hate him now? He closed his eyes, dread pelting him like a violent, unrelenting storm.

Aric and Drake each came to stand by Kieran's side and took

one of his arms, hoisting him to his feet.

"Your father is dead as well," whispered Drake.

A stone's throw away, Kieran saw Desmond on his back, a blade protruding from his belly. Sighing, Kieran closed his eyes for a moment, finding a tangle of regret for the death of the sire who had never been a father to him.

He could not mourn the loss of the father he'd never had.

"We have dead and wounded to tend. You have a grieving wife." Aric nodded toward the ruins.

Maeve. Pain lanced Kieran as he swerved his gaze to his wife, sobbing silently as she knelt by her brother.

Heated feeling came in another blast. Kieran closed his eyes, wishing he could sink to the ground and find a moment's oblivion, for he could not face Maeve's blame and loathing, sure to come.

Refusing to succumb to such weakness, Kieran took slow steps toward his wife until he reached her side. "I am sorry. I never wanted—never meant—"

Maeve suddenly rose and threw herself into his embrace. Kieran knew not what to say. Her slight body molded itself to him, and he sensed her tears in her trembling, knew the confusion and fear, so evident in her fierce grip.

"I never meant to see it end this way." His voice was a low vow, willing her to believe him.

Still, he knew 'twas unlikely she would ever take him back.

Maeve released her grip on him and stepped away. She answered with a brisk nod, her chin trembling as she held in tears.

"How fare you?" asked Aric as he approached Maeve with a concerned touch to her shoulder.

Kieran watched closely as Maeve gave his friend a shaky nod. But he was not fooled. She had yet to really understand what happened this night. Once she did, Maeve would despise him always.

"Maeve, I am Drake," said his other friend as he approached his wife with the blanket from his saddle. "Get you warm, lass." He looked at Kieran. "We need to be away. Colm is hurt, as are you."

Casting his gaze down, Kieran found the shallow gash across his chest that was already beginning to clot. He had no concern there. But what of Colm? A moment later, he found his young squire clutching a jagged wound in his shoulder. 'Twas deep and would need stitches and a poultice quickly if he was to keep the arm. Damnation! What was he to do? He could stitch wounds if he must but had no needle and thread. And poultices, he knew precious little about them.

"Ismenia back at Langmore could help," said Maeve.

Kieran nodded. "Let us be gone then."

He directed a handful of the other soldiers to stay and bury the dead. The few Irish soldiers still alive surrendered with peace, and Aric tied them behind his mount. Kieran took a last glance at his father and Maeve's brother, wondering why they had been so foolishly willing to die for their violent cause.

Tearing himself away from the scene, he turned to Maeve only to find Drake had already taken her to the waiting horses. And though he knew in his gut she would likely never have any more to do with him after this night, he wanted to feel her against him one last time, tell her once more how sorry he was for the manner in which she had lost her brother.

Before Drake could see her mounted on his horse, Kieran made his way to the pair and grasped Maeve by the arm, leading her to his own mount. Drake smiled. Maeve cast him a wary glare before allowing him to hand her up into the saddle.

Moments later, Drake brought Colm to his mount and the party left the scene of Balcorthy, more haunted now for the tragedy that had taken place there. Yet he knew it was like a grave—now it would be left to rest in peace.

Finally, Kieran mounted behind Maeve, and the small party was on its way. He placed his arm about her waist, knowing as she leaned against him that she did so only out of weariness. Still, he relished the opportunity to touch her, fearing it would be his last. He could detect only the slightest thickening of her middle, but still, knowing he would always share the bond of the child with her, the remembrance of the happiest moments he'd ever spent in a woman's arms, pleased him.

"I understand it not," Drake said, breaking into the weighty silence. "What did the rebels intend to do with Langmore if Kieran surrendered it? All this blood, and for what? To regain his home?"

"I know not," said Kieran sadly.

"I know," Maeve said suddenly, looking at Drake, then Aric just beyond him. "You must warn your king that Margaret of Burgundy has found a new pretender, a boy named Perkin, I think. She and her followers plan to bring him here to Ireland within the week, put an army behind him, pass him off to the English people as Richard, the missing Duke of York. Langmore was to be the base of their operation."

Kieran, Aric, and Drake all exchanged alarmed glances. They knew full well that the young prince Richard, Duke of York, had been murdered by his late uncle, Richard III. And though Henry Tudor shared their knowledge of the tragedy, no one could produce the corpse of the young boy, and his elder brother, Edward, to convince the English people that no male descendants of the House of York still lived.

And until they could, the new Tudor throne would always be vulnerable to these pretenders. This Perkin was not the first Ireland had supported.

War was ever a threat.

"I suppose if this boy came to power, he agreed he would then pull the soldiers from Ireland and let you rule yourselves?" Kieran asked.

Maeve nodded. "As I understood Flynn, aye."

"Thank you," Aric said. "Once we reach Langmore, I will find a fresh horse and ride for London."

"I will journey with you," Drake offered.

Aric nodded his thanks, then turned his attention back to Maeve. "I know that cannot have been easy for you, telling an Englishman of such a plot that may gain Ireland freedom."

"And cost what in lives?" asked Maeve. "I could not live with the knowledge that such a secret would be the death of innocents."

"You are an extraordinary woman, sweet Maeve," Kieran whispered in her ear.

"I am a woman weary of death," she corrected.

Kieran had no illusions that she spoke of her brother's demise and would give him the full force of her tongue-lashing once they were alone.

He sighed. She would probably cast him out again. But this time, before he went, he would tell her he loved her. If she still wished him gone then…he would ride to London with Aric and Drake. God knew what he would do with his life after that. He yearned to stay at Langmore, by Maeve's side. Yet he feared nothing he said or did would convince her to open her heart to him—ever.

* * * *

The weary group rode through the night in silence. Maeve did what she could to curb Colm's bleeding when they stopped for a brief rest and a meal.

Dawn began to streak across the sky in vivid oranges and purples when Langmore rose into their view. As they approached the bridge over the river and trekked down the dirt path, he remembered his first day here. Lord, how badly he had wanted to leave then, to turn away and ride from his fate.

Now he could think of no fate he would like more than to stay at Langmore with his bride for the rest of his days.

Given that Maeve had said next to naught during their long ride home, he had lost all hope she would wish to share that fate. Aye, not only had he killed Flynn, though to save Maeve, but he had taken part in the confrontation, engaged in the war his wife despised. That was plenty of reason for Maeve to hate him always.

Finally, they stopped their mounts in the lower bailey. The soldiers Kieran had left behind to guard the castle swarmed the small party, begging for details of its outcome.

"Are ye badly hurt, milord?"

"Did ye win the battle?"

"Where be Flynn?"

The questions came in an endless stream. Their enthusiasm gladdened him, for he recalled the days when they wished him nothing but gone and felt sure they would stick a blade in his back upon their first opportunity. To see them now so loyal made him proud.

Still, he had not come to celebrate now. He must speak with Maeve.

"I am unharmed. Aye, we won the battle. And Flynn is dead," he answered in a rapid stream.

With that, he thrust Lancelot in the direction of a soldier. "Care for him."

Then he looked around for Maeve, only to see the last swish of her skirts as she disappeared inside the keep, an injured Colm beside her.

He sighed. Colm needed care now. His conversation with his wife could wait a few moments. But it chafed him. He did not regard her silence as a good one, and the idea of never hearing Maeve's sweet voice address him again—even in anger—chilled him.

"We leave now," Drake said from behind him.

Kieran whirled to find his friends standing beside fresh mounts, bags and blankets already attached. "That was quick."

"Time is of the essence," Aric explained. "We must warn King Henry of this Perkin boy. He cannot be allowed to sway the country into believing him the rightful heir. The wars in England are over. Peace and prosperity are beginning to settle over the land. Henry is a good if stern king. 'Tis important all stays such."

Kieran nodded. "I wish you well, then. Both of you."

"As we wish you, brother," Aric said, then mounted. "Go to your wife."

Drake paused. "You hesitate at that notion. Go to her and share what is in your heart."

Casting his gaze down, Kieran wondered how, why, loving Maeve had changed him so much. "She has no wish for what is in my heart. Much as I yearn to share your fate and Aric's, wedded bliss will not be mine." He sighed. "But I will tell her anyway."

"She embraced you after the battle," Drake pointed out.

"She was frightened and confused." Aye, and Maeve had pulled herself from his arms quickly enough.

With a hearty clap on the shoulder, Drake smiled. "She may surprise you. How many women can resist a man's confession of undying love and devotion?"

Kieran shrugged as he watched Drake mount. He exchanged waves with his friends—so like brothers to him—as they rode again out of sight.

Drake's words lingered. 'Twas true that few women could resist deep professions of love and loyalty.

But he felt sure Maeve was the kind of woman who could.

* * * *

When Maeve entered the chamber she still shared with Fiona that afternoon for a much-needed nap, she was weary from the long night's ride, as well as the grueling task of assisting Ismenia in stitching Colm's arm and seeing him comfortable.

She was also stunned to see Kieran sitting on her bed, his gaze fastened upon her, holding her in place as surely as shackles.

Why was he still here?

Her heart picked up speed, racing in her chest as if anticipating his embrace.

Foolish, it was! Pining for a man who had never wanted her, could never love her, nor settle into a simple life with her in the country he resented. By the saints, how she wished she knew why he felt thus. Perhaps then she could combat his dislikes…

Nay, if he wanted so badly to leave her and Ireland that he would lie and manipulate his way into her bed, then she would grant him the freedom he needed. They would only be miserable—both of them—if she tried to make him stay.

Wondering if knowing of her love would make a difference in Kieran's mind was killing her, but she stifled the words. He wanted her not. And that was that.

"My lord," she greeted finally. "I had thought you would leave with your friends."

"Not until I spoke a word alone with you, Wife. Come." He took her hand.

Maeve did not resist, chastising herself for enjoying the feel of his warm, rough palm against her own, enveloping, making her feel so secure.

He led her to his chamber, the room they had briefly shared, where they had made love—and conceived their child. For what purpose did he bring her here now?

He sat her at the small desk against the wall, then faced her, looming above her. His furrowed brow and taut jaw bespoke his turmoil. Maeve frowned in concern.

"Kieran?"

He nodded, then sighed. She saw the fists clenched at his sides, and her concern mounted.

"I wanted to tell you again how very sorry I am about your brother. I did not wish him dead, truly. Please believe—"

"You *saved* me. I know thus." She bit her lip. "Absolve yourself of guilt on that score."

"You do not hate me for it?" He sounded shocked.

Maeve swung her gaze to him again. Clearly he *had* believed she would hate him for the deed. At one time, she would have.

"Nay," she said, then touched his arm in a comforting gesture, though she knew it to be unwise. "Flynn was not the same brother of my youth. The—the war…it had…*changed* him until he was someone I feared. I will miss the boy he used to be and mourn the man he might have been. I will not mourn him. He would have killed me, killed many, for his cause."

"Sweet Maeve," Kieran whispered, kneeling to her. "You astound me always. Your strength, your understanding. Men all over the world would wish for your character, myself included."

The fervency of his words took Maeve aback. Then he took her hands in his and squeezed.

"I do not deserve you. I know thus. I-I should have told you before we wed about the bargain with King Henry, but I knew if I told you, our marriage would be forever chaste and no babe would be conceived. I put my freedom above yours, and I am sorry for it."

Did he mean those words? Could he? "Kieran—"

"Let me finish," he urged, shaking his head. "It wasn't until you ordered me gone that I saw all I had lost in losing you. I realized"— he paused, gripping her hands even more tightly—"I had allowed my parents' marriage to color my judgment."

"Your parents?"

Kieran swallowed, forcing himself to face the past he had spent years avoiding, facing the ugly times at Balcorthy for Maeve's sake—for their sake.

"My parents wed because of a royal decree. I know not why the match was arranged, but it was calamitous from the first. They had not a civil word to say to one another through the whole of my youth, for he was wont to battle and bosoms. My English mother was a quiet woman of reflection, religion, and study. I suppose, somewhere in my head, I imagined myself too like my father and you like my mother."

"And you doomed us from the start?"

He nodded. "I could not see any other possible ending, and I feared their fate would become ours."

"What happened?"

"After years of bitter feuding, my mother wrote her family and begged them to come take her away. Her brother agreed and brought an army to Balcorthy for the task. Desmond was infuriated and beat her near to death for her perfidy."

"And you saw it?"

Kieran nodded. "'Twas not the first time. He accused her of leaving him for a lover. She had none. I think she merely wanted freedom. She hated this country."

Understanding began to dawn on Maeve's face.

He continued on. "Desmond was ready for my mother's family to arrive, and he trounced them in battle, killing my uncle."

Maeve gasped at the eerie similarity.

"But my mother would not be denied this want. Before she even learned of the battle's outcome, she set Balcorthy afire, picked me up amongst the flames, and took me to England. I-I had not been back to Ireland since that day."

Recoiling in shock, Maeve felt at that moment how difficult his return to this land must have been and all the reasons why he had sought freedom so recklessly.

"She told me my father died in battle, left me at Guilford's doorstep, then took herself off to a convent. I saw her but once more before she died."

Maeve wanted to cry for him, for the confused boy who had lived such violence and betrayal, abandonment and uncertainty.

She touched his face. "Oh, Kieran. How I wish I could take that from you."

"You can," he whispered, his gaze delving to her eyes, willing her to feel his care. "Let me stay."

Shock transformed her features. "You want to live here?"

Kieran nodded, his stare unending. "After I left, I realized I—I love you."

Maeve gasped, then lapsed into a stunned silence. Could he mean thus? His earnest expression, those blue-green eyes tangling with hers, seemed so sincere.…

"I know I have much to learn as a husband. If you will have me, I will stay here, lay my heart at your feet, and love you always."

With those eloquent words, Kieran turned to her a face so earnest Maeve knew not what to say. He wanted to stay and he loved her? She swallowed against confusion. 'Twas all so quick. But her heart knew for certain she loved him as well.

"I know we still have the matter of politics between us," he said, rushing into her silence. "And I cannot fight for the Irish cause. Such would bring harm to Guilford, Aric, and myself, as well as betray my honor. But I can vow to do my very best to be the voice of reason with the other Palesmen. I will do all I can to see the rebellion ended in diplomatic ways whilst encouraging the English to leave you in as much peace as can be. I will do all possible to avoid the shedding of anyone's blood. This I promise."

She believed him, felt so connected to his heart, his soul. Maeve knew he would live up to each of his promises.

"But," he went on, his voice growing taut, "if you wish me gone, I will go now and never bother you again. The choice is yours alone, sweet Maeve."

Her choice? For a man of Kieran's ilk to give her such power over his life, his future… Aye, he loved her well indeed. As she loved him.

Tears stung her eyes as joy washed over her in towering tides. She stood and flung herself into his arms.

"If you ever leave me again, you'll not have to worry about the rebellion, for I will kill you myself."

Maeve's broken voice and ardent declaration were the sweetest sounds Kieran had ever heard. He drew his arms around her and held tight to his wife, this amazing woman he loved with all his soul.

"Never will I leave," he whispered as he clasped her warm, freckled cheeks in his hands. He was stunned to see tears making silent silver paths down her face. "Nay, do not cry."

"I cannot stop. I am overwhelmed by my good fortune. I love you."

He pressed his forehead to hers, closing his eyes, inhaling her springlike scent. Relief and joy filled him, and yet he needed to know all of what lay in her heart. "You're certain you can love *me*? You no longer wish you had wed Quaid?"

Maeve shook her head. "Quaid and I were promised from the cradle, and he was my dear friend. But he never made me feel…whole. I never loved him as I love you."

Kieran sighed in relief. "Oh, my sweetest Maeve. I cannot stop loving you."

With a heartfelt smile, she met his gaze, love warming her golden eyes. "I never thought you could love me. I never thought you would love at all."

"Nor did I," he whispered, soothing her with the gentle touch of his thumbs across her cheeks. "But I do, so much."

She drew in a ragged breath. "I wondered why you could not love me, why you could not stay...."

"'Twas hard for me to believe such joy could come from so forced a union."

"But it can," she whispered.

"It has," he agreed. "And with you at my side, I have no doubt I will always know joy."

Smiling through her tears, Maeve rose up to the tips of her toes. Kieran met her halfway and sealed their union with a kiss destined to last a lifetime.

EPILOGUE

Langmore Castle, Kildare, Ireland
March 1491

Kieran smiled as the group, so like a family in all the ways that mattered, gathered around the cradle.

"She is beautiful," whispered Gwenyth, sending him a misty-eyed gaze. "And look! Her little mouth moves as she sleeps."

"She is lovely. I see why you are such a proud papa," said Averyl, placing a sisterly kiss on his cheek.

"Aye," Kieran answered. "But I cannot take much of the credit. Maeve had the biggest hand in Elinora, even down to the red hair."

His wife cast him a rueful grin. "Aye, you had the diverting part."

"Isn't that always the way?" Averyl asked her, hazel eyes dancing as she juggled a dark-headed boy not yet six months old on her hip.

Laughing, Kieran took the few steps to stand beside Aric, Drake, and Guilford, all recently arrived to see his new addition to their informal clan.

"What news brings you from London?" he asked the group.

Aric answered first. "Beyond the usual court intrigues, King Henry is keeping an eye on the rebels' pretender. Perkin Warbeck appears to be the lad's real name. With his Irish backing disarmed now, Margaret of Burgundy is rumored to be taking the boy to France, to seek support there. But I'm sure naught will come of it,

258

now that the king is prepared."

"Aye," said Drake. "And old Henry was so happy for the information, Aric has become quite the favorite at court."

"Rumor has it," said Guilford, "that he will even make Aric the godfather of his coming child, to be named Henry after his father if 'tis a boy. I would call that an honor indeed."

Aric's face flushed with color. "If the king is pleased and England is well, that will satisfy my ambitions. I have much more interest in home and hearth these days."

Upon hearing his words, Gwenyth glanced up at her husband, then, smiling, went to his side. "I have much interest in you, too," she whispered.

Laughing, Aric kissed his wife and tucked her under his arm. Their daughter, soon to see her first year done, toddled about their feet.

"And what of you, Drake? 'Twas a mighty long winter with little word from you and Averyl."

"We spent much of the winter at Abbotsford, Averyl's home. The keep's repairs are nearly complete; the crops are again flourishing. And her father took a widow to wife close to Christmas, so we simply remained there for a time."

"She is a wonderful woman. And best of all," said Averyl as she approached, "no one at Abbotsford will starve this winter—or any other, I believe—and the Campbells and the MacDougalls have ceased their petty squabbles."

Drake took his younger son from her arms, then looked at his other two children standing near. He flashed his wife a contented smile. "That's right, wench. You learned the value of a good MacDougall man at your side."

Averyl rolled her eyes at the teasing. "Nay, you boaster. 'Twas the love of a good Campbell woman that made you worthwhile."

He ran a tender thumb across her fair cheek, brushing the golden hair at her nape. "You are right, love."

In the sweet moment of silence, Drake kissed his infant son's forehead. Averyl added her affection by patting the boy's shoulder—and looking at his father with love.

"Now we are glad that you came to your senses and took Maeve to wife," Averyl offered.

"And that we *finally* had the opportunity to meet her,"

complained Gwenyth with a grin.

Maeve, certainly the loveliest lady in the room by Kieran's estimation, joined the group, completing it. "As I am finally glad to meet you. I will look forward to hearing tales of these three ruffians."

Collectively, the trio groaned.

"I could start with that tale of the day I caught you boys watching the bathing castlewomen," Guilford offered, winking at the wives. "Not a single one of them under forty, and these lads were barely thinking of becoming men."

The women all laughed. The men groaned again.

"'Twas an accident," Kieran pleaded. "Have mercy!"

Guilford joined in the laughter. "As you wish. Have no doubt I am well pleased, Kieran. Maeve will keep you in line, and well you need it."

Kieran reached for Maeve and placed a soft kiss on her mouth. "She does, I do, and I could not be happier."

"Well, this is a fine state." Guilford's blue eyes snapped as he thrust his hands on his hips. "Here we have three warriors—well trained, I might add—utterly tamed by love. What have you to say?"

"The battle was a sweet one," said Aric, watching Gwenyth.

"Aye, beyond a doubt," added Drake, smiling at Averyl.

Kieran reached for Maeve's hand. "I agree, and it seems fitting that God has blessed us all in love—and friendship."

"God willing, He always will," said Guilford with a smile.

AUTHOR'S NOTE

Dear Reader,

As depicted in *His Rebel Bride*, Pro-Yorkist supporters in Ireland indeed tried twice to oust Henry VII with a pretender to his throne.

In May 1487, Lambert Simnel (real name unknown) was crowned in Ireland's Dublin Cathedral Edward VI of England, claiming he was Edward, earl of Warwick, a nephew to the late King Edward IV. Simnel was a boy of eleven and of humble origins, and a pawn of the pro-Yorkist forces. Henry VII, enraged by this turn of events, brought the real Edward, earl of Warwick, from the Tower of London for all to see, but support for the pretender grew in Ireland anyway. The pro-Yorkist forces attacked the English in June 1487, at the Battle of Stoke, where they were decisively beaten. King Henry pardoned the boy afterward and put him to work in the royal kitchens. Eventually, he rose to the role of king's falconer. He died peacefully in 1525, at the age of fifty.

In 1491, the second such pretender, Perkin Warbeck, emerged. He was the son of a French official and, while working in Ireland, gained the support of the Yorkists. After a time, he claimed to be Richard, duke of York, the youngest of the "Princes in the Tower." For the next few years, Warbeck traveled with Margaret of Burgundy, sister to the late King Edward IV, gaining support and recognition from many governments, including that of Maximilian I in Germany. In October 1494, Warbeck proclaimed himself Richard IV and returned to Ireland to raise an invasion force. Henry VII, however, had already arrested most of the English nobility who supported Warbeck. In 1496, he turned to the Scottish for help, which resulted in nothing more than a brief border skirmish. He tried again with Cornish backing in September 1497, without success. He was captured a month later and placed in the Tower, very near Edward, earl of Warwick. Together, these two young men plotted a conspiracy, for which they were accused of treason and executed at Tyburn in November 1499. Warbeck was then aged twenty-five.

The English-Irish conflict began heating up in earnest in 1495, when the Drogheda Parliament bound Ireland firmly to English control, ending independence for the Irish parliament. But I like to think Kieran and Maeve could brave the rough waters of politics and remain steadfast in their love.

I sincerely hope you enjoyed *His Rebel Bride* and the entire "Brothers in Arms" series.

Shayla Black aka Shelley Bradley

THE LADY AND THE DRAGON
By Shayla Black
Coming November 11, 2014

A Runaway Heiress

Lady Christina Delafield was as bold as she was beautiful.
When her overbearing grandfather threatened to tame her in a Swiss
finishing school, Christina stowed away on the first ship leaving
London harbor, determined to make her own way in life. But the
mysterious captain of the Dragon's Lair was a seductive reason to
relinquish her independence–and embrace desire.

A Gentleman Pirate

Drexell Cain had lived for four years as the merciless Black
Dragon, the scourge of the seas. Bent on rescuing his brother from
the British Navy, Drex would do anything to return him to his wife
and son in Louisiana–even kidnap the Lord Admiral's granddaughter
for ransom. A lovely blonde stowaway was an unexpected
complication, until he discovered her real identity–and her
passionate claim on his lonely heart.

HIS TO TAKE
A Wicked Lovers Novel
By Shayla Black
Coming March 3, 2015

Racing against time, NSA Agent Joaquin Muñoz is searching for a little girl who vanished twenty years ago with a dangerous secret. Since Bailey Benson fits the profile, Joaquin abducts the beauty and whisks her to the safety of Club Dominion—before anyone can silence her for good.

At first, Bailey is terrified, but when her captor demands information about her past, she's stunned. Are her horrific visions actually distant memories that imperil all she holds dear? Confined with Joaquin in a place that echoes with moans and breathes passion, he proves himself a fierce protector, as well as a sensual Master who's slowly crawling deeper in her head…and heart. But giving in to him might be the most delicious danger of all.

Because Bailey soon learns that her past isn't the only mystery. Joaquin has a secret of his own—a burning vengeance in his soul. The exposed truth leaves her vulnerable and wondering how much about the man she loves is a lie, how much more is at risk than her heart. And if she can trust him to protect her long enough to learn the truth.

Excerpt

"…What about you? You're with another government agency, so you're here to . . . what? Be my lover? Does Uncle Sam think you need to crawl between my legs in order to watch over me?"

Joaquin ground his jaw. She was hitting low, and the logical part of him understood that she was hurt, so she was lashing out at the messenger because she didn't have anyone else. But that didn't stop his temper from getting swept up in her cyclone of emotion. "I'm not here on anyone's orders. In fact, I'll probably be fired for pursuing this case because Tatiana Aslanov isn't on my boss's radar. When it became obvious the agency intended to do nothing, I couldn't leave you to that horrific death. So here we are. But let me clue you in, baby girl. Uncle Sam doesn't tell me who to fuck. I can't fake an erection, even for the sake of God and country. That kiss we almost shared? That was me wanting you because just being in the same room with you makes me want to strip off everything you're wearing and impale you with every inch I've got."

When he eased closer to Bailey, she squared her shoulders and raised her chin. "Don't come near me."

That defiance made him wish again that he was a spanking kind of guy. He'd really like to melt that starch in her spine. If she wasn't going to let him comfort her, he'd be more than happy to adjust her attitude with a good smack or ten on her ass, then follow it up with a thorough fucking. A nice handful of orgasms would do them both a world of good.

"I am so done with people lying to me," she ground out.

That pissed him off. "You think I'm lying to you? About which part? Your parents being agents? That I'm sorry? Or that my cock is aching to fill your sweet little pussy until you dig your nails into my back and wail out in pleasure?"

Her face turned pink. "You're not sorry about any of this. I'm also not buying your sudden desire bullshit."

"I will be more than happy to prove you wrong right now." He reached for the button of his jeans. "I'm ready if you are."

In some distant corner of his brain, Joaquin realized that combating her hurt with challenge wasn't going over well. On the other hand, something about arguing with her while he'd been imagining her underneath him hadn't just gotten his blood flowing, but boiling. If fucking her would, in any way, prove to her that he wasn't lying, he was beyond down with getting busy. If she let him, he'd give it to her hard and wicked—and repeatedly.

"No!" She managed to look indignant, but her cheeks had gone rosy. The pulse at her neck was pounding. Her nipples poked at her borrowed shirt angrily.

He put his hands on his hips. If she looked down, she'd see his straining zipper. "Do you still think I'm lying?"

"I'm done with this conversation."

"If you're telling yourself you don't want me at all, then you're the one lying."

"Pfft. You might know facts about me on paper, but you don't know me."

"So if I touched your pussy right now, you wouldn't be wet?"

He'd always liked a good challenge. It was probably one of the reasons he loved his job. But facing off with her this way made his blood sing, too.

"No." She shook her head a bit too emphatically. "And you're not touching me to find out. Leave me alone."

"You're worried that I'd find you juicy. You're afraid to admit that I turn you on." He stalked closer, his footfalls heavy, his eyes narrowing in on her.

"Stay back," she warned—but her eyes said something else entirely.

"Tell me you're not attracted to me." He reached out, his strike fast as a snake's, and gripped her arms. He dragged her closer, fitting her lithe little body against him and holding in a groan when she brushed over his cock. "Tell me you want me to stop. Remember, you don't like liars. I don't, either."

She didn't say a word, struggled a bit for show. Mostly, she parted her lips and panted. Her cheeks heated an even deeper rose. Her chest heaved. Never once did she look away from him. "I'm involved with someone else."

"If you think whatever you've got going with Blane is going to stop me . . ." He didn't bother to finish his sentence; he just laughed.

"So you're not listening to me say 'no'? You're not respecting my feelings for another guy?"

"Let's just say I'm proving my sincerity to you." He tightened his grip. When she gasped and her stare fell to his lips, triumph raced through his veins. "I'm also testing you. That pretty mouth of yours might lie to me, but your kisses won't."

Joaquin didn't give her a chance to protest again. Normally, he would have. Women 101 was never to proceed without express consent, but this thick air of tension electrifying his blood and seizing his lungs was something entirely new and intoxicating. Their fight seemed to be helping Bailey forget her shock and sadness, not to mention the fact that it revved her, too. She wasn't immune to him—not by a long shot. Thank fuck.

Thrusting a fist in her hair, he pinned her in place and lowered his head.

CHERISHED
By Lexi Blake
A Masters and Mercenaries Novella
Coming October 28, 2014

A doctor living a double life

By day, Dr. Will Daley is one of Dallas's most eligible bachelors, but every night he dons his leathers as one of Sanctum's most desired Doms. He's sworn off looking for a long-term relationship but is captivated by the club's newest member, Bridget Slaten, even though they couldn't be more different. She comes from a world of privilege and he was raised in poverty. When he discovers she needs a date to her sister's wedding, he makes certain he's literally the only man for the job.

A woman no longer willing to live in the shadows

For most of her life, Bridget hid herself behind her laptop. She can write romantic, sensuous lives for her characters but not herself. Having Master Will as her date to the wedding is a thrilling prospect but he has a special request. He wants her to accept two weeks of his services as a Dom, a lover, and expert in BDSM, and that is an offer she can't refuse. Their sexual chemistry is undeniable, but it's in the tender moments that Bridget realizes she's falling for a man who might never trust her with his heart.

A love strong enough to cherish

Together in paradise for a week, Will realizes he can't imagine his life without Bridget. As the wedding approaches, ghosts from their past come back to haunt them and threaten to ruin the peace they've found. With everything exposed, they will have to risk it all to claim the love that can set them both free.

* * * *

"I thought you were staying for dinner." He moved in, taking up all the space. This close, she could see that he had a five o'clock shadow across his perfect jaw. She was a sucker for a square jaw. Damn it. Even his ears were hot. She kind of wanted to lick them to see if he was ticklish there.

"I think that's a bad idea."

"Because I'm not looking for anything serious? Does everything have to be serious? Do you go into every relationship looking to get married?"

"No. I don't think about getting married much." Her parents marriage was so bad she often couldn't stomach the idea. "But I'm getting too old to do the one-night stand thing."

He moved in closer and she nearly forgot to breathe. He smelled so good. Clean and masculine. Sandalwood. He'd likely washed with it. All over. A vision of him soaping that body made her mouth water. "I didn't say anything about one-night stands. I just said maybe you shouldn't take every relationship so seriously. Bridget, I want to spend time with you."

And her nipples were hard. Yeah, they wanted to spend time with him, but her brain was still in charge. "My sister's getting married in Hawaii."

Oh, her brain was a traitor, too.

He loomed over her, his body inches away. His lips curled up in the sexiest grin. "Really? That sounds like fun. When is that happening?"

He was going to kiss her. His lips were going to touch hers and she had the sudden and deep fear that she wouldn't be the same afterward. Still, she couldn't quite seem to move, couldn't get the will worked up to step back. She only managed to run her tongue across her lips to make sure they weren't bone dry. "Soon. Next week."

He sighed, his hands finding her shoulders. "Oh, I guess you're going to be out of town then. I was hoping to see you while I was on vacation next week."

She was mesmerized by his eyes. This close, she could see how green they were. His hands moved to her neck. "You could come with me. I need a date."

Now she was kind of happy everyone else had turned her down.

It seemed right to ask him, good to be here with him.

There was the sound of a phone ringing.

He shook his head as his hands sank into her hair. The way he was taking his time did something for her. The men she'd been with before had all just gone for it and would likely have already been pawing her boobs by now, but Will was moving with languid seduction. It was like a dance. "You need a date?"

The only thing pulling her out of the sensual haze was that stupid phone. Who had a landline these days? "I do. Shouldn't you get that?"

His nose touched hers as his fingers ran along her scalp, sending pleasurable shivers through her body. "Don't worry about it. The hospital requires I keep a house phone. And a pager. And a cell. If it's really important, they'll page me. This is more fun than answering the phone, don't you think? Bridget, you know I won't be able to keep my hands off you if we go to Hawaii together."

She didn't want him to. She was fairly certain she was going to fall into bed with him in the next ten minutes. Maybe he was right. Maybe she took everything too seriously and she should just have some fun for once in her life. Maybe she could handle it. "Will?"

His mouth hovered right over hers, and there was no way to mistake the satisfaction coming off him. He wanted her. God, he really wanted her. "Yes, Bridget?"

ABOUT THE AUTHOR

Shayla Black (aka Shelley Bradley) is the New York Times and USA Today bestselling author of over forty sizzling contemporary, erotic, paranormal, and historical romances produced via traditional, small press, independent, and audio publishing. She lives in Texas with her husband, munchkin, and one very spoiled cat. In her "free" time, she enjoys reality TV, reading and listening to an eclectic blend of music.

Shayla's books have been translated in about a dozen languages. She has been nominated for career achievement in erotic romance by RT Bookclub, as well as twice nominated for Best Erotic Romance of the year. Additionally, she's either won or been nominated for the Passionate Plume, the Holt Medallion, Colorado Romance Writers Award of Excellence, and the National Reader's Choice Awards.

A writing risk-taker, Shayla enjoys tackling writing challenges with every new book.

Connect with me online:
Facebook: https://www.facebook.com/ShaylaBlackAuthor
Twitter: http://twitter.com/Shayla_Black
Website: http://shaylablack.com/

Visit Shayla's website to join her newsletter!

If you enjoyed this book, I would appreciate your help so others can enjoy it, too. You can:

Recommend it. Please help other readers find this book by recommending it to friends, readers' groups, and discussion boards.

Review it. Please tell other readers why you liked this book by reviewing it wherever you purchased your book or on Goodreads. If you do write a review, please send me an e-mail at interact @ shaylablack.com so I can thank you with a personal e-mail.

SHAYLA'S BOOKSHELF BY SERIES

EROTIC ROMANCE
THE WICKED LOVERS
Wicked Ties
Decadent
Delicious
Surrender To Me
Belong To Me
"Wicked to Love" (e-novella)
Mine To Hold
"Wicked All The Way" (e-novella)
Ours To Love
Wicked and Dangerous
Forever Wicked
Theirs To Cherish
Coming Soon:
His to Take (March 3, 2015)

SEXY CAPERS
Bound And Determined
Strip Search
"Arresting Desire" – Hot In Handcuffs Anthology

MASTERS OF MÉNAGE (by Shayla Black and Lexi Blake)
Their Virgin Captive
Their Virgin's Secret
Their Virgin Concubine
Their Virgin Princess
Their Virgin Hostage
Their Virgin Secretary
Coming Soon:
Their Virgin Mistress (April 14, 2015)

DOMS OF HER LIFE (by Shayla Black, Jenna Jacob, and Isabella LaPearl)
One Dom To Love
The Young And The Submissive
Coming Soon:
The Bold and The Dominant (February 10, 2015)

STAND ALONE TITLES
Naughty Little Secret (Shayla Black writing as Shelley Bradley)
"Watch Me" – Sneak Peek Anthology (as Shelley Bradley), Coming this fall!
Dangerous Boys And Their Toy
"Her Fantasy Men" – Four Play Anthology

PARANORMAL ROMANCE
THE DOOMSDAY BRETHREN
Tempt Me With Darkness
"Fated" (e-novella)
Seduce Me In Shadow
Possess Me At Midnight
"Mated" – Haunted By Your Touch Anthology
Entice Me At Twilight
Embrace Me At Dawn

HISTORICAL ROMANCE (Shayla Black writing as Shelley Bradley)
The Lady And The Dragon, Coming this fall!
One Wicked Night
Strictly Seduction
Strictly Forbidden

BROTHERS IN ARMS
His Lady Bride, Brothers in Arms
His Stolen Bride, Brothers in Arms
Coming Soon:
His Rebel Bride, Brothers in Arms (September 15, 2014)

CONTEMPORARY ROMANCE (as Shelley Bradley)
A Perfect Match